FIELD OF FLOWERS

⊛ greenhill

https://greenhillpublishing.com.au/

Wilkin, Carol (author)
Field of Flowers
ISBN 978-1-922957-57-3
FICTION | THRILLER

Typeset Calluna 11/16

Cover photo by Envato Elements
Cover and book design by Green Hill Publishing

CAROL WILKIN

MUSIC. DRUGS. CORRUPTION.

FIELD OF FLOWERS

A THRILLER

FOR THOSE WHO WANTED TO KNOW,
YOU'RE ABOUT TO FIND OUT.

1969 CRIMSON KING

I'm home. I sink into the permanent hollow in the soft kid leather of the sofa, attributable to my weight gain in the last few years, according to the tabloids. I am aware I have been labelled 'pudgy' lately, a term I don't appreciate, and it is of course an exaggeration.

I turn on the six o'clock news. Watching anything on my large colour television brings some life to my otherwise dull world. I have a glass of good red wine. I watch the headlines, mostly for the novelty of the colour but suddenly I sit up. My interest is piqued. Pictures of a redhead are flashed across the screen, young, pretty, in a hippie, 'Age of Aquarius' sort of way. I am watching images of an ambulance, a pop concert and screaming fans, then a close-up of the girl's face. The colour screen emphasises the pallor in her cheek, her pale lips, and blue eyelids, sharply contrasted by the mass of flaming red hair, as she is placed in the ambulance.

I absently put the glass down and lean forward. She looks young, too young. I strain to see more. I narrow my eyes and peer intently attempting to glean more detail simply by needing it. I smile, the smile I have been told engenders fear rather than affection. I can't help myself.

I pick up the white Ericofon and dial the number.

'It's me. We need to talk. I've seen something I like.'

JULY 1969

BONNIE

'A Whiter Shade of Pale'
Procol Harum

Robert slid into the front passenger seat of the black Zephyr. His offsider joined him in the driver's seat. A Whiter Shade of Pale played on the radio.

'Step on it son. This could be a bad one.'

Alby stepped on it, the tyres squealed, and they pulled out of Scotland Yard onto Victoria Embankment, and then executed another tyre squealing left onto Northumberland Avenue. Just an ordinary Wednesday morning in London.

'What have we got this time gov?'

'Another drug OD, maybe multiple. Hippy den in Notting Hill. Reports are one dead, others in a bad way. Got the ambulances on the way and ME is waiting. Nobody's saying but we could have somebody well known, apparently a teenaged pop star. Oy watchit!'

Alby swerved as a taxi pulled out in front of them.

'So, is it like her, you know, the popstar that's deceased?'

'No information on that yet. Nearly there. Ladbroke Drive.

Here we go.'

Ladbroke Drive looked to be an affluent area with four story Georgian terrace houses, most of them neatly kept with fresh paint, ornate porticos, and wrought iron railings. It was obvious where they were stopping. There were ambulances and squad cars, uniforms and medical personnel milling around. The Zephyr ground to a stop as close as Alby could pull in. The two men got out and walked up to the uniformed officer guarding the door. As they approached, ambulance officers carried out a stretcher bearing a young woman who was alternately moaning and yelling abuse.

'DCI Turner and DS Coates.'

They showed their badges and walked through the door into the substantial entrance hall. What would have been an elegant entry only recently, was now a shambles. Painted flowers decorated the walls along with peace symbols, and graffiti extolling the benefits of LSD, free love and the anti-establishment. Robert and Alby stepped over a flock mattress and numerous rugs and pillows strewn over the polished floor. An ornate Victorian pendant decorated with strings of beads cascaded from the high ceiling. A pungent smell immediately assaulted their senses, a mix of incense, fried food, alcohol and the cloying odours of unwashed bodies and pot. Emanating from every room, a thick fug of choking smoke filled the passage. A man, or was it a woman, was droning tonelessly to a guitar which badly needed tuning. Somewhere in the house, someone was shouting slurred abuse. A constable beckoned them up the stairs.

'Up 'ere guv.'

As Robert and Alby passed the rooms, they saw more mattresses. Young men and women so gone that they knew nothing of what was going on occupied some of them. Small huddles of men and women, their eyes unfocussed and bleary, shared tiny joints, filling the rooms with more pungent smoke. No doubt some of the occupants had been 'with it' enough to scarper at the first sign of the cops.

The two detectives climbed the wide staircase and emerged onto a spacious landing from which several doors opened. In the room straight ahead, through the open door, a medical team could be seen performing resuscitation on a young woman.

'Not there, sir. That one still has a chance. Massive overdose but she might pull through. She's that pop star, Bonnie Summer. Poor lass.' The officer shook his head. 'In the bathroom 'ere, sir is the one who didn't make it. Another girl, about seventeen or eighteen. Couldn't be much older. OD'd. Found 'er in the bathroom. She'd been sick everywhere and we couldn't rouse 'er.'

Both Turner and Coates had seen scenes like this before. They were becoming more and more common, but it never got any easier. This girl lay on her back on the floor in front of the toilet, her long blonde hair matted in her own vomit. The ambulance men were still there packing their gear up. The girl was motionless, her colour drained, her clothes roughly torn where the ambulance men had been working on her in vain.

'Do we have an ID on her?' Robert asked the two men who were packing up.

'Yes, they tell us she went by the name of Harmony. Yeah, just Harmony,' he added as Robert looked askance. 'Lived here. Supposedly a singer in Bonnie Summer's pop group. Not any more though. She was gone when we arrived, completely unresponsive, no pulse. We tried for fifteen minutes but nothing. Called it at 11:20 am. ME should be up here in a minute, then we'll take her to St John and Elizabeth down the road.'

'Right. Alby, you go down and ask around the ones still here. See what you can find out about her. She must have family somewhere and her real name would be handy. I'll go and find out if Miss Summer has managed to pull through.'

Robert returned to the room at the top of the stairs just in time to see the girl carried out on a stretcher. Her long red hair fell in unkempt ringlets from the stretcher. Covered by a sheet, her pale face protruded, her hands were crossed over her stomach. Robert raised his eyebrows to the men carrying her. *Still with us?*

'She's going to be alright. Pulse is weak. She's not in great shape but she'll get over it after she has her stomach pumped. She'd been taking LSD and plenty of booze thrown in. God knows what else. We're taking her down to St John's and St Elizabeth's. These bloody pop stars. Too much money and no sense. Only sixteen you know. Sixteen! What on earth is her mother thinking?'

The ambulance officer shook his head. 'Got a daughter the same age, I have.'

They began taking her down the stairs. Robert followed, finding Alby in the entrance hall.

'We're taking a couple of them in,' said Alby. 'One of those men is nearly fifty years old and another not much younger. They're clearly up to no good, sharing rooms and beds with young women, supplyin' 'em with drugs and booze. We're holdin' 'em on suspicion of unlawful sex with underage girls and trafficking. Neither of 'em is talking.'

As they spoke, two uniforms came in and yanked one of the older men to his feet to handcuff him. He put up no resistance, merely holding two fingers up in a 'V' and saying over and over, 'Peace, man. Peace and love.'

'Right,' said Robert to Alby, 'we'll get on down to the hospital, see when we can talk to Miss Summer. Has everyone been warned to keep her identity under wraps? No press and no interviews.'

'Yes, guv, they have, but there have been reporters sniffing around. They must have got wind of something. Don't know how long we can keep a lid on it.'

They climbed into the car.

'What a bloody mess, eh?' commented Robert.

***

Later in the day, Robert sat in his office, contemplating the events of the morning. At the hospital, he had been told there would be no interviewing Miss Summer until the next day at the earliest. She was on a drip and being closely monitored, particularly due to her young age. He already had a pile of notes and a couple of reports from zealous constables. Plenty of reading to do and he felt disinclined to start. Instead, he found himself questioning, not for the first time, how these kids got themselves into such a mess.

He, Robert, had not had the best of starts. He could have easily 'run off the rails', coming from a family with an abusive father and a weak and defenceless mother who had no power to change their situation. His older brother had done just that and had paid the ultimate price.

The bitter memories never completely submerged hurtled back to haunt him at the oddest moments. Such as now. He could still hear his mother's cries, then weary sobs, his father stomping up the stairs and cracking the walls with his fists. Hadn't he had his very front teeth knocked out by the man at the age of five? He would never be able to remove these memories, but the death of his deviate brother had simply strengthened his resolve to fight for such people as his mother. He would help turn the tide against such mindless violence. He had thought at an early age that the best way to do that was to become a policeman, and from that day onwards, he had worked tirelessly to achieve it. He tried hard at school, endured beatings for being a 'smart little bugger, too big for his boots'. He had passed his O levels and gained entry to the police force. Over the years, he had risen through the ranks to Detective Chief Inspector. His specific interests lay in families in crisis, people suffering the long-term effects of trauma, using violence against their families as his father had. In recent times, the growing subculture of mostly youth, the 'hippy scene', had sparked an interest and he had spent much time reading and studying the current philosophies.

So, sitting here at his desk, he wondered, what had happened to make a sixteen-year-old girl abandon her family and live like this? Their inquiries with the other semi-coherent individuals had not revealed her real name or family details. *'We're her family'* they had said. He had asked a young constable to find some pop magazines to see if this Bonnie Summer was a real pop star. The lad came back with the latest editions of *Petticoat* and *Fabulous 208*. It did not take long to find an article about Bonnie, the headline, 'Bonnie Summer talks pop culture'. Inside, the article was very thin on detail or truth for that matter but brimming with the sixteen-year old's supposed inner ponderings on materialism and repression, advantages of communal living and how experimenting with freedoms had lifted her and her music to a higher plane. The photographs showed her driving a yellow VW Beetle cabriolet decorated with large flowers. Her long red hair was blowing in the breeze, held only by a brightly coloured bandana. Her face, fresh and young wore a wide smile showing perfect white teeth. A pink guitar sat in the back seat. The picture was the epitome of youthful vitality, freedom, and all things beautiful. Nowhere was there any mention of family, where she hailed from or her real name. He felt doubtful that 'Summer' was her proper surname, but you never could tell.

The more Robert looked at the face in the photo, the more intrigued he became. There was something about her which held his attention, but he could not pinpoint it. Something about the eyes, was it? It might come later. She almost seemed familiar. Robert shook his head, conceding to himself that she looked like any other teenaged girl you would find on the streets of London these days. He would wait until he was able to talk to her in person. Meanwhile, he needed to sort out what to do with a couple of dirty old men he had locked up in the cells for the night.

EARLY JANUARY 1953

She lay on the daybed staring at the window, her eyes glazed, unblinking, her mouth slack, a ribbon of drool tracing a wet stain down her jaw. Nothing outside the window interested her. Nothing inside the room could capture her attention. After just a few short weeks, she had found that keeping her mind blank and unresponsive was the only way to keep the horror locked away where she could not feel the pain.

Her mother tried to make her eat. Food made her gag. If nothing was placed in front of her, she would not eat or drink, but she was able to sip water or tea, which her mother sweetened to give her some energy. Most of the time she just felt sick.

Most of her physical injuries were healing well by now enabling her discharge from the hospital. The doctor deemed her mother Joan would be capable of seeing to her requirements at home. On admission, the doctors had discovered her swollen eye was masking a fractured eye socket, her nose was broken, and her jaw fractured in two places. The internal damage, while appearing severe at first was not as bad as first thought. Doctors told her she would not suffer any lasting physical effects.

Despite their reassurances, Petunia Jackson knew something was terribly wrong. She *felt* wrong. Different. Aside from feeling ill all the time, she just felt *not right.*

It was now four months since her incarceration, torture, and repeated rape by a local man. Twelve weeks since she had killed him, murdered him by strangling him with one of the chains he had used to shackle her in his barn. Sixteen long weeks since she had lived a life worth living. Christmas and New Year had come and gone. It had passed with no celebration or acknowledgment for Petunia. She saw the beginning of 1953 from the same daybed she now occupied. She felt an empty shell of a woman, only thirty-three years old and incapable of seeing any future for herself. Never again would she stand in front of a class of forty youngsters and teach them spelling, arithmetic and religious instruction in the Catholic School where she had been employed for her whole adult life. How could she? She had seen the very worst of human behaviour. She wrestled inwardly questioning how her God could possibly have created such a man. The horror she had experienced had been unimaginable before this. She had been a virgin, hadn't she? She had never seen a naked man let alone the things the man had shown her and done to her. No wonder she felt sick. No wonder she needed to push the present away and live within herself.

She stared at the window. Her mother came in the room with a tray. Petunia neither turned her head nor acknowledged her in any way.

'Tea, Petunia. Just vegetable soup. You need to eat some. You've hardly eaten for two days. The doctors have told me that you should start to feel much better soon. I'll leave it on the table.'

Petunia did not move. The room was getting darker as the outside light faded. She made no effort to get up and turn a light on. She did not look at the tray of food. Joan returned with a cup of tea and some dry biscuits.

'Petunia, you must eat something. How can you expect to get strong enough to go back to school? Your class is waiting for you to come back. Look, I have a stack of get-well cards from each and every one of them. They miss you.'

Petunia turned her head and sighed a deep sigh. She moved the tea trolley closer to her daybed, leaned over, took the spoon, and scooped up a spoonful of the soup. She slurped it. Much of it spilled down her nightgown. A small amount went in her mouth. With obvious effort, she managed to swallow it. She tried again. After a few spoonfuls, she pushed the trolley away and sat staring at the dark window.

'That's better!' Joan said. 'Try a bit more later?'

Petunia dropped her gaze and suddenly vomited the soup down her nightgown.

'Oh Petunia!' Joan snapped. 'Why did you have to do that? Couldn't you get up? Now you will have to clean yourself up. It's about time you pulled yourself together.'

With that, Joan stalked out shaking her head. This was all she needed after the last few months. What with all the to-do with Petunia, then the whole village turned upside down with the investigation, and their tiny village all over the papers when the bowling green was dug up, she was at the end of her tether. She too found it difficult to leave the house. People tried to be sympathetic, to say nice things but she could tell that underneath the pleasantries, they were thinking dark and terrible thoughts about her daughter and probably her too. She had not even been to church and had been ignoring the ringing telephone. Nevertheless, right at this moment, she felt she needed to talk to someone, and the only choice was Father Michael. He was the one who had helped her when Petunia had disappeared. She would call him.

The telephone was ringing on the other end. She waited. 'Click'
'Father Michael, St Angela's, speaking.'

'Oh, thank God. Father Michael, I don't know what to do. Who can I turn to? I could only think of you.'

'Mrs. Jackson? Is that you? I have tried to ring you several times to see how you both are. How are you?'

The floodgates opened and Father Michael listened patiently as Joan poured the whole sorry mess out, finishing up with the current situation and adding that she was at her wit's end.

'Mrs. Jackson, I think I need to come and see you both. How about tomorrow morning at ten? Alright? Good, I'll be there. We've missed you at church. Perhaps we can aim for next Sunday?'

'We'll see. Ten tomorrow morning then Father?'

Joan ran her hands through her increasingly greying hair and rubbed her face. The weariness penetrated every fibre of her, constant and unrelenting. Some days she felt she did not have the energy to get out of bed let alone tend to Petunia. She went to the bathroom, ran a sink of hot water, and soaked a flannel, then she sighed deeply again and returned to the living room where Petunia had not attempted to move. She sat staring at the wall covered in her own vomited up soup. Joan cleaned her up, brought her another nightgown and finally retired to bed exhausted. Tomorrow could not come soon enough.

✳✳✳

The green Rover crunched over the newly laid gravel driveway and pulled up. Father Michael knew of the excavation, which had taken place before Christmas, when a bulldozer had destroyed the whole area by repeatedly chopping up the surface. Efforts to repair it had been minimal leaving the stark severity of plain gravel, unbroken by any shrubs or borders, which had once edged the Old Vicarage driveway. It served as un-welcome reminder of recent events.

Father Michael knocked on the front door and called out, letting Joan know who was there.

Joan opened the door and peered around it, then satisfied, she let him in. Michael was shocked at her appearance. She looked years older. Her expression spoke of a complete depletion of spirit. *She has almost given up* he thought.

'Come on in Father. Petunia is in the sitting room but before we go in, I must warn you that she is not the woman you know.'

You are not the woman I know either thought Michael. He entered the room and was immediately conscious of the smell. There was no doubt in his mind. The room smelled like a ward for highly dependent people in aged care or a mental institution. He knew the smell very well. Many a time he had been called to give the last rights in such a place where it was the all-pervading odour. This was the same and yet, this was Petunia.

The subject of his visit lay on a daybed, her nightdress partially covered by a candlewick dressing gown. She faced the window, her back to the door. He could see lank hair and slumped shoulders.

'Petunia,' said Joan briskly, 'Father Michael is here to see us.' Petunia did not move.

'Good morning, Petunia!' Michael greeted her brightly and moved towards the bed. 'How are you feeling today?'

He came around so that she was able to see him. She continued to stare out of the window.

'I have come to see if there is anything I can do for you or your mother. I am also here to pass on many well wishes from the parishioners. Everyone is eager to welcome you both back to our fold.'

Petunia turned to face him. Once again, he was shocked. The pale, gaunt face bore little resemblance to the bright, self-confident woman he had known as the Junior School teacher up at the Catholic School. Her dull, sunken eyes found his and for a second, he thought he could read a plea for help. Then her eyes dropped to her lap again. Michael spoke to Joan in a whisper.

'Joan, do you think I could have a little time alone with her?' Joan tutted and left them.

'I can hear you.' Petunia's voice, contrary to her appearance, was sharp.

Michael nodded gently. 'Go on.'

'I can speak, you know. I just don't want to, especially to her.'

'Then talk to me, Petunia. Your mother is so worried for you.'

'I could eat,' she said, 'but it makes me feel sick. I could get up, but I just don't want to. I don't want to go on doing anything. Nothing. If I do, I risk letting it all back in and I simply can't live with it.'

'I trust you have been taking comfort in God's presence as he watches over you. I can help you with some prayers. Or would you like to take confession?'

Petunia threw him a dark look.

'No, I do not! If I had anything to ask forgiveness for, I would. I need no penance, Father. I am the one who has been abominated. And as for the Heavenly Father, I no longer feel His presence. He was not there when I needed Him the most!'

Father Michael leaned in towards Petunia. 'Petunia, who gave you the strength and the will to overcome the evil? Do you truly think that came from within you alone?'

Petunia cast her eyes down and Father Michael saw a single tear spill down one pale cheek. He took her limp hand in his.

'My child, you must give thanks for your life. Your children are eagerly waiting for you to take up your position again, to guide them into their lives along the right path. You must start to eat and become strong again.'

'I told you I don't eat. Everything feels so wrong. *I feel wrong.* I know everyone just wants me to get over it. They don't understand. Can't you understand Father? What that monster did to me has undermined my whole belief, my faith, my place in this life? How can I worship a God of goodness and forgiveness? What happened to me does not allow it. I can never have *my* life back. Do you see? What is there left? All I can do is wait until the horror of this life is over and then what? Certainly not the Heavenly existence I have always believed in.'

Michael listened. He was beginning to understand that Petunia's mental state might require a little more than he could offer.

'Petunia, have you told anyone else about your feelings, a doctor at the hospital, your mother?'

'No, I haven't spoken to anyone, barely at all to mother. I can't.'

Michael thought that she had lost a great deal of weight. Although she was swathed in nightclothes, the wrists, and ankles visible were painfully thin and her face was sallow, the skin stretched tautly over her bones.

'Petunia, I think you may need more help than I can give you.'

'NO. Leave me alone!'

'By help, I mean a doctor or a therapist. You may be sick. You might have an infection. There must be a reason why you feel so ill. Your mother told me that the hospital doctors expected you to be well on the road to recovery by now. Won't you let me call my doctor? He is a very good man; one I trust completely. May I call him?'

Petunia grudgingly agreed to see Father Michael's doctor.

***

Two days later, Doctor Flaherty arrived at the Old Vicarage, armed with the information Michael had provided to him. The doctor was the archetypal country doctor, mid-fifties, unruly shock of silver hair, tweed jacket, a big smile, and a jolly demeanour. He could have made a perfect Santa Claus at anyone's Christmas Party.

Petunia had made a huge effort to dress in day clothes, a skirt, blouse, and woollen cardigan. Joan had aired the room and the smell had dissipated somewhat.

After greeting them both, Doctor Flaherty did some perfunctory examinations, blood pressure, pulse, and temperature. All normal. He asked to examine her to determine some reason for her sickness and lack of appetite. He knew her history, had telephoned the hospital and spoken to the doctor who treated her there. He had been informed regarding the injuries from the rape, specifically that they were not thought to be severe enough to cause any lasting effects. However, Petunia agreed to an examination, and he asked her to move her blouse up so that he could palp her stomach, which in contrast to her wasted body was round and firm. As he pressed gently, he asked her to tell him if it caused pain. She simply stared at him, while laying rigidly on the bed, obviously fearful of being touched in any way.

'Please try to relax Petunia. I'm just going to feel here.'

When he finished, he asked her to sit up.

'Petunia, I do not think you are ill. I would like to take some blood to be sure, but I think I know what the result will tell us. You are pregnant. About four months, I'd say.'

1969
HUGGY PAPA

'Come Together'
The Beatles

Robert and Alby sat facing the man across the table in the Interview Room. Looking at him reminded Robert strongly of the Beatles song, Come Together. Here was 'old flat-top' himself. After spending the night in the cells, nothing about his attitude yesterday had changed. He lolled on the chair, lanky, waist length hair, streaked with grey, draping across his shoulders and across the surface of the table. He sported a benign, vacant smirk while he regarded the two coppers through semi-closed eyes. Robert noted the grubby feet clad in leather sandals, scruffy jeans, and a loose shirt. He had so far declined to offer any cooperation, preferring to repeat his mantra, 'peace man.'

Robert fixed his eyes on his. 'This interview is being recorded. You know the drill. Anything you say may be used as evidence against you in a court of law. Do you understand? What is your name, your real name, I mean?'

The man gently nodded to some internal pulsing rhythm and remained silent; his eyes fixed on a spot somewhere on the wall behind Robert.

'Look, Mr Huggy Papa, apparently that is the name you prefer to go by, you could be in a lot of trouble. Let's start with abduction of a minor, incarceration of a minor, illegal sex with a minor...'

'You can't prove that!' interjected the man.

'Oh, so you are listening! How about supplying alcohol and narcotics to a minor, securing an underage girl for sexual exploitation, shall I go on? You're risking the prospect of spending a long stretch in Belmarsh. I suggest you start answering our questions. So, I ask you again, what is your real name?'

'You don't have anything on me, man. We're just doing our thing.'

'Name!' Robert barked, slamming his open hands on the table. He took a notepad from his top pocket, flipped it open and showed the man a name scrawled on it. 'Is this your name?'

Huggy peered through lazy unfocussed eyes as if trying to decipher hieroglyphics.

'Might be. Maybe in a past existence of which I have little memory and even less interest.'

'Peter Bramley? Peter Findlay Bramley?'

The man formerly known to them as Huggy Papa, raised his shaggy eyebrows and nodded again. 'Yeah, I guess that's me.'

'What is your relationship with the people we found in the house at Ladbroke Drive?'

'I'm their guru, their protector, a father figure. I take care of them. They are my children. I love them all.'

'Feeding them drugs and booze is not my idea of 'taking care of 'em!' Robert leaned across the table. 'Neither is sleeping with them. How does that work then?'

'What they choose to do is out of my control.'

'Mr. Bramley, you have only just told us that you take care of them, you think of them as your children. Many of them are too young to be deciding for themselves. You are their self-proclaimed guardian and as such are responsible for their care and protection and now, you're saying what they do is none of your concern. I think we need to start again, don't you?'

Changing tack Robert continued. 'Are you aware that Harmony has died of a drug overdose? Who gave her the drugs? Where did you meet Harmony?'

He watched Bramley unwaveringly. Was that a momentary flicker of fear in his eyes, Robert wondered. Yes, the man had averted his look and hesitated.

'She was in the band.'

'Whose band, yours?'

'Yeah, I suppose you would say that.'

'Your band, yes or no.'

'Yeah, at the moment. I do lots of different stuff. The band has only been going twelve months.'

'And... where and when did you pick her up?'

'Look, man, what happened to her has got nothing to do with me. I travel around you know, doing gigs. I saw these two girls at a country fair up north. One of 'em could sing and play, I mean *really* sing. I wanted her in my band, but she wouldn't come without her friend. She called herself Bonnie. Her friend was Harmony. That's how I met her. I never asked her if she had another name. Like I said, not my concern. Bonnie, well I didn't know if it was her real name or not. She never told me.'

'Bonnie Summer. So, you met the two of them at this fair and what, you just put 'em in your van and drove 'em to London?'

'No, they went home, packed up a few things and we went on the road. I've got contacts in the music business, you know, and I took them both to see my man. He really liked Bonnie and thought she could make it. We got her in the studio, and she put down some tracks, you dig? You must have heard her first single,

Field of Flowers?'

Robert's taste in music did not run to pop music, preferring modern classical such as Mahler and Britain. No, he had never heard the song but realised thousands must because she was famous enough to feature in the teenage magazines.

Huggy continued, 'It was released in September last year and by Christmas it had been in the Top 40 for eight weeks. We put down some more tracks and released an EP. She was in such demand we arranged some concerts. She never even did gigs as back-up to say *The Who* or *The Stones*. She shot straight to number one status, headlining her own gigs. I can't believe you've never seen her! She's everywhere man! She's advertising cars, pop mags, perfume, pop drinks, you name it. And only sixteen! That's why her next hit, *Sixteen in Love* went crazy, 'cause she *is* sixteen!'

Robert cut him off right there. 'And that is where the trouble starts for you, my friend. Just as a matter of interest, how did she sign a legal contract with a record company without her parents' consent?'

Huggy had now kicked off the grubby sandals and had one leg crossed over the other, giving Robert the dubious pleasure of studying the blackened sole of one foot. He shrugged his shoulders. Robert shook his head and turned to Alby.

'Got a smoke, man?' Bramley asked expectantly.

Robert slammed the notepad on the tabletop. 'What is the name of your contact in the music business?'

'Rick Chambers.'

Alby, who had so far remained silent, only observing the proceedings, interrupted.

'I've heard of him guv. He's one of those hot shot record producers. Isn't he always being photographed hanging around with the likes of *Herman's Hermits* and such.'

'Different record company, man,' responded Bramley scornfully. 'Not your style of music I wouldn't think!'

Alby shrugged. 'Can you give us an address for this Rick Chambers, please Mr. Bramley?'

Bramley looked to be drifting away, completely oblivious that Alby had spoken to him. Finally he replied, 'no, not really. I can sort of tell you where it is, the building I mean,' he slurred. 'Sorry, man.'

He resumed swaying his head side to side to the personal soundtrack playing in his addled mind.

'I need a smoke, man.'

'Stop the tape.' Alby did so. 'We'll leave it for now. Lock him up. Give him time to get himself together.'

'You've got nothin' on me, man. You can't keep me here.' Bramley slurred.

'I can and I will. We can keep you for as long as we think we need to, while we conduct investigations into your operations at the Notting Hill location, Mr. Bramley.'

He flicked his head to the door indicating to Alby to take him out.

＊＊＊

Later in the office, Robert conferred with Alby.

'Right, you find out all you can about Mr. Bramley. I'll follow up on this contract with the record company and Rick Chambers. I'll go and see Bonnie again and see what she is doing when she leaves hospital. I want to make sure she doesn't go back to Notting Hill. Perhaps we'll pay a visit to her parents too. Find out if they even know where their daughter is!'

'Right guv, I'm on to it. I'll find out where they live. When do you want to go?'

'Let me know when you've got the address, son.'

Robert wondered why he felt he *needed* to know Bonnie Summer's back-story.

1953 FORSAKEN

'Oranges & Lemons' (say the bells of St Clements)
Children's Nursery Rhyme

Petunia stared at the doctor. 'You are wrong. I know I am not…. that!'

'Well, I will do a blood test to be certain. We should know by tomorrow. I will give you a call. Would you like me to call your mother in now?'

Right on cue, Joan appeared at the door.

'I heard voices. Sounded like you Petunia, raising your voice at Doctor Flaherty. Is everything alright?'

The doctor took out his handkerchief and polished his glasses before replacing them on his nose after which he put his stethoscope, thermometer, and sphygmomanometer back in his black bag and fastened it. He rose and offered his hand to Petunia who ignored it.

'Well, I'll be off then. I'll be in touch as soon as the blood test comes back, probably tomorrow. Petunia, you need to explain to your mother. You will need some support, no doubt. I'll see myself out Mrs. Jackson. Goodbye.'

With that the doctor left the room and could be heard leaving by the front door. Joan eyed Petunia. Considering her daughter had hardly spoken for weeks, Joan was very curious to know what had transpired between the two and why Petunia had suddenly found her voice again.

'Well? What was all that about? What do you need to tell me?'

Two bright spots of colour had appeared on Petunia' cheek-bones, a terrible contrast to her greyish complexion. Her eyes were glittering like flint, and she clamped her thin lips together.

'What do you think? I'm pregnant!' she spat. 'Pregnant to that foul creature. A demon straight from Hell has planted his seed and that is what I have in me. A demon seed!'

Joan's expression froze. Seconds passed as she grappled with the shocking revelation.

'Oh, dear God!' She sagged visibly. 'Dear, dear God, I cannot believe it!'

Petunia sneered. 'Believe it. I knew something was terribly wrong. I will not go on carrying this spawn. I must rid myself of it or I shall kill myself. I do not know what I have done in this life to deserve this punishment, but I cannot carry it into the next, even in Hell.'

Joan was stricken with shock and grief listening to Petunia. Although she had reared her daughter as a good Catholic girl, she had never subscribed to such a radical perversion of their religion. The words coming out of Petunia's mouth horrified her.

'Petunia, stop! Stop talking like that! You know that every child is a gift from God, no matter from whence the seed came. That child is innocent and unblemished. All babies are born pure. Only the living can turn them. You must have the child and cherish him, raise him as I have raised you. I will not hear any more of that rubbish.'

'I will not!' Petunia screamed at her mother. 'Already it's taking its toll, making me ill, sick. It's only going to get worse. It will kill me if I don't kill it. Can't you see what it's done to me already? I can feel the evil growing. I didn't know what was happening to me, but now I know. I don't need any blood test to confirm it. I can *feel* it here.' She prodded her own belly.

'I will not rest until it is out of me. I know there are places I can go. I have heard of them before. You must find someone who will do it, or I will do it myself. I have money.'

Joan was beside herself. Petunia's ranting was out of control and a baby's life under threat. She knew she must try to calm her daughter, make her see the right thing to do.

'Listen to me,' she soothed calmly. 'You're in shock. This is something neither of us had ever even imagined. It will take time to adjust. But rest assured, I'm here for you and the baby. Perhaps we should consider moving away from the village, make a new start where no one knows us. You could say your husband was killed, leaving you to raise a child alone. In any case, we can do it together. You mustn't think you're doing this on your own.'

Petunia slumped onto her chair. 'Leave me alone. I don't want to talk any more. I need to sleep.'

'But... alright then. Would you like something to eat?'

'No.'

Joan shrugged and left her alone. She would try to talk again in the morning.

Petunia slumped. For some unaccountable reason the nursery rhyme about London churches, Oranges and Lemons began to spin dizzily around in her head, over and over...

FEBRUARY 1953
STRIKE 1

'Don't Sit Under the Apple Tree'
The Andrews Sisters

Joan woke slowly. The room was bright light. Birds chattered outside. Everything made note of a morning well advanced. She moved her head to the side and saw that the curtains had not been drawn last night. She had been wrung out. Not surprisingly, she had fallen into bed and into a deep sleep. What time was it? Craning her neck, she saw the bedside clock. It read a quarter past nine! Joan rubbed her eyes and sat up, swinging her feet around and into her slippers which she had remembered to place thoughtfully right where they would be needed. She switched on the radio which sat atop her bedside table, automatically, as she did every morning. 'Don't Sit Under the Apple Tree' played its cheery tune. Joan hummed absently along thinking to herself that the dogs would be wanting to go outside, and Petunia would be wanting something to eat or at least a cup of tea. She put her dressing gown on and got up from the bed to let Hugo and George out, then, the realization hit her like a brick. Petunia! Petunia, pregnant, the baby, her hysteria yesterday. She threw the door open and both dogs scrambled against each other to get out before the other, claws scrabbling futilely on the tiles.

'Petunia!' she called as she approached the living room where her daughter had been spending night and day for the last two months. 'Tea dear?'

Petunia didn't answer. *Must be asleep still. Surely not.* She opened the door.

'Petunia, will you have a cup of....' Joan stopped mid-sentence.

The room lay silent, except for the faint jazzy rhythms of the Andrews Sisters coming from her bedroom. Petunia sprawled on the floor, her nightgown and dressing gown smeared with blood. Her arm was thrown out to the side, beside her hand one of Joan's long knitting needles, also smeared with blood. She was not moving other than the faint rise and fall of her chest. Joan's hands flew up to her face.

'Oh my God, no! Petunia, how could you?' She rushed to her daughter and patted her on the face. 'Petunia, it's me, mother. Wake up. What have you done?'

Joan knew fully well what had happened, she was just having difficulty accepting the enormity of what she was seeing. Petunia's eyelids fluttered slightly, and a small moan escaped her lips.

'Thank God, you're still here. Stay there, don't try to move.' Joan went to the kitchen, picked up the telephone and dialed 999.

The ambulance arrived within ten minutes. She showed the officers in and gave them a very brief explanation. Petunia remained semi-conscious while they carefully lifted her onto the stretcher and loaded her into the ambulance. Joan, who was not even dressed yet, quickly found trousers and a jumper and climbed into the ambulance with her. They crunched out of the driveway with lights and bells and sped off down St Lawrence Road. Once again, the old biddies on the Snicket oohed and aahed and speculated as to 'what was goin' on now then?'

'She'll be alright, won't she? And the baby?' asked Joan as they jolted and rattled towards the hospital.

'Mrs. Jackson, when we get her to the hospital, the doctors will take over. You will have to wait until they can give you any news,' replied the ambulance officer who was monitoring Petunia on the narrow bed.

'But surely you can tell? She didn't lose that much blood, did she?'

'She lost a bit, but I think she'll be alright. I'm sorry, but you will have to wait until she has been examined and they can determine how much damage has been done. There is really nothing I can tell you now.'

***

Joan sat in the waiting room. Like all hospital waiting rooms, it was bland, decorated only with posters encouraging women to train to be a nurse, pleas to use a handkerchief, *'Coughs and Sneezes Spread Diseases'* and advice on washing hands before eating. The floors were dull green, the walls, an even duller grey and the seating hard and unforgiving. There were at least twenty others in the room, parents with young children who plainly could not read the coughs and sneezes poster at all. An elderly couple who beseeched anyone in a nurse's uniform how their son was. The over-riding smell of disinfectant made Joan feel like sneezing. People talked amongst themselves, but every voice echoed off the hard surfaces. Joan sat, not speaking to anyone, not leaving her seat for nearly four hours. People had come and gone. Still, she sat.

'Mrs. Jackson?' A middle-aged nurse rustled towards her in her starched uniform and winged hat. 'The doctor will see you now, about your daughter, Petunia? Follow me.'

She bustled off down the corridor, *swish, swish.* The swinging doors led to Wards 5A to 10A. Joan followed her to Ward 7A where Petunia was resting in bed number 2, curtains drawn around it. The nurse pulled them aside and Joan went in. A doctor was waiting with a clipboard in his hands. Petunia lay on her back, slightly propped up. A tube fed liquid from a bottle on a stand into her arm but otherwise, she simply looked to be asleep.

'Please take a seat, Mrs. Jackson. My name is Doctor Mason.'

'Is she alright doctor? When can I take her home?' asked Joan.

'Your daughter has suffered quite a nasty injury. She lost some blood and was in shock. She is sedated and has some intravenous antibiotic going into her arm. She will be here for a couple of days,' replied Doctor Mason.

'So, she's not too badly hurt then? And the baby?'

'Mrs. Jackson, I cannot emphasise how lucky your daughter is. What she attempted to do could have easily killed her and or the baby. Due to her extreme lack of understanding of her own anatomy, she has succeeded in badly perforating the lining of the vagina, nothing more. The needle did not penetrate far enough to pass the cervix and into the womb. The bleeding will stop, and the womb is intact. The baby is completely fine. Petunia will also make a full recovery. However, Mrs. Jackson, there will be further investigation into her attempt to harm the baby. Your daughter's mental state has obviously come into question. When she has recovered well enough physically, a psychiatrist, here at the hospital, will examine her before she can be discharged. You do understand that the police have been notified?'

Joan nodded disconsolately. When would this nightmare end? It was difficult to remember a time when she simply lived life, Petunia went to work at the school, they walked the dogs and attended church. What in God's name had happened to them?

'Thank you, Doctor Mason. Why the police though?'

'Any attempted suicide must be reported. Don't worry too much about that. Take care of your daughter. Good day.'

The doctor left the cubicle and the nurse smoothed Petunia's sheet.

'Now, Mrs. Jackson, you must go home and rest. Petunia needs her rest too. You may come in tomorrow. Visiting hours are from two to four in the afternoon and six to eight in the evening. Can you find your way out? Good. Petunia will see you tomorrow then?'

Joan walked out of the hospital and sat on a seat near the main doors. She sighed deeply. She felt so weary, but she knew she must go home. Her dogs would be waiting. She stood up and searched for a taxi.

JULY 1969

'House of the Rising Sun'
The Animals

London was already heating up. The weather was very warm. The only place to gain some cool relief was near the riverbank. Traffic was already snarly; people were moving around beginning another busy business day in the capital.

But the real heat, Robert thought, was the sharp rise in the anti-establishment movement, the drug culture, the protesting university students, and commune living hippies. Blame America! It had really arisen there, partly because of the Vietnam war and partly because young people were so disillusioned with the way their parents' generation had led the world in recent years. Looking back, he realised, Americans had seen a much-loved President assassinated, their own people sent to fight a foreign war across the world, the Cold War with Russia, and the rise of unrest in the black communities, and despite all this, they were very close to putting man on the moon. He could understand how confused the youth of today felt.

England had come on board with its own burgeoning counterculture. Drugs such as LSD and marijuana had become easily obtained and commonplace. Pop music, art and film fuelled the rebellion against the establishment while the introduction of the contraceptive pill had given women freedom for the first time. Hippies had embraced the sexual revolution enthusiastically. Young people were realising that they had power, the power of numbers, and were standing up against everything the older generation held dear. Cops like Robert saw the dirty, desperate, and hopeless side of this revolt. He and his team were the ones who had to pick up the malnourished, diseased and drug addicted victims of their own quest for freedom.

As he drove through the busy streets, fittingly listening to *House of the Rising Sun* on the car radio, he wound the window down and loosened his tie. Eight o'clock and already the temperature had soared into the high seventies. He pulled into the carpark and headed for the office.

His offsider DS Coates, Alby, was already at his desk poring over a sheaf of paper. 'Mornin' guv. Managed to find out Miss Summer's real name sir.'

'Morning Alby, fill me in then.'

'I got in touch with her record company. With a bit of persuasion, they told me. Her real name is Bronwyn Coleman. Not exactly a pop name, is it? She came from up north, a town called Menston in West Yorkshire. Apparently, she has some family up there. I've got a couple of uniforms onto it. Going up today. Those two old chaps we brought in are a luverly pair of unsavoury characters. They both claim to have studied under that Swami chap, meditation an' such and have set up the 'House of the Rising Sun' to save young people who've left their 'other materialistic, regimented life behind'. If you don't mind me saying, what a pile of codswallop, sir.'

'House of the Rising Sun? Think they could have been a bit more original, couldn't they? Get on to it then. We can't do a thing unless we can prove they've been using the girls for sex or holding them against their will. See how many of the girls you can find out about, their ages first and then whether they've been threatened, abused, or supplied drugs and who by. Did we get any names and addresses yesterday?'

'We talked to as many as were still there when we arrived but most of 'em wouldn't say a thing. Some couldn't because they were too drugged out to know what was goin' on, and them as did gave us made-up names, I'm sure. Nobody in their right mind would call their kid 'Earth Unit' or 'May Butterfly'! Anyway, we'll get on to it. Drug Squad are interviewing 'em today.'

'Have those two coppers left for Menston yet?'

'Dunno sir, I can check if they've signed out a car.'

'Yeah, do that. I might go up myself. Something about that young girl. She doesn't seem like the others. Maybe it's because she's so young or because she's got money and fame. I don't know but I want to find her parents and talk to them.'

'Righto guv. On to it.'

'And Alby, tell one of the uniforms he's got another job. I want you in that car with me. Alright?'

'Yes guv. Thanks.

FEBRUARY 1953

ALICE

'Marche Funebre' (Funeral March)
Chopin

Ivy Crabtree, who lived next door to Cherry Tree Cottage on the Snicket saw the taxi bring Joan home, despite her affirmations that she was no busybody and did not spend her time peering out of her windows to see what was going on. Ivy promptly went next door to tell Gertie the latest news who then passed it on to Molly in number seven. Molly in turn told the whole story, as she knew it to the lady in the greengrocers, Mrs. Greenwood who promptly informed anyone from the village who came to shop that day.

One of those was Mary Waterhouse who lived next to the Vicar. The story she heard was that Petunia Jackson was most likely dead as she had been taken in an ambulance yesterday and had not returned with her mother. The story went that she had killed herself because she simply could not live with the terrible goings on that 'the egg man' had inflicted upon her but more so because she herself had committed a murder and God could never forgive her.

She was a devout Catholic, wasn't she?

Shocked, Mary went home and discussed it with her husband, Alan, after the two girls had gone to bed. Mary and Alan did not want their elder daughter Alice to hear anything of it, as she had suffered enough in the last year and was slowly beginning to get back to her old self. Alice had visions. She claimed, and her parents now believed her, that she could talk to those who had passed on. She had spoken or communicated on several occasions with her Uncle Charles, who had disappeared twelve years ago and whose body was only recently recovered from the Old Vicarage bowling green. Alice had told them where he was buried and true enough, his body had been recovered in the precise spot.

Alice had stopped having 'turns' and visions. Mary didn't want anything to upset her recovery. The next day, when Alice and her younger sister Elizabeth returned home from school, Elizabeth burst in the door, flushed, rosy, red cheeks and full of exciting news.

'Mum, guess what? That Petunia lady across the road killed herself, with a knife. She went to hospital and never came home!'

Eyes wide with surprise, Mary then frowned.

'Who told you that Elizabeth? Somebody at school?'

'Everybody knows, mum. They're all talking about it, even the teachers. I even heard Mrs. Titmus and Miss Guest saying about it, weren't they Alice?'

Alice nodded. 'I don't believe it though, mum.'

'Good girl, Alice. Don't listen to gossip, you two and don't pass it on!'

Alice looked uncomfortable. 'I'm pretty sure Petunia's not dead.'

Rising panic filled Mary's throat. *Oh God, not again!* She thought. *What now, just when things were beginning to get back to normal.*

'Why do you say that, Alice?'

'Because...you know I have feelings about things. Usually, I can tell if somebody around here has, you know, died. I don't tell you because I know it upsets you, but even when old Mr. Parsons from church died just after Christmas, I knew, because I saw him in the churchyard, and he told me he was going to meet his wife. He was happy, just like Uncle Charles was. I haven't had anything like that about Petunia. She's alive and so is her baby.'

Mary listened, dumb founded. Shaking her head slowly she said, 'Her baby? Alice, what are you saying, that Petunia is expecting? How do you know...?' Mary stopped. 'I wish you had told me that you still have these feelings or visions or whatever they are... We've had enough secrets in this family, Lord knows! Alice you must not say anything about any of this to anyone! Do you understand me?'

Alice nodded. 'Yes mum, of course I do but I only said it because I didn't want you to think the wrong thing. I'm sorry.' Alice cast her head down dejectedly. 'I sometimes wish I *didn't* have them, the visions I mean.'

'It's alright Alice, don't worry yourself about it. Now both of you, don't listen to gossip at school and don't say anything about what you've told me to anyone. I'm sure everything will be alright.'

Petunia, however, was not alright, as it turned out.

JULY 1969

'Mrs Brown, You've Got a Lovely Daughter'
Herman's Hermits

The three policemen drove out of London to interview Bonnie's parents. Taking the M1 straight through to Leeds, they took the quickest route through Horsforth, Rawdon and finally to Menston. Robert sat in the passenger side while Detective Sergeant Alby Coates drove and Constable Antony Preiss sat in the rear with a map unfolded on his lap, giving directions.

'Go left here, then first right. Yep, now up there to Cleasby Road. Keep going, keep going, there it is.'

The car stopped in front of a substantial three story attached house with a steeply pitched, grey slate tiled roof and freshly painted white trims. It was the end house of a row of three terraces and as such had a generous garden at the side in addition to the small front garden bordered by a stone wall.

'Nice looking place, very neat,' commented DS Coates. 'Colemans aren't short of a bob.'

'Right,' said Robert, 'Let's see why Miss Summer felt it necessary to leave this perfectly nice neighbourhood, change her name and live like a squatter in London shall we?'

DCI Turner and DS Coates got out; Preiss stayed in the car. They walked up the short path. The white door had a doorbell, which played the Westminster chimes.

'Nice.' Alby looked around noticing the neatly trimmed flowering shrubs, borders, and a small patch of grass.

The door opened. A woman of about fifty stood behind the door in the shadows.

'DCI Turner and this is DS Coates.' They both flashed their badges. 'Mrs. Coleman?'

The woman gave them a puzzled look.

'Yes, what can I do for you inspector?' she asked, deliberately avoiding addressing the more junior detective.

'Could we have a word? May we come in?'

Mrs. Coleman took a quick look both ways down the road, presumably to check that no-one saw her let two strange men into her house, then opened the door further and waved her hand impatiently for them to come inside. With one last check for onlookers, she shut the door with a sharp slam, then turned to face the men, bunched her dyed strawberry blonde hair, straightened her wide bottomed trousers, and led them into the first room on the right, a pleasant sitting room. Mrs. Coleman stood and did not ask them to be seated. Robert thought she had the look of a woman who had once been the vibrant blonde, life of the party and aware of her own good looks. Her expression now bore the hallmarks of cynicism, or perhaps discontent, her mouth pinched, her cheeks drawn, her eyes cold.

'Mrs. Coleman, I'm afraid we have some news regarding your daughter Bronwyn Coleman.'

Mrs. Coleman's reaction was certainly nothing Robert had expected. He had done this sort of thing many times in his career and generally the recipient of such a statement would produce a sharp intake of breath, a look of panic and an immediate plea for more information, particularly asking, 'was the child alright'. The woman in front of them bunched her hair again with her left hand while dismissively waving her right.

'Not surprising I suppose given her recent antics. I assumed it would happen eventually. In the morgue, is she?'

Robert frowned.

'Mrs. Coleman, your daughter was taken to hospital after a massive drug overdose, but she is going to be alright, this time. She is in a fragile state and when released, she will probably need to come home for a while.'

'Not my daughter!'

Mrs. Coleman, the woman, the mother, who spent her days at home dressed in a fashionable tailored pantsuit and wearing full make-up, regarded the two detectives down her powdered beak of a nose, with intensely dark eyes.

Robert studied the woman carefully. He had seen deference before, usually meaning that the child had been 'disowned' because of their wayward behaviour. However, watching her cold expression, he thought this was different.

'Can you explain what you mean by that Mrs. Coleman?'

At that moment, the door opened, and a man entered the room. Shortish and stocky with a balding head, he was wearing a grey suit and a forced smile. Everyone turned towards him. Mrs. Coleman tipped her chin upwards and turned away to look out of the window. *No love lost there*, thought Robert.

'Good morning, gentlemen. Robert, 'Bob' Coleman.' He held his hand out and shook enthusiastically with both men. 'Bob can save you a bob! TV ad?'

'DCI Turner and DS Coates, Scotland Yard. We were just informing your wife about your daughter Bronwyn.'

Coleman cut in. 'Our daughter? Why what has she done?'

'She has suffered a massive drug overdose. She was taken to hospital in a serious condition but is recovering as well as can be expected under the circumstances. She will be released in the next couple of days. We need to ask you both a few questions.'

'Is she alright?' Bob looked worried, more than could be said for his wife. They were all still standing.

'She is in very good hands. She will recover, I am told. Er, may we sit down?' Robert asked. Mrs. Coleman did not reply.

Robert 'Bob' swept an inviting arc towards the sofas. 'Of course, of course, please do.'

After being seated, Mrs. Coleman continued to appear uncomfortable, more so since her husband had entered the room. Robert observed her quietly, mentally noting that all was not a bed of roses in this family.

'Mrs. Coleman has just made a statement that I would like to clarify. She claims Bronwyn is not her daughter. Can you confirm that Mr. Coleman?'

Bob's expression remained cemented in the car salesman's grin, the one he had adopted on entering, but his eyes darted towards his wife, a subtle flicker conveying a hidden meaning undecipherable to the two detectives.

'Deirdre, whatever have you been saying?' Turning to face Robert, his expression now one of puzzlement he offered, 'she's in shock I should say. Of course, Bronwyn is our daughter!' He indicated the mantle upon which several framed photographs were displayed. 'She is our only daughter. There she is on the beach with her mother. Her eighth birthday and her first day at grammar school. She attends, well, did attend a very good school and always topped her class. A very good student.'

Bob puffed his already expansive chest out. Deirdre Coleman continued to stare out of the window.

'Mr. and Mrs. Coleman, did you know where Bronwyn was living? Were you in contact with her?' asked DS Coates.

Deirdre Coleman chimed in. 'Bronwyn chose to leave us nearly a year ago, inspector. She was still fifteen, only turning sixteen last month. She was lured by fame and fortune by people who make their money out of exploiting young, vulnerable children. We tried to stop her, reason with her, but she packed her bags and her damn guitar and left with two men in a van full of other hippie, drugged out young people. Of course, I understand you probably know the rest. Changed her name, the name we chose not good enough, somehow impressed a record producer, and became a 'pop star'. We did our best, gave her everything she could possibly want, the best schools and of course music lessons. She had done her grade five piano, passed with Honours, and then dumped that to play a folk guitar. Can you believe it?' Deirdre slumped in her chair, the explanation obviously draining her.

'Do you say that Bronwyn was under sixteen when she left?' asked Robert.

'Yes. I said so didn't I?' snapped Deirdre.

'Why did you not contact the police immediately? Your underage daughter takes off with a bunch of people you don't know, some of them clearly much older and you don't think there is something very wrong there? Enough to call the police?'

Robert was incredulous. How stupid could some people be?

'We didn't want any trouble. My husband runs a large business and cannot afford to risk our reputation.'

DS Alby Coates sucked air between his teeth, an audible indication of his disgust.

'What kind of business do you run, Bob?' he asked.

'He's a car salesman!' chipped in Deirdre.

'I own a large dealership in Leeds, one of the biggest. I supply fleets and offer corporate leasing to large companies, worth thousands of pounds. I cannot afford any negative press. I was quite relieved when Bronwyn changed her name. None of my people connect Bonnie Summer to me.'

His people Robert thought. *How deeply did this man's feelings of self-importance run?*

'And you have no idea who these people she went away with are? She never mentioned any names?'

Both parents shook their heads.

'Did she have a boyfriend?'

More headshakes.

'Do you know if any of her girlfriends went with her?'

'No! We don't inspector.'

'Have any of her school friends called or asked after her?'

'Obviously not! She left them just as she left us, without so much as a 'goodbye'!'

'Does she have any sisters or brothers who might know something?' Alby asked.

'No, she doesn't.' Mrs. Coleman's pressed her lips tightly together. 'Didn't my husband just tell you she was our only daughter?' She took a sideways glance at Bob.

'Mind if we take a look in her room?' Alby asked.

Mrs. Coleman shrugged.

Mr. Coleman shook his head. 'Up the stairs, first on the left.'

As they left the room, Robert told Alby to fetch Preiss. Three sets of eyes are better than two.

The men climbed the stairs and opened the door to Bonnie Summer's bedroom. Most grieving mothers whose daughter had taken off usually leave their rooms untouched, feeling that when the child returns, everything will be as they left it. This room had been cleansed, fixed up, neutralised.

There were no real indications that a teenaged girl had ever occupied this room. It had the appearance of a guest room, with plain bed covers, no posters, ornaments, stuffed toys, or schoolbooks, in fact, no paraphernalia of teenage life to be seen. Even the air seemed dead.

'Where has she put it all?' muttered Robert.

He lifted the bed's valance. Nothing under the bed. Checked the wardrobe and found only bare coat hangers. Even her clothes are gone! Incredible! Almost as if the poor girl had never existed.

Alby pointed to the wall beside the bed. 'See? She's taken lots of posters off the wall; you can see the brighter patches where they've been.'

Preiss was in the bathroom, which had been equally sanitised. Nothing in the cupboards. He checked the toilet cistern for hidden drugs. Nothing. The basin did not even have a bar of soap. The mirror above had no obvious fixing points and Preiss assumed it was glued to the wall. He felt around the edge. Sometimes things were slipped behind mirrors. Suddenly the mirror popped open like a cupboard door. It had concealed hinges and a spring-loaded catch which worked by pushing the edge of the mirror to release it. Behind the mirror was a shaving cabinet, but more interestingly an envelope tumbled out. Preiss called out, 'In 'ere guv. Found something.'

Preiss passed it to Robert who used his handkerchief to open it, revealing a hand-written letter. He unfolded it and read the first line: *Darling, sweet, sweet Bonnie, come away with me...*He skimmed to the end. It was signed off in similar style by *Your Huggy Papa, forever in this life and every life...*

'I think we have something here. 'Huggy Papa' could be a much older man than her, but the letter leaves us in no doubt that whoever he is, he's not interested in her singing career, is he? Look at the date. She was still fifteen! Better have another talk to 'Huggy Papa'!'

Robert passed the letter back to Preiss who carefully replaced it in the envelope and bagged it. Robert sighed resignedly.

'You'll take that and get forensics to test the envelope and the letter for prints? Thanks. Should get something. Did we fingerprint those two men? If not, get 'em done. Alright, I think we've finished here for now. Better go and tell the devoted parents, eh?'

Downstairs once more, Robert explained what they had found concealed in her bathroom. The Colemans were shocked and claimed they had no idea she had a boyfriend. When quizzed as to why the room had been cleared of all their daughter's personal effects, Deirdre replied that she could see no reason to keep any of it. Bronwyn had made the decision to leave everything behind and had given no indication either where she was going or whether she would ever be coming back. When asked if they would be bringing her home from the hospital, Deirdre had balked. Hadn't she got friends who would be better off looking after her in London, people in the music business? She, Deirdre, was not good at that sort of thing anyway and Bob was always at work or off somewhere on business.

Alby addressed Bob. 'Does she have a godparent or a grandmother she could go to? She really needs somewhere away from 'the scene', somewhere where she can recuperate for a couple of weeks.'

Bob looked askance at his wife. 'I suppose she could go to my mother's for a while. She is down in Devon though. I can contact her. Would someone drive her down?'

'Please do your best and make sure you let us know. Yes, someone can take her there. Mr. and Mrs. Coleman, I must say your attitude to your daughter's situation is less than encouraging. She is your only child, after all. May I remind you that you had a duty to care for her at least until she reached sixteen. Please think about what we've told you. We'll see ourselves out, thank you.'

Out in the car, Preiss was first to voice what they were all thinking.

'No wonder she ran away with a bunch of happy-go-lucky friends about as far away as she could run! I would too. What a pair!'

As they drove off, several of the neighbours were peering through the curtains watching the car leave. Most would have known it to be a police car as the uniformed cop had finally gone inside the house. The other two were 'plain clothes', detectives. Definitely something going on with the Colemans. She was a funny sort anyway, too good for the likes of her neighbourhood and he was just a glorified car salesman. Curtains gently fell back into place. The gossips of Cleasby Road had something juicy to share for a few days.

JANUARY 1953
DEMON SEED

'Rock a Bye Baby'
Children's Nursery Rhyme

On the Friday that Petunia returned home from hospital, Alice Waterhouse turned eight years old, and a party was in full swing at their house after school had finished. The weather was very cold, so the festivities were taking place inside in the 'front room', the large drawing room facing the street. Contrary to the laughter and excited squeals of a dozen eight-year-old girls, the mood at the Old Vicarage was sombre.

Joan Jackson had collected her daughter after the hospital had discharged her with a sheaf of aftercare instructions and letters of referral to a psychiatrist, a gynaecologist, and a maternity hospital.

Petunia's demeanour had not improved since her attempt to rid herself of the pregnancy. A social worker at the hospital had spent some hours with her. Petunia had been given information regarding several different options, surrendering the baby for adoption or foster care until such time as she was mentally able to rear the child herself. But given Petunia had a mother who was more than willing to help her raise a child and wanted her to live in their home for as long as she wished, Petunia was advised that this might be the best outcome for both. Petunia refused to enter into any conversation on the subject, preferring to stare sulkily at the walls as she had done at home for weeks. Although she was recovering well, physically, she seemed unable to pull herself out of her mental malaise. The baby however, had a strong heartbeat and the midwife pronounced it to be in good health as far as they could tell.

Joan brought Petunia into the living room and placed her few things on a chair. George and Hugo, the two enthusiastic retrievers, on hearing them arrive came bounding into the room to greet them with overzealous licks.

'Now then Petunia, I have made your bed up freshly and tidied up in your room. I think, for the sake of getting back to normal, you can sleep in there. No need to keep living out here for twenty-four hours every day. It's not natural. So, you can pop your things away now. Have a bit of a nap before tea. We'll eat at the normal time. Alright, I'm going to leave you to it for a bit while I see to a few things. Come on dogs, outside.'

She left Petunia standing in the middle of the room staring blankly after her.

Inside her head, her mind twisted and turned. Foul and graphic images, sickening memories and morbid predictions for the future if she were to allow this foreign demon to thrive, haunted her. She did not want to carry this thing. If she were ever to have married, the children would have been gifts from God. This was an evil seed planted by a minion of Satan. She had been thwarted once but she would not fail again. She had decided in her muddled mind that she must kill herself to finally rid the world of this sickness inside her.

Across the road, there was a party going on at the Waterhouse's. She could hear the children from over here. Good Lord, they must be loud! Perfect. She looked at the time. Nearly five o'clock. Pretty soon parents would be coming to pick the children up to take them home. She had better make her move now. As she contemplated her intentions, a slow smile formed, the first one since the awful events of last August. What she was about to do was the perfect revenge on the Devil's seed. She went into the kitchen and grabbed her coat and boots from the boot room. Her mother was out somewhere with the dogs. No-one would see her leave. She selected a sharp knife from the kitchen drawer and slipped it inside her coat. She left by the front door. She was feeling remarkably good.

Alice had opened her presents, played 'pass the parcel' and allowed her friend Elise the triumph of winning, cut her cake and handed out small bags of sweeties to her friends. Now she leaned on the settee gazing out of the window at her friends leaving in dribs and drabs. As she watched, she saw someone dressed in a long brown coat and scarf leaving the Old Vicarage. She watched, not thinking a great deal about the person, as they walked up to the crossroad where St Lawrence Road met the Snicket on the right and High Street on the left. The figure looked around furtively and turned into the Snicket. Alice was sure it was Petunia Jackson. She simply had a feeling about it and then as if she had been struck by a blow, she reeled back from the settee.

'Mum!' she yelled. 'Mum, come here, quick!'

Mary ran into the room, panicked, ready to spring into action. Seeing her daughter staring out of the window again, she stood, hands on hips.

'What is the matter, Alice? I thought you had hurt yourself!'

Alice turned to face her. Mary read her panicked expression.

'Alice! Tell me. What's going on now?'

'Sorry mum, but I was watching Petunia Jackson walk down the Snicket and I had one of those really strong feelings in my head. I think, I *know* that Petunia is going to do something very bad, again! Why is she going down there?'

'Petunia? But she only came home today. She's been in hospital. It must have been Mrs. Jackson.'

'No mum, I know it wasn't her. It was Petunia and she's going to the Egg Man's Farm to do something terrible. I can almost *see* it. Mum, you need to go and find out!'

Mary shook her head. 'Ohhh no, not again! Not me. What I saw in that barn, well it was awful. Look, I'll call the police. They can sort it out. She's no reason at all to be going over there anyway, now that Eric's gone, and the place is empty.'

Alice looked distraught. Mary could see it in her eyes, and she knew that her little girl was once again dragging them into a continuation of the horror that had beset the whole village last year.

'Oh, alright, but dad's going with me. Will you be able to take care of Elizabeth for ten minutes?'

'Yes mum, 'course I can. I'm a grown-up girl now.'

Yes, you are, Alice. You certainly are thought Mary.

'Alan!' she yelled. 'ALAN!'

JULY 1969

'Where Do You Go to My Lovely?'
Peter Sarstedt

Bonnie Summer, pop star, teenage heart throb of thousands of young boys, pin-up girl and beloved icon of the young generation, shifted uncomfortably on the hard hospital bed. She felt like none of those things right now. In fact, she had never felt less groovy, less with it. She had asked the nurse to give her a hairbrush, some make-up, a mirror, but they had told her she needed more time to recover, and they needed to see her natural colour because it was an indicator of many things medical. Like what? She thought.

Her hair felt matted and unclean. Her stomach felt very sore. She knew she had had it pumped to rid her of much of the booze and pills she had taken. She hadn't known a thing about it at the time but now she was reaping the rewards. She still felt terrible. The hospital staff had declined to let anyone other than her parents see her, which was fine with her, as she didn't want fans seeing her like this. Her parents clearly didn't want to see her like this either as they had not set foot inside the hospital, so far. Bonnie Summer was feeling extremely miserable when a nurse pulled the curtain aside.

'Someone to see you, Miss Summer. A Detective Turner.'

She stepped aside and a tallish, well-built, middle-aged man with greying hair which still showed sandy in places, came in and sat in the chair next to the bed. He smiled, a smile which crinkled the corners of his eyes and immediately had the effect of putting Bonnie at ease. He was probably the same age as her father, but the two men were worlds apart in every way. This man warmed the room whereas her father made it cringe.

'Miss Summer or can I just call you Bronwyn?'

Bonnie was taken aback. It was quite a while since anyone had addressed her by that name. She levered herself into a sitting position with a small groan.

'Still sore?' asked Robert.

She nodded. 'Call me Bonnie. So, you found out my real name then. I don't like it and it wouldn't look good on a record label, would it? People would think I was a gospel singer or something.'

Robert smiled and observed the girl as she spoke. Although she had turned sixteen, sitting in the bed, she looked no more than fourteen. Her pale, almost transparent face, framed by long, untidy ringlets of rich red hair, held wide eyes, the colour of a summer sky. Her small hands were folded on top of the coverlet as she smiled timidly at him. Nothing came to mind to explain it, but he had felt an immediate connection as soon as he had walked in. He remembered seeing her photograph and how her eyes had captivated him. Not that he had *those* kinds of thoughts about her, his feelings were more of wanting to protect.

'Alright Bonnie, we have been to see your parents. I must say, they seemed relatively unconcerned about you.'

Bonnie flapped her hand across the bed cover.

'They hate me, and I hate them.'

'They are very strong words. Why do you say that?'

'Didn't they tell you? I've never been the daughter they wanted. Our family has never really felt right.'

'Wait a minute, explain what you mean by 'not right'. Why don't you start from the beginning? I've got plenty of time.'

Robert glanced at his Seiko wristwatch and thought he didn't really, but he didn't want to discourage her from talking. He very nearly took that flapping hand in his but stopped himself in the nick of time.

Bonnie began talking. She spoke about her early years and how she always tried to be the very best to make them proud. The words tumbled out in a torrent.

'I'm not saying they haven't given me everything I wanted. It's not that but, you know, is that *love?* I always did well at school, and they were soooo proud, trumpeting to anyone who'd listen how clever I was. I passed my eleven plus when I was only ten and got into that posh grammar school. I was supposed to be a doctor or a lawyer or a teacher. Dad paid for music and ballet lessons. I went to art classes. I loved all of that, you know, but could I study any of those things at school? No, yet they gave me a guitar for Christmas one year. It's the best thing they ever gave me. I taught myself a bit and sang a few Peter, Paul, and Mary songs. I was quite good at those, just simple stuff.'

'Go on,' urged Robert. 'How did you get to be living in that place in London? You couldn't have just done that on your own.' Mindful of how time was creeping on, he wanted to get to the important parts. *Why did you end up like this?*

'Yeah, I'm getting to that, gotta give me time, man. So, I went to our Country Fair with some friends. They had people singing on stage, you know, a group. They sang 'Lemon Tree' and I knew that song. I was right up the front, you know, singing with them, really getting with it, 'cause, you know, I love that song. One of the guys told me to come on stage and sing it with them. He asked me if I played guitar and I said I could play that song, so he handed me one, a guitar I mean, and stuck me on the microphone with him. He was groovy. Our voices, you know, blended soooo perfectly together.'

Bonnie paused. To Robert's consternation, her eyes were glistening as she remembered. She took a sip from her glass on the side table and wiped her eyes with the heel of her hand.

'Can you go on Bronwyn, Bonnie? What was his name, do you know?'

'Yeah, like he was hip, you know, but his name was Peter. Anyway, then they sang *Where Do You Go to My Lovely'*. Do you know it? The chords are easy, so l stayed up there and played along and he sang just like Peter Sarstedt. You know, l ended up staying up for the last few songs. My friends were clapping and dancing to the music we played. Do you get it? The music *we* played! l just felt at home. That's where l belong.'

'Anyway, when they finished their set, Peter asked me to hang around. My friends stayed too, but it was me Peter wanted to talk to. He asked me to join the group, right there, you know? Wow! He said l had a voice like an angel, and l should be their lead singer. He said l would earn some bread, can you dig it?'

'To cut a long story short, he asked me to go with them. l said l would if my friend could come too. Peter said she could be like a back-up singer, you know? 'Course when l told *them* they threatened to lock me up!'

'You mean your parents?'

'Yeah. So, l packed a bag and Peter brought his van around and picked me up.'

Robert sighed, visions of young women, girls who had been picked up on the side of the road in various conditions; beaten, raped, drugged. No matter how many messages the police, the government, doctors, and teachers tried to use to educate these young people, they continued to find themselves in deep trouble by 'following their dreams'.

'Bonnie, you are very fortunate to have made it alive and in one piece. l can't tell you how many l have picked up who did not. You took an enormous risk.'

Bonnie screwed her face up. 'It was just Peter and what else was I supposed to do? They wouldn't listen to me. They don't care what *I* want. They only care what their stupid, rich friends think. Anyway, I proved them wrong. I've earned more money than my dad, doing what I love.'

'Is this what you wanted? Being stuck in a hospital? Stomach pumped? Feeling sick?'

Bonnie shook her head and began pleating the bed sheet with nervous fingers. 'It was all so cool when it started. Peter was my manager and made me a solo star, got me a record deal and we went touring. He looked after me. He *cared* about me!'

'Well, I'm sorry Bonnie, but this doesn't look like he *cared* enough!'

'I was handling it, you know, the drugs. He just gave me what I needed to keep my music groovy. He didn't let it get out of hand. It was when we came to London and there were so many other singers and groups, I begged him for a bit more. I was losing my vibe a bit and the pot and LSD were not doing it for me. Peter told me he had something that would really help me out, but I wasn't to tell anyone, not even the others. He gave me this other stuff, better than LSD and I went on some trip, man. I think this happened then. I think somebody gave me other stuff as well, but I didn't know and I had lots of booze. I'm confused, man.'

'So, you're telling me that this Peter, your manager, was giving you drugs and alcohol? Were you sleeping with him as well?'

'Of course, I was, am. We all do. He's like our guru, you know, he protects us, loves us, and watches out for us!'

'Bonnie, where is Peter now? Can you give me his full name and address?' Seeing the horrified look on her face he hastily added, 'we'll need to interview him to corroborate your story. He's not in trouble...yet'

Bonnie shook her head. 'I don't know his other name and the only address I know is where we all live. Sorry.'

'OK then. Anyway, we're going to leave it there for today. You've been very brave telling me this. Of course, it will be kept confidential, but I will need to talk to you again. You rest and get well, and I'll be in touch. Bye-bye Bonnie.'

Robert left her cubicle. He planned to head back to the office to check on what Alby had found out about this Huggy Papa character. He and 'Peter' were one and the same. Bonnie had freely admitted he was giving some of the girls drugs and that he was sleeping with them, but did that mean having sex with them? He made a mental note to check if she had been swabbed on arrival at the hospital. God, she's only sixteen, he thought. How bloody sad.

He knew he would have trouble sleeping while this investigation was going on. He would have dreams of young, vulnerable girls. He would be twisted up in the dreams, not knowing if he was the one enticing them and seducing them or someone else. The dreams always ended with him waking drenched in sweat. Often, he would give up on the idea of sleep, make himself a coffee and go out to the sitting room of his spacious flat where he would work until the morning. It had the effect of keeping his mind occupied, keeping him sane. *It wasn't me. I wasn't the one who did those terrible things. Or did I? Sometimes he wasn't so sure.*

JULY 1969

'Space Oddity'
David Bowie

Bob dialled his mother's number. He rarely called her and saw her even less often. He held the phone to his ear waiting as it rang on. Then a click. His mother's voice.

'Rae Coleman speaking.'

'Mum, it's Robert. How are you?'

Bob could see her expression almost as if she were transmitting it on a television wavelength. Puzzlement, quickly followed by suspicion.

'What a surprise,' she said, her voice loaded with sarcasm. 'How long has it been, Robert? Let me see, did you call me at Christmas, Easter, on my birthday? I can't remember therefore I don't think you did.'

Her voice, her words made him cringe.

'I'm not sure, mother. It has been a very upsetting time, what with Bronwyn taking off and Deirdre beside herself. We must come down to Devon soon, while the weather holds.'

'What do you want, Robert? Can't be money, can it? After all you're the big shot car dealer on the TV, aren't you? 'Big Bob, he'll always save you a bob'. Isn't that it?'

Robert switched the hand piece to his left hand, took his handkerchief out of his pocket and gave a good honk into it.

'Deirdre and I were wondering if Bronwyn could come and stay with you for a couple of weeks. She's got herself into a bit of trouble and must get out of London for a while.'

'Why can't she come up to you then? What kind of trouble is she in?'

Robert could picture her squinting eyes, full of accusations directed at him and his wife. He always felt cowed by his mother. She had never let him forget that he had not managed to independently become a businessman. He had barely passed O levels and had left school to clean cars in a car sales yard. Marrying Deirdre had been his ticket to success as her family had bankrolled his whole business. As far as Rae was concerned, he had lost any dignity when he became a kept man.

'She took some drugs and she had to go to hospital. She'll be fine but needs to stay somewhere quiet, away from the 'scene'. Mum, can she come down to you? I know you've still got her room ready. We'll pay her way for food and board.'

'I ask you again, what's wrong with you and Deirdre?'

Robert sighed. 'You know how Deirdre is. She's not good at this sort of thing. Look, it would be doing us, *me*, a great favour if you could have her. She's always got on well with you. She'll feel at home.'

'Says a lot, doesn't it?' Rae sneered on the other end of the phone. 'Alright, when is she coming?'

'I'm not sure yet. I'll have to get in touch with the hospital to see when she can be discharged. I'll let you know. Thanks mum.'

Bob hung up and stared at the handset. Although the phone lay dead, he could feel the admonishment and criticism streaming through the line. He felt that if he touched that phone again, his hand would burn. Why had things turned out this way? All those years ago when he and Deirdre were starting out, they had loved each other, hadn't they? They couldn't wait to start a family, but nothing happened. They both thought Deirdre was barren, unable to conceive but all the tests showed it was him. From that day onwards, their lives had never been the same. He had known that Deirdre blamed him for depriving her of having her own children. She became cold, disinterested in him. That was when he suggested adoption. She was not keen. She wanted, *yearned* for a pregnancy, to deliver her own baby, but eventually she agreed, and they adopted a baby girl, Bronwyn.

Deirdre never really took the little girl to be her own, while Bob flapped around wondering how to deal with her. They managed to present a decent approximation of a natural, loving family and it was fair to say Bronwyn wanted for nothing. But Bob knew and so did his mother, that genuine love was missing between adopted daughter and mother at least.

Bob left his study and called out to his wife who was watching the TV in the sitting room. The news all over the TV and papers was the forthcoming moon landing.

'I'm watching the three astronauts going up towards the capsule on top of the rocket, Bob. Come and have a look. What do you think? Do you think they can really do it?'

Deirdre looked up. She had a cigarette in a bone holder in one hand and a glass of sherry in the other. She tapped ash into a crystal ashtray on the side table.

'Deirdre, I have just been on the phone to my mother asking her if she can take *our* daughter in while she recuperates. I can tell you she is non too impressed! She thinks we should be doing it, but I managed to sweet talk her into it.'

Deirdre turned back to the television where the three astronauts had reached the top of the platform. They were waiting while photographs were being taken before being given the all-clear to climb into the capsule.

'Good,' she commented.

'For Christ's sake woman, we're talking about Bronwyn here! Can't you at least show some interest?'

'What do you want me to do Robert?'

Bob sighed.

'We must go to the hospital and see Bronwyn. We need to talk to the doctors and find out when she can be discharged and what needs to be done for her while she is recovering. It's the least we can do. You cannot seriously expect my mother to do that!'

Dierdre got out of her chair, carefully and pointedly placed the half-drunk sherry on the table and stubbed the cigarette, then flounced over to the television and switched it off.

'There! Happy? Alright, when do you want to go? Tomorrow? I will make a reservation at Claridge's and then I will go and pack.'

1953

PETUNIA GOES BACK

'Il ne revient pas' (He's not coming back)
from Faust, an opera by Charles Gounod

The wind bit with icy teeth, penetrating the long gabardine coat she wore. She shivered, wishing she had taken her scarf. Head down, shoulders hunched, she walked across the road and turned right into the snicket. The farm was on the left, deserted since police and forensic teams had vacated it. Petunia had no idea if any of Eric's family had claimed the property or if anyone might be in the cottage, but it was not her destination. She slipped through the gate and made for the barn, the scene of her entrapment and torture; the place of conception of the demon she was carrying. Wind whistled around the eaves, blowing flurries of dead leaves and remnants of straw around her feet. The animals had gone. The only sounds were the relentless wind and rattling shingles on the roof. Everything looked deserted, abandoned. Another gust shook the huge wooden barn doors.

Petunia approached the great doors which had so recently been padlocked against her. There was no padlock now, simply an iron bar through the hasp to stop the doors blowing open. She shoved it free and opened the door just enough to squeeze inside. She stopped, letting her eyes adjust, as she had done before. She remembered how her eyes hurt when they brought her into the daylight. The light in here was comforting allowing her to gradually see the interior of the barn. Straw was still scattered across parts of the floor. There were the hooks where her chains had been held. The chains were gone. Looking up she saw hooks on the ceiling beams. She remembered they were the first things she saw when she opened her eyes, lying on her back, chained to the floorboards. She stepped inside the barn feeling an odd familiarity, unsettling, yet now an irrevocable part of the fabric of Petunia Jackson. A surprising flush of pride swept over her as she recalled the unexpected strength and utter determination which had allowed her to be the one who had survived. For a fleeting moment, she saw herself as a strong woman with a future, then reality crushed her spirit like a leaden blanket. *The spawn. She must destroy it.*

Somehow it felt right and just that the act should be undertaken here. The ultimate retribution on that vile man, that his progeny should be aptly disposed of at the very spot it came into being, and in the very same way he had intended to dispatch her. The thought gave her great satisfaction.

Petunia removed her coat and placed the knife carefully next to one of the hooks in the floor. Next, she looked around for a hay rake or large broom and found none. All taken for forensic examination and not returned, she assumed. Not to worry. She began pushing with her feet and gathering in her arms as much straw as she could, placing it between the four hooks, exactly where she had lain just over four months ago. After she had made the bed of straw, she sat on it to catch her breath.

The constant whistling through the gaps in the walls and roof was almost deafening, while the hinges of the doors which were now unsecured, screeched as they swung back and forth. It was freezing in the barn, but Petunia no longer felt it. She knew she must take all her clothes off and lay naked on the straw. The cold wouldn't bother her for long. She began to undress, throwing her clothing items into the corner where *he* had done so. Finally naked, she lay down and spread her arms and legs as he had. She had placed the knife at her left hand, which was the one she had managed to free and had eventually strangled the beast with.

She was ready. In a former life she would have prayed. She did not. No God could help her now.

***

Alan and Mary stepped out of their back door and were immediately assaulted by the gale, nearly pushing them off their feet. Alan took Mary's arm and together they made their way towards the snicket and the now defunct Turner Farm. There was no rain, but the icy air stung like knives, slicing through the exposed skin on their faces. Tucking their heads down, they approached the farm. The wooden gate stood ajar. The vacant cottage crouched against the howling wind. The barn behind loomed. The doors had blown open and now swung back and forth banging repeatedly against the walls. Inside, a dark cavity yawned.

***

Petunia's breathing steadied. She felt calm. She took the knife in her hand, placed her right hand over left on the handle and held the knife above her exposed and slightly distended belly, the curved blade just touching the skin. She knew what to do.

***

Alan approached the furiously swinging doors with caution. He realised the wind possessed the doors and catching one of them to secure it was out of the question. They were solid, heavy, battering rams. Getting past them would be like a game of Russian Roulette. He yelled to Mary to keep well back. He stood watching the doors swing, trying to see a pattern. There was none. The wind played a random game.

'Be careful Alan, please!' Mary shouted against the roar.

He saw a chance and sprinted through the gap just as both doors slammed together.

'Alan!' screamed Mary. She saw he had succeeded in entering the barn by the skin of his teeth. Now she must wait.

Petunia raised the knife. At the penultimate moment she uttered a last prayer. 'Forgive me Father'.

'Petunia, STOP!' yelled Alan, aware that his voice would be drowned out by the bellowing gale outside.

He sprinted towards her across the floor, which was strewn with hay, some of it whipped into furious flurries which flew in his face, stinging and blurring his already limited vision. In slow motion, through the melee, he watched in horror as the knife came down. He saw the smooth arc it took towards her belly. The sharp point touched her skin, indenting the soft flesh, but her hands were shaking so badly that she hesitated for a moment. It was enough. His strides felt like tiny steps as he tried to cover enough ground to reach her in time. Alan slid the last two feet towards her and lashed out with his hand to knock the knife away. His arm connected with the blade. The knife sliced downwards on his forearm, straight through the jacket sleeve and peeling away the skin underneath in a long, bloody strip. At the same time the point tore across Petunia's bare stomach. She screamed and wrestled to regain her hold on the weapon, but it slid away from her, clattering across the wooden floor.

Blood was now welling copiously from Alan's arm and Petunia's abdomen. Alan kicked the knife across the floor to the farthest corner. Petunia was shrieking at him but the wind noise through the open, flapping barn doors was deafening. She scrambled to her feet and made for the knife.

'You can't stop me! Get out of my way and let me do what I have to do!' she screamed.

Alan caught her around the waist and held her in a bear hug as she grappled with him, hitting out, punching, and kicking. But Alan was stronger than her, even with her newfound will, and he held her tightly until she gave up and slumped, sobbing.

'Why couldn't you just leave me alone?'

Her words were lost to him in the ricocheting gusts eddying around the barn. They shuffled, still locked together, across to where she had thrown her clothes and finally releasing the hold on her, he picked her coat up and handed it to her. Helping her to gather it around her naked and bleeding body, he walked her to the doors.

He put his face close to her ear and shouted, 'Got to get you out of 'ere. Hang on to me and go with me. Alright?'

She nodded.

Outside, Mary took shelter around the side of the barn in the lee of the strengthening wind. She waited. This was the worst kind of waiting, nothing like the queues at the bus stop or in the grocers. The end of this waiting was unknown, and each second felt like an hour. She stamped her feet to try to keep them warm, but she could feel burning, the start of chilblains, she thought miserably.

Suddenly Alan appeared in the storm, supporting Petunia who wore only her brown coat. Mary saw as the coat flailed in the wind that she was naked underneath. She saw blood, again, bringing the memory of the first time she had entered the barn back into sharp focus. That moment when she had discovered the ravaged Petunia with her attacker laying across her, both covered in blood, had been burned forever into Mary's mind.

Oh God, what had she done now? Then she saw the blood all over Alan, his jacket sleeve, and the front of his shirt. She ran to him hysterically shouting, 'Alan! Are you alright? You're hurt!'

'Help me get her back to the vicarage, Mary!' Although they were shouting at the top of their voices, the wind swallowed the words. 'Come on, help me!'

Petunia half slumped between them as they each grabbed an arm and pulled her along towards her home. Their eyes stung, assaulted by flying dirt, leaves and other detritus whipped up by the gale. Trying to shield her eyes, Mary let go of Petunia's arm. Unsupported, Petunia collapsed to the ground. Mary saw the cut across her stomach and screamed.

Alan picked Petunia up and continued to drag her home. Just as they reached the gate, Joan Jackson and the two dogs were coming from the High Street across St Lawrence Road, themselves fighting the buffeting of the wind. When Joan realised what she was seeing, the brown flapping coat, her daughter's naked body underneath with streaks of blood, she too screamed, a long, desolate howl. Dropping the dogs' leashes, she sprinted towards them.

'Help us get her inside, Joan. Just help!'

Alan pushed, dragged, and lifted Petunia to the front door. Joan opened it and the three of them got her into her bedroom where at last the roar of the wind was a duller whine outside.

Petunia moaned. Alan explained what had transpired, how he had prevented a much worse scenario. Petunia whimpered. Joan sobbed. Mary was shaking uncontrollably. Joan thanked them and told Alan he must go home and get his arm seen to. Mary thanked Joan and grabbed Alan's good arm.

'Joan, can you manage?' Alan enquired. 'If you need anything, just ring. We're in the telephone directory.'

Joan nodded. Mary guessed Joan neither wanted nor needed a third party while she dealt with Petunia. Mary and Alan left.

'It's not too bad love, just a bit of skin off me arm, that's all,' Alan comforted Mary. 'Come on, let's be getting' on home. Alice must be wondering where we are. Said we were only going to be ten minutes and 'ere we are, gone half an hour.'

On returning home, they found Alice and Elizabeth playing in the kitchen. Neither appeared worried, nor distressed.

'You're home,' commented Alice. 'I told you Petunia was going to do something bad. But she's alright, isn't she?'

'Yes, chick. She's alright.'

'Get that jacket off,' commanded his wife, 'I want to see if you need stitches!'

1953

STRIKE TWO

'Tears on My Pillow'
Little Anthony and the Imperials

Joan called the doctor. She had examined Petunia's wound after carefully cleaning it with some cotton swabs soaked in Dettol. The wound was superficial, however one small section about three inches long looked a little too deep to not need stitches. Joan had applied a thick pad of cotton gauze over it and used tape to keep it in place. Petunia was quiet. She had not offered any explanation of her actions and Joan had not insisted.

An hour later, Doctor Eglington arrived. Joan took his coat and hat and showed him into Petunia's room. Without his hat, the doctor's bald dome shone, broken only by a thin fringe of hair just above his ears. His glasses perched precariously on the end of a long, narrow nose, under which he sported a neatly trimmed moustache. Dr Egg, as he was known in the district, looked weary and none too impressed at being called out this late on a Friday night.

'Thank you, Mrs. Jackson. Now then, how are you feeling Miss Jackson? May I have a look at the wound?'

Petunia nodded, making no eye contact.

The doctor carefully undid the padding Joan had placed over the wound. It stuck a little and as he pulled it free, Petunia winced, but said nothing. The cut was long but only deep right at the centre. The bleeding had stopped but it was still weeping.

'I think a couple of stitches are needed, just to hold it right here.' He pointed to the cut. Opening his bag, he took out antiseptic, gauze, forceps, scissors, and sutures. 'I'm going to give you some local anaesthetic and then I'll stitch you up.'

Petunia nodded again, lethargically. The process was over in a matter of minutes. The doctor peeled off gloves, placed them with the used gauze swabs, and the empty suture packets and wrapped everything up before putting it in his bag to dispose of at the surgery. He had put a dressing on the wound, instructing the patient to keep it dry and she must come into the surgery on Monday to have the dressing changed. Doctor Eglington regarded Petunia quizzically.

'How did you come by this injury?' Petunia clamped her mouth shut. 'I am aware, Miss Jackson that you are pregnant and that you were recently hospitalised for a similar injury, which I am informed, was self-inflicted.' The doctor, perched on the side of the bed. 'I think you need some help, my dear. You are obviously not coping with the situation and...' The sentence hung in the air.

Petunia glared at him. 'Situation? No, I am not coping with the 'situation'! Do you know how I came to be in this 'situation'? That animal across the road stripped me naked, chained me up and repeatedly assaulted me. If I hadn't strangled him while he was on top of me, I would be dead by now. To find out that he has done this to me is unbearable. I want this thing out of me, and no-one will do it for me, so I had to try myself. I don't care if I die. I have no life now. Don't you see? I have nothing, I *am* nothing. I can't live here among people I have known all my life. I can't face my priest, my fellow church goers, my school children. No-one. I will find a way out, eventually. I don't care how long it takes or how.'

Doctor Eglington patted her hand. 'I'm sure you don't really feel like that, dear. What you need is some rest and time to adjust. Mrs. Jackson, I'd like to consult on this with a colleague of mine, would you mind? I think he may be able to help your daughter. Meanwhile, when she settles down a little, she can have something to eat and make sure she gets a good night's rest. Things always look much brighter with a new day! I'll see you on Monday then.'

With that the doctor left with a benign smile. Petunia stared after him. She sighed a deep sigh, shook her head miserably and closed her eyes.

***

First thing on Monday morning, Jonathon Eglington called up his friend and colleague, Doctor Andrew Floyd, MBCS, MRC Psych. Jon Eglington often marvelled that he and Andrew were still friends after university, Jon in his lemon shirt, brown slacks and tie and Andrew who much preferred the starched open collar shirt with cravat and pin striped tailoring! Jon gave the psychiatrist a synopsis of the situation, explaining all that he was aware of. Andrew listened carefully.

'Sounds like she should be one of ours, old man. Why wasn't she referred by the hospital after the first episode? Did anyone speak to her?'

'I'm not sure. I'll ring them, find out what the wash-up was afterwards. Look, I'm seeing her this afternoon, so I might find out a bit more from her mother, but to tell you the truth, they are both a bit odd. Anyway, how are you doing, old chap? Keeping up with it all? How is your delightful wife?'

After a short conversation regarding their respective wives' health and welfare, Jonathon rung off. He dialled the number of the hospital where Petunia had been taken and asked to speak to one of the doctors who had seen her. All the doctors were engaged. He spoke to the matron on ward 7A, who remembered Petunia well.

'Poor girl. Yes, she did see our resident psychiatrist. He gave her a referral to a doctor closer to her home, but she flatly refused any help. Her mother said she wanted to help her with the baby, you know, help her raise it and she was very convincing. In the end we discharged her in the care of her mum. The police were notified, but they didn't want to pursue anything, considering she was going to be cared for at home. Has that helped at all?'

'Oh yes, it has. Thank you, Matron.'

Jonathon rang off. He dialled Andrew again, who answered immediately. He repeated the matron's words.

'Well, what do you think?' he asked.

'I think she needs to be hospitalised in a psychiatric institution until such time as she shows a significant change in her mental stability, or the baby is delivered. If you would like to refer her, I can take it from there. She would be better off with us. She could go to the Mental Health section of the Menston Hospital. They are very, very good.'

'Good. I'll speak to them both when they come in this afternoon. I'll be in touch.'

Jonathon rang off. Petunia's appointment was for 3pm. He made a note in her file regarding Dr Floyd's recommendation. He then penned a letter of referral to Dr Floyd and added it to her file.

***

She grudgingly had to admit to herself that she was not feeling so sick in the last few days, but Petunia's feelings about the child she was carrying had not changed. She fancied she was being consumed by it from the inside, slowly picking away at her body and her mind, its evil claws digging deeper and deeper into her psyche. Sometimes her mind was not her own, the times when the voice inside her head told her to eat and drink and feed it well. She wanted to starve it, but against her subconscious will she forced herself to eat. Many times, the food was regurgitated, not because she felt ill but because she needed to rid herself of the nutrition which was propagating the thing.

Petunia was living a hellish nightmare every hour of every day. She saw no redemption, no forgiveness, no future, and no eternal life in the arms of her Saviour. She did not want to live. For the last two days she had hardly left her room, only to visit the bathroom. Her mother would bring food and speak to her in vacuous placatory terms with no understanding of how Petunia felt. Speaking to her mother was something she found impossible to do, so she remained silent.

On Saturday, Father Michael had visited. Unlike the day before, she was also unable to speak to him. No-one could do anything for her. After a short but heartfelt prayer, he left assuring her that things would improve soon, and she would start looking forward to the birth.

Today she lay on her bed. Joan had been in and checked her dressing, left her breakfast, and offered to take her to church. Petunia had spat one word at her, NO! Now she was alone in the house as Joan had left to go to the church.

She lay there, her stare fixed on her increasingly swelling belly. With utter disgust she realised her breasts were also enlarged and a little tender. Her body was becoming an abomination and she was almost powerless to do anything about it. Almost. The house was empty except for the two dogs, George, and Hugo, both of which were in the kitchen, probably snoozing on their beds. Tears stung as she contemplated dismally the life she had foreseen before. She had loved her teaching, her students. That she had not met a suitable partner mattered not one iota. If it was right and meant to be, it would have happened. After all she was young enough. She had plenty of time. But she didn't. Not now. Everything in her existence had been ripped away from her.

She levered herself from the bed with a slight groan. The wound was still tender, after all, the cut had been quite deep. She opened the door and padded down the hall to the kitchen. Both dogs' tails twitched at the extremity but otherwise, they remained still. She went to the kitchen drawer where the knives were kept. It was empty. A frown drew her face into a grimace. Realisation that the knives had been removed to prevent her from repeating her actions last Friday infuriated her. She slammed the drawer shut. *They've got to be somewhere. Where has she hidden them?*

Petunia began pulling every drawer open, rifling through looking for the knives. Nothing. She opened all the cupboard doors. Nothing there either. Moving into the dining room she yanked the dresser drawers and doors open, then the secret drawer in the long extension table. They were nowhere to be seen. The two retrievers watched her with interest, probably expecting her to find a ball to play with them. By now Petunia was seething with anger and resentment. How dare her mother assume she could control her daughter's life like this? She continued to ransack the house to no avail.

Stopping for a moment, she had a sudden thought. *The garden shed! That's where they'll be, and even if they aren't, I'll find something in there!* She threw on her coat and boots and let herself out of the back door. Both dogs scrambled up and raced to get through before she closed it. She made her way down the path between beds of spinach, carrots, parsnips, and trellises of runner beans. The small shed stood at the end of the path next to a glasshouse and the potting shed. The dogs raced ahead, exuberant with anticipation. The little shed was quite dark inside, the small window, stained with years of grime, let minimal light through. George and Hugo barked excitedly, tails wagging furiously. Petunia's eyes scanned the interior, struggling to see in the dimness. There were shelves on the walls packed full of tools, both gardening and workshop, trays, gloves, watering cans, packets of fertilizer, seeds, and insecticides. There were shovels and spades, forks, rakes, a large crowbar, and post diggers. Taking up the bulk of the floorspace, a wheelbarrow sat full of loam. The knives were not there. She began studying the tools. There were some screwdrivers, hammers, and such but then she spied a pointed spike with a wooden handle. The spike was about eight inches long and looked to be quite sharp. This would do, she thought and grabbed it from the wall bracket.

By now all rational thought had deserted her. She saw the 'Egg Man', Eric Turner, looming out of the past, his face creased into a gruesome grin of victory; victory over her! Even in death, he had prevailed, forcing her to carry his progeny. There was nothing else for it. She must destroy it and to do that, she must take her own life. It was the only way. She took the spike in both hands.

The two dogs were still barking at the promise of a game or a walk when the door flew open. Joan stood silhouetted against the dull late autumn day. She saw Petunia standing there in her overcoat and boots, the spiked tool held towards her belly, positioned ready to plunge and stab.

'Petunia!' Joan shrieked and lunged for the tool. She succeeded in knocking it out of Petunia's hand, sending it spinning across the dusty floor.

'You hid the knives!' screamed Petunia at her mother. 'You have no right!'

She pushed past her mother and ran back down the path, past the back door, picked up her pace along the side of the house and sprinted down the front path to the gate. Through the gate she made for St Lawrence Road, losing Joan. However, George and Hugo, who thought this was the best game, were right alongside her, barking joyfully. A green car appeared, coming in the opposite direction towards the top of St Lawrence when Petunia suddenly left the pavement and hurtled herself in the path of the oncoming car. Tyres screeched but the car connected with Petunia, bouncing her off the front right-hand mudguard. She fell screaming and rolled to the gutter. The driver flew out of the driver's seat.

'Oh my God, Petunia, what are you doing?' Father Michael bent to the screaming woman and looked up helplessly as Joan arrived, breathless. The dogs cavorted and barked. 'She ran straight out in front of me! I couldn't stop!' he uttered desolately.

1969

Bonnie sat on the headland, a fresh breeze sending her auburn ringlets streaming behind her. Far below, the sea rolled and receded leaving a hollow echo each time the waves struck the rugged shoreline. Gulls wheeled overhead against the clear blue sky. Down in the village the temperature had been warm, summery. Up here she felt she was half-way to the transparent moon where the air was cool, fresh, and clean. Fixing her eyes on the pale and translucent disc in the midday sky, she studied the dark and light shades, 'the man in the moon'. Images of the moon lander on that surface had peaked Bonnie's interest sharply. She gazed upwards, wondering how the astronauts must be feeling, looking out of their window seeing the dusty surface of Earth's only natural satellite. She wondered whether they would make it back to Earth, to their families and friends. Thinking of families brought melancholy feelings and guilt that she had abandoned her own family. Would she ever go back to them?

Bonnie had only arrived yesterday, brought to her nanna's in an unmarked police car. Their arrival in the village created no interest.

It was the high season when picturesque coastal villages such as this one in Devon were overrun with tourists. She had spoken briefly with her dad, who had rung the hospital, to explain where she was going and with whom, on her release. He had told her how her mother was not well and that although they had planned to come and see her, it had become impossible to organise it. They would try to get down to Devon soon. Bonnie had thought she would be going home to Menston, but having had no visits from her parents, she was not surprised to be heading down to Devon. She loved it there and she adored her Nanna. She thought she would be okay recovering for a few days in the beautiful coastal village.

Nanna's house was in a row of mismatched cottages which climbed raggedly up a steep hill overlooking the coast. Her house was about halfway up, which meant it overlooked the ones below her, and the ones above peered straight into her windows and small garden. Most of the cottages were painted white with slate tiled roofs, tiny casement windows and colourful doors. Everyone had baskets of highly coloured petunias, lobelia, and pansies. The gardens were bursting with lupins, delphiniums, hollyhocks and climbing honeysuckle. The road, which was not wide enough for motor traffic, served as a walkway from the top of the village to the wharf, where fishing boats sat idle, waiting for the next foray into the bays and coves. Running along the quay was the main street, which was home to the local pub, a general store, post office, fish and chip shop and the home of the village's lifeboat and radio room. There was a tiny tearoom, serving proper Devonshire Teas with real clotted cream for which the tourists clamoured, and a popular seafood restaurant.

Bronwyn, as Nanna Coleman insisted on calling her had been discharged from the hospital without any fuss, bundled into the car and they had slipped out un-noticed. The fact that she had disappeared off 'the scene' had drawn attention from the pop magazines and the press. Headlines had begun to appear asking 'Where is Bonnie Summer?' 'Bonnie Summer Expecting a Christmas Baby' and 'Teenage Pop Star Elopes to Greece with 57-Year-Old Boyfriend'. Her songs had skyrocketed in popularity because of the speculation. Everyone wanted an interview with her. Her agent had known she was in hospital and had been repeatedly calling them asking for details of her whereabouts. DCI Turner ordered that no information must be divulged to anyone other than her parents.

Bonnie had settled in quickly. She had always loved coming down to Devon as a young child. Many school holidays had been spent here and when her grandad had been alive, she would go fishing off the quay with him, crabbing on the beaches and exploring the rugged coast on their long walks. He had suffered a heart attack out on the lifeboat, and they had not been able to get him back to shore quickly enough. He had gone before they made the wharf. She missed him very much but was very fond of Nanna. Bronwyn had had her own room since she was little. When she had arrived last night with her few things and plonked them on the bed, suddenly she had felt very young again. Her life of the last twelve months felt like someone else's. She had tucked into a hearty meal, sat in the cosy sitting room and talked with Nanna about nothing and everything not related to her pop star life. Nanna had not pushed, probed, or questioned allowing Bronwyn to gradually become her old self. She had slept soundly for the first time in many months.

Bronwyn sat on the tussocks of grass, the wind in her hair, gazing at the faded moon, when she heard footsteps behind her. Nanna had climbed the path from the top of her road to the headland. She sat on the grass and silently shared the view with her granddaughter. Eventually she turned to her.

'How are you feeling, Bronnie?

'Alright, I suppose.'

'No,' insisted Nanna, 'How are you really? You're here with me for two weeks and I deserve to know if there's anything I need to understand. Are you going to go through withdrawal from the drugs?'

'I wasn't doing that much! Just enough to give me an edge, you know?'

Rae Coleman shook her head, 'No, I don't know. The last I heard about you from your mum and dad was before you left home. You were doing well at the Comprehensive School, doing well in your piano and ballet. I didn't find out about you leaving for months. Typical of them, I suppose. Down here, we live in our own little world, a long way from the pop music scene. Can't even get a decent telly signal sometimes, so we don't bother. I didn't even know you could sing let alone make a record! So, tell me. No judgement here Bronnie, just someone who loves you and cares about you.' Rae put her arm around Bronwyn and hugged her.

'I don't want to say really. My mum...well you know, she's got her own life and friends and well...'

'It's alright love, I know what your mum can be like. She never really took to being a mum but I'm sure she loves you! It just doesn't come naturally to some folks and she's one of them, but you've never wanted for anything have you?'

'No, nothing like that. It's just that I...'

Tears sprung up and coursed down Bonnie's cheeks. She wiped them away with the heel of her hand and then swiped across her nose.

'It was not what I wanted to do. The minute I went up on stage with Peter, I knew where I wanted to be, where I want to go! I knew they would never let me. They always had visions of me being you know a doctor or a lawyer, you know, letters after my name. They don't get it, how groovy it is to sing and people dancing, singing with you, yelling, and screaming for you to come out on stage, and everyone loves you. I'm in all the pop mags and on the TV and everything and I earn money, lots of it.'

'So, you've earned a lot of money? Where is it? Do you have access to it? Who manages everything for you?'

'Nanna, I'm still a bit young to have full control. That's what they told me, but they promised me that when I'm twenty-one, it will all be handed over to me.'

'That's why I'm asking. Who are 'they' Bronnie? Who has control right now?'

'Peter has a friend who has a big record company. They signed me up and manage all my earnings. It's all in a... is it a Trust Account? Yeah, I think that's what they called it. They give me my spending money; a lot more than I was getting from dad. Peter used to give me some pot and a bit of acid just to help me write good songs. I'm not an addict, if that's what you think. Somebody else in the house gave me the stuff that got me sick. I can handle the other stuff. I'm not going to get all weird with withdrawal although, I do miss it a bit. It's pretty harmless, you know? Peter would never give us bad stuff.'

'So, this Peter guy, is he like your boyfriend?'

'Oh no! He's my friend, my guru. I started singing with his band, then they ended up being my backing band. Cool, eh? We, the band, all live together with a few other people. It's really great! Everyone loves everybody. We're all free and happy. I love that I don't have to go to school, do homework, do everything mum says and I'm famous!'

'So, you are all living together. Who does the shopping, cooking, washing? Who pays the rent, electricity? Do you have your own room, your own place when you want privacy?' Rae heard herself and regretted sounding exactly as young people expected the 'oldies' to sound.

'Well, we all love being together *all* of the time. We usually eat whatever somebody brings in from the shops or the chippy. There's always plenty of food and drink. Don't worry. Peter makes sure of that! Everybody sleeps with everybody else, except Peter. He's got his own room. I've slept in his room sometimes when he asked me to. Sometimes there's others in with him, sometimes it was just me. He told me I was his special lady. He wrote me love letters you know, beautiful poetry.'

Rae listened, revealing nothing of her growing internal turmoil. This child, her beloved Bronnie, had obviously been trapped into a situation by this 'Peter' character and was oblivious to the legalities, exploitation, and danger she had been subjected to.

'I'm glad you're here with me for a couple of weeks, anyway, love. I'd love to hear you play your guitar and sing sometime. Meanwhile, we'll concentrate on getting you as fit and healthy as we can. I think mum and dad are planning to come down in the next few days.' Rae pursed her lips and raised her eyebrows thinking, *won't count my chickens*. 'I'm going back down now. Got to do some grocery shopping for my elderly neighbour two doors up. She can't manage the steep path with bags anymore. So, I'll see you when you come back down, OK?'

'Thanks Nanna. I'll come back soon. It's so lovely up here.'

Bonnie sat, soaking in the sight and sound of the rushing swells out in the bay, feeling the breeze through her hair. She closed her eyes and smiled contentedly. She didn't hear the sound of a vehicle driving up the lane behind the hill. It stopped, a door opened and slammed shut. She turned around. A figure was coming towards her across the dry grass. Long hair tangled in the wind, striped linen pants and a T-shirt printed with a peace sign identified him immediately. Bonnie sprung to her feet, racing towards him, and throwing her arms around his neck.

'Peter! Oh Peter, I was hoping you'd come to see me! Oh, I'm so happy! How did you know where I was?'

'Don't worry about that, Bon. I have my spies! I've come to take you back, back where you belong. Your fans are screaming for you. Come on. The van's over there.' He hugged her and led her away from the headland overlooking the ocean, back to the van.

'Where are we going? I should let Nanna know. I need my stuff too.'

'Don't need to worry about any of that. I've got you. We're heading back up north where you'll be safe.'

Once in the van, he turned to Bonnie. 'We'll go find somewhere where you can get back to your old self. Somewhere quiet where you can do some writing. I'll leak it to the press that you've gone into a hiatus, a break from everything because you were exhausted. You're recovering and using the time to do a new album. Perhaps we can record and release a single, just to keep you at the top of the game. I'll look after you, baby.'

'Oh Huggy, I know you will, but I think I should let Nanna know what I'm doing!'

She reached across and pecked him sweetly on the cheek. Huggy was acutely aware of her, so young, naive, and pure. Those incredible blue eyes meeting his with simple unadulterated love and trust. As she smiled at him, pleading with him to allow her to inform her Nanna, Huggy imagined her still immature form under the peasant clothing, and it was all he could do to stop himself pulling her to him across the front seat. So vulnerable. He must hold back because he knew the final reward would be worth it. Probably set him up for the foreseeable future.

1953

STRIKE THREE – OUT

'Prelude in E minor'
(a piece which represents true despair)
Chopin

Once more the ambulance sped up St Lawrence Road, coming to a halt where people were gathered around a green car which was parked askew across the road. A woman lay on the ground, people hovering and fussing around her. Someone had supplied a blanket, others were acting as traffic wardens to direct traffic around the accident, not that there had been any, other than the ambulance. The two ambulance officers jumped out, one grabbed a bag, the other went straight to the woman.

'Can everyone please move back now? Give us some space to do our job. That's right, move back. Thank you. Who called us?'

An older woman who was talking to a priest, spoke up. 'I did. Joan Jackson. This is my daughter Petunia, officer. She has been hit by the car. She bounced off. I don't know how badly she's hurt. And...she's pregnant.'

The man moved to kneel next to Petunia. 'Petunia, can you hear me? Can you tell me what happened?'

Petunia moaned. She was lying on her back covered by the blanket. The officer moved around to her head and carefully supported her neck.

'Do you have any pain, Petunia?' She nodded.

'Is it here, your head or neck?'

'No, in my hip and leg.' She indicated her right hip.

A soft brace was placed around her neck. The ambulance officer then moved around to her right side, pulled the blanket down looking for obvious dislocation or severe fractures and found no indications. There was no blood to be seen. He could see that she was lying with both legs straight. He tried gently raising her leg at the knee, just a little. She drew breath sharply and winced.

'On a scale of one to ten, how bad is the pain, Petunia?' he asked.

'I can put up with it!' she snapped. 'Bears no resemblance to the pain I've suffered.'

'Alright luv, we're going to take you to the hospital, get you all checked out and make sure your baby is fine.'

Seeing the horrified look on the woman's face he hastened to reassure her. 'Don't worry, I'm sure it will be. Looks like you'll have some bruising and soreness, but that's all. We'll get you checked out though. OK?'

Everyone turned as a police car arrived on the scene. The two officers got out, surveyed the scene, and immediately took the number of the green car. The priest, Father Michael, on seeing them at his car, shook his head, muttering to himself and hastened over to them to talk to them.

'Is this the car then?' asked one officer to the group gathered around the scene.

Father Michael strode up and offered his hand which the police officer declined to shake. 'Father Michael, St Angela's Catholic Church.' He introduced himself.

'Is this your car?'

'It's my car. I hit her or rather, she ran straight out in front of me! She wanted me to hit her. I couldn't do anything about it. She was too close and running right at me!'

The officer took out his note pad.

'I was coming to see Petunia,' Father Michael continued. 'She has been unwell recently. I have been supporting both her and her mother. They are members of my parish.'

The priest gave the police officers a brief synopsis of Petunia's situation. Both officers had heard a little about such a woman, gossip around the station, but had not made the connection.

'And you say she ran out in front of you without warning? Was she trying to flag you down, attract your attention?'

'No! Nothing like that. She was running *down* St Lawrence Road and when she saw the car, she changed direction and came straight at me, *meaning to hit me!*'

Michael turned to speak to the closest officer, lowering his voice in a conspiratorial tone. 'She has had a recent history of trying to harm herself and the baby. This is her third attempt. The hospital will have the history. I am absolutely certain that this is precisely why she threw herself in front of my car.'

'I see,' replied the police officer, rapidly noting all this down. 'Thank you, Father. We may need to interview you further. Can we contact you at St Angela's?'

'Yes. Of course.'

The ambulance made its way from the scene with Petunia and Joan on board. Father Michael waited while the two constables examined his car, looking for damage or evidence of the impact. There were no obvious signs, dents, blood, or scrapes. He was permitted to take his car.

At the hospital, Doctor Eglington was called as soon as Petunia arrived. Consulting his notes, he spoke to Joan in the Emergency Department where Petunia was being assessed.

'Mrs. Jackson, in light of recent events, I have a referral for Petunia to attend a consultation with a Mr. Andrew Floyd, a psychiatrist who is a friend of mine. He consults here at the hospital, and I can arrange for her to meet him tomorrow.'

Joan sagged visibly, her greying hair tousled, her complexion sallow and shapeless. There appeared to be no fight left in her. She was depleted. 'If you think it's what she needs, doctor.'

'I do, Mrs. Jackson, for her sake and for the safety of her unborn child, I think she needs to spend some time in a facility which can care for them both. Naturally I will leave those considerations to Doctor Floyd, however, I think the hospital at Menston has an excellent mental health wing, and I know he recommends it and consults there himself. It's for the best. I must go and talk to Petunia now and we will speak later.'

1969

'Mr. Tambourine Man'
Bob Dylan

Peter 'Huggy Papa' drove out of Clovelly with Bonnie on Thursday evening. Rae Coleman had not worried at all when she didn't come down for tea. All her things were still in her room, and she was sixteen years old after all. She had probably found some of the friends, made when she had been staying down here before. Rae went to bed expecting to see her asking for breakfast in the morning. Instead, Bonnie spent the night on the grubby mattress Huggy had in the back of the van, fighting for space with piles of rubbish, clothes, his guitar, and a selection of drug paraphernalia.

***

In the early light, the Thames van rattled along the narrow roads making for the main road to Barnstaple. Huggy drove hunched over the nearly horizontal steering wheel as if trying to urge it along. Bonnie sat, her face leaning on the cold window as she watched the countryside rush past.

'What's wrong Bon? Are you crying?' asked Huggy.

'They told me about Harmony, you know. The police did.' Bonnie sobbed a little and wiped her eyes with her hand. 'Why did she have to die, Huggy? Why?'

Huggy placed a hand on her arm. 'I don't know Bon. She must have had something wrong with her. I don't know. The coppers didn't tell me anything. I'm sorry. Stop crying. I'm taking you away, somewhere nice where you can forget all about everything. Alright?'

Bonnie sniffed, wiping more tears away.

'Huggy, why wouldn't you let me get my clothes and guitar? And why can't I tell Nanna where I'm going? She will be so worried!'

'Bon, you know that they would have stopped you coming with me. They don't get it. They always think they know what's best, but they don't. I had to get you away and fast. What we're going to do is dump the van and I'll buy an old car in Barnstaple. They'll be looking for this van, so I'll get something completely different but common, you know?'

Bonnie opened her mouth to protest but Huggy held his finger up to shush her.

'When you're reported missing, we're going to have a problem. The cops had to let me go. They had nothing on me, but they might put two and two together, thinking I might have come down to see you. I just don't want to take a chance of being pulled over. Leave it to me. I'll keep you safe from them. Now, sing me a song, one of yours. No, you don't need your guitar. Use mine.'

Bonnie climbed through into the rear onto the cluttered mattress. On top of all the stuff was Huggy's guitar. Bonnie grabbed it and climbed back into the front seat. By turning sideways in the seat, there was enough room in the van for her to just squeeze in playing the guitar.

'Which one, Peter? *Fields*?'

'Yeah, do that one. I love your voice when you do that breathy vibrato when the flowers die.'

Bonnie sang, even though Huggy's guitar was not as good as hers and badly needed new strings, she still managed to enchant him.

The roads were busy with summer traffic. Several police cars passed going the other way. Each time Huggy pulled his cap down, but none paid any attention to the old van.

'Huggy, I need the john. Can we stop soon?'

'Nearly there. We'll stop in Barnstaple and while you do that and get us some food, I'll get us another set of wheels. I'll just park the van and we'll leave it there.'

'Why do you need another car? What about all your stuff in the back?'

'Don't you worry about that. I'm sure that by now, the cops know what I drive. They've probably got the number. They might have put two and two together and worked out that I might come and find you.'

'Yeah, I know, you already said that Huggy. Are you alright? You're not doped up, are you?' asked Bonnie.

'Huh? No, not really. Why, do you want some?'

'No. I really wish I had my things though. Why would the cops want you Huggy? And why would they think you would come for me?'

'Because coppers always think the worst. The only good thing is that they wouldn't know that I had the means to find out where you were. As for the stuff in the van, there's nothing I need really. I've got everything right here.'

He glanced across at the girl but refrained from further comment. She had not reacted but remained watching the road and absently strumming.

They were on the outskirts of the town now coming up to the River Taw. They crossed it and turned left onto Mill Road where factories and a variety of trade outlets lined the left, while the quay was on the right. Old wooden boats, fishing boats now high and dry lolled lopsidedly on the bank. They drove a short way before Huggy pulled into the side and stopped the van.

'Right, up there a bit is a café. Not posh by any means but you'll get a sandwich and a drink. Just down this lane is a used car place I know. I'll leave the van here. You take the keys and here's some money to buy supplies. I'll meet you back here when I've got us some transport. Alright? You'll be OK?'

Bonnie nodded. She took the money and the keys. She locked the van and began walking in the direction of the café, wondering as she did, how Huggy knew this area so well. He had never talked about where he came from or his past. Perhaps this was his home-town? He really didn't have the Devon accent. Why was he so keen to get her away from Nanna Coleman? And why had he not allowed her to bring anything? Also, he had been behaving a little strangely. She had caught him surreptitiously watching her as he drove, but she had pretended not to notice. It was creeping her out a little.

She arrived back at the van with a paper bag packed with egg sandwiches, two Chester squares, and two bottles of Coke. She unlocked it and climbed into the front putting the bags and the drinks on the floor. There had been one moment when the girl behind the counter had squinted at her as if she recognised her but had said nothing. With her hair bundled in a ponytail, no make-up and sunglasses, Bonnie assumed she looked very little like her on stage persona. While she waited for Huggy to return, she rummaged around in the back and found a woven, embroidered bag. It looked very much like the one her friend Harmony had, but she was dead now, wasn't she? Bonnie had not had time to have given much thought to the day they were all busted in Notting Hill. Remembering seeing Harmony in such a terrible way made her feel sick. The interior of the van suddenly felt claustrophobic, like the walls were closing in, crushing her. She had to get out. She threw herself out onto the pavement and leant against the van, panting, trying to catch her breath as the world swam. What was she doing and where had her former 'normal' life gone?

'What's going on, Bon? Are you sick?'

She lifted her head and flung herself into Huggy's arms, sobbing. 'Oh Peter, what are we doing? I want to go home. Please take me home.'

She snuffled into his shirt which smelled faintly of pot, sweat and the remnants of incense. From that first day when he had invited her on stage and handed her a guitar, she had felt comfortable and safe with him. She loved him and he loved her. She thought of the letters he had given her, always promising to take care of her. For her, she had a substitute for the father who had always been distant and inept.

Huggy liked her to refer to him as Huggy Papa, yet his hands were caressing her now in such a way that she pushed him away and knuckled her eyes to wipe away the tears.

'Don't!' she mumbled. 'Where is your new car?'

'Just around the corner. Grab what you need out of this, and we'll get going.'

'Are you taking me back to Menston, to Mum and Dad's?'

'Why do you want to go there? They've never done anything for you. They don't get you at all. I can give you everything you want and more. Just grab the food and we'll go!'

'I don't want to, Huggy. My Nanna will be worried. I'd say she's reported me missing. I want you to take me home!' Bonnie began huffily shoving the food into the bag. 'I'll hitch. Don't worry about me!'

Huggy grabbed her by the arm hard enough to cause her to cry out.

'Ouch, you're hurting me! Let go!'

'You're coming with me.'

Huggy yanked her away from the van and began marching her around the corner where a pale blue Mini panel van sat. Scanning the area around them, he saw that there were no onlookers to question what might be going on here.

'Get in!' He swung the rear door open and shoved her in the back, then slammed the door and locked it from the outside.

Bonnie felt numb. How could someone change so much in an instant? What had she done wrong? Their journey 'up north' began, though Bonnie was sure it was not going to be to Menston.

***

The blue Minivan drove up the M5. Huggy was taking it easy, confident that no-one knew where he was or indeed, that Bonnie was in the back. His plan was to leave the motorway near Ayshford and travel the 'B' roads to Taunton where he would find somewhere to stop for the night. His ultimate destination was Birmingham. He had a flat above a corner shop in Rotton Park. Huggy smirked as he thought of the name. How fitting!

In the back Bonnie sat on the bare metal floor, leaning against the side, trying not to get knocked around too much when the car took corners or braked. She had tried to climb into the front seat, but Huggy had threatened her viciously. She was so confused. Where was her beloved Huggy Papa? This man was gruff, cruel, and very nasty to her. She had cried and sobbed. He had told her to 'shut it'! She had pleaded with him, and he had ignored her.

'You know they'll be looking for us soon?'

'We'll have a day or so to drop out. Don't worry, I'm doing the best for you.'

Bonnie said nothing more. She was beginning to wonder how she was going to get away and hitch home to Menston. Absently, she ate her sandwich and Chester square, declining to give Huggy his. He had not made himself popular with her back in Barnstaple. He could go hungry!

1969

'Keep on Running'
Jackie Edwards

Huggy and Bonnie drove through Taunton on to Glastonbury, where Huggy easily found his way around. Once again, Bonnie wondered how he knew so much about this part of the country. During the uncomfortable drive, she had tried several times to talk to him, asking him to please take her home, even to stop so that she could find a public toilet, but he had simply told her to be quiet. She had no windows in the back part of the Mini, so had a very limited view of their whereabouts at any given time. As they drove through the centre of Taunton, she had asked him to let her into the front, if only to relieve the pain in her back from sitting propped against the hard metal sides of the van. He had refused. Now they were leaving Taunton. Bonnie caught glimpses of fields and farms again.

'I thought we were stopping in Taunton!' she said sulkily.

'No. We'll keep going a bit longer. I know a place we can park for the night where we won't be bothered.'

'Huggy! Why are you being like this man? What have I done? I thought we were going somewhere where I could relax and write, somewhere safe. I don't feel safe! And I need the john. Desperately!'

Huggy turned his head to the back. 'Jesus! Can't you stop whining? I told you; we'll be there soon. There are public conveniences. Now shut up.'

Bonnie slumped back against the side. She stared at the back of his head; the matted hair topped with the grubby cap. The purposeful set of his shoulders un-nerved her. She found herself chewing her bottom lip and her forehead creased into a frown. *Why was he being like this?* A small stab of something she hadn't felt before pierced her mind and she clenched her fists. As she bounced along in the bare rear of the van, a feeling she had not previously experienced began to stir deep down in her psyche.

***

Huggy had parked the car in the corner of a carpark in Glastonbury. The parking area was for visitors to King Arthur's Tomb during the day, but at this time of the evening, there were only two cars left. High walls surrounded the car park on Silver Street, which looked onto the industrial backs of a row of shops and businesses on the High Street. All was quiet there as shops were closed and the last rubbish had been emptied into the rows of bins. Most workers' vehicles had left.

Bonnie saw the Public Convenience building at the opposite end of the park. She pushed her way past Huggy and sprinted for them.

'Make sure you come straight back! I know this area and I'll be watching!' growled her former protector.

Once inside the toilets, Bonnie sat down and puzzled over her situation. Only a matter of days ago, she had been hanging out with her 'family' at the Notting Hill flat, feeling loved, appreciated, and special. She had been enveloped in a slightly druggy haze making her happy and relaxed. Her next big gig was to be in Manchester at the beginning of August. Everything was going her way, or at least the way Peter 'Huggy' Bramley, her manager, had planned.

She had some incredible competition but was holding her own against Lulu and other chart toppers such as The Bee Gees and Herman's Hermits.

Thinking about the concerts, the crowds and fame made her sad, but just as quickly, thinking of how Huggy had treated her in the last twenty-four hours made her angry. She had to get away from him and find her way back to London. She would see the man Huggy had introduced her to when she had signed up with the label. He would find someone else to manage her and that would serve Huggy right! And, she had to let her nanna know she was OK.

'Bonnie! Come out! We need to get something to eat. You're hungry, aren't you?'

'I'm coming.' Bonnie walked out of the ladies; her eyes fixed on the man who was standing right near the door as if he had been listening. She walked straight past him to the car.

'We can walk through to High Street and then on to Magdalene Street where there are cafes and other places to eat. What do you fancy, Bon?' He put his arm around her, seeming to Bonnie to be trying to make up for his former unpleasant manner by feigning fatherly affection.

'I don't care. You go. I'll stay here.' She twisted away from him.

'Ah, no, I don't think so. You've been a bit off. I don't think I trust you. You're coming with me. Grab that bag of yours and let's go.'

'That *was* Harmony's bag in case you forgot about her!' she snapped.

He opened the back door so she could reach in to retrieve it. Bending over and stretching across the floor, she had the sudden feeling that he was watching her. She straightened and spun around. He was standing so close, his hips nearly touching hers. She backed away. Ugh! That was weird!

'Come on!' Huggy's voice was gruff as he took her arm and pulled her into the street with him. 'Now walk with me and don't give me any trouble!'

***

Back in the car, they ate chips wrapped in paper and soaked with vinegar. He was right. She had been hungry again. He had bought two pop drinks, a cola for him and a lemonade for her. Unscrewing the top of the lemonade, he added something out of a small hip flask he pulled from his trouser pocket.

'It's just a shot of booze to make it taste better. Don't worry, it will relax you. You're too freaked out. Here drink it.'

'No, I won't. Let me have yours.'

Huggy roughly grabbed her arm again. 'Drink it!' he ordered. He pushed the bottle towards her mouth and shoved it against her lips. Bonnie tried to push it away, but he forced her mouth open and poured the drink down her throat. She spat and coughed. Some of it ended up all over Huggy's already grubby and stained shirt, but most of it she swallowed simply by reflex, and against her best efforts to resist.

'That's better! Now just cool it girl. Try to sleep.'

Bonnie stared at him, her eyes welling with tears. His face blurred and everything became indistinct, sounds, the interior of the van, her thoughts. She knew the feelings. Drugged! It was too late to protest and fight back as the drug kicked in. Instead, she slumped into a deep sleep clutching Harmony's bag to her chest.

Peter Bramley observed quietly. When he was sure she was out, he got out of the van, locked all the doors, and walked off down to the High Street again, this time to find a telephone box. After he had made his calls, he walked casually along to The Crown. He was in familiar territory yet again and leaned against the bar. The barman greeted him jovially.

'Hey Pete! Where you been man? Haven't seen you around for a while. Looking a bit different my man. What are you up to now?'

'Give me a pint and I'll tell you. You won't believe it, oh and have you got a pair of scissors?'

***

Two hours later Peter Bramley, aka Huggy Papa walked out of The Crown wearing slacks and an open necked shirt, clean shaven with a fashionable Beatle style haircut. The scissors were tucked into his back pocket. Looking at his watch, he realised he might be running out of time. He hurried back to the Minivan, where he found Bonnie still slumped in the same position in the back.

Good he thought. He climbed into the back, removed the scissors, and gathered a handful of the red ringlets. The scissors hacked through the hair, raggedly chopping it within an inch of her scalp. He continued until the whole lot was cropped short. *Tomorrow, we'll get some hair dye and then no-one will recognise the ordinary man with his gamin daughter. Also, tomorrow, the Daily Mirror will run the story that 'according to a close friend, Bonnie Summer has suffered a mental breakdown. She is recovering in a secret location. Her manager was hopeful that she would be ready for the Manchester concert, so ticket sales should go ahead.'*

He grinned and grabbed the newspaper the chips had been wrapped in. He was about to wrap the hair up when he spotted a headline on what was the front page of yesterday's paper. The headline blared that Bonnie was in Devon with family, recovering from exhaustion. Huggy swore. His plan for releasing his own version of what Bonnie was up to was now dead in the water. He angrily screwed the hair up into the paper, got out of the van and dumped it into one of the large industrial bins across the road.

He pulled out a joint, lit it and inhaled deeply, waiting for the effect. He knew exactly what Donovan meant when he wrote about 'mellow yellow' because that is exactly how the stuff made him feel. He, Huggy, had never believed the song was about meditation! But now what? The cops would soon be crawling around Devon assuming it would have been him who took Bonnie from Clovelly. Shit! Better keep low. They wouldn't know about the Mini, but he didn't think it would take long for them to discover the dumped van. Then they would start asking questions around Barnstaple. Shit again. Why hadn't he dumped the van somewhere less obvious? Right around the corner from a used car lot! Jesus, that was not smart! Huggy started the car. He thought he still had a little time to make some distance to where they could lay low for a couple of days. He knew a place. Then, he needed to start thinking about changing their ride.

1969

'You Were on My Mind'
Crispian St Peters

He took the crystal decanter, poured himself a drink in a matching crystal whiskey glass and dropped into his plush leather, modular sofa, designed in Denmark. A lithe, black shape leapt to his side and settled next to him; Midnight, the cat a former lady friend had given him. He had never thought he would have a pet, but he had to admit he quite liked the cat. His leather shoes lay kicked off at the foot of the sofa, his expensive jacket thrown over the back. Robert enjoyed life's little luxuries and some of the big ones too. He had a manageable mortgage on a modern apartment. He drove a nice Mercedes Benz, which was securely garaged under the apartments and was accessible from the lift. His life appeared to be very comfortable looking from the outside.

Robert picked up the copy of *Fabulous 208* which was open to the double page spread on Bonnie Summer. He studied the pictures of her. Here was a young girl who seemed to have the perfect life, *looking from the outside,* he thought. The world was a strange place. Bonnie had a secure family and yet they didn't seem to care for each other. When Robert was a child, his family was ripped apart by war, illness, and violence and yet beneath all that, his mother had tried her best to keep them together. In his adult life, Robert had experienced plenty of this kind of family trauma with his work, but his personal story had never been shared with his colleagues.

After his older brother Eric had denied any involvement with the murder of a local girl, and supplied an incontestable alibi, Robert who had been two years younger, had known that it had all been lies. The brothers, being close in age, had spent a lot of time together after school and in the streets, when unthinkable things were happening at their house. Robert had contributed to some of the terrible animal slaughters around the village, simply because, he told himself, he had not known any better. Those killings preyed on his mind to this day. When it came to the girl, Freda, he had known that Eric had not been at a dance with his friend Sam because he had told Robert to 'cover' for him, to tell mum that he was out with Sam. Robert did so but when the body was discovered, he heard the village gossip about the knives, the cuts in the stomach and the intestines, immediately he had known. It had been all so familiar. He had never admitted any of this to either the police or family.

He poured another measure of whiskey. With the alcohol loosening his thoughts and memories, the guilt rose in his throat like hot acid. How could he possibly be putting others behind bars when he was as guilty by default as they were? Although he had tried over the years to compensate, becoming a police officer, graduating until reaching Detective Chief Inspector in the Homicide Division, his past and his family shame haunted him. Sometimes he thought he could sense evil in himself, lurking under the surface, waiting for the right moment to break through. Those were the times when the whiskey bottle was finished in one night so that he might fall asleep, nightmare free.

The phone rang, jolting him into the present. He placed the glass on a stylish teak coffee table and walked over to the wall to answer it.

'Evenin' guv.' It was Alby. 'Sorry to disturb you on a Sunday. I just thought you might want to know that Bonnie Summer has gone missing, reported about half an hour ago.'

'What, by who? She was only released from hospital last week and went down to Devon to stay with her grandmother for a couple of weeks.'

'Mrs. Rae Coleman, her grandmother, reported her missing when she failed to come home.'

'I'm coming in, Alby. Stay where you are.'

As Robert collected his briefcase containing the case notes on Bonnie, grabbed the car keys and let himself into the corridor where the lift waited, he once again pondered why this one girl-child should have such an impact on him. He simply could not fathom it. The Mercedes screamed out of the garage, exploding into the quiet Sunday street, and was gone in a flash. DCI Turner was in a hurry.

***

'Well, what have we got? Fill me in Alby.'

Alby dropped a large folder on the desk in front of Robert. 'Rae Coleman called in about an hour ago. Thursday afternoon, she had been talking to Bonnie somewhere near her house, I gather, up on a hill overlooking the ocean. She left. Bonnie said she'd be down soon for tea. That was about...' Alby ran his finger down a page in the folder. 'Here, 6:30 pm. Bonnie never came back.'

'So, she's been gone for two days, and she didn't let us know until now?' Robert asked incredulously.

Alby shrugged, 'She must have thought she was going to come home.'

'Why on earth didn't she report her missing earlier?' The question purely rhetorical.

'Don't know guv. She might be still in the village, perhaps? Or maybe Mrs. Coleman thought she was with friends or something.

Anyway, she's not there now, so what's the plan?'

'I think we'll go down there. Grab some gear. We might be staying the night. Do we have an address?'

Once more Alby scrutinised the sheaf of papers. 'Here it is guv, 34 Smuggler's Lane, Clovelly in North Devon.'

'Right, we'll get going first thing in the morning, I'll meet you back here at six.'

1969

Rae Coleman put the phone down and flopped into her armchair. So, Detective Turner was coming down to Devon. He should be here very soon.

I hope he can do something to find her she thought. Rae felt devastated that she had left it so long to report that Bonnie was missing. That night, she had gone home after doing her neighbour's shopping and then prepared tea for her and Bronnie. Her granddaughter had settled in easily on her arrival and had seemed very happy. She had her own room from when she had visited during school holidays, and already it had taken on the untidy, carefree appearance of a modern teenager's room. When Bronwyn had not returned that evening, Rae wasn't too concerned, thinking she must have found some of the friends she had made during her former visits. She was only sixteen after all, and after the life she had been living for the last year or so, the last thing she would want to do is hang around with her Nanna.

Rae had eaten her tea and gone to bed assuming Bonnie would be there in the morning. She wasn't, so Rae walked down to the village centre to see if she could find her. After walking the High Street and the Quay, investigating the fishing boat ramp and the local Co-op, she called in at the small police station where she explained her growing concerns. They were sympathetic and promised to follow it up. Nothing had happened until Rae decided to call Bob. Bob had been furious and railed at his mother, telling her she should have known better, that Bronwyn couldn't be trusted and now she had probably gone and got herself killed or something. He gave her the phone number of the Metropolitan Police DCI Turner who had been on Bronwyn's case. First thing Sunday morning, Rae had called him and now, she was expecting the doorbell any minute.

She showed the two men into her small living room and indicated the chintz sofa. Both detectives bent their heads to avoid the ceiling beams and graciously accepted the offer of a seat on the sofa. Robert introduced his partner, as Detective Sergeant Coates.

'Would you like tea?' asked Rae.

'Yes, thank you, that would be very nice.'

Alby had insisted on stopping in Taunton to grab a drink and a sandwich for breakfast, but it had still been a long drive on roads getting busier by the minute, as commuter and holiday traffic woke up. Thankfully there had been no traffic jams or hold-ups and they had arrived on Rae's doorstep a few minutes before midday.

While Rae busied herself around the corner in the kitchen, Robert surveyed the room. Typical of many of the older cottages, it had low, beamed ceilings, tiny casement windows and an uneven floor covered with worn Axminster floral carpet. A large rough hewn timber beam supported the wall above the cavernous inglenook which was dead in this warm summer weather. Rae returned with tea for all of them.

'Mrs. Coleman, why didn't you report your granddaughter's absence earlier? It's going to be hard for us to pick up her movements now.' Robert voiced his puzzlement.

'I really didn't think there was anything to worry about. I felt sure she would be home when I got up in the morning. What do you think has happened to her Inspector?'

'We would only be guessing, wouldn't we?' Alby's voice betrayed a hint of sarcasm. Robert raised an eyebrow in his direction.

'Mrs. Coleman, Bronwyn ran away from her home twelve months ago to live with a group of hippies, including some quite unpleasant characters, two of whom we have had in custody until Friday. We'll be investigating their current whereabouts. Have you seen a white van around the village at all in the last couple of days? He pulled a photograph out of his inside pocket. 'Or this man?'

Rae squinted at the image. She shook her head. 'No, but I don't go out much, only down the High Street. There are a lot of people here because of the summer season. I try to stay at home as much as possible, Inspector. I can't say I have or haven't seen him. I don't take any notice of the tourists. The van, well, that could be anybody's couldn't it?'

'Yes, it was only an off chance. After all, there must be quite a few white vans around the district at any one time. When was the last time you saw Bronwyn?'

'On Friday evening. She had gone for a walk, up to the top of the cliff. I went up there and talked with her for a while. She told me she would be down for tea shortly, so I came back home to prepare it. But I had a bit of shopping to do for my elderly neighbour first, so I don't know if she came here, and I wasn't home and left again.'

'We'll check in with the people around here to see if anyone saw her come back at about six, did you say? So, how did she appear to you? Distressed, worried, maybe angry?'

'Oh no!' Rae protested, 'nothing like that. She was happy! Well mostly happy. She settled down quickly after arriving. She used to stay here often in the school holidays, you know. She loved it!'

'What do you mean by 'mostly' happy Mrs. Coleman?' asked Alby.

'Inspector, please call me Rae. She *was* happy but I asked her a bit about her life in the last twelve months, you know, about the drugs and also where her money was, who was in control. She got a bit defensive. She told me about how they all live together and share *everything!*'

'Anything else?'

'She said her earnings were in some Trust Fund until she turns twenty-one. She admitted taking drugs and smoking pot but assured me she knows what she's doing and she's no addict.'

'I'm afraid they all say that Rae. Addict or not, she ended up in hospital in an extremely serious condition from an overdose of a cocktail of drugs. She had to have her stomach pumped and she was very ill for a couple of days,' replied Robert. His mind flashed back to the image of her sitting in the hospital bed, looking so pale and fragile. He remembered how his heart had lurched and he had been flooded with inexplicable emotion at the time. 'Did she give any indication that she had plans to go somewhere? Or that she might be meeting someone?'

'No, nothing. Like 1 said we were talking about what she had been doing since she left home. But she took nothing with her. Her clothes, her bags and her guitar are still in her room. 1 don't think she even has any money!'

'Does that sound like her, to leave without any of her things?' Robert queried.

Rae wrung her hands and fixed her eyes earnestly on Robert's. 'I'm sure she wouldn't inspector. She has always been such a responsible girl. 1 can't understand it! She must be hitch hiking home or something. I'm so worried!'

Robert placed his cup and saucer carefully on the table and rose. 'We'll be staying here for a couple of days. Where would you recommend?'

'The Red Lion just down the road here. Clean and cheap but not high end so quite often they have rooms even during the summer season. Shared facilities though.'

'Sounds fine. We'll look into it. Do they do meals?'

'Yes, they do midday meals. You can get a nice Ploughman's there. If you want dinner, you'd best go to the seafood restaurant on the quay. Bit pricey though.'

'Right then, we will leave you for now, Mrs. Coleman. Please don't hesitate to call my office if anything turns up. Maybe she will just come back or perhaps she is heading home to Menston. In any case, we'll do our best to make sure she comes home safely.'

'Oh, thank you Inspector. I will call you if she comes here.'

Robert and Alby left to pursue their accommodation and some food, realising they had not eaten for hours.

The Red Lion sat on the high side of High Street giving it good views of the harbour and coast. The two detectives sat on a small balcony overlooking the bay, enjoying a pint and a pork pie. They were attracting a few inquisitive looks from the people in the crowded bar, attributable no doubt to their suits and ties. A fresh breeze off the ocean kept the temperature on the cool side, while it whipped up frothy waves which were casting spray on the rocks below as they broke. The soundtrack to a perfect day on the coast; gently rushing waves and the continuous cries of the gulls as they rode the wind currents.

Both men were keenly observing the comings and goings of the people in the pub. Robert was hoping he might spot 'Huggy Papa' but it was a long shot. He took the photo out of his inside jacket pocket and made his way to the bar. He ordered another pint and flipped the photo to the barman.

'Have you seen this man around here at all?' The barman studied the photo and shook his head.

'No mate, sorry. He hasn't been here as far as I know. Wait a minute, I'll ask Eva. Hey Eva, come over here a sec.'

The barman's Australian accent sounded out clearly above the Devon buzz.

Eva looked at the image Robert held up. 'No, I don't zink so,' she replied in a Nordic accent. Then, 'vait a minute, he looks like a man

I saw in Barnstaple yesterday. He vas buying a car. My boyfriend vorks at ze, vat do you call it, vere zey sell ze cars? I was vaiting so ve could have...food, yes!'

'Does he really? Are you sure Miss er?' smiled Robert.

'Eva Yansen.'

'Are you certain Miss Yansen? This is the same man?'

'Yes, I vas zinking, 'how he should buy ze nice little car? He looks like a, um, hippie!'

'Do you know what kind of car he bought, Eva?'

'Yes! It vas a Minivan! Zat is vat Brian said. It was blue.'

'Brian being your...boyfriend?' asked Alby. Eva nodded.

'I don't suppose you know the registration number?'

'No, but Brian knows. He can get it for you. Oh, you could ring ze boss!'

'Yes, we could. Could you give us the name of the business?' Eva wrote it down and handed it to Robert.

'You have been more than helpful Eva. We may need to speak to you again. Will you be in Clovelly or Barnstaple?'

'I live in Barnstaple, but I vork here sree days, so I stay here, zen I go home. I vill be here til Vednesday.'

'Thank you very much Eva.' Robert returned to the table and re-told the details of his conversation at the bar.

'Finish your drink Alby, we're going to Barnstaple.'

1953

INCARCERATION

'I'll Never Smile Again'
Tommy Dorsey

Petunia limped, courtesy of the huge bruise on her hip after running into Father Michael's car. Head bent and arms sagging by her side, she slumped along the neatly gravelled path from the car park towards the double doors. Her mother walked alongside, her shoulders hunched, her expression care-worn, her eyes dull. The burden she carried had little to do with the suitcases in her hands.

The building was a relatively modern brown brick building, built on four sides with a large garden style courtyard in the centre. The main doors featured a gabled roof attempting to create a mock Tudor style.

Petunia cared nothing for the appearance of the building. The arched Tudor entry did not impress her. What took her eye and caused her to heave a sigh of resignation, were the grim iron bars across every window.

In reception, the process for admission was completed quickly. Petunia would be placed in a secure ward as she was deemed to be a risk to herself and the baby. While the doctor and admission staff spoke to Joan, Petunia sat, silent, staring at her feet. She was unresponsive when questioned and refused eye contact with anyone. No-one appeared concerned or perturbed. Many of their patients were like her and worse. At least this one was quiet, not screaming or throwing herself at the staff. Petunia and Joan were ushered away from reception down a long, green lino floored corridor, Petunia dragging her feet. If she was aware of her surroundings, she failed to show it.

Joan was by now, beyond her capacity to deal with any of this. Thoughts of loving a tiny grandchild had evaporated after her daughter's third attempt to kill it. All she could hope for now is that Petunia would see the pregnancy through, here, under the ever-watchful eyes of the staff. Joan prayed that she would come out of it at the end, alive and able to begin rebuilding her life. These thoughts constantly roiled around and around Joan's head, depriving her of any meaningful sleep or peace of mind. In the last months, she had lost weight, her hair was almost pure white, and she had ceased any socialising, in particular, going to church. She often felt she should be the one admitted to an institution.

In addition, this hospital was over forty miles from the village which meant Joan would not be able to visit every day. Besides, she knew she was not a confident driver and the thought of travelling that distance on the motorway unnerved her.

'Alright Miss Jackson, here we are.'

The young orderly bustled in, plumped the pillows on the bed and straightened the coverlet. 'Petunia, this is your room. You're sharing with Miss Bloom. I'm sure you two will get along. If you would like to unpack your things, You'll see you have wardrobe space, a chest of drawers and a small table with four chairs by the window. Not that there is much to see, only the rear carpark and rows of houses!'

She chuckled. 'Miss Bloom is in the TV lounge. She'll be back soon but for now you should have time to get acquainted with everything. You have a bathroom through there. It's shared between two rooms, so four girls. If you need anything urgently, there is a bell, push the red button but let me advise you that it is only for emergencies! This is a very busy hospital. The staff are always here, there, and everywhere! So, I'll leave you to it, shall I?'

The girl left the room. Petunia stood, arms by her side, eyes cast down. Joan flopped onto the bed, undoing all the young orderly's good work.

'Well, here we are,' said Joan.

As she spoke, another orderly entered the room carrying Petunia's suitcase and a toiletry bag. 'Here are your things, Miss Jackson. You can unpack them and put them away now, please.'

'I'll help you do that, Petunia, and then I'll have to be going,' offered Joan. 'By the time I get the bus and get home it will be well past six and George and Hugo will be wanting to get out.'

Joan opened the case and realised that everything had been removed and hastily re-packed. The toiletry bag had likewise been emptied. Missing were such things as scissors, nail file and even the small compact with mirror. Oh well, thought Joan, hopefully they are doing their job and Petunia will be safe.

'Help me, Petunia. You will have to buck up soon. Here take these and hang them up.'

Petunia threw her a morose look and reluctantly grabbed the clothing. There were no wire coat hangers, only wooden ones which were permanently hanging, threaded onto the rigidly fixed wooden rail in the wardrobe. Joan watched her for a few moments but could bear it no longer.

'I'm going to have to get going now. I'll see you soon.'

Whatever was going on in her daughter's mind, Joan had little idea of it. She left the room and the hospital wondering what was to become of them both. What had become of hers and Petunia's lives?

1969

'Reach Out I'll Be There'
Four Tops

Robert was fuming. The news was out that Bonnie Summer had gone to Devon to stay with her relatives. Every daily had her picture on the front page. Every TV news service was running the story as the headline item. 'Bonnie was drying out'. 'Bonnie was going through withdrawal'. 'Bonnie was pregnant and was to have the baby in Devon'. He had no clue where the leak had come from, but suspected it had to have been the Colemans. Other than the doctors, they were the only ones who knew.

Now their operation to find her could be in jeopardy. He had no doubt that wherever she was, whether she was with Huggy Papa or not, she would have seen the news somewhere and had probably gone to ground. Even down here in Clovelly, the buzz had begun.

Robert and Alby had returned from Barnstaple and were sitting in the seafood restaurant on the quay, waiting for their risotto with prawns and mussels. Going the whole hog, they had ordered the delightfully piquant and almost salty Picpoul French wine to go with it.

'So, we have the make, model, and registration number of the car, but we only know this Huggy character bought it. He used his real name. No sign of a young girl and he made no mention of anyone being with him either. He arrived on foot, paid cash, and drove away in the direction of the quay. Typically, the Minivan only had a quarter of a tank of petrol, so we need to get someone onto checking petrol stations within say fifty miles. Also, we'll need someone doing the immediate area, along the quay, checking to see if there are any shops along there he might have visited.'

'I'll get onto that, guv. I'll get on the 'phone to the local DS in Barnstaple. They can get cracking. The photo of this Huggy character should be across the country by tomorrow.'

'I want to get the details of the car out to all divisions as soon as possible. He won't get far once we get pandas out there spotting. She's got to be with him. Why else would he be in this area, buying a car? And Alby, while I think of it, tell 'em to find the van. It wasn't at the car lot so he must have dumped it somewhere.'

'Yes guv. I'll get onto it first thing tomorrow morning. Here it is!'

Their food had arrived. The wine waiter poured their drinks and wished them 'bon appetit'.

'I'm in heaven!' grinned Robert. 'Dig in son!'

* * *

The dinner finished, Robert and Alby thanked the waiter and asked him to pass on their appreciation of the food to the chef. Robert left a five-pound tip.

'Right Alby, we have a couple of hours daylight left. Let's do a door knock around Rae Coleman's place, see if anybody saw Bonnie go up to the house that night. By the way, did we get any prints off those letters yet?'

'Haven't heard guv, another thing I'll do tomorrow.'

They walked back to their digs at the Red Lion and after a quick stop they set off up the tiny roadway towards Rae's cottage. The sun, still well above the horizon, continued to provide residual heat, making the evening warm and humid down by the water. As they climbed, the views of the cove and harbour became more spectacular, the archetypal picture postcard scene. Tiny people milled around the quay. The cobalt sea lapped at the rocks and breakwater. The temperature cooled slightly the higher they walked.

'I can see why people come here in summer. Pretty nice, isn't it?' commented Alby, admiring the view before them.

'Yeah, it is. Pity we 're here on a case!'

'We'll start next door and work down, and up. You take 'up'!'

'Righto.' Alby walked up to the front door of the cottage above Rae's and knocked on the door.

1969

'Don't Worry Baby'
The Beach Boys

The black Zephyr sped along the M4 towards Reading and London. Robert and Alby had left Clovelly early to avoid the worst of the commuter traffic. Now, travelling in the fast lane doing over 100 miles per hour with the blue light flashing, they were making excellent time.

'I must apologise to your delightful wife for high jacking you again,' commented Robert. 'She must get tired of you being away.'

'She understands, guv. How about you? What are you up to these days, you and the cat?'

'Oh, not much. I don't have much time for anything outside of work. And I'm quite happy that way, thankyou Alby.'

'Guv, I've got tickets for the Spurs in January. Deborah doesn't like football much. I wondered if you'd like to come with me? Do you follow the league?'

Robert chuckled. 'I have watched it on TV Alby, but it's not really my game. More of a cricket man myself. Looking forward to watching The Ashes next year. Hopefully we can win 'em back from the Aussies, but with them playing at home, they have an advantage. Do you follow cricket Alby? It's very popular in your part of the world!'

'Yep, both football and cricket. 'Course they'll win this time! Aussies fell apart against South Africa, and we've just come out unbeaten against the Windies and New Zealand. Think we've got a chance!'

'Well, well Alby, I didn't know! You're quite the font of information! And you support England! Well done! What do you think of Illingworth then? He's done well recently, as you say. He'll captain us next year and I reckon he'll bring 'em home!'

'I've lived here most of my life, guv. Of course, I follow England! I agree. The Ashes will be coming home at last!'

'Thanks for asking me to the Spurs game, son. How soon do you need to know? It might be just what I need, a bit of raucous cheering and chanting, flag waving and beer swilling!'

***

The door knocking had revealed only that Rae's neighbours kept to themselves during the peak holiday season. None of them had seen Bonnie come back to the house that Friday night. None of them recognised the photograph of Peter 'Huggy' Bramley and not one of them could say they had seen the white van. Now the two detectives were returning to London to follow up the latest on the case.

'What a stroke of luck finding that barmaid in The Red Lion! Without her, we'd be a long way behind. As it is, we have photos of the Mini and the registration out across the country. Shouldn't be too long before we get something on it. They've got to stop somewhere.'

'Yes, you're right, Alby. I wonder what they've turned up on this Huggy character. We know he's been in trouble before, but they've never pinned anything too serious on him. I might pay a visit to the record company. Find out what connections he has to them.'

The radio in the car buzzed into life as their call sign sounded. Robert picked up the hand piece.

'Turner. What have you got for me?'

The voice crackled on the tiny speaker.

'We've got the van, sir. Dumped only about a hundred yards from the car yard in Barnstaple. It's getting loaded as we speak; coming back here for forensics to go over it.'

'Thanks for that. We're not far out now. Should be there in an hour. Any luck in the local area? He must have bought petrol somewhere or food?'

'Nothing yet. There's a lot of places to cover in that area. We'll keep you posted.'

'Thanks. Out.' Robert used his index finger to find Barnstaple on the map.

'Where do you think he's taking her Alby? Back to London? Up north? Could be going anywhere. Until we find out more about him, we're flying in the dark.'

***

Back in the office, Robert sat at his desk, upon which mountains of paper, memos and other paraphernalia had accumulated over the two days he had been away. He got himself a cup of coffee from the machine against the wall and took it back to the desk. Taking a few minutes while he sipped the too hot drink, his thoughts turned to Bonnie Summer. In his mind he collated the information he had so far.

Bonnie had grown up with everything but parental love. She had been lured by her love of and natural ability with music to leave her home. She was only fifteen at the time, naïve, impressionable, trusting. Although she left with people her parents did not know, they did not try in any way to do anything to stop her or find her. Robert struggled to understand this part. Surely most parents would be doing everything they could to bring their child home!

There was something about that family, something different. Mrs. Coleman had just about erased all evidence of Bonnie's existence from their home, hadn't she? Mr. Coleman was more concerned about what 'his people' might think.

Robert had never been a parent. He had no personal experience with children. He did have two surviving siblings, both of whom had children, but he never saw them. The family had drifted apart after their parents had passed away, his mother from a heart attack in her fifties and his father from complications of exposure to mustard gas in the first world war. He knew his sister and her husband and kids lived somewhere near the village he grew up in, but he had never visited or been invited to. His other brother lived in a council estate on the outskirts of the village. He had a couple of minor convictions for break and enter and one for aggravated assault. He had done time for that one, leaving his wife and kids to fend for themselves. He had pleaded with Robert to help him out, but younger brother Detective Inspector Turner, had ignored his snivelling protestations of how the family just needed money for food. The apple didn't fall far from the tree, thought Robert bitterly.

As a result of his family history, Robert had always harboured the belief that he did not deserve the right to be responsible for caring for children or indeed a wife. The evil trait in his family could surface any time and he feared he would not be strong enough to control it. He hadn't as a child. He had tried in the past to convince himself that he had only been along for the ride, however, increasingly he feared he had *allowed* himself to *enjoy* those terrible deeds. What would it take to bring it all back? No, far better to keep to himself and do the work he did to at least try to balance the scales.

So, why had Bonnie's parents behaved with such detachment regarding their daughter's situation? It was almost as if they had fallen into parenthood by mistake. Did they not want any children and Bonnie was an unwelcome surprise? He decided to investigate her birth records, to find out where her birth had been registered and if the Colemans were her natural parents. It occurred to him that if Bonnie had simply stayed at her nannas, recovered, and returned to her former life, he would have no reason to be following any of this up. He realised he was perversely grateful that he now had a legitimate reason to focus his attention on the girl. He shook his head and drank the coffee which had reached a temperature slightly below boiling.

***

After a simple search of the UK National Birth Records, Robert found twenty-three records of a Bronwyn Coleman born in 1953. Searching Births, Deaths, and Marriages he found the marriage of Robert Edwin Coleman and Dierdre Fay Swindon. He found no record of a Bronwyn Coleman born to that couple. Interesting. What was that telling him? Bonnie was not their natural child. So, he needed to look at adoption records from June 1953 onwards. That was a little more difficult as they were sensitive and restricted records. He would need to apply to the courts, but he could expect little chance of success without the consent of the Colemans or Bonnie. Bonnie did not know she had been adopted. Did he have enough reason to legally pursue this? After all, her heritage had nothing to do with her alleged abduction by Peter Bramley. It was simply that Robert *needed to know.*

***

DS Wright plonked more papers on the top of a pile of others on Robert's desk. 'Here we go guv. 'ere's a report from a preliminary examination of the white van.'

Robert glanced up as Wright spoke recognising the familiar Yorkshire accent, though somewhat watered down, it was unmistakeable. Robert knew DS Wright had begun his career near where he used to live and had risen up the ranks swiftly. He was a good detective, thorough and everything by the book. *Very trustworthy,* thought Robert, *more so than me.*

'Fingerprints everywhere, all over inside and out,' continued Wright. 'Peter Bramley's and dozens of others. Do we 'ave Bonnie Summer's prints on file? Anyway, he must 'ave used it to carry the whole lot of 'em around. Found no blood or other bodily fluids anywhere but strong traces of multiple drugs plus drug taking stuff in the back. 'E left most of his clothes and 'is guitar in it. Still waiting on two clear sets of fingerprints from that. Doesn't look like anything of 'er stuff though.'

'No, Rae Coleman told us she had left everything behind in Devon, including her purse, clothes, and guitar. One reason Rae was not concerned enough to report it straight away.' Robert took the files and opened them to peruse the printed findings. 'So, unless we can get a fingerprint match for Bonnie, we can't prove she's ever been in the van.'

'No, guv. But the question begs, why did 'e dump it and buy another car? People only do that if they're trying to escape something, don't they?'

Robert scratched his chin and tried in vain to suck the last drop of coffee from his empty cup.

'Want another?'

DS James Wright stepped over to the coffee dispenser. He was so tall and thin, his beige suit hung in folds from his skinny shoulders, the back of the jacket pulled up while the front drooped down. He had one of those vulture necks, hanging forward so that beneath his collar you could see the top vertebrae protruding. To add to his slightly comical appearance, he had a ring of collar length hair around his bald head and sported longish sideboards as was the current trend.

'Ere you go, guv, nice and 'ot!'

Robert grinned. 'Thanks, Jim! What else have you got? Any more on Bramley?'

'Ah yes, Bramley.' DS 'Jim' Wright pulled up a chair and sat, draping one long and bony leg over the other allowing both feet to touch the ground. He relaxed into the chair.

There's nothing of him, mused Robert. *Wouldn't be able to swat a fly!*

'Our friend Bramley is an interesting character to say the least. Born and bred in Somerset, a tiny village called Butleigh Wootton in 1921. 'E was a troublesome kid. One of those entrepreneurial types, always schemin' to make a penny. By the time 'e was eighteen when World War Two broke out 'e was well into petty crime, but not as the perpetrator, oh no, 'e managed other people. Let them do the dirty work. Therefore, 'e was never pinged.'

'Hmm. Did he fight in the war?'

'Yes, 'e did enlist but records show 'e went AWOL. Couldn't cope and disappeared.'

'He's had plenty of practise then! With disappearing!' commented Robert. 'Was he ever caught up with and charged with desertion?'

'Don't know. Couldn't find anything. 'E just disappeared. Might 'ave gone overseas. Years later, 'e turned up in Birmingham, using the name Reginald Mountford. 'E was managing some er, ladies of the night there and finally got caught up with when a couple of girls went missing and were found dead. Apparently, they were keeping money from 'im.'

'What happened?'

'It wasn't 'im. But he was not an innocent party with regards to the deaths of those women. He did time. They shut down the 'business'. In the last few years 'e's been into the drug scene, dealing. 'E's been using several names and changing 'is appearance. 'Is latest is this Huggy Papa character, 'managing' pop artists. So far, this bit seems sort of legit. After all, he got Bonnie to the top of her game.'

'Yes. He can do anything, eh Jim? But it doesn't appear that he's happy just being 'legit' does it? What does he want with Bonnie, I wonder? She has the fame, the money. No doubt he's right in the mix there. What else does he want?' *Does he want to hurt her?* 'I'm going off to talk to the record company.'

Robert had to get out of there. He didn't like that unspoken voice in his head.

'Alright, guv.'

Or is he part of a bigger operation?

1953

Floyd – *'High Hopes'*
Frank Sinatra

Doctor Floyd waited in the consulting room at the hospital. His appointment with Petunia Jackson was imminent. She was to be delivered to his room by staff in a few minutes. Meanwhile he was reading her history so far.

This woman had suffered major trauma at the hands of a man she had hardly known, although he had lived directly opposite her home. She was a teacher - he raised his eyebrows at this – an intelligent woman then. She had taught at a local Catholic School. Deeply religious, he assumed. Never had a relationship with a man. Thirty-three years old! OK. He read on. Chained up, naked, raped and beaten. My God, no wonder she's traumatised! She fought him off and managed to strangle him with one of her chains. To the death! There was a detailed description of how she had achieved this, which he skipped over, as he had discussed some of this with the family doctor. She had conceived a child.

Floyd read the next part, skimming through as he was more familiar with the most recent events. Since finding out she was pregnant, Petunia had tried three times to either kill the baby or herself or both. She had constantly referred to the child as the demon seed. She had been admitted to Menston Mental Facility to protect her against herself, and to protect the pregnancy, which was now in its sixth month.

There was a quiet tap on the door. Petunia was wheeled into the room, her hands and feet secured to prevent her getting out of the chair or using her arms. The orderly took a chair in the corner of the room. Petunia refused to look at the doctor.

'Good afternoon, Miss Jackson, or may I call you Petunia?'

Petunia shrugged slightly.

'Good. How have you been feeling?'

Petunia shrugged again.

'I have been reading your case notes Petunia. I think I have an understanding of the trauma you have recently suffered.' He paused, trying to discern if she was listening. With no outward indication that she was, he continued. 'I can never pretend to know how you feel about all this. Those feelings are yours and no-one else's, and my job is to try to help you to deal with them. Our aim is not to erase them, deny them or change them, rather, to give you ways of living with them. Do you understand?'

Petunia eyed him. Did he detect the slightest spark of interest?

'In order for me to help you, I need you to talk to me. I realise you haven't felt like talking to anyone. I assume you are tired of people telling you to 'get over it', yes?'

Petunia pursed her lips together and nodded dejectedly.

'Do you think we can have a conversation, you and I?' asked Floyd.

Contemplating the doctor carefully, she finally spoke mournfully. 'I suppose so. I can't get away from you. You'll just persist, and they'll keep on bringing me here anyway, so I might as well give in.'

'Thank you, Petunia. I want you to understand that I am here to help you. Regardless of what happens with the baby, I want you to come out the other side with a meaningful life to live.'

'Well, at the moment, I cannot *possibly* see how that can happen,' retorted Petunia. 'Everything I ever valued has been ripped away from me. I have no concept of how I might go on, *after.*'

'That's where our conversations over the next few months will be focussed.'

'One question, doctor. Why must I be restrained?' Petunia's eyes flicked nervously around the room as if expecting something to jump out. 'It brings back all the memories of...what happened in the barn.'

'You know why Petunia! You have a habit of using weapons against yourself. You must show us we can trust you.'

'How can I if you won't untie me?'

Doctor Floyd motioned to the orderly. 'Undo the restraints, just the wrists at this stage.'

'But I can't! I'm not allowed to!' she protested.

'Do it. I'll explain. I take responsibility!'

The girl reluctantly undid the wrist straps, all the while glancing furtively at the doctor. *You'd better stand up and take the blame when she does something!*

'How does that feel, Petunia?' Floyd asked.

'Better.'

Doctor Floyd settled back into his chair, displaying his complete assurance that he trusted her. She noticed and visibly relaxed too.

'Tell me about your home, the village, anything. I want to hear the good stuff. I've read enough about the other! Is it a small village, where you grew up?'

Petunia tipped her head to one side, her greying hair flopping over her eyes. She didn't attempt to brush it away, then realising her hands were free, she wiped the hair off her face. The doctor nodded and smiled.

'I feel like I mustn't remember the good things. I feel unclean and not fit to keep those memories. I have pushed them away in the last months.'

'Is there one good memory you can share with me today?'

Petunia contemplated her swollen belly. 'I used to dress nicely. For school. I was a teacher you know, at a Catholic school. I always made an effort to look nice.'

'Would you like to look nice again, Petunia?'

'I suppose so, but I never will!'

'I will arrange for you to see a hairdresser. Would you feel better with your hair done?'

Petunia ran her fingers through her too long, lifeless hair. She nodded. 'I regularly had my hair cut and set, at least every two weeks. I don't know. It might be alright in here. I wouldn't feel like...I wouldn't feel as if I was trying to...' She faltered.

'You wouldn't be. We both know that deep down, don't we? You are still the same person you were despite your trauma. In essence, we don't change. All the values you held are still there, only they have been challenged and it's up to us to win that challenge. Are you ready to do that Petunia?'

'What about this?' She tapped her belly.

'My concern is with *you* Petunia. For the next three months you are merely a vessel which is needed to see this child through to birth. The child will be taken care of. I assume you have talked about giving it up for adoption?'

'I suppose people have been talking to me about different things. I haven't paid attention because I just wanted it out and gone, even if that meant I was gone too!'

Floyd listened not betraying his delight at her words. *I just wanted it out.* She had used the past tense. A significant step in the right direction, he thought.

'Plenty of time.' Floyd assured her. 'For the time being, I'll organise the hairdresser and I'll see you again next week. I've enjoyed our chat. I hope you have too.'

Floyd indicated to the orderly to take Petunia back to her room. He scribbled some notes. On his way out, he stopped at the nurses station in Petunia's wing and requested a visit from a hairdresser for Miss Jackson. He left with a spring in his step. The first session had gone well.

1969

Robert and Alby stood at the foot of the multi-story modern building, which was the home of Bonnie's recording company. It was located on a corner, the glass walls sweeping an elegant curve. Emblazoned across the top level was the name. Robert knew it to be one of the largest in the world with origins in the United States. Many of the most famous current artists were produced and marketed on this label. He entered the glass building.

After showing their ID and speaking to a doll-like receptionist, they were making their way in the lift to level three, where Ricky Chamber's office was situated. A skinny young man with long unkempt hair, well below his collar and parted in the centre, hurried before them. He appeared nervous. He wore tiny round glasses which gave him an uncanny resemblance to John Lennon. *Wrong record company* thought Robert.

'Is it about Dave? The girl?' the youth asked, looking back to the two detectives. He spoke with a whiney, cockney accent.

There goes the Lennon image thought Robert.

'No,' Robert replied, unaware of who 'Dave' might be and caring even less about what he might have been up to with 'the girl'.

'What is it then? Rick is real busy, man. It better be somefing real important!'

Robert ignored him and watched as the lift reached level three where a soft chime indicated the doors were opening. The youth stepped out and led them down the corridor to a door where he pressed an intercom.

'He's here, Sharon.'

'Is he feeling groovy? 'Cause Ricky Chambers is!' came the reply.

The man opened the door and indicated the desk where a stunningly modern girl greeted them. Blonde hair teased into a six-inch beehive on top of her head, long false eyelashes, full lips wearing pale pink lipstick and a mod outfit made of what looked to be white plastic. Robert felt sure he had seen her on TV, Coronation Street perhaps? In any case she bleached him with a thousand-watt smile and pouted coquettishly as he once again showed his badge.

'A *real* Detective! So exciting! I'll bet you have some real groovy stories.'

She batted the eyelashes and pulled her lower lip with a long pink fingernail, her way of trying to appear seductive.

Alby raised his eyebrows. Wow, Robert certainly was the flavour of the day!

'Is er, Rick in? As you say, I am a *real* detective and a very busy man dealing with my groovy schedule. Could you tell him I'm here, now?'

The skinny youth smirked and nodded, reminding Alby of the latest craze, nodding plastic dogs in the back of cars. Nod, nod, nod; his head as vacuous as the plastic dog's. The girl pressed the intercom.

'The Detective's here Rick.'

The two detectives are here, Rick, thought Alby.

'Send him in.'

The voice sounded like gravel on the intercom. Three went into the inner office leaving the Lennon lookalike in the outer office. Rick's office was spacious with panoramic windows providing stunning views of London. The central desk was mahogany, the chairs white vinyl and up to the minute style, a huge drinks cabinet nearly covered one wall. Above it, framed photos and gold discs displayed the man's successes in the business. Another smaller desk to the side, was now occupied by the blonde, who began examining her nails. Across the windows was a fur covered sofa which could comfortably seat six. The entire scene spoke of phony luxury and insincerity.

Rick lounged against his expansive desk. He appeared to be a middle-aged man with a face which painted a portrait of a life in the fast lane. Long creases formed his brown leathery skin into deep folds. Underneath the prolific facial hair, thin lips, sculpted by years of smoking, parted to reveal large yellow teeth, which looked to Robert as if the man only brushed them spasmodically. His hair curled over his collar but was visibly thinning on top. Robert judged him to be in his late fifties or early sixties. Nevertheless, he was still lean, wiry and wore a psychedelic orange Indian style shirt over hipster jeans and Cuban heeled boots. He was sporting a large gold medallion on a gold chain around his neck.

He held out a wrinkled hand adorned with multiple chunky gold rings, glinting with diamonds. 'Pleased to make your acquaintance, detective...?' He looked around at the girl seated at her desk asking her to fill in the detail. Robert helped her out.

'Detective Chief Inspector Turner, and this is Detective Inspector Coates, Rick...?'

'Yeah! Oh, right. Yeah, Rick Chambers. What can we do for you? Is this about Dave again?'

Rick turned to his desk, grabbed a packet of Benson and Hedges Special Filters, and lit up using a gold lighter. He declined to offer them around. Robert didn't smoke, but the girl took her own packet of Rothmans out and lit up.

'I've sorted it, man. He won't even look at her again.' The tip of the 'gold standard' cigarette glowed. 'She's gone anyway.' He exhaled smoke to the side and grinned. 'For good.'

Robert waited. 'What can you tell me about Bonnie Summer?'

Rick looked surprised. 'Bonnie? What about her? Oh, you mean that little incident in the hospital? Look, she made a bit of a mistake and she paid for it, but she's OK now. Down in Devon I believe with some old folks, grandparents, yeah? She'll be back next week. Got her big concert in Manchester. Tickets are sold out.'

Rick sucked on the cigarette, held the smoke then exhaled theatrically towards Robert. He perched on the edge of his desk, crossed one booted foot over the other.

'Tell us about the day you signed her to this label, asked Robert. 'Who was present? Who acted for her, considering she was fifteen at the time?' Robert kept his focus on Rick who took another long drag on the smoke.

Rick shifted: swapped legs. He looked uncomfortable. 'Oh man, that was a while ago. Let me think.'

'Surely you have records, documents here?'

'Yeah, yeah, of course. Hon?' he addressed the blonde at the desk, 'get the contract, yeah?'

Hon minced back into her office with Alby following, where she rifled through the filing cabinet and found a folder. Returning, she walked over to Rick, her plastic dress squeaking as she moved, her long white plastic boots performing a duet with it.

'Ta, baby.'

Rick moved behind his desk and sat, spreading the folder's contents out. Robert stepped behind him, looking over his shoulder.

'Right. OK.' Rick pointed with a yellowed finger. 'Here. Bonnie's manager was acting on her behalf in the absence of her parents. They had signed over to him, here.'

He pointed to a document which appeared legal where two signatures gave authority to 'Peter Farmer' to act on behalf of Bronwyn

Coleman. The signatures had been witnessed by a solicitor; a name Robert did not recognise but the signature was stamped correctly.

'As you can see detective, all above board and legal, yeah? Yeah.'

'I'd like a copy of this 'if you don't mind. Do you have a Xerox?'

'Er, yeah, yeah. Hon?'

Hon took the sheets into the other room and the Xerox machine could be heard humming.

'How well do you know Peter Farmer? Does he manage any of your other artists?'

'Oh, no not really. Well, not at all. But he's done a fab job of Bonnie, don't you think? I mean from a nobody to number one in six months! Quicker than The Beatles!'

Back in Rick's office, Alby chipped in. 'Bonnie is raking in the money, I understand. She informed DCI Turner that you have set up a Trust Fund in her name. May we see those documents too? Could we have a copy as well?'

Rick was now shifting in his chair, no doubt wishing he could drop through the floor. He stubbed out the filter of his cigarette and lit a new one.

'It would take a bit of time to do that. Held by the bank, you know.'

'Which bank?' Alby asked.

'Umm, Hon?'

Hon fluttered her lashes and hit Robert with that floodlight smile again. 'I don't know Ricky. That's not part of my job!'

'I'll make enquiries then,' said Robert, picking up the Xerox copies. 'In the meantime, Ricky, I'll leave you to sort out a few things, get your ducks in a row, and I'll be back. You can count on it.'

He turned to the girl, giving her a departing nod. 'Hon.'

***

Back in his office, Robert called in Wright.

'Jim, I need you to see if you can find the name Peter Farmer in any of our records. It's another alias of this Huggy character but I need proof. If he's on record as Peter Farmer, let's see why he's there. Look into bank accounts in his name, property, other record companies. See if he has been doing this elsewhere. The more I find out, the more worried I am about Bonnie. Have we heard anything? Has that Mini been sighted yet? Petrol stations, shops?'

'No. It's almost as if they've disappeared off the face of the earth. I'll get into those files guv.'

Robert knew that Wright would approach the tedious task with determination and would persist into the night if necessary.

Alby came in with a flurry of folders and papers, looking flustered.

'What do you have there, Alby?' said Robert as Alby flopped the pile onto his already crowded desk.

'All the reports on door knocks around Barnstaple near the car dealer's place. Nothing much came up. Only the barmaid and her boyfriend who corroborated her story that this character bought the Minivan. He paid cash and was alone. We've had a few claiming to have seen him but pretty vague; not really reliable.'

'What did you think of Mr Ricky Chambers, Alby. First impressions?'

I think he's putting on an act. I don't trust one word that came out of his mouth if you want my opinion. Just something about him.'

'Ye-es. I know what you mean. He did not seem too overly concerned that his top artist is away somewhere unknown to him only days before her biggest concert to date. Very dismissive about it wasn't he?'

'While I'm checking out Farmer, I'll have a look into Chambers as well. See if anything turns up on him.'

'Thanks Alby, get onto it.

1969

Bonnie lay in the back of the Minivan. Her eyes felt glued together and she struggled to force them open. They were on the move again. She wondered how long she had been out to it and where they were going now. As full consciousness returned the memory of how he had forced the drink into her mouth and how cruel he had been came rushing back. Lifting her head slightly, her vision swam in circles for a few moments before steadying. She frowned. Who was driving? She slowly levered herself up a little. All she could see was a man with smooth neatly cut collar length hair and a tan shirt. Her head felt light somehow; a very strange, cold, and airy feeling. She put her hand up and felt short tufts of hair. Running her hand over her scalp, she screamed.

'What happened to my hair? What have you done?'

The driver told her to 'shut it' without slowing the car. The same words Huggy had used.

'Huggy?'

'Shut up and keep out of sight.'

'Huggy! What's going on? You've changed! Where are you taking me?'

'I told you to shut it or else I'll have to put you to sleep again until we get there.'

'Get where? And why have you cut all my hair off?'

Huggy half turned and leaned his arm over the back of his seat.

'I'm warning you. I told you this is all for your own good. I want to get you to Birmingham, where I have contacts and a place for us to lay low until we can get things sorted out. Now, either you cooperate, or I'll find ways to make you.'

As he turned back to drive, he noticed a panda car going the other way. For a second, he wondered if they were going to turn around, but he saw it continue on its way in his rear mirrors. He kept driving.

****

Robert was in the process of wading through the many reports on his desk, trying to piece together a multitude of diverse facts which appeared disconnected, but Robert thought they were interwoven like a grisly spider web. The phone rang. He picked it up.

'DCI Turner.'

It was Alby on the line.

'They've spotted the car guv. Uniforms in a panda car. He's heading north on the Bristol Road, just south of Chewton Mendip.'

'How soon can we get squad cars there? Is the panda following?'

'They're sending cars down from Bristol. Yep, he's following him at a distance. Doesn't want to alarm him. Can't see anything much. Only one in the front, the driver. No sign of a passenger. She must be in the back. We don't know until we stop the car.'

'Righto Alby, keep me informed.'

Robert hung up. All he wanted to do was go home, open a bottle of single malt, and calm his frantic thoughts. Images conjured up by Alby's suppositions all too familiar; more than thoughts, they felt like *memories,* his own memories! He almost felt he was at one with the man in that car with Bonnie. The hairs stood up on his arms. *What was wrong with him?*

Robert finally walked into his up-market flat at nine thirty and opened an expensive bottle of single malt whiskey, possible only because he had been very good in his career at putting the worst of humankind behind bars. He, the brother of the one of them. The guilt rose again, and suddenly his arm hurled the crystal whiskey glass at the wall, causing Midnight, the cat, to yowl and flee into the bedroom. Glass sprayed across the carpet like a million diamonds. He put his head in his hands. Why hadn't he taken Susan's advice, given out of concern and probably even love, to seek counselling? No, he had rejected the idea, assuming she felt in danger from him and his unpredictable behaviours. He had never hurt her. Never! Not physically anyway, but he knew deep down that he had done so emotionally, being unable to allow himself to love her. Because he had no right, did he? His heritage was not one worthy of sharing with anyone, let alone someone he had feelings for. Perhaps that had been the start of the decline. He took a plain water glass from the kitchen cupboard, poured another drink, and hoovered up the crystal fragments. He flooded the whiskey stain on the cream shag carpet with soda water, but he could see it was going to require professional cleaning. Damn!

***

They were through the village of Chewton Mendip, when Huggy realised they would need to stop for petrol. He knew there was a fuel station at Farrington which was only minutes up the road. Turning once more to Bonnie, he warned her again.

'Stopping up here for petrol. Don't move and don't make a sound. Or do I need to stop before we get there and make sure you don't?'

Bonnie shook her head. How odd if felt without her long hair. 'Good, here we are.'

Huggy pulled over into the station next to a pump. A lanky lad sauntered over to the car, unhitched the pump, and shoved it into the filler. While the lad did that, Huggy walked into the office where there was a small selection of chocolates and potato crisps. He grabbed a couple of each and two bottles of pop. He was waiting at the desk for the attendant to come in when he saw his picture taped up behind the cash register. He still had long hair and a beard but concerningly, there was a photo of the Mini Van and the registration number! The youth returned. Huggy pulled some cash out of his pocket and shoved it at the lad.

'Keep the change.'

The youngster was so taken aback with the extra money he grinned and thanked Huggy. He did not appear to have noticed the car or made the connection between it and the photo right next to him. Huggy ambled slowly out to the car, cool as a cucumber, jumped into the driver's seat, fired up the little car and gunned the motor. Out on the road he glanced in the rear-view mirror. Was that the coppers way back in the distance? He couldn't be sure, but he needed to decide and quickly. He executed a complete U-turn back to the crossroads where he turned hard right into Ham Lane and sped off through the outskirts of Farrington and into the countryside. Keeping a sharp eye on the road behind he was sure after a few minutes that he had not been followed. Their situation might have just become a whole lot more complicated.

1953

THE PSYCHIATRIST

'Stormy Weather'
Lena Horne

Doctor Floyd walked down the corridor to his consulting room whistling. He raised a few eyebrows as he passed the nurses station. Whistling was not something common to this institution.

Inside the rooms, he settled at his desk and checked his notes for the day. He noted Petunia Jackson at 2 pm. There was a brief entry recording the hairdresser's visit. Then a more disturbing one detailing another attempt by his patient to harm herself. He knew she was going to be a challenge. But to his first patient, a woman who had inexplicably lost three babies at only weeks old. Interesting.

At two o'clock, Petunia was wheeled into his rooms by the same orderly, the young girl who was with her last week. She looked quite different physically, but he noticed her shoulders slumped, her expression still vacant.

'Good afternoon, Petunia.' Floyd waited.

Petunia sighed and gave a disconsolate nod in his direction.

'Good afternoon, Doctor,' she replied.

She sat with wrists and feet secured again. Floyd noticed her hair had been cut into a shoulder length bob. He fancied she had had a colour too as it seemed a more vibrant chestnut.

'Your hair looks very nice. They did a good job, I'd say. Do you like it?'

Petunia shrugged. 'I suppose it's better than it was.'

The doctor rubbed his hands together. 'Alright, what is next for Miss Petunia Jackson? Maybe it's time to get out of that chair and into some ordinary clothes, do you think?'

The orderly in the corner looked horrified. She tried to attract Floyd's attention.

'Yes, I read the notes. Now Petunia, how has your week been? Remember, we are going to talk, you and I!'

'Terribly exciting!' replied Petunia sarcastically. 'There is just so much to do, I don't know how I find the time! And then there is this!' she prodded her expanding belly. 'Now it's kicking me from the inside out.'

'How do you feel about that?'

'I can't pretend it's not there anymore.'

I need you to understand that this child did not choose to be conceived...'

'As I did not choose it to be either doctor!' hissed Petunia.

'In the meantime, may I see your wrists? I heard you suffered some injury?'

Petunia rolled her eyes. Yes, she had tried to saw through the skin on the edge of the table. She had only succeeded in bruising them as the table edges were not sharp, and her roommate, Miss Bloom, had called for help.

'I was under the impression you wish to get rid of the restraints and we need to trust you. What do you need to do to achieve that, Petunia?'

'Stop trying to hurt myself, I suppose.'

'Correct! Alright, let's try another week with them and see how our next session goes. Later in the week, the hairdresser will pay you another visit. By the way, has your mother been to see you?'

'No. She doesn't want to drive all this way and catching the bus is too difficult. Also, she doesn't like leaving the dogs alone all day.'

'Has anyone been to see you at all?'

'No. I don't want them to, either. I don't think my mother has told anyone in the village where I am.'

'Would you like to see her, your mother?'

'I don't know. The last time I was at home, I was furious with her.'

'Can you tell me what caused you to feel so angry with her?'

'She hid all the knives.'

'So, she thwarted your plans. You were not able to carry them out. Has your mother always been controlling?'

'I don't know, really. Yes, probably, since my father died.'

'How old were you when he died, Petunia?'

'Seven.'

'How close to him were you?'

'I don't know. I remember him. He worked in a bank, I think. He was killed by a horse and cart. I don't know much about it. The horse must have spooked and reared, then took off across the pavement. Hit my father and killed him.'

'You were only seven, Petunia. Do you remember going to his funeral? Quite often children were not permitted to attend funerals to say goodbye. Still to this day!'

'No, I didn't. What has this got to do with anything, doctor? I'm not suffering from the lack of a father in my childhood. My mother more than made up for it. She has always been a very strong, purposeful woman. She and the church have guided me on a righteous path through life...until now!'

'And how do you see yourself now?'

'The person sitting in front of you doctor is not me, not Petunia Jackson. I feel like a vessel for something I cannot even imagine. I feel wrong, in every sense of the word. My faith has evaporated. I question a God who could allow one of his servants to suffer as I have. When I think of the rest of my life, however long or short it might be, I feel deeply saddened, desolate, abandoned. I see no reason to continue. I will see this...this child to its birth and after that stretches an eternity of darkness for me. No-one can help me. Not even Father Michael.'

Doctor Floyd contemplated Petunia thoughtfully. She was going to be a tough one, but he had had worse. He would win the fight for her. That was why he was in such demand.

'Petunia, we are going to find a light to guide you through this, together. It may only be a flickering candle at first, but it will be a beginning. One day, and I promise you this, you will find the sun again and you will experience love, laughter, and life. Trust me Petunia, I can see the glimmer already, in your eyes. You are not as lost as you think you are.'

Petunia met his eyes briefly, and there it was, a flicker of hope. Floyd rose and motioned the orderly to come.

'Our time is up, my dear, I will see you next week. Our aim is to get you out of those bonds, remember? Goodbye.'

Dr Floyd left. He called into the nurse station to ask them to make a note to contact Joan Jackson by telephone and arrange for a couple of maternity dresses and some underwear to be brought in for her daughter. Andrew wanted Petunia to begin to feel like a normal woman again.

Petunia was wheeled back to her room. Another week of reluctantly supporting the life she felt she still despised inside her.

***

Two days later, Petunia had just arrived back in her room after seeing the midwife, when there was a knock on the door. Miss Bloom, who was not secured in a chair as Petunia was much of the time, waddled to open it, holding her rotund belly with one hand and twisting the door handle with the other.

Joan Jackson entered the room laden with shopping bags and her handbag.

'Oh, hello Miss Bloom. Hello Petunia. I've brought you some things.' She walked over to the little table and plonked the bags down, then took a seat.

'Oh?' said Petunia.

'How are you getting along dear? Your hair looks nice. Have you had it cut?'

'Yes, I get the pleasure of a hair-do once a week. Lucky, aren't I?'

Joan sighed. 'Well, it does look very nice. And how are you Miss Bloom? Looks as if you're not far off now.'

Miss Bloom, who had tried starving herself to hide her pregnancy for fear that her father would kill either her or her boyfriend or both, was now looking ripe and rosy.

'Just a couple of weeks, they tell me. Then this little chap will make an appearance. Of course, I must give him away. My mum says they'll take me back after. They'll tell everyone I went to finishing school in Switzerland.'

'Oh, I see.'

Looking at the girl, Joan thought she might only be fifteen at the most. *Poor thing* she thought.

'Petunia, I have a couple of new things for you to wear. I went shopping. I also brought in your own hairbrush, hairspray, and make-up. You do have a mirror? Oh yes, I see, in the bathroom, on the wall.' She handed the things to Petunia, then seeing her hands were still secured, Joan hastily took them back.

'I had a telephone call from Doctor Eglington. He wanted to let me know how you were doing. Doctor Floyd is the best there is in his opinion. Floyd is very pleased with your first two sessions. I was very happy to hear that. So have you changed you mind yet about keeping the baby and us raising it together?'

Petunia rocked her chair in fury. She screamed a scream of pure frustration.

'NO! I have not! Don't you dare ever ask me that again! This foul thing will be delivered and that is the sum of my responsibility to it. Someone else can have the pleasure of grappling with the devil child! Now, if you insist on annoying the HELL out of me, you can leave!'

Both Joan and Miss Bloom stared at Petunia, Joan taken aback at her daughter's language as she continued to fume and rock the chair, almost threatening to turn it over. Miss Bloom rang the bell for a nurse, again. Joan hastened to the door.

'I'm going then. I won't be able to come again for a while.'

And with that she pushed through the door and disappeared into the corridor. The nurse had squeezed past, marched up to the writhing woman in the chair and jabbed a needle in the top of her arm.

'This will make you feel better, Miss Jackson. Now, just relax.'

1969

'Mrs Robinson'
Simon & Garfunkel

Robert was driving up to Menston again to pay a return visit to the Colemans. As he drove, his thoughts again turned to Bonnie and her captor. He was sure Bramley had her, even though they had no concrete evidence yet that he had anyone with him. Robert had some coppers doing the rounds in Taunton and Glastonbury, asking at all the pubs, shops, and petrol stations if they had seen either Bramley or the car. They were specifically asking if anyone had seen him with another person. So far, nothing. He instructed them not to show pictures of Bonnie. He knew that there would be an uproar if the public found out she was missing and not 'down in Devon with her folks'. So far, they had kept a lid on it, and it was thought she would be ready for her Manchester concert in just under a week!

The Mini had disappeared between Chewton Mendip and Farrington. The panda car had them in their sights but were a long way back when the car simply vanished. They had searched all the side roads, but all were essentially lanes through farmland. The car had gone. The constables had enquired at the petrol station on the main road, but the manager had been out, and the young driveway attendant had not been much help. He thought there might have been a Mini but wasn't sure. All he could remember was some smart-looking businessman giving him a tip. When shown the photo of Huggy, he was certain he had never seen him before.

Robert sighed. She *had* to be with him, but where and what were his intentions? A shudder rippled through him. A sudden flash, a vision like a sharp blade pierced his thoughts and was gone. *I remember, how it was, the anticipation!* The thought arose unbidden. *I need a coffee* he thought. He stopped in a small village where he spotted a tea-room. He found they served coffees as well as tea, so he ordered a strong black coffee with two sugars and a Bakewell tart. He sat at a tiny table eating his tart and drinking his coffee. It was her eyes, wasn't it? They captivated him. The colour, like the deepest of blue summer skies. When he had looked into them in the hospital, he had felt a deep connection and had no idea why, but he knew he had to find her. He had looked into eyes like that before, somewhere in his past, but where and to whom had they belonged? Finishing his coffee, he returned to the car and continued up towards Menston.

'Come in Inspector.' Deirdre Coleman once again looked up and down the street, ushered Robert in hurriedly and cast a disparaging glance at the black Zephyr parked on the kerb.

'Good afternoon, Mrs. Coleman.'

She led him into the same sitting room, but this time invited him to take a seat. Bob Coleman stood and shook hands before they all seated themselves. 'What can we do for you, Robert?'

Coleman used his name as if they were old golfing buddies.

'Have you heard from Bronwyn?' asked Robert.

Both looked askance. Deidre pushed her hair up and curled it behind her ears.

'No, of course not! The last we heard is that she went missing from Bob's mother's place on Friday night and the stupid woman didn't think to report it to anyone until Sunday! Bob gave her a piece of our minds, didn't you dear?'

'I passed on our concerns, yes. So do you have any news yet?'

'We are following a number of avenues. Naturally, I am unable to divulge the details as it may compromise the situation. I'm sure you understand. I am here to ask you a couple of personal questions which might have a bearing on our inquiries.'

'Oh, personal, and what might that be?' asked Deidre, her pointy nose tilted up so that she regarded Robert down the length of it, her pink lips pursed.

'Mrs. Coleman, I can find no records of Bronwyn's birth. I have searched the files for relevant years and there is no record of a Bronwyn Coleman born to the pair of you.' He saw the sharp intake of breath from Deirdre, the darting look to his wife from Bob. 'So, my question is, whose daughter, is she?'

Deirdre exhaled loudly and turned to Bob. 'You tell him, Robert. After all, it was all because of you!'

'She was adopted, Detective. Adopted just after she was born. Me and Deirdre, we couldn't have children of our own...'

'So, *you* decided Robert, that we should adopt someone else's child! We did. She was a week old.'

'Did you know who her natural parents were?'

The discomfort between these two gave Robert the same urge to escape as if a swarm of wasps had buzzed into the room.

'No. All we knew was that the mother was single and could not keep her.' replied Deirdre.

'It would help us greatly to know something of her natural parents. Maybe she does know who they are. Is that possible? Could she be with them?' Robert asked.

'Definitely not. We have never given her even the slightest hint that she is adopted. In any case, she would have to wait until she turns twenty-one to try to find them, even if she did know!'

'I can get a court order to search adoption files, but it would make things much simpler if I had your permission. Do I have it?'

'Well, what can we do? You'll get our permission; however, I fail to see how this can help find her if she is unaware of her 'connections!' snapped Bob.

'Which adoption agency did you use? Do you even know the district from where she came, the hospital perhaps?'

Bob sighed. 'I suppose I might find the papers if you gave me time. They're in a safe in my office, but I don't think those details were on them. The whole thing is that when you adopt, the child is yours. No-one else can claim them after they are adopted. You understand that we were told that many of these mothers were very young or had been raped. Some wanted to keep their babies and weren't allowed to, others just wanted them gone. Some were in physical danger if they stayed with the real mother. It's all a very sad story. We have no idea what situation Bronwyn could have been in, or where, but rest assured, she has had the best of everything with us. Couldn't have asked for more.'

Except love! Isn't that what Bonnie had said?

'Thankyou Mr and Mrs Coleman. I will have the documents sent to you. You'll find your signatures need to be witnessed. It's all explained. Then if you could post them back to me. I'll give you an address.'

Robert scribbled on his notepad and handed Bob the piece of paper. 'Also, I have given you the private number at my office. You can telephone me direct if you have any questions or if you hear from Bronwyn.' Robert withdrew an envelope from his inside pocket and opened it. He passed the Xerox sheets to Bob.

'Do you recognise this, Bob?'

Bob scowled as he quickly skimmed over the top paper. 'What is this, a contract of some sort?' He took reading glasses out of his pocket.

'It is indeed. It is the contract between Bonnie Summer and the recording company. If you take a look at the second page, I would be interested in your thoughts on that,' said Robert.

Bob scowled even harder. 'That's my signature! And Deirdre's! We never signed this! What is it… signing over the power of attorney to, who's this, Peter Farmer?'

'Precisely. Peter Farmer is Huggy Papa, the one who wrote the letters, also known as Bonnie's manager. It appears you signed these giving him control over her money.'

'We certainly did not!'

'Are you saying these are not your signatures?'

Bob scrutinised them. 'Well, they look like them, but we didn't sign these papers, Inspector!'

'May I?' asked Dierdre. She flipped the page and skimmed it.

'I think I recognise this. We were given a document to sign but this last page was attached to something else, to do with her leaving school, I believe. If you look, Inspector, page two has only our signatures and the witness on it. Very clever! Who is this Alan J Giles? We don't know him. I can't remember having to have our signatures witnessed at the time. This must have been done at some later date. I assume then, that Bronwyn is unlikely to see any more of her money?'

'You are telling me that you did sign this document but under false pretences? To your knowledge, you were signing her withdrawal from her school?'

'Yes, that's right.' replied Deirdre. 'You remember, Bob?'

'I do. I felt devastated that she would not finish her O levels, in fact I wanted her to go on to A levels and University. She is more than capable Inspector. More than capable!'

'I'm sure she is Mr. Coleman. I think I have enough for now, Mr. and Mrs. Coleman. Meanwhile, if something turns up, and I'm sure it will soon, I'll let you know.'

'Thanks Robert.'

Bob shook his hand again and indicated the door. The two watched Robert leave from behind the curtains.

'I hope none of this gets out,' said Bob. 'My reputation would be in tatters.'

Deirdre tossed her head.

'Pfft. Grow up Bob. You over-estimate your reputation. After all, you are just a car salesman!'

'Oh, go and have another drink, Deirdre!'

As Robert drove away, the Motorola telephone in his car rang. He picked it up. 'Yep.'

'Alby, guv. Just got a call in from a barman at The Crown in Glastonbury. He wasn't there when our lads called in but saw the photo of Huggy pinned up at the bar. He was there on Monday, and we've got a new lead now. This character says he went into the gents and when he came out, he'd cut his hair, shaved, and changed into slacks and a plain shirt and tie. He thought it was a bit odd but didn't think much of it until he saw the poster. Another thing, guv, he was askin' the manager for scissors! It looks like Bramley and the manager of the pub know each other quite well but when our guys asked him, he denied ever having seen him. What do you think Bramley's doing with scissors?'

Robert listened as he negotiated his way out of Menston back towards Leeds.

'Alby, have you got someone going to Glastonbury to interview this bloke?'

'Yep, onto it guv. I asked Wright to go tomorrow.'

'Right, so we're looking for somebody very different now. Can you get one of the Identikit artists to go with Jim? He might be able to do up a sketch of what Bramley looks like now. The sooner we can get that out the better. How did Wright go looking for Peter Farmer?'

'We've got it all for you when you get back. You were right. Farmer is another alias of Bramley's, plus he has a few more. He certainly has been around, plenty of very dodgy dealings through the years. I think what you'll be most interested in is his history of associations with young girls and women. He's escaped convictions many times. He must have quite a network of pawns willing to take his raps.'

'OK. I'll be back in London tonight, but I'll get all the latest in the morning. Tell the lads from Bristol to have another look around the outskirts of Farrington. He could have dumped that car by now. He's a slippery one alright! All we can hope is that Bonnie is still alive and unharmed.

'Righto, will do. Do you think he might have cut her hair off to change her appearance too?'

'Spot on Alby. I'm sure he has. She's probably a blonde by now. Either she's doing this because she wants to, or, and I think this is probably the case, our Mr. Bramley has abducted her, for what purpose I dread to think. Look I'm coming into some traffic now. I'll see you tomorrow.'

'Right you are, then. Take it easy in that traffic!'

Alby rang off. An icy cold chill of fear crawled over Robert's skin.

Where are you, Bonnie?

1969

Rick Chambers paced agitatedly in front of his desk. He lit up a smoke from the butt of the last one and blew smoke to the ceiling. He wore blue tinted glasses and a psychedelic orange shirt open to his waist baring a greying hairy chest, with a large gold peace symbol nestled into it.

'For Christ's sake where is she, pet? Three days and she's on! And I don't mean the bloody Manchester concert. No sign of her. No word; nothing from Pete. What the fucking hell does he think he's doing?'

He paced, smoked, and uttered repeated expletives. 'Everything was ready to go after the concert!'

Sharon, his baby-doll, blonde secretary stood beside his desk watching him rant.

'I've got people waiting. I've got the best paying customer I've ever had waiting with a fistful of money. And where has that idiot taken her? Why hasn't he called me since Glastonbury? Gone AWOL again with our merchandise!' He paused his pacing just long enough to take another long drag on the cigarette. 'Sharon! Get me that long drink of water in here!'

Sharon, who had been filing her long false nails as she watched him asked, 'Who, Ricky? Stevie?'

'Yeah, yeah, Stevie! Who else, baby? Get him in here!'

'OK Ricky. I'll call him.'

Sharon tottered into her office on platform boots which rose above her knees. Her white mini dress showing most of her thighs as she wiggled her way out. Rick could hear her on the phone calling Stevie. In a matter of minutes Stevie arrived with Sharon right behind him. Again, Rick had to remind himself that this was his personal assistant and not John Lennon, the likeness was so close.

'Stevie! You've gotta find Bonnie! Get out there. They're in a blue Minivan. Last I heard from them they were in Glastonbury. I don't care how you do it but find 'em and then get down there and drag her back by the hair if you have to. I will not put up with this shit when there's so much riding on her!' Geez!' he guffawed at his own joke.

'But Ricky, the coppers have got a blanket ban on any info about her, man. Nobody knows where she is, only that she's in Devon, which we know she's not. Somerset's a big county! And you know they're looking for Peter! I can't get a hold of him!' protested Stevie.

'Yeah, yeah, I don't care! Find out, however you can. I have thousands of pounds riding on this. Now get out and get going and don't come back until you've got her!'

Stevie backed out of the office throwing his hands in the air in frustration. How was he going to find out where she was and bring her back in time? Three days! *Such a has-been,* he thought. *With his super mod, trendy gear, and wrinkled face. Jesus, why do I put up with him.* He knew why. Sharon! He thought he was in love with her, but she hadn't given any indication she might feel the same...yet.

Stevie went back down the corridor to the little hidey-hole he called an office. The room, he was sure, had once been a broom closet. There was barely enough room for a small desk, a chair and a couple of filing cabinets. To open the drawers, he had to shift the chair to the side of the desk. He could only open the door three quarters. Luckily, he was very slim. A 'long drink of water' as Rick was wont to call him at times.

The tiny desk was strewn with newspapers and magazines, empty coffee cups and screwed up paper bags which had held donuts or cream buns. A couple of empty Rothmans packets and one which lay open with two remaining cigarettes also joined the rubbish party on the desk. Stevie grabbed one and lit up. He exhaled the smoke and burst into a fit of coughing. The closet had no ventilation, window or otherwise and with the door closed, one drag was enough to cause a choking fog. Stevie hastily stubbed it out and opened the door to fan the smoke away.

'Damn it!' he said aloud. *Right, where were those articles in the paper about the silly little bitch?*

He spent the next ten minutes scanning through the piles of print until he found what he was looking for. 'Detective Chief Inspector Robert Turner' had led the bust at Notting Hill. Buried among the garbage on the desk was a telephone, somewhere! He found it and dialled the Metropolitan Police Headquarters, then asked for DCI Turner.

'May I ask what your call is regarding?' The voice on the other end sounded weary as if she had fielded too many irrelevant calls today already.

'Yeah, I'm calling on behalf of Bonnie Summer's recording company. We need to speak to DCI Turner regarding her big concert on Saturday in Manchester. She hasn't been in touch wiv us at all. Maybe the Inspector could give us some idea where she is and what the h… what she's doing?'

'Inspector Turner has only returned to London late yesterday and is extremely busy. He is not taking calls. However, if you give me your name and phone number, I can pass it on to his office for you.'

Stevie silently swore at the 'cow' at the other end of the line. 'Stevie Wonder, and the number is…'

'I beg your pardon?' came the distant voice through the line. 'Did you say Wonder?'

'Yeah, yeah, I changed it. Pretty groovy, don't you fink? Anyway, my number.' Stevie gave the number.

'Thank you, Mr. Wonder. I will pass it on.'

Stevie jammed the phone down and swore. He did not for two seconds think DCI Turner's office would get back to him. Who else? Well, that wierdo, Pete, her manager. But of course, he was missing and on the wanted list! No good. Did they know her parents? Did Rick know who they were? Maybe? He picked up the phone and dialled the internal number for Sharon.

'Hello, are you feeling groovy, 'cause Mr Rick Chambers is!' she said.

'Sharon, it's me.'

'Oh, yeah, Stevie. What?'

'Do you have the names and address of Bonnie's parents? Rick has given me only free days to find her and get her back here, ovverwise she's in breach of her contract and she's too big a loss financially to let that happen. Anyway, I fought maybe I could contact 'em. They would know somefing surely?'

'I think I do have their phone number, because they had to witness that document giving Peter Farmer authority to manage her affairs. Just a minute, I've got it right here, um, never put it back after that inspector was here. Um, yeah, here it is. Their names are Mr Robert and Mrs. Diedre Coleman, but the address wasn't on the document. Oh, there is no phone number, just the names and their signatures.'

'OK, who was the witness?'

'Umm, I can't read the signature, but printed underneath is 'Alan J. Giles, Solicitor and Notary Public.' There is a phone number and a business address in greater London. Come up and you can call from here.'

Within minutes Stevie was back in Sharon's office. He nodded to the closed door to Rick's office. 'He in?'

'Ricky's busy. Here's the number.' She pushed the papers across and handed Stevie the handset.

Stevie rang the number. He rolled his eyes at Sharon as the tone for 'number disconnected' sounded. 'Got a map of London?'

Sharon wobbled out to her office in a most ungainly manner, nearly turning her ankle at one point. Stevie watching her marvelled at the boots, thinking what a sexy little piece she was. She returned with a map and handed it to him. He tried looking up the address, but no such place existed on this map anyway.

'What's Rick been up to? Or was the contract all organised by Peter Farmer, alias, Bramley? Another dead end, because he's missing, wanted by the cops. Do you fink it's because of this, fraud, or somefing to do with Bonnie?'

'I don't know, Stevie. I'm not much for the news, only the pop mags.'

'Back to square one. Do you want to go out wiv me? We could go somewhere after work.'

Sharon batted her ridiculously long, black lashes and pouted. 'I can't. I've got a boyfriend. Anyway, you're too old for me, Stevie, otherwise...'

'Damn! See you 'round like a Lifesaver then!' as he slammed the door on the way out. *Jeez, I'm twenty-free for God's sake!*

1969

'Runaway'
Del Shannon

The little Minivan swung into a narrow two-rutted lane, bouncing on its worn out suspension, finally pulling into a gate. The deserted yard, populated with derelict barns, sheds and animal pens appeared to have been abandoned many years ago. Huggy drove around to the left where an old, dilapidated cottage sat, the windows boarded up, the chimneys fallen in and the front door now bare timber and rotting. An ancient old Ford sagged into the ground, one intact headlamp glass winking in the sun, giving the appearance of a drunken old man collapsed in the parched weeds, the rusted crank handle, his ancient pipe.

Bonnie lay in the back of the Mini, her hands and feet bound, her eyes wide with fright and shock too. How had things come to this? The van stopped. The 'new' Huggy got out, came around to the back and opened the rear doors.

'Out you get. I'll untie your ankles. Wait a sec.' He undid the ties.

'I don't understand Huggy. Why are you doing this to me? What do you want?'

'Bon, if you had cooperated from the start, we wouldn't be in this mess. All I wanted was to get you away from all the oldies who think they know what's best for you, but all *you* did was whine and complain! You should have shut up and trusted me. Now you have wrecked your chances. Probably wrecked your career and my income, not to mention your own! You won't be doing Manchester. In fact, you won't be doing anything until I find out what Ricky wants me to do with you.'

'You can't just keep me like this! People will be looking for me. I'm famous. When famous people don't turn up for gigs, people go looking!'

'Just watch me!' Huggy growled.

'I think you should take me home,' stated Bonnie matter-of-factly.

Huggy turned to look at her. Her tone of voice had changed subtly with that last comment. Did he detect *defiance?* Her eyes penetrated his, unblinking. Suddenly, they didn't seem so gloriously blue, but steely.

Huggy pushed the old and rotting cottage door in and dragged Bonnie inside. No-one had been here for a long time. The room wore a cloak of aging dust and faded memories. There was nothing left but an old wooden chair in the first room. The ceiling had fallen in places, the walls crumbling plaster and the fireplace empty. Someone had raided the cast iron range long ago. Only a pipe remained protruding from the wall where the sink had once been. The adjoining room, which had been the sitting room, was similarly bare and cobweb-ridden, except for a sepia photograph in a broken frame, a pathetic reminder that this had once been a family home; the couple staring forlornly into the camera.

Up the stairs, in one of the bedrooms there was a rickety iron bed with a mattress which had long been the home of rats, mice and other vermin. Huggy pushed Bonnie onto it.

'Stay there until I get back. I'm going to hide the van and bring up a few things.' He tied her ankles again.

Bonnie listened to his descending footsteps on the stairs. When she heard the door scrape, she tried wriggling her wrists. The ties were not that tight, but she thought it would take too long to work them free. Then what? She knew they had not travelled very far after getting petrol, so it was possible she would be able to make it to Farrington and get help, but she doubted her chances of getting out of the cottage in one piece. She heard the Mini start up. He was in the car. She tried the restraints again, but her ankle ties were tight. She reasoned that if he came back and found the wrist ties loose, she might be in more trouble.

Think this through. OK. It's now Wednesday. The police would have been alerted that she was missing, surely. Nanna would have told them she had left everything behind. That would mean they would think her disappearance was suspicious. Did they even know she was with Huggy? Did anyone see him or the white van in Clovelly? Or did they think she had simply run away for some reason? She was supposed to be in Manchester rehearsing as of today, so wouldn't Rick Chambers and everyone at the record company be wondering where she was? Had Huggy been telling them some far-fetched story about her?

Since leaving Clovelly, she hadn't seen a newspaper or any television and had no idea what had been said, assumed or believed about her. Whatever Huggy was planning for her remained a mystery, but she really did not like the drastic change in him. She was certain she needed to try to get away from him but how? The front door banged shut. He was coming up the stairs, each step sounding hollow on the old timber risers, except one which squeaked. Bonnie was still shocked at this different man when he entered the room. He looked like a bank teller or a businessman. Very strange. He casually tossed Harmony's bag on the bed. Bonnie hugged it to her. It gave her a measure of mild comfort. She looked inside and found one of Harmony's guitar picks. She slipped it in her jeans pocket. It was a token, a reminder of her friend.

'Right, first off, I found a basic bathroom out back where there is some running water and a basin. Come on, we're going to bleach your hair,' announced Huggy.

'What? Why?'

'Obviously, so you can't be easily identified until I get you to Birmingham. Now, come on. Let me take those ties off. Afterwards, I got us some food, well snacks, at the petrol station. It'll do for tonight while I think what to do now.' He kept talking almost to himself as they squeaked and thumped down the old stairs.

'So, the coppers are looking for the Minivan, they must have realised you're with me and that we dumped the white van. How did they find out about the Mini though? Going to need another car or van. After we've done your hair, we'll go for a walk while it's still light. See if we can find anything close by.'

They were now at the back of the cottage where the rudimentary bathroom was tacked on to the stone building. Everywhere was draped with dusty cobwebs which had become pendulous with dirt.

'Ugh!' exclaimed Bonnie as she collected one across her face in the doorway.

'Over here. Do you know how to do this?' He showed her the bottle of hair bleach.

'I'll do it!' she said grabbing the bottle.

Only ten minutes later, her white-blonde hair was dry. Huggy dragged her outside, where he poked around the sheds and barns looking for any vehicles which might be a viable option. There was nothing, only an old lorry, the drunken Ford, and the remains of a wooden cart. They returned to the cottage, ate the crisps and drank the pop.

'Alright, I'm going out for a while. To make sure you don't scarper, I'm going to give you the sleepy juice again.'

He poured a few drops into the remainder of her drink and offered it to her. She knew now not to refuse. Better to just drink it. *After all,* she reasoned, *he is not going to hurt me now.*

'Sleep tight!' he said as he sat on the edge of the bed, waiting for the drug to take effect.

1969

Robert was early. Another hot one was to be expected in London. He wanted to avoid the morning rush. Sitting in traffic, wearing a suit, waiting to move a few yards as the temperature climbed was no fun in anyone's language.

Inside the building, it too was beginning to heat up. Although they had some portable fans, no such thing as air conditioning existed. He remembered a few years ago when an American FBI team had been over conducting a major investigation; a double murder involving a couple of their compatriots. It had been mid-summer and quite warm. They had found it unbelievable that the Brits had not seen fit to install the creature comforts of air conditioning. They had complained constantly, not only about the buildings, but the cars too. They had refused to dress appropriately for the job, and furthermore, spent more time in the locals than in the Met.

Robert pushed the door to his office open, walked in and took his jacket off, hanging it over the back of a chair, then loosened his tie. Alby was at his desk. Without looking up he greeted Robert.

'Mornin' guv.'

'Mornin' Alby. You beat the rush too? You got a coffee or a tea?'

'Yep, got one, thanks.'

Robert moved over to the machine and made himself a milky coffee with two sugars and grabbed a couple of custard cream biscuits.

'Good breakfast, boss!' commented Alby. 'On your desk is Jim Wright's report on his findings on Bramley's various other names and his past misdemeanours. There's a copy of the Identikit picture of Bramley from that barman at Glastonbury as well. Should be pretty accurate since he just overlaid it on our picture of him. The guy had a good memory too! He was sure that Bramley and the Manager knew each other. He was very worried that he was going to get fired for contacting us. What else? Oh, there was a message from Rick Chambers' PA asking for information on Bonnie Summer's whereabouts. He said they're getting nervous about what to do if she doesn't turn up to do the Manchester concert. It's probably much too late now anyway. They tell me she should have been rehearsing with the band, doing sound and staging checks, outfits, and all. How did your visit to the Colemans go?'

Robert swivelled his chair to face Alby. 'Mrs. Coleman is a most unpleasant woman. In my opinion, I think Bob was caught in her spider's trap, fooled by her attractiveness and flirtations. She in turn was fooled by his brash over confidence and sense of self-importance. He has certainly done well in his field and provided a moderately lavish lifestyle for her, but she clearly is of the opinion that he hasn't quite made it far enough up the ladder to fulfil her expectations. Furthermore, once they discovered that it was he, who was unable to father children, I think she simply began manipulating him to maintain her status quo, but it's certainly not a happy home.'

'So, Bronwyn isn't theirs?'

'No. Adopted just after birth. She doesn't know. She must have wondered where her flaming red hair came from. Also, both parents have dark brown eyes. The chance of her having those incredible blue ones would be low.'

'One in four, guv, and considering she was the only child, yes, unlikely I suppose.'

'Is that right Alby?'

'Yep, A level Biology, sir. Genetics.'

'Oh yes, Alby, I forgot you were an educated man!' said Robert wryly and grinned. He picked up his phone and pressed a couple of digits. 'Yeah, Turner. Have you got those documents I asked for, ready to go? Thanks. Can you get them off to the address I gave you? Yes, Menston. That's right. Thanks.' He replaced the phone.

Addressing Alby, he said, 'Those documents they supposedly signed handing over Bonnie's affairs to Peter Farmer were fraudulent. They signed them but thought they were signing her exit papers for the school!'

'So, who set all that up? '

'I would be making a wild guess; Peter Farmer, aka, Huggy Papa, aka, Peter Bramley! So, how are we going with Bristol, looking for the Mini? Have we got uniforms onto it?' he asked Alby.

'They should be there I would think. They've been instructed to knock on the door of every farm, cottage or otherwise and search empty sheds. If he's dumped it or still around that area, they'll find him, guv.'

'Have we had any reports of a girl travelling with or without him?'

'No, not yet.'

'I think it's time to do a press conference. We need to let the public know. It's the only way we can start to get information. I'd like to get the Coleman's to put out a plea for help. What do you think the chances are?'

Alby snorted. 'Huh! How sincere would they look? I can't imagine Deirdre, can you?'

'Not really but we need to do something. The press will go bonkers, of course. Get a team together and get in touch with our Bob and Dierdre. Tell them what we need. Contact Rick Chambers. Inform him what we're doing. He'll have to deal with the backlash. I'll contact the BBC and ITV. We'll try to schedule it for 10 tomorrow morning. I'll get on to writing a spiel, get Wright to prepare the photos, then we'll take some questions for ten minutes and that's it. Hopefully, the phones will start running hot with sightings.'

As Robert was talking to Alby, he was mentally grappling with underlying jabs of panic, thoughts of evil and a feeling of losing the fight against time for Bonnie. What were they doing? Where were they? Why did he have this persistent feeling that there was a much darker reason behind her disappearance than first thought? And why did this particular case stir him at the core? Surely, Bramley had not just taken off with her for a bit of fun with a young girl! He had all that anyway, Robert suspected, though Bonnie had denied it. No, there had to be something of which they hadn't thought. Why would this Huggy Papa character sacrifice his share of Bonnie Summer's fame unless there was something much bigger, more valuable at stake?

He took the file containing Wright's report on him and began to read it. It was a substantial rap sheet for Peter Findlay Bramley, aliases, Peter Farmer, Peter Formby, Reginald Mountford, and Lane 'Chip' Byrd. Robert frowned. Where did he come up with *that* one? There were more than likely others but these names were the ones Wright had found on their records. *Right, let's see what you've all been so busy doing in the last forty years.*

Robert spent the next hour poring through a myriad of petty crimes mostly around small time fraud, theft, and prostitution. The first serious one came when he was in Birmingham under the name of Reginald Mountford, where he was discovered to be a silent partner in a brothel. Two young girls were found dead, both severely beaten and had had their throats cut. He had been elsewhere at the time, but his association with the person who was identified as the perpetrator put him fairly in the hot seat. He was jailed for accessory and receiving monetary benefits from an illegal business. The business was investigated. Robert read that it was found to be more of a backyard brothel, poorly run, employing only a few girls. No substantial money trail was found. It seemed to be an utter dead end. After doing time, 'Reginald' vanished. The girls' killer was imprisoned for life. The case was closed and forgotten.

So, then what for our Huggy character? pondered Robert. Reggie popped up again in the mid-sixties in Manchester as Peter Farmer. Apparently, he had suddenly acquired musical skills and had formed a folk group. They travelled around playing country fairs, festivals, and pubs. They couldn't have been making much and yet, Robert discovered, Peter Farmer was paying land taxes on a large country house in Suffolk on some acreage. The owner was listed as Lane Byrd. Robert began looking for anything on him, occupation, business and found he purported to have come over from the US but there were no other details. The property was not mortgaged. *So where was he getting all this money?* Lane Byrd had slipped up once in the small village near his property, getting into a scuffle at the local pub. It resulted in half a dozen men being taken into custody. They were all finger-printed and bingo! Lane's were a match with Bramley's and Mountford's, all one and the same. The man they knew as Huggy Papa was running around in an old kombi, dressed like a hippy, long straggly hair and all the while had a house which would have been worth thousands of pounds. He had no registered business or taxable income except his earning as Peter Farmer in the music business. What other businesses was he a 'silent partner' in? There was much Robert needed to find out about this character.

He looked at the clock and was surprised to see it was already one o'clock. He saw Alby's desk unoccupied. He must have been so engrossed; he had missed him leaving. Half the day gone, and he still needed to set up the press release for tomorrow. He made himself another coffee, went back to his desk and began making phone calls.

1953

WAITING ROOM

'The Great Pretender'
Elvis Presley

Petunia sat in her chair gazing dismally out of the window. Miss Bloom had delivered her baby some days ago and had been moved to a post-natal ward to recover from the birth and receive drugs to dry up her milk supply. The baby had been surrendered immediately. Despite Petunia's refusal to interact with Miss Bloom, she missed her idle chatter and presence. The bathroom was now shared between only two, one girl on each side which was significantly easier for both.

Petunia's pregnancy had continued without any complications. Now in her eighth month, she had been receiving weekly sessions with Doctor Floyd. She was free to move around in her room or visit the recreation room to watch television. Floyd congratulated himself on her progress, noting that she rarely flew into a rage or gave the staff cause to sedate her. On recommendation from him, Joan was to keep her visits short and refrain from mentioning the baby at all. Joan had conceded that this would be the best thing to do and had complied. Everything was progressing satisfactorily towards the delivery. In fact, Dr Floyd was ready to begin reducing his sessions to one every two weeks, he was so pleased with her turnaround. When no-one was around, however, things were quite different.

Petunia was wont to sit staring blankly out of the window to the car park. She was marking the days and weeks until such time as she was rid of this thing inside her. She constantly relived those final moments of Eric's life, when she had tightened the chains around his neck further and further, even when she had known he was already dead. She remembered the feeling of triumph as she had watched his eyes glaze over. She remembered thinking, *not for you the heavenly chorus, the welcome into the Heavenly Father's arms. No, you are now on your way to Purgatory and eternal damnation!* At that precise moment life left him, she had felt she had won the fight against evil. Then, minutes after Mary Waterhouse had discovered her in the barn, she realised how wrong she had been. She too could be blamed just as he was. Had she not been looking for something? If not, why had she turned towards his cottage to see if he was looking for her? Responding to him had appealed to her lustful needs, one of the seven deadly sins. She thought she could claim envy and pride as well; envy of other women her age who had found the perfect companion for a marriage within the church, and pride in her own need for perfection.

The more she had contemplated these things, the more withdrawn she had become to the point that her mother had not been able to cope with her at home. Added to this, the discovery that she had become pregnant had driven the last nail in her coffin of self-loathing.

Now she had become very adept in masking her true feelings. She knew exactly what Floyd was doing. She was not insane. Far from it. She had him figured out after the first couple of sessions and had quickly learned how to manipulate him. Inside, Petunia still considered her life over. She knew in her heart that she would never be worthy again. Once she was released from this place, her plan was to kill herself as soon as the opportunity arose. She had no remorse thinking this way. She simply wanted out. Meanwhile, she would acquiesce, appear to have accepted her past and to be ready to resume life on the outside after the birth.

A small smile played on her lips. *Not long to go now!*

1969

'Maxwell's Silver Hammer'
The Beatles

Bonnie lay on the rotten mattress fast asleep. Farmer aka Bramley and Huggy knew he had only a short time before she would begin to stir. He needed to find a telephone but was reluctant to go back into Farrington. Instead, he set off up the road looking for a farmhouse or cottage which might have one. Telegraph lines running the length of the road meant telephones! Today, a warm southerly breeze and intermittent clouds cooled the sun. The road was a two-lane track with weeds growing in the centre of two roughly paved and worn strips. Bramley walked on the bitumen trying to think what he needed to do. Before long he saw a cottage on the right, set back from the road a little. It looked to be well kept and he noticed the telephone line connected to the corner of the house. Great. He opened the white-painted paling gate, walked up the gravelled path and pressed the doorbell. As he waited, he looked around noticing the well-tended flower beds, the polished windows and fresh paint. He rang again.

The door was opened by an older gentleman with thick, white hair, a luxurious moustache and reading glasses perched on his nose. He carried a newspaper under one arm and leaned on a walking stick.

'Can I help you?' he asked.

'I was wondering if I could use your telephone. My car has broken down just up the road.'

'Where abouts is it?' The man took his reading glasses off, carefully folded them and put them in the breast pocket of his cardigan.

'Just a bit down the road, not far from that derelict old cottage. Could I use your phone to call a friend?'

'Well, wait a minute, what's wrong? Have you run out of petrol?'

Bramley hid his growing frustration. 'No, I don't think so. I just got petrol in Farrington. It just stopped. If you could see your way to let me use your phone...'

The old man smiled benevolently. 'I was a mechanic before I retired. It can't be too much wrong then. Probably the points have closed up. Simple! I'll come and have a look for you. Just a tick, I'll tell the wife and grab some tools.'

'Margaret!' he called out. 'I'm going out for a few minutes. Just grabbing my tools from the shed and...'

That was all he managed to say before Bramley came up behind him, grabbed him around the neck and held a kitchen knife to his throat.

'Shut up you stupid old fool. I don't want the car fixed. I need the telephone. Now where is it?'

The wife, who had heard some of what the old man had said, came shuffling down the passage. On seeing her husband in a headlock, she stood, paralysed, whimpering to please let him go. Bramley motioned her to turn around and lead them back into the living room.

'Where's the telephone?' he demanded.

The man tried to speak, but Bramley tightened his grip.

'You,' he nodded towards Margaret. 'You show me where it is.'

The woman, Margaret, indicated the kitchen door with a shaking hand. She was too terrified to speak, her eyes like saucers.

Bramley forced the man through into the kitchen. 'Sit down!' he barked at Margaret.

She sagged onto one of the dining chairs. Bramley forced the man down onto another, still with the knife hovering perilously close to his jugular.

'Go and find some rope, grandma. If you're not back in five minutes, I slit his throat. Got it?'

'Go on Margaret, do as he says. There's some in the garden shed out back. It's hanging up on the wall, dear. You can't miss it. Use it!'

Margaret nodded to her husband and looked questioningly at Bramley.

'Go and get it. Hurry up!'

'What kind of car is it?' asked the man.

Huggy glared at him and narrowed his eyes. He looked at the newspaper the old man was still holding on to.

'Let me see that!' He grabbed the paper and unfolded it. There on the front page was a picture of the Mini, the number plate and Huggy's photo, as he had looked before cutting his hair. The man was studying him.

'What do they want you for? Must be something serious for you to be on the front page.'

Huggy, punched the old man. 'Shut up!' The man's head lolled, and his eyes rolled upwards.

Out in the shed, Margaret new exactly what Howard had meant. There was an extension telephone hanging on the wall for when her husband was messing around in there with his motorbikes. She lifted the handpiece and tentatively listened. Was that horrid man on the other phone? No. She heard the dial tone. She dialled 999. It took seconds for the operator to answer.

'Hello,' she whispered, 'Police please. There is a man here threatening my husband with a knife. I need help.'

'Madam, what is the address?'

'It's 14...'

Bramley hit her over the head with a hammer he had picked up from Howard's workbench. He heard the crack and knew as she collapsed to the ground, she wouldn't be getting up. He felt for a pulse and couldn't feel one. The phone hung from the wall, a tiny voice on the other end repeatedly asking for an address. He slammed it back into its cradle then returned to the kitchen.

'Where's my wife? Where's Margaret?' Howard asked in a trembling voice.

Bramley strode up to him and shoved the knife into his midsection before the old man had time to realise what was happening. He sagged to the floor.

'What have you done to my wife?' he gasped before closing his eyes for the last time.

Bramley picked up the phone and dialled. 'Hello? Yeah, it's me. I need you to send somebody to pick me up.' He gave the address. 'I've got the merchandise with me. Let 'em know she's available. She's clean and untouched. Yeah. Top notch goods. He's got good taste! So, we'll sort the details and payment when I get to Birmingham. I'll talk to you then.'

He replaced the phone. Looking around, he found a dishcloth on the sink, ran hot water from the tap, squeezed it out and thoroughly wiped the phone, then he returned to the shed where he wiped the handle of the hammer, the shed door handle and then the kitchen door handle. Backing out of the front door, he made sure to wipe both sides of the door, the doorbell, and the front gate latch. He checked to see if he had left any footprints in the dirt and retraced his steps, keeping to the bitumen. Now to wait.

***

Meanwhile, back in London, the press conference was aired on both BBC channels and ITV. Alby had failed to secure the Colemans help and therefore Robert ran the press release with his team. Alby Coates was alongside him describing the perpetrator in both his recent iterations, supported by photographs and the Identikit image. Then Robert dropped the bombshell news that Bonnie Summers had been abducted by this man and had been missing since last Friday night. Alby provided a photograph of Bonnie with her long hair, then a drawing of her with short, cropped hair. He then added the picture of the Minivan. They appealed to the public for any information regarding sightings of the pair. Robert threw it open for questions from the press. After ten minutes he thanked them and walked away from the cameras.

In Howard and Margaret's living room, the television provided all the details to a dead man who could no longer do anything to help. In the shed, Margaret lay still but a fluttering heart still beat in her chest.

1969

'I Love the Flower Girl'
The Cowsills

The black car sped along the motorway heading south, keeping with the flow in the fast lane. Inside the car, the humour was as dark as the vehicle itself. Neither of the two occupants spoke. No music played on the radio, or the 8-track player installed under the dashboard. Eyes were ever watchful for police, though they need not worry. No-one was looking for a plain black Mercedes. The single goal: pick up the merchandise in one piece and the moron who fucked up the initial delivery. It should have been in Birmingham two days ago.

The customer was livid. He was a very high-profile man, one who could not and should never be kept waiting. He was a returning customer, paid extremely well and was ultimately discreet, as he needed to be in his position. He had become aware of the pop star several months ago but had been otherwise occupied, playing out his paid role in the public arena. In some circles he was revered almost as a god. Fans would bow down to him in their masses when he made an appearance. Recently he had approached his 'suppliers' and demanded they secure this prize for him. Knowing they would find it difficult to pull off with her being such a high-profile celebrity, they agreed to a fifty thousand pound down payment, another fifty to be paid on delivery. This was an unheard-of price, but the customer agreed and paid the deposit. Now the pressure was on to deliver.

Unfortunately, the news had broken this morning of Bonnie Summer's abduction by her manager. This had thrown a spanner in the works to say the least. Yesterday, no-one was concerned about her whereabouts. Today, they were looking for her. Farmer had contacted them from his current hiding spot near Farrington, but they knew the cops would be swarming around the whole west coast and probably all the main arterial roads looking for the Mini as shown in the pictures. Hopefully the idiot had ditched it and it was well hidden. The driver looked at his watch. They had been on the M5 making good time but were now caught up in a major traffic jam on the motorway, the result of roadworks. He swore profusely. The other man glowered at him.

'Shut up!' he snarled. 'Won't change anything.'

'Fuck you!'

The driver, Ed, thumped the steering wheel with the heels of his hands repeating the expletive over and over. Stopping repeatedly, the car crawled on to its destination.

*** *

In the old cottage, Bonnie slowly came to, finding her hands and ankles still tied up. Huggy was sitting on the edge of the bed, smoking.

'Hello sunshine! Back in the land of the living, eh?'

She stared at him, bleary eyed.

'What's the matter, Bon? You hungry?'

Bonnie shook her head. She had asked Huggy over and over why he was doing this, now realising that this was no simple road trip.

Something much more sinister was afoot which meant she needed to start thinking differently about him and her situation. Today was Friday. Her concert was tomorrow. Reason told her that everyone must be looking for her and Huggy. There must be police scouring the country for their car. Huggy had hidden the car. He was hiding her here in this derelict cottage. Where did he go when she was drugged, asleep? Did they know that he looked different now, that she did too? Did they have any idea what part of the country they were in?

'What's up baby, cat got your tongue?' Huggy asked.

'Where did you go while I was asleep?' countered Bonnie.

'Just for a look around, see if I could pick up some transport. Not much around here.' Huggy sat on the edge of the bed, one foot hooked over the other leg and studied the sole of his shoe.

'So, what are we going to do? We can't stay here. No food, no bathroom, nothing close by. We'll have to leave here soon.' Bonnie twisted herself uncomfortably as the ties restricted so much movement, she was quite stiff. 'Can I have these off for a while?'

'No, I can't trust you. Just stay here for now.'

'But I'm stiff from just lying here. I need to get off this bed and stretch. We have to get away from here because you know the police will be looking for us. It won't take long for them to figure out we're somewhere around here.'

'We will. I've got a couple of friends coming to pick us up.' He looked at his watch. 'They should be here within the hour, all being well.'

'How did they know?'

'You ask too many questions. I told you; they're coming. That's all you need to know.'

'I think I know more than you would like. When I get out of this, you had better watch out. I will make sure you pay for doing this to me, making me miss a major concert, keeping me drugged and tied up. You will probably go to jail!'

'Shut it, bitch!' Bramley raised his hand to hit her across the face when he stopped and reconsidered. He could not deliver damaged goods. He swore. 'I'll be downstairs.'

Alone again, Bonnie replayed the last couple of minutes in her head. OK, she had taunted him. He was going to hit her but stopped himself. Why? What was he afraid of, that someone would see a bruise? Considering what he was already guilty of, an extra bruise would not make much difference to the outcome for him. No, there had to be another reason why he didn't want to hurt her. Where was he taking her?

She tried the bindings. He had tied her ankles up with his tie and her wrists with his belt. She tried wriggling her hands. Although the belt had been wrapped tightly around them, she found she could move them and felt the belt loosening as she did. It only took minutes for her to free her hands. She untied her ankles and sat wondering what to do next. The only way out was down the stairs. She knew at least one creaked, and she would not be able to get down without him hearing her if he was still in the cottage. She stepped across to the window taking care not to make the floorboards squeak and peered through the dirty glass. Too big a drop for her without getting hurt, possibly breaking an ankle. She looked around the room. The only furniture, the old bedstead topped by the ruined mattress. Filthy, bare floorboards and crumbling plaster walls completed the picture. Not even a light bulb hanging from the ceiling.

Bonnie listened for the slightest sound coming from downstairs. She could hear nothing. She crept to the door which was half open. Cautiously she peered around the door. The cottage was a long house, so the stairs were at one end and the rooms all went off the passage. She could see two more doors. Keenly tuned for the slightest sound, she still heard nothing. Perhaps he was asleep? Ever so slowly she moved around the door into the passage, stopped and step by step she began towards the next door. A board groaned. She froze, waiting. No sound. She took the next wary step and the next until she reached the door. It was open. She peeked in.

The room was identical to hers without the bedstead. The fireplaces in both rooms were simple caverns in the wall. She looked at the window. Her heart leapt. There above the window, a curtain rod with the ragged remains of curtains hanging! She had to force herself to remain calm and tread very carefully and lightly over to it. The rod was supported by brackets. She could see she would be able to lift it off easily as the windows were low. Reaching up she was able to grasp the dusty curtain-draped rod, and very gingerly lift it clear of the brackets. A flurry of dry dust fell, raining on her face. She coughed a small cough and had to work hard not to sneeze. With the rod down she slid the remains of the curtains to the floor. More dust puffed up, further exacerbating her need to cough and sneeze. She felt the weight. It was an old cast iron rod with an ornate, spiked decoration at one end, in total about three feet long. The other spike had come off long ago and lay on the floor under the window. Would she be able to use this makeshift spear against Huggy? She thought so.

Just as that thought formed, she heard a sound. Huggy was coming up the stairs! She hid behind the door, the curtain rod at the ready. He reached the landing.

'Bon, you awake? Very quiet up here!' Then, 'Fuck!'

Bonnie steeled herself. He would be here any second.

'Bonnie,' his voice wheedled. 'Come out wherever you are. Big mean Huggy is coming for you.'

She heard his steps. He was at the door. She stiffened, prepared, behind it. He came into the room. Bonnie lunged with all her might, thrusting the pointed spike into his lower back, *aiming for a kidney,* she thought, shocked at how easily such a violent thought arose.

'What the fuck?' he cried out. 'That hurt you bitch!'

As he spun around, she lunged again, this time connecting squarely with his midsection. She pushed as hard as she could. He screamed with pain and fell to the floor. The man who used to be her 'Huggy Papa' writhed in agony on the floor. She felt nothing. A fire burnt behind her eyes, a *need, a blood lust!* With no other thought than wanting to thrust again, she shoved the pointed spike into his stomach. He lay writhing in pain, cursing while blood began to seep through his shirt. Bonnie ran out of the room, taking care to take the spike with her, lest he gather himself enough to take chase and use it against her. *Or, I might have to finish him off with it.*

She ran into the other room, grabbed Harmony's bag, and pounded down the stairs, out of the front door where she hurled the curtain rod into the verge. Not knowing which way to turn, she headed left down the lane, hopeful that she might come across another house where she might get help. She ran, constantly looking behind her. He was not following. *Maybe I killed him.* She grinned.

Up ahead she could see a cottage set back a little off the road. *Thank God!* She sprinted the last yards, through the gate and rapped on the front door. No-one answered, although she could hear the television. She walked around the back and found the back door open.

'Hello? Hello, I need a telephone! Hello?'

No answer.

'Help.'

Bonnie heard a small, raspy voice. She turned around. It was coming from the shed.

'Help me.' There it was again. She opened the door.

'Oh God! What happened?' she cried.

'Is my husband alright? Is Howard alright?' Margaret was leaning against the work bench. She had a nasty lump on her head, her grey hair was matted with blood.

'Let me help you.'

Bonnie gently helped the woman onto her feet. She was a little wobbly but steadied with help from Bonnie. They slowly made their way into the house and through to the living room. Howard lay on the floor; a large bloodstain had spread beneath him soaking the carpet. He was motionless. Bonnie felt his neck for a pulse. He was dead and cold. Margaret collapsed into an armchair and began to cry, great racking sobs of unimaginable grief. Bonnie touched her arm.

'Do you have a telephone?' As she asked, she spotted it on a desk. She dialled 999.

'Police and ambulance. This is Bonnie Summer. Yes, that's right. I'm just outside of Farrington in a cottage on Ham Lane. A man has been stabbed, he's dead. His wife is injured. Please hurry.' She hung up the phone and let out a huge breath as if she had been holding it for minutes. She went over to the woman again.

'Don't worry, I've called the police and an ambulance for you. They won't be long, and you'll be alright. I am so sorry about your husband. I think I might know who did this to you.'

The woman, gasped and stared at Bonnie, raw fear in her eyes.

'It's alright, I fixed him. He won't be coming back.' The woman's fear mounted. Bonnie tried to reassure her.

As she spoke, she heard a car pulling up at the front of the cottage. Bonnie peered through the curtains. It was a black car. Two men got out. Neither of them was Huggy.

'Thank goodness! That was quick.' said Bonnie running to the front door.

1969

Robert and Alby rode the lift to level three again. This time they came un-announced, hoping to catch Rick Chambers off-guard. They entered the outer office. 'Hon' sat at her desk reading a pop magazine. She looked up as they entered. Today she looked positively drab in a powder blue pantsuit, her hair teased into a mountain held by a powder blue ribbon. She took only seconds to switch on the blinders and focus them on the disinterested Robert, and then more fiercely on the younger DS Alby Coates.

'Inspectors, we weren't expecting you today. Ricky, he's busy. He won't be able to see you right now.' She flapped the black, impossibly long eyelashes and pouted. Robert walked straight past her desk and opened the door to Ricky's enclave.

'No!' squawked 'Hon' jumping out of her chair. 'You can't…'

Alby turned round and shrugged.

'Yeah, he can!'

Ricky was indeed 'busy'. He was currently occupying the long, fur-covered sofa with a young lady who was in a state of partial undress, specifically, she only wore tiny panties. When the door opened, Ricky yelled without breaking concentration on the task at hand. 'Hey Sharon, I told you, an hour, OK?'

'Mr. Chambers, DCI Turner, and DS Coates. Would you mind?' Robert announced.

'What? Oh man, what are you doing here? Did we have an appointment? Sharon!'

'No, no we didn't. We would like to have a few words following the press release on Bonnie's abduction and some further information which has just come to hand.'

The young thing had jumped up off the couch and was attempting to put her clothes on. She eyed Robert and Alby. She looked to be terribly young, no more than sixteen or seventeen.

'Would you mind introducing us to the, er, young lady, Mr. Chambers?' asked Robert.

'What? Oh yeah, Molly Wilson. She's, aah, we're looking at signing her, aren't we baby?' Ricky gave the girl an encouraging nod.

'Is this how all your artists 'sign up' then? Is this how you signed Bonnie Summer?' Alby could not contain the sarcasm.

Robert spoke to the girl, 'Go and put your clothes on. Wait out in the office with Sharon. DS Coates will be with you in a few minutes.'

The girl, Molly, who by now looked terrified, grabbed the rest of her clothing and boots and followed Sharon into her office. Robert turned back to Rick.

'Now, Mr. Chambers, sit down please. We're going to have a chat. Let's start with how you know Peter Farmer?'

Ricky was cornered and he knew it. He tried every ploy he could think of. He wasted time lighting up a cigarette and gazing out of his window, commenting on the views. He refused to make eye contact. Robert knew the signs. People who were lying often displayed all these traits. Ricky was trying to remember what he had said previously. The trouble with lying was that you dug yourself deeper into the pit of deception with each answer. Eventually, the web of lies became so convoluted you would inevitably slip up.

Robert didn't want to waste time watching Chambers reach that point here. He had had enough.

'Alright Mr. Chambers, you seem reluctant to cooperate. I think we will continue this conversation back at Scotland Yard. Escort him Alby.'

On the way out, Alby took details from the young girl and explained that they would want to speak to her later. She agreed on seeing Ricky being forcibly led out of the office. She appeared relieved.

***

Back at the Yard, Ricky sat in the Interview Room with Robert and Alby. He lit up a cigarette, lounged back on the chair and stared at the ceiling. Robert read the ubiquitous script regarding his rights. Ricky had heard it all before and continued smoking thoughtfully. Robert started the tape recorder, stating the date, time, and subject.

'How long have you known Peter Farmer?'

Rick flicked his hand. 'A while.'

'Is that the only name you know him by?' Robert saw it in Rick's fleeting expression. He knew his real name and probably some of the others too.

'What do you mean?' In control again, Rick shrugged.

'I mean, Peter Bramley, Lane Byrd, Reg Mountford. Ever heard of any of them?' There it was. Ricky was surprised the coppers knew those names.

'No.'

'Mr Chambers, when was the last time you saw Peter Farmer?'

Ricky was thinking hard. 'Um, must be weeks ago, when we were planning the Manchester gig.'

'Mr Chambers, as you must be aware, we suspect that Bonnie Summer has been abducted by him. There has been an incident in the south, possibly involving him. There have been a couple of triple nine calls made from a cottage down there, one of which was made by Bonnie herself. An hour ago, a call was made from that same telephone to your office. Can you tell me about that?'

'I don't know, I don't take the calls, Sharon does,' replied Chambers.

'Oh, come now, Rick! Sharon would have told you even if she didn't put them through! It was an hour ago! Who made that call? It was Farmer, wasn't it? What did he want?'

'I don't know. I didn't take the call!' insisted Ricky.

Ignoring him, Alby said, 'Let's go back to Bonnie Summer's signing with you. Did Peter 'Farmer' approach you or were you aware of Bonnie and asked him to bring her to you?'

Ricky remained silent. Alby grinned. 'Come on Chambers, how did Bonnie come to your office?'

'Peter Farmer rang me up and told me he'd found a real singer, outta sight, if you dig it?' The man still avoided eye contact and Robert *knew* there had been more to it than that.

'Did you know she was under sixteen at the time?' he asked.

'What? Oh, no man!'

'And you didn't think to ask, considering your 'reputation' in the music industry? I would have thought that would be one of the *first* things you need to know, along with her name!'

Rick shook his head. 'I leave all those details to the guys who find the kids.'

'And is Peter Farmer one of those guys?'

'Yeah, he finds 'em. Ones who can sing or play. 'Course, none of 'em have made it like Bonnie!'

'How old is the young lady you were with this afternoon?'

'Eighteen. She's old enough. She was the one who wanted it, you know.'

Robert regarded Rick with undisguised disgust. 'Wanted what Mr. Chambers?'

Ricky shifted awkwardly and stared at the ceiling. 'A recording contract. What do you think?'

'I don't know. Why don't you elaborate? I must say her reaction when we arrived appeared to be one of relief. She couldn't get off that couch quickly enough.'

'What, you think I was shagging her?' Ricky stubbed his cigarette.

'Obviously not at that precise moment but will you please explain what else you were planning with most of her clothing removed?' countered Robert.

'Look Inspector, I don't know anything about these girls. Pete just brings 'em to me. All I do is sign 'em up and do the promos and gigs. He does all the rest. I don't know where he finds 'em. What can I say? Some of 'em find me, you know, attractive, yeah? Sometimes, they make it in the music biz, most times not.' Ricky nodded towards the door. 'That one, nah!'

Robert was fighting an inward battle to refrain from decking this abominable man, deciding instead to change tack.

'Does Pete secure young girls for anyone else, or just you, Mr. Chambers?'

Ricky shifted uncomfortably on his chair, reached for the gold packet, and lit up another cigarette. 'How would I know?'

'I think you do. I'll tell you what I think,' said Robert. 'It's my opinion that you could be part of a whole group of elderly men who pay a lot of money for young girls and boys. I think Pete is just a pawn in a larger game. How much do you pay for say, a girl like Bonnie, Mr. Chambers?'

Ricky feigned shock and personal offence. 'Elderly! Ta very much. Listen, I don't pay anyone for girls. I am a record producer. Check me up. You'll find out I'm telling the truth!'

'I'm quite sure you are, in part. I also think there is a lot you are not telling me but rest assured Ricky, we will find out. What is Peter Farmer doing with Bonnie?' Robert snapped. 'That's why he rang you wasn't it? He wanted directions! Where is he taking her Chambers?'

'I don't know. I wish he would bring the precious little popstar back. I've lost a lot of money, a *lot* of money over this!'

'How do you mean?' asked Alby.

'From the Manchester concert!' Ricky explained with exaggerated patience. 'We've spent a fortune on the venue, staging, personnel, back-up artists and band. Thousands have bought tickets and we'll have to refund them. Oh yeah! I've lost a lot of dosh!'

'I'm sure. Again, how long have you known Peter Farmer and where did you first meet him?'

'I met him about, aah, three years ago, yeah.' Ricky nodded to himself, cigarette balancing on his lower lip.

'And where did you meet him?'

'Where? Probably at a party, yeah, a party.' He flicked ash into the overflowing ashtray.

'Whose party?'

'Bloody hell, what does it matter? I can't remember!'

'It may well matter Mr. Chambers!'

Alby could see Robert losing patience. He could see his hands clenching by his side. He jumped in. 'Try! Try to remember.' He urged, watching Robert's fists.

Ricky sighed and searched the ceiling for the answer. He gave the name of a famous American movie star.

'It was an Oscars party. There were lots of film stars, rock stars and even politicians.'

'In America then? When exactly? What year?' asked Alby.

'Yeah, yeah, of course. You know this record company is based in the US, yeah? I think it was 1966.'

'So, you met him in LA. Were you living in the US at the time?'

'Yeah, yeah, workin' for this company but, you know, but they offered me the chance to come home to London and work. I couldn't turn it down, could I?'

'Did you ask Mr. Farmer to come and work for you?' asked Robert.

'What? No! He doesn't work for me. I never met him again until about twelve months ago when he came and saw me. I remembered him but didn't know he'd gone into management. That's when he brought me Bonnie.

'I see. Was this the first time he had brought you someone? You just told us that he had brought you others, but they had not been as successful as Bonnie.'

Ricky rubbed yellowed fingers across his forehead, and flicked ash. 'He found a couple of others at the same time, but they didn't make it. Okay? Bonnie was the big one, you know.'

'In your opinion, what was his relationship with Bonnie Summer at the time?'

'He was her manager!'

'Do you think there may have been more than that? A personal relationship?'

'Well...you know how things are in the music industry.'

'No, I don't. Why don't you fill me in?' Robert's patience was wearing exceedingly thin with this unpleasant man.

'I don't know. But it's none of my business. All I'm interested in is selling her records and filling her concerts.'

'Alright, Mr. Chambers, we'll leave it there. Interview suspended at 1:10pm.' To Ricky, 'You're free to go but do not go anywhere. We will have further cause to speak, you can count on it.'

Once Chambers had left, Robert collected the file and notes and turned to Alby.

'You know, Alby, I think we've stumbled across something a lot bigger than just the disappearance of a pop star. I'm beginning to get more and more concerned for Bonnie. Whatever Peter Bramley aka Farmer is caught up in, he's dragging her along with him, I'm sure of it and I don't like it. It could have become a race against time to find her before something much worse eventuates.'

The phone rang on his desk. He picked it up.

'Turner. Are they on the way? Tell 'em not to spare the horses! We're on our way too. Alby get the car. We're going to Farrington.'

'Right guv!'

1953

DELIVERY

'Over the Rainbow'
Judy Garland

Petunia was in the delivery room in the Menston General Hospital. The imminent birth had begun much earlier than expected; Petunia was approximately thirty-seven weeks. The doctors reassured her that three weeks early was not unusual, and the baby was a good size, appearing robust and healthy. Petunia secretly thought she might have had some impact on the early birth with her constant feelings of hatred and yearning to be rid of it throughout the pregnancy.

When the contractions started, Petunia had not known what was happening as no-one had discussed the actual birth with her. She rang the bell when the pain became almost too hard to bear. The nurse on duty bustled in, recognised contractions, and organised for Petunia to be taken across the car-park to the general hospital on a stretcher. Once inside she was wheeled into the Delivery Ward, down a long, green corridor where cubicles held single, high beds. Many of the beds had women lying on them, some crying, some screaming and some cursing. Petunia was placed on one of the beds. Another nurse came in.

'Just going to see how far along you are, dear. Just relax.' The nurse thrust a gloved hand deep into her. Petunia tensed and gasped with pain. 'Now then, keep still or you will make it worse young lady.' Petunia took some deep breaths. Then it was over.

'You've got a bit to go, yet.' The nurse wrote something on a chart. The matron, an insipid woman, wearing a permanent sneer, walked past and on seeing Petunia, asked about her progress.

'Only two and a half inches dilated.'

The matron sniffed and shook her chinless head on its scrawny neck. She reminded Petunia of a plucked chicken. Petunia had no idea what 'dilated' meant with reference to birth. The two nurses left without any explanation. There was nothing to distract her from the pain when the contractions came. No-one came to her or looked in on her. She was one of a row of baby production machines. That is how she saw herself and she hated it. Because there were no clocks and she had not been allowed to have a wrist-watch, Petunia did not know how long she lay there enduring the pains which seemed to be getting closer together and more intense.

Eventually, a different nurse came in and repeated the horrible procedure to determine her progress. This one was a little more friendly with a rosy, interested face.

'You're coming along, dear. Won't be long now. I'll let matron know.'

Once more Petunia was left alone. The pains were now only minutes apart. She could feel the heaviness in her stomach which heralded another wave of the awful pain. It was now lasting longer, and Petunia was aware of a bulging feeling between her thighs. *Oh, dear God, what did I ever do in my life to deserve this?* Suddenly, the bed was soaked, and she didn't know why. Despite her best efforts, she let out a cry. She had no knowledge of the process of a birth, so the wetness came as a complete surprise. The feeling that she needed to expel something became enormous, to the point she thought she would explode.

A nurse had heard the cry. She came to Petunia with another woman who was introduced as the mid-wife. Again, the dreaded gloved hand but this time the examination was followed by rapid action. Suddenly her legs were pulled apart, lifted above her, and secured into stirrups.

'Your baby is coming Petunia. You mustn't push until I tell you. We need you to do it when the contraction is the strongest,' urged the midwife.

Petunia was in a world of confusion and pain. She had never felt so vulnerable, even when Eric had been having his 'fun' with her. A pain began. The mid wife cautioned her not to 'push'. As the contraction increased, she was instructed to push. She didn't really understand what was expected of her.

'Push hard Petunia, as if you're trying to force something out of you! As hard as you can!'

The contraction was over, and her body relaxed a little.

'That will never do, dear. When I tell you, you must take a deep breath then hold it and push down as hard as you can. Do you understand?'

Petunia nodded dismally. 'It hurts so much.'

'Well dear, no reward without the pain. They do say that the pain of childbirth is the worst any woman can feel, but totally forgotten after the birth. Alright, here we go again. Now just as I said.'

Petunia had no concept of time or how long the terrible process went on. She began to float in and out of consciousness. Her strength was waning and with each contraction, she felt she simply had nothing left. At one stage, she was dully aware of a stinging sensation and opening her eyes she saw the midwife with a pair of surgical scissors and swabs.

Another contraction began.

'This is the one Petunia. Get ready...now PUSH!'

Petunia pushed as hard as her body allowed. She felt as if something enormous squeezed out. She thought she screamed in pain, but couldn't be sure, then it was over.

'Well done, dear, nearly there. Here we go, one more!'

Petunia heard, groaned, and was overcome by the pain again. She pushed but felt as if she had completely run out of energy. Tears streamed down the sides of her face.

'I c...can't!' she moaned.

'Well done!' trumpeted the midwife. 'You have a beautiful baby girl! She is perfect!'

The nurse took the baby, which produced an utterly alien squawk, to the table where she went about wiping her and then weighing and measuring her. Meanwhile someone else was doing something down there, which Petunia did not understand.

'Just the afterbirth dear. Now we'll stitch you up. Might hurt a bit.'

'Is it out?' Petunia managed to whisper. 'Is it gone?'

The midwife who was busy with bowls and instruments gave her an odd look.

'Whatever do you mean, dear?' The question was moot since Petunia had fallen into an exhausted sleep.

The tiny baby was removed to the post-natal ward where she was to be taken care of by the staff until such time as a foster family or adoption couple claimed her.

1969

'Psychotic Reaction'
Count Five

Bonnie raced out of the front door of the cottage towards the car, waving and shouting to the men to come inside and help. Suddenly she stopped. Realization dawned. These two were not here to help. They were neither police nor medical people. Dressed in denim jeans, black leather jackets and wearing dark sunglasses, they stood, legs apart, simply observing her antics. A terrible feeling of dread rose in Bonnie's throat. She turned and darted back through the door, slamming it shut and throwing the lock.

She stood, leaning on the door for a few seconds before remembering the back door was wide open. Too late, she flew down the passage, through the kitchen only to find the two men standing at the door waiting for her.

'Who are you?' she demanded. 'What are you doing here? I called the police and an ambulance. They'll be here in a few minutes!'

'Get her!' snarled one of the men to the other, 'and don't damage anything! Be careful!'

The man strode towards Bonnie. Panic took hold as she about faced and ran back up the passage. She scrabbled at the door, trying to hastily unlock it when she was grabbed around the waist, from behind,. A voice in her ear urged her to 'calm down'. The man had a smooth cheek and smelt of cologne. It was difficult for Bonnie to connect the two, the pleasantness of him physically and the fact he was tightly restraining her.

'We're not going to hurt you. Just going for a little drive, that's all.' The voice had a certain gentleness to it. Bonnie jabbed her elbows backwards trying to connect with his ribs, but he was simply too strong.

'Now that wasn't called for Bonnie!' He tightened his hold on her while the other had now unlocked and opened the front door of the cottage. They walked out, Bonnie's captor marching her in front of him in a tight hold, leaving the door of the cottage wide open.

From a crack in the cupboard door under the stairs, Margaret Banbury watched the two men march the young girl out of the front door to what looked like a dark coloured car. She stayed in the cupboard.

Outside, at the car, the boot was unlocked, and Bonnie was forced into it. The boot lid slammed shut. She was in near perfect darkness, but she heard the car doors open and shut, then the engine start, and the black Mercedes moved off. Bonnie could not tell which way they were going. Lying cramped in the boot in the darkness, she felt totally disorientated.

There were now four occupants in the car, one of them lying on the back seat holding a jacket over his stomach, moaning, and floating in and out of consciousness. The two in the front had done little else to help him. He was simply a nuisance now. They had the goods and were on the way to delivery.

Margaret heard the car leave and gingerly opened the door to the cupboard under the stairs where she had been hiding. Her head was throbbing, and she felt very dizzy, but she managed to find the telephone and dial 999. Once more a call was received from the cottage on Ham Lane. The ambulance was already near Farrington, the police were with them.

***

Robert and Alby were still some distance away when the car phone rang.

'Turner,'

'Another call from that same address, sir, this time the resident, a Mrs. Margaret Banbury. She reported two men in a car took the girl, the one who made the first 999 call. She didn't know her name. She didn't know the make or model of the car or which direction it went as she hid in the cupboard under the stairs when the men came to the door. She heard a bit of a scuffle but not much else.'

'Get the squad cars to give me a call when they get there, will you? Thanks.'

'Doesn't give us a lot to go on, guv.'

'No, it does not, Alby. But we do know that previous call came from Bonnie. Get the map out, son. The cottage is on Ham Lane. Find it. Must be not far along from the turn-off. So, if the car turned around, it would get straight back onto the Bristol road. If it went the other way, where would that take it? Since the only thing we know about this car is its colour, all we can do is keep an eye out for a black car or any sightings of Bonnie, now we know she's with them.'

'Looks like it does a sharp right onto a Green Lane and back to Bristol Road, so we're a bit in the dark as to where they are. There are quite a few houses along the lane, so it wouldn't be unusual to see cars. Bugger!'

Alby continued to pore over the map. 'I wouldn't think they would be going back down south, guv.' He added. 'And if they are heading east to London, we've probably passed 'em!'

'Alby, step on it! Let's try to get some answers. Maybe Mrs. Banbury knows something! Some of the other residents may have spotted a car they didn't recognise.'

'We could be in luck. It doesn't look as if the two lanes are used as a through road, except for local traffic. Somebody might have noticed something' replied Alby.

Robert sat tensed in the passenger seat. He knew they were still thirty minutes or so from Farrington. His thoughts focussed on Bonnie again. Why her? Why Bonnie Summer? She was no different from thousands of other sixteen-year-olds except...what? She was a wealthy pop star. Would there be a demand for ransom money? Robert didn't think so. He felt certain that one would already have surfaced. There had been nothing. Why else would a pretty, young girl be taken? His horrible creeping suspicion was planted firmly and growing. He knew that certain criminal syndicates had been adding child prostitution to their rap sheets, but it was still not commonly prosecuted under the law. Robert hoped Bonnie had not been abducted for that reason. However, the image of a pretty girl being secured as a sex toy for some wealthy man persisted, almost as if he could 'see' it. This man could be a very high-profile person, maybe in the music industry, maybe politics! Was Bramley merely the means to an end? Or was he part of a ring of paedophiles himself? If he was the spotter, the one who found and delivered, is this how he managed to fund paying for the house in Suffolk. *The house in Suffolk!* Was it here that these clandestine affairs took place? Had Bonnie Summer been 'purchased' by some ridiculously wealthy person for purposes which could range from keeping her as a 'pet' to imprisoning her for the use of violent, sexual exploitation and torture?

Robert shivered involuntarily. The car phone rang. 'Turner.'

The voice came through, tinny but clear enough. The squad cars and ambulance had arrived at the cottage. One dead, an elderly man, stabbed. The woman was alive but suffering concussion. Bonnie, Bramley, the Mini or the mystery car nowhere to be seen.

'We're just coming into Farrington now. Out.'

Robert signed off as they turned into Ham Lane and immediately saw the collection of police vehicles and two ambulances. On the left they passed the derelict cottage. Up a little further on the right police were everywhere. Yellow police tape had been strung across the front of the cottage. It was now being used routinely to prevent contamination of evidence at the scene of crime. Gloved officers were moving in and out of the cottage as Robert and Alby drew up in front. They got out of the car, showed their cards, and introduced themselves to a couple of plain clothes detectives who were in control of the scene.

The older one introduced herself as Detective Jones and his partner Detective Davies.

'The husband was stabbed. The wife was hit on the back of the head. ME said she has a compressed fracture of the skull. Luckily, he used the flat side of a hammer, not the head. We found the hammer on the bench in the shed. Looks like it had been wiped. They've got to get the woman to hospital to check for bleeding and what-not. Hopefully she'll be OK.' volunteered Jones.

'Knife?' asked Alby.

'Haven't found a knife yet. We're currently searching the cottage.'

'Does the old lady remember what happened?'

'Spoken to her briefly. She recognised our picture of Bramley. He came here asking to use the phone last night. Said his car had broken down. We've got her preliminary statement, but she's off to the hospital. We might be able to talk to her later.'

'And the car? The Mini or the other car?'

'Not yet. Got officers going to all the houses, knocking on doors to see if anyone saw a car they didn't know or the Mini.'

'Right,' said Robert. 'Have they searched that old cottage down there?' He indicated the run-down buildings back down the lane.

'Yep. Someone's in there as we speak.'

'Okay. Alby, go down there and report back to me on the search. It seems to me it would have been an ideal place to hide with Bonnie. I'll bet the Mini is hidden there somewhere.'

'Right, guv.'

Alby headed off down the lane. Robert took gloves out of his pocket and pulled them on before entering the cottage. Officers were dusting all the doors, handles, the telephone. Robert looked at the older man on the floor. The ME was currently with him.

'What do we have?' Robert asked.

'Well, he was stabbed from the front, straight in and upwards under the ribs. The poor fellow would have been standing right in front of Bramley who just took him by surprise I suppose. About a six-inch blade which we haven't found at the scene. One other wound, a bruise on the lower mandible, left side. Looks like he was punched upwards by a right-handed man. Looking at it, I'd say this happened before he was stabbed as the bruise had time to form. Means he was still alive.

'Did he try to resist, to fight 'em off?'

'Nothing to suggest a struggle. No defensive wounds or scratches. Looks like the perpetrator attempted to knock him out, then came back later and finished him off. Cold-blooded murder.'

'Time of death?'

'I'd say sometime between six and eight last night. Can't be sure yet. I'll know more after the PM.' replied the ME.

'At this stage then, Bramley is the prime suspect as identified by Mrs. Banbury. The other car didn't arrive until this morning. Thanks.'

Robert left the crew to do their work, looking for hairs, fibres, and anything else which might identify Bramley or the other two men. Meanwhile, Alby came jogging back to the cottage.

'We've got it, guv. The Mini. In an old shed back there.' He glanced back to the derelict cottage. 'He and Bonnie were definitely there. Evidence everywhere. They used an upstairs bedroom. Out back is a washroom with an old sink where it looks like someone bleached their hair. The empty bottle still there. Inside, chocolate bar wrappers and empty pop bottles. Looks like one of 'em pulled an old curtain down; it's been dropped on the floor, but the rod is gone. Officers looking for it around the house and yards. One spiked end still under the window. There's blood on the floorboards near the door. Looks like it was used as a weapon, but by which one, we don't know. They're bagging everything.'

'So, Alby, we know where they've been but not where they are now or where they are going! And, there is a possibility that one of them has an injury, maybe from the curtain rod. My money is on Bramley. I have a feeling that he would not be very popular if he hurt her.'

Alby threw him a perplexed look. 'Why, what are you thinking?'

'I think Bramley is the delivery boy. Someone with a lot of money is waiting for Bonnie, somewhere, but who and where?'

'Right, so he wouldn't want to bring back damaged goods?'

'Exactly. I think that Bramley has fallen foul of our little Bonnie. He has really screwed up and the others will be damned furious that they have extra problems to deal with now. I also think Chambers has more to do with this than meets the eye and I think it's a distinct possibility that the mansion in Suffolk might play a part. I really need to spend time just putting everything in place and thinking, Alby. I need to get *my* ducks in a row! And fast because I fear Bonnie may be in great peril!'

1969

'Young Girl'
Gary Puckett & The Union Gap

Bonnie had been in the boot of the Mercedes for what seemed like hours. The car had been driving on a motorway, she was certain of it because of the relatively smooth ride. It had not stopped once. By now she was feeling that she needed a toilet stop but was so cramped up that she was not sure if she would be able to unfold herself and stand up! Both her feet and lower legs were numb. She attempted to shift position. She was not a big girl, nevertheless, turning over was impossible. Her knees were bent up and trying to turn over they jammed against the boot lid. She turned her head to the side to the rear of the car. There was some light penetrating the taillight lenses and piercing through where the bulbs were screwed in. That was all, but enough to see the inside of the boot dimly since her eyes had adjusted. For the first time, she was grateful that her hair had been cut! It really would have got in the way.

She felt around as much as she was able. She found the two tension rods at the back of the boot which allowed the lid to lift and stay up. She didn't understand exactly how they worked but as she felt around towards the driver's side hinge, her fingers found an extra cable which was flexible. It snaked inside the boot lid, along the sides of the boot towards the lock mechanism. The framework of the lid made it possible for her to feel the cable on its way there. Now her fingers grasped the cable right at the centre of the lid and she was able to tug it a little.

She tugged again, very carefully and sure enough, the cable was connected to the lock. This was it! She felt sure that if she tugged hard, the lid would flip open but then what? They could be travelling at eighty miles an hour or more! So, she had to be ready when the car slowed enough. Could she pop the boot, jump out on her numbed legs, and get away before they had realised what was going on? Would she be seen, and would someone come to her aid?

The discovery had given Bonnie new resolve. She began to plan. Once again, the feeling of power she had experienced when thwarting Peter was surfacing. It was an un-solicited response. To her it felt as if it had always been there, buried deep in her psyche, ready for a trigger. Huggy's attacks on her had triggered it and now her incarceration in the boot of this car repeated it. Adrenaline flowed, she felt charged. She attuned her ears now, listening for changes in engine pitch, even fragments of conversation in the cabin. She thought she heard a low moan, right there in front of her. Someone was on the back seat. Huggy? Was he badly injured? She smiled and waited.

***

The lift on the third floor opened. This time DS Wright stepped out, unaccompanied and walked into the outer office of Rick Chamber's suite. Sharon sat at her desk, leafing inattentively through a magazine. On hearing the door, she looked up.

'Hello, are you feeling groovy, 'cause Mr Rick Chambers is! Can I help you?' she asked in a voice she had cultured to sound soft, sexy, and inviting.

DS Wright held up his ID. 'DS Wright. I'd like to talk to Mr. Rick Chambers please. I'm quite sure he's not feeling as groovy as he was last week!'

'Do you have an appointment?' Sharon skimmed over a diary page with a long, glossy pink fingernail. She shook her head.

'Is he in?'

'Well, no. No, he's not in detective. He's...out!'

Wright made a move, but Sharon leapt up and flattened herself against the door, preventing his entry.

'You can't just show up and burst in! I'll call the security guy!' she cried; her voice tremulous. 'I told that other guy!'

'Alright, I'll get a warrant and I'll be back later,' replied Wright coolly.

Sharon was backed into a corner now, her eyes darting around the room as if she might like to discover a secret exit.

'Meanwhile, I'd like to have a look through your files, or do I need to wait for the warrant for that too?'

Sharon shook her head and remained rooted to the spot, incapable of deciding. Eventually she volunteered, 'It's just a job. I do as I'm told.'

'Would you find the files relating to all the girls who have come to Mr. Chambers to sign up for a record contract? Let's say in the last twelve months.'

Sharon appeared very unsure as to what she should do. She shifted her eyes to Ricky's door for a split second. 'So, if I don't get them for you, you'll come back later with a search warrant anyway?'

'That's correct.'

'Alright.'

Today, Sharon was balancing on impossibly high heeled, platform, pink patent shoes. Her white mini skirt barely covered her underwear, and she was wearing a pink plastic short-waisted jacket nipped at the waist with a wide plastic belt. The result was a cacophony of squeaks and groans, scratches, and squeals as she walked. DS Wright observed all this squeaking and squelching in a detached manner, scratching his chin. *I'm glad my wife doesn't choose to wear plastic clothes!* he thought.

After ten minutes or so, Sharon came back over to her desk with a pile of folders. 'There, I think that's all of them, going back as far as you asked.'

Wright picked them up. Thanks. I'll bring them back when I've finished,' and he began to leave.

'Hey! You can't take them!'

'I'm taking them for examination back at the office. Oh, and while I'm here, can I have Rick's telephone directory with his contacts?'

Sharon rolled her eyes and handed him a Rolodex.

'Thanks. Any questions, direct 'em to DCI Turner. Goodbye!'

Back at his desk, DS Wright took to the task of unravelling where the girls had come from and with whom, with a will. This was just the sort of detailed police work he thrived on, crossing every 't', and dotting every 'i'.

***

Meanwhile, as Turner and Coates were returning to the car to drive back to London, the black Mercedes was still on the M5 but approaching the outskirts of the city of Birmingham. Rotton Park was on the west side which meant they avoided having to cross the city centre, although traffic would still be heavy everywhere at this time of day. Their destination was a flat above a corner grocery store in a shopping area on Dudley Road. Bramley, still laying in the back seat, was now pale and sweaty. He continued to moan periodically, however, he had spent less time moaning and more time sleeping in the last hour. The two in the front seats ignored him. There had been no sound from the boot. That was good. Perhaps she had been asleep too. Off the M5, the car was negotiating traffic with frequent stops and starts.

In the boot, Bonnie was keenly aware that the car was now in traffic. The frequency with which they were slowing and stopping must mean lots of people! Could she pull this escape off without killing herself? She felt the cable again. She tried to construct in her mind how it might play out when she pulled it. First, the boot lid would pop ajar. She had limited experience with operating cars, but her dad was a car salesman, wasn't he? And she had seen him open many a boot. They rarely flew right open, so, she would be able to see out of the gap enough to see if it was safe to get out, *if* she could get out! She would wait for the car to stop, hoping that the occupants did not hear or see the boot open. Then it would get tricky, because she would have to open the boot up enough to climb out, hope the car following would see her and stop, hope that they might help her, hope the men in the car didn't have guns or other means of stopping her, hope that she didn't get halfway out as the car took off! Another horrifying thought occurred to her. What if the men had another carload of thugs behind as support? Bonnie lay there waiting for the right moment. The car was crawling along now, then she felt it make a left turn as the yellow blinker glowed inside the boot. They were moving slowly now, as if looking for an address. The road surface was noisier, perhaps cobbles? She heard murmuring in the front, then saw the brake lights.

Bonnie could hear distant traffic, people-sounds. The Mercedes came to a halt. Suddenly, every part of her, every sense, every muscle focussed on escape. Without a second to waste, she yanked on the cable, and it worked! The boot lid popped open. Taking no time to survey the scene through the gap, she pushed it up and began to unfold herself from the cramped space. She felt the cobbled road under her feet and threw her arms in the air screaming 'Help!'

The car had stopped in a narrow laneway completely enclosed on both sides by the back yards of terraces. There were a couple of cars parked down one side, the lane too narrow for parking on both sides. No-one was around though Bonnie could hear the busy humdrum of the city in the background. Just as she realised there was no-one to call out to or help her, strong arms grabbed her again. A gloved hand was shoved over her mouth and nose while the other arm held her around the waist in an iron grip. The man propelled her into one of the rear yards, urging her to keep quiet. She could see the other was roughly pulling someone out of the back seat of the Mercedes. She knew it was Peter. She had enough time to see he was not in a good way. He was badly hurt then.

They went through the back door of the building where a staircase led to the first floor. She heard the man pulling Huggy along call her captor, 'Ed'.

'Get her up to the flat Ed, I'll leave him here and go and dispose of the car. When I get back, we'll have to decide what to do with him.' He nodded towards Huggy slumped against the wall.

Ed took Bonnie up the stairs then shoved her through a door into a parlour where she was encouraged to sit on a velvet sofa. Ed still held his hand over her mouth. 'You gonna be quiet or do I have to give you something to keep you quiet? If you do as you're told, you won't be hurt. Understand?'

Bonnie nodded, her eyes fixed on his, trying to read his real intentions. He took his hand away. She remained silent and continued to study his face. It was a pleasant face, almost kindly. He looked to be in his thirties, dressed like a thug but he could have been a concerned big brother. He had dark eyes and a square jaw with dimples at each side, even when not smiling. The dimples gave him a disarmingly attractive look. Bonnie was no longer afraid. Something inside her had changed since Huggy had taken her to the old cottage. The moment she had taken the curtain rod to defend herself, she had resolved to use all her instincts and inner strength to rise above her situation and she had succeeded! Now she faced a new challenge, but she was feeling mentally stronger than ever before.

'What are you staring at?' he demanded irritably.

Bonnie said nothing but kept her eyes fixed on his. He turned away. *He's nervous,* Bonnie thought. *He's scared of doing something wrong. I must be valuable somehow. He's not going to hurt me. But who is? Why me?* She ran her hand through her short blonde tufts of hair. It still felt alien, but she would get used to it. She hadn't even seen herself in a mirror to know what it looked like.

'Excuse me,' she said.

Ed spun around.

'What?'

'I need to go to the toilet.'

'Oh, alright, in there, through the door, first on the right. Don't try anything. We're two stories up, all the windows are barred.'

Bonnie found the bathroom. It was beautifully equipped with a luxurious bath, gold taps and a mirror worthy of any dressing room she had ever used. She stared at her reflection. Without make-up and little proper food or real sleep in the last week, her eyes were hollow, her cheekbones protruding and her skin translucent. With the short, boyish haircut, she looked all of thirteen or fourteen at the most. Her image reminded her of a crystal skull with shining blue gems for eyes, sapphires, she supposed.

Bonnie used the toilet all the while marvelling at this bathroom, in a terrace house, which from the outside appeared like all the others, old and run-down. Even the parlour had seemed out of place with plush velvet sofa, thick carpet, crystal decanter and silver candlesticks.

'Oy, time's up!' yelled Ed through the door.

Bonnie flushed and washed in the marble sink. The towels were top quality, thick and soft. She opened the door.

'Good girl. Now come and get something to eat. You must be hungry.'

Bonnie followed him into the parlour and through into a kitchen-diner where a selection of food and drink had been laid out.

'Should be something you like here. Help yourself. There's pop over there or tea if you like.' Ed sat on a chair away from the table.

'Aren't you going to eat?' she asked.

'No. That's for you. Go ahead. You look a bit pale and sickly. Got to get your colour back, yeah?'

Bonnie regarded him quizzically. She cocked her head on one side. 'Why did Huggy abduct me? Was he always going to bring me here to you? And why? Are you asking my parents for money?'

'Shut up. Don't ask so many questions.' Ed snapped. 'I told you, eat something!'

The door to the parlour opened and the other man came through into the kitchen. He gestured to Ed to follow him out of the room. When they left, Bonnie put her ear to the door and listened keenly.

'He's not going to be any more trouble. I changed my mind and took him with me. He was too far gone anyway. He's going to be found dead from an overdose across town by morning. Cops won't think anything of it. He's a seasoned addict. He's got all the hall-marks; needle lines and his bloody nose is ruined. I dumped the Merc nearby. Don't worry, I gave it a thorough going over. Poured petrol all around it and under it, then as luck would have it, I heard somebody coming so I ducked behind an industrial bin. Blow me, the bugger walked past and flicked a ciggy butt in the gutter. Bloody car went off like a bomb, took the guy with it! Cops will be looking harder for the girl now though, once they figure out who the dead junkie is, so I think we need to get her to the pick-up sooner rather than later. Is the client waiting?'

'Yeah, he's already there, with the other fifty. We're good to go.'

'Right, the boss has organised a vehicle. Pick up is tomorrow morning at 5 am, city centre. I'll fill you in on the rest of the details after supper.'

'Right, better go and check up on her, see if she's eaten anything. Have we got clothes for her?'

'Yep, all organised. Sharon is an ace. Dumb as shit but does as she's told. She thinks she's shopping for some wanna-be pop starlet! Shopped on Carnaby Street. All that gear will be at the house when we get there. He should be very pleased with how we turn her out! I hope that idiot Bramley rots in hell. Think of the wasted miles! Without him we could have gone straight across but no, he had to come back to this ridiculous flat to 'process her! What does that mean?'

Bonnie heard the other man mutter something indistinct. Nothing more was said. She wondered what 'processing' was. Anyway, it didn't sound like it was going to happen now because Huggy had gone.

Bonnie kept listening but nothing more was said. She slipped back to the table and selected a dainty sandwich. She was eating when the men entered the room.

So, I'm to be delivered to a man who is paying an awful lot of money for me. For what? I guess first of all, I'll have to give him a private show or something. Bonnie ate and pondered. She felt no threat from her captors. They were only the delivery boys, just as frightened as she. The main event featured someone else. But who? She ate quietly.

1969

It was getting late when DCI Turner and DS Coates arrived back at the Yard. Robert was once again thankful he had no wife or family waiting at home with a hot dinner on the table. He was free to work for as long as he needed to, and tonight was going to be one of those nights. Time was getting away from him with so many things he wanted to do. Alby had a wife, Deborah, Robert reminded himself, who would be waiting for him.

'Go home Alby. I want to spend some time sorting out what we know, what we don't know and what we still need to follow up on. I think I just need some quiet thinking time.'

'Are you sure, boss? I don't mind if I do! I've been a bit *in absentia* lately and I'm not sure Deborah appreciates it.'

'Absolutely, son. I'll see you in the morning.'

After making himself a strong coffee and taking a handful of biscuits from the jar, Robert sat down at his desk and contemplated the neat piles of papers and folders. Where to start? Well, what he had said to Alby was a good place to begin, wasn't it? What do we know?

Robert took a legal pad and his fountain pen. He wrote:

BONNIE SUMMER - she has the bluest, sapphire eyes I have ever seen!!

He struck out the last. Underneath he wrote a list of short items:

- *Vulnerable, unhappy home, disinterested parents, lured to leave home by Bramley at country fair.*
- *Fraudulently signed up with xxxxx by Rick Chambers when 15!*
- *Bramley, alias, Farmer, fraudulently given power of attorney over her money.*
- *Supplied drugs and alcohol by same. OD'd (Was this an unforeseen slip-up?)*

Robert thought about this. If he hadn't attended that drug OD at Notting Hill, would Bonnie have ever come to his notice? After all, he was not usually in the business of missing persons. Perhaps Bramley's actions had been a blessing in disguise. He continued:

- *Removed from Chambers and Bramley's control to hospital, then Devon.*
- *Abducted by Bramley (Why was it so important to get her back since he didn't return her to do the concert in Manchester? Something more important? Must have been worth the trouble!) Both changed their appearance*
- *Bramley knew we were on to him*
- *Probably murdered Mr. Banbury, assaulted Mrs. Banbury*
- *Bonnie fought back, overcame Bramley (My kind of girl!!!)*
- *Bramley had accomplices, took Bonnie in a car, unknown brand, colour black or dark, reg?*

RICK CHAMBERS - Worked for xxxxx in US before coming back to London. Knew Bramley or met him there. Met him again 12 mths ago. (Is this a coincidence? I don't think so!) Seems to have a propensity for very young girls. How many young lads has he 'signed up' or

'interviewed'? Probably none. Is often 'unavailable' and yet is not
actually out of his office. Very evasive, fake
PETER BRAMLEY: AND ALL HIS ALIASES - Has not in his adult
life held a regular job. Deserted from the army. Been involved in
brothels. Been in prison for aggravated assault and accessory to crimes
associated with two murders. Owns a large property in Suffolk under
false name (Lane Byrd). Pays taxes on property in name of Peter Farmer
yet doesn't seem to have a legal income to support it. Does not reside
there. Peter Farmer also owns a flat in Rotton Park near Birmingham.
Where is his money coming from? Recently formed a band and travelled
the country, (looking for impressionable, vulnerable young girls?)
(Why?)

Robert contemplated his notes. Alright, what don't we know.
Becoming tired , he gave up trying to keep his scribblings neat. He
printed in capitals:

WHERE IS BONNIE NOW?
Where is Peter Bramley now?
Who are the men in the car which took Bonnie?
Did they take Bramley as well?
Are Bramley and the other two working for someone else? Who?
Is Chambers mixed up in all this somehow?
Have the places in Suffolk or Birmingham got a role to play?
Why are the Colemans so disinterested? Have they even contacted us?
What we need to follow up:
Calls re sightings or info from the public since the press release.
Check hospital admissions for Peter Bramley. There was a fair amount
of blood in that upper bedroom, and it was not Bonnie's. Curtain rod,
was it found? Fingerprinted?
What was the outcome of re-interviewing the manager and barman at
the Crown? Did he know Bramley? In what capacity?
DS Wright's findings on contracts drawn up in last 12 mths, how many
were signed, how many have recorded? Where are they all now?
More info on Lane Byrd alias and the house.

Robert stopped scribbling. Lane Byrd, Rick Chambers, USA. When Rick said he knew Bramley in the US, was Bramley then operating under the name of Lane Byrd? He wrote underneath:

- *Need to get FBI onto this, checking up Lane Byrd's associations with Rick Chambers. I've been working on the wrong partnership!*
- *Check out Bramley's flat in Rotton Park*
- *Go to Suffolk and check out the house.*
- *Do any of Bramley's aliases or even Chambers have Swiss Bank Accounts?*
- *Check airlines for their names, also train stations and the channel ferry. Have they left the country?*

Robert contemplated everything he had written, picked up his coffee cup, discovered it was empty and glanced at his watch. Eight o'clock. What could he do right now? Not a lot. Most of these tasks he would delegate to others tomorrow. He took the pile of papers which were sitting on his desk and leafed through them. Ah, here was Wright's report on the girls.

Robert spent the next hour sorting out the girls into different piles. What he came out with at the end were four girls who had been in Rick Chambers' office and had then disappeared completely. All but one had been reported missing. The other had turned up dead, apparently from a drug overdose.

A cold shiver of dread coursed through his whole body, creeping up his throat. He felt like he was suffocating. Four girls! He couldn't believe what he was seeing, and why had no-one ever connected the three disappearances to the record company and in particular Rick Chambers? He pulled up the file on the dead girl. Sixteen years old, originally from Bakewell, had gone to several 'meetings' which were documented in the file, then had been mysteriously found dead near Birmingham from a drug overdose. ODs were so common these days that often they were simply processed and forgotten. The family were on record admitting the girl had had a drug problem for a few months, quoted as saying 'the music scene had destroyed her'.

As he contemplated the file, the word 'Birmingham' jumped out. *Jesus Christ.*

He picked up the phone and dialled Alby's home number. It was picked up after three rings.

'Hello, Mr. and Mrs Coates residence.'

Robert sighed and shook his head sadly.

'Hello Deborah, It's Robert Turner. I am sorry to disturb your night. I wonder if I may speak to Alby?'

'Well, we were just about to have dinner, Robert, but...'

'Alby here guv, what is it?'

'Alby, I think Bramley may have gone to Birmingham, Rotton Park to be precise. I don't know if Bonnie and the other two are there, but I think we need to go. Might be our best chance of catching him. Then we'll focus on finding Bonnie. Will you meet me at the office in say half an hour?' Robert could almost see the look on Deborah's face, her disappointment over the meal she may have spent half the day preparing, the opened bottle of wine. He waited.

'I'll be there boss.' Alby rang off.

Robert busied himself writing down the address and finding it on the map. He then called the Birmingham police and put them on alert as to what he planned to do. He had to know back-up was available if needed. He enquired if they had anything on the address that he had given them. It came back negative. Alright, no-one would be expecting a visit.

Let's get up there and see if my hunch is right. It must be. For my Bonnie's sake.

Robert put his head in his hands and rubbed his temples. There it was again, that automatic feeling of connection, a feathery, indistinct intrusion on his rational thoughts. He shoved it to the back of his mind, the better to focus on the task at hand.

Alby arrived in less than thirty minutes. Robert picked up his jacket when the phone rang.

'Turner.' He indicated to Alby and mouthed 'Birmingham Police'.

'Right. Whereabouts? Close to the Rotton Park address I gave you? No. Positive ID? Right. Get a couple of squad cars over to that address, will you? You'll need a warrant. You're looking for two men and Bonnie Summer. Anything even remotely suggestive of trafficking young girls, drugs, prostitution. Got it? I want a full report as soon as you can get it to me. Dust the flat, all the usual stuff. Thanks. I'll be up there tomorrow.' Robert replaced the receiver.

'They've found Bramley. OD'd. Dead. He had a significant wound to his stomach. Looked like he had been bleeding for quite a few hours. Found across town from the flat. Anyway, you can go home Alby. Give my apologies to your wife, again! I'll see you in the morning.'

Robert felt strangely relieved that he no longer needed to waste his time on the arrest of Bramley for murder. Now he was able to pursue his true passion; finding Bonnie Summer before it was too late. *I might as well go home for a few hours' sleep. I think wherever Bonnie is going, the immediate intention is not to physically hurt her...yet.*

1953

CHOPIN

'Piano Concerto No 1'
Chopin

Petunia Jackson spent her days, alternatively staring morosely out of the window into the side garden where the roses were in glorious bloom or sleeping. She had been home now for a month. The first couple of weeks after the baby was born had been terribly difficult. She had been very sore both from the cut and her milk coming in. Not only had she been in pain, but totally disgusted as well. She was secretly still unable to come to terms with what her life had become. She was under the illusion that she had successfully hoodwinked Dr Floyd into thinking she would be quite ready to leave the Menston Mental Facility and go home. Dr Floyd had agreed but had arranged to continue to see her on a weekly basis for the time being.

Today, Andrew Floyd was due to arrive in the afternoon for their session. This was the only day Petunia bothered to get properly dressed, brush her hair, and sit out in the kitchen. She still did not converse with her mother. Joan had made no bones about her disappointment in Petunia relinquishing the baby and she had been unable to find any common ground with her daughter. She had complied with Floyd's request to keep anything which Petunia might use against herself out of reach. Joan was sickened by having to do this. She simply could not understand why, months afterwards, Petunia had not begun to return to normality. Floyd arrived on time and Joan welcomed him in with a tired smile.

'Nothing much has changed doctor. Still the same, miserable woman we have come to know. Is there nothing you can do to speed up the process of making her well?'

'Good afternoon to you, Mrs. Jackson.' He walked straight into the sitting room where Petunia was perched on the edge of the sofa. Joan closed the door.

'Well, my dear, what have you been filling your time in with this week? Walking? Cooking perhaps? Gardening? Reading? Studying even? Doing your homework for me?' He knew the answer.

'Not much. I don't feel motivated.'

'Petunia, I set you things to do, did I not? We had a deal, you, and I, that you would talk to me, and you would do as I ask.'

'We did. I have been too tired. I can't see the point,' replied Petunia. *I'm even too tired to do what I know I must do.*

'Alright, we will do it now. Here is a notepad and a biro. Now write down for me a heading, 'things I like to do"

Petunia did.

'Now list five things you like to do, or if you like, five things you *used* to like to do. You have two minutes, starting now!'

'I can't...' Floyd held up his hand. 'Don't waste my time, write!'

Petunia wrote:

> *Teach children*
> *Church*
> *I don't know*
> *I don't know*
> *I don't know*

She thrust the paper back to the doctor.

'Good!' he said. 'Let's look at the last three. When you were not at school or church, what did you do?'

'I used to volunteer at the community hall, organising jumble sales and baking sales to raise money for the poor.'

'Excellent!' Petunia raised a cynical eyebrow.

'And...?' he asked.

'Walk the dogs.'

'Good, and...?'

'Take my mother to concerts in Rotherham or Sheffield.'

'See, Petunia? Nothing is lost. Everything you have held dear is still there and can be accessed again now that you are free. What kind of music do you like?'

'Classical, of course, doctor. I never had time for this new rock and roll!'

'Champion, my dear, Wait there.' Doctor Floyd opened the door and called Joan.

'Do you have a newspaper at all, preferably a current one?'

Joan hurried off and returned with the requested newspaper. Floyd flipped through to the pages advertising performances in the district.

'Do you like Chopin? His piano concertos?'

Petunia nodded.

'Alright, we shall go! I shall organise the tickets, just you and I, this time. Next Saturday, it's a date!'

'But, I...' protested Petunia. 'I can't go out. I have no clothes that fit me now.'

'Don't worry about that. I'm sure you and your mother can sort that out before Saturday. Petunia, you don't realise how much weight you have lost. I am guessing your clothes will be too loose! If so, take them in. I know you will make it happen. This is your homework. So, I will collect you here at seven pm for the eight o'clock concert in Rotherham.' Doctor Floyd rose, left the sitting room and Petunia could hear him speaking in a low voice to her mother. She sighed. *What can it hurt? Nothing will change.*

***

Joan had worked hard to modify a dress for Petunia, whose shape had completely changed. She had lost a great deal of weight, but her breasts were still larger than before. Joan had to take out some darts and take in the waist. In her opinion, she had made a very pleasing effort. Petunia gave nothing away, but Joan thought she may have seen a slight reaction when she stood in front of the mirror in the dress, her hair done and wearing pink lipstick.

Floyd arrived on time. He was wearing an impeccably tailored evening suit, highly polished black shoes, and black bow tie. At the last minute, Petunia grabbed a fur stole her mother had offered to loan her and they drove to Rotherham in silence. The doctor left it to her to open any conversation but nothing was forthcoming. He didn't insist.

On arrival, they seated themselves in the concert hall. Petunia remained silent. The lights dimmed and the orchestra could be heard tuning. The stage was dark, but the silhouette of a grand piano could be seen in the centre, the orchestra's instruments periodically glinting as the musicians settled themselves and finished tuning up. Petunia looked at the program. She did not recognise the pianist. She stole a surreptitious glance at Dr Floyd. He was intently studying the stage with a satisfied expression on his face.

The lights came up, the audience immediately hushed, and the conductor walked onto the stage. The orchestra rose as he bowed to the audience and indicated the players. They seated themselves. The conductor faced the wings. A spotlight moved to the side and the soloist walked to centre stage and seated himself with great theatre at the piano. He flicked his coat tails behind the stool and positioned himself to play. The orchestra raised their instruments as the conductor raised his baton. The lights on the stage dimmed slightly, the spotlight on the soloist.

The powerful opening chords of Piano Concerto No 1 began, the determined pulses of the march-like rhythms drawing the audience into the opening passages of the concerto. Petunia leaned forward slightly on her chair, her focus solely on the music. The strings rose and fell in graceful arpeggios. Petunia was carried with them. The pianist fell on the piano keys as Chopin's notes rained in drifts and swirls across the keys. His long fingers teased them to pour over the edge of the instrument like sparkling droplets of pure perfection and out into the audience, where Petunia was enfolded and transported by them. Her breathing responded by alternately pausing or sighing as the music breathed with her. Floyd watched her, a smile playing on his lips. He might have discovered a key.

After the last strains had played, the conductor had taken his bow acknowledging the orchestra, and the soloist had received the deserved accolades four times over from his appreciative audience, the lights came up and it was time to leave. Petunia turned to Dr Floyd.

'Did you enjoy my dear?' he asked her.

Petunia cocked her head to the side as she regarded him. After a moment, she spoke in a harsh whisper, 'I despise that beauty, joy, even glory still exist. You may be congratulating yourself that you have broken me, however, I feel very deeply and sincerely that I do not deserve to be amongst these people who are free to enjoy, free of the evil which pervades me. So, thank you doctor! Now take me home please.'

'Just before we leave, there is someone I am meeting backstage… oh, there he is!'

He waved out. The pianist saw the wave and almost bounded across the floor towards them, bestowing a wide, friendly smile on the doctor. Dark tendrils of glossy black hair fell across his forehead, escaping the bulk of thick waves which swept backwards. He was very tall and slim, giving him a gangly, youthful awkwardness. He held out a large hand with perfectly manicured, long fingers.

'Doctor Floyd! You came!' He withdrew his hand and stepped back slightly as if suddenly realising he might be over-stepping in his exuberance.

'Yes, my dear boy, of course. An exemplary performance, as always. I see you are doing Liszt next month! Bravo!'

The doctor placed his hand on Petunia's back and gently ushered her forward. 'I have someone I would like you to meet. Philippe Gauthier, Miss Petunia Jackson.'

Philippe paused as if to gather his courage, then took Petunia's hand in his. 'Very pleased to meet you, Miss Jackson,' he said formally, awkwardly shifting from one foot to the other.

'Thankyou. Congratulations on a wonderful performance,' she replied dryly.

'I owe everything to the doctor,' Philippe said, indicating Floyd. 'He brought me to where I am today. If it weren't for him, I would be in an awfully bad place.'

'How are you getting home Philippe? Would you like a lift?'

'I would call the taxi.' Philippe said. 'My mother will be waiting.'

Floyd placed his hand quietly on Philippe's shoulder. 'Nonsense my boy. I will take you home. Gather your coat and meet us at the front doors.'

Petunia and Floyd walked out together. She did not ask questions, but the doctor volunteered.

'Philippe has been a patient of mine for many years. A wonderful performer is he not? Come, here he is.'

1969

Robert flopped onto his bed after removing his tie and shoes. He immediately fell into a deep sleep. It seemed like only minutes later, he opened his eyes and checked the time on his digital clock. 1:34 am. He lay there, closed his eyes with the intention of drifting back to sleep, but his mind insisted he stay awake and mentally re-visit his list of things to do. Every item on the list came into sharp focus as he lay there, and each one led him on a dozen different byways. Each path his thoughts took was paved with dark, evil foreboding. He shivered and looked at the time again as the leaves flipped over to 1:42 am. Groaning he got up and padded into the kitchen where he ran a glass of water.

Somewhere between drinking the water and visiting the bathroom, he remembered he needed to contact the FBI regarding Chambers and Lane Byrd aka Bramley. He opened the second drawer down in one of his kitchen cabinets where he kept a diary giving all the major city times against GMT. He calculated that it must be around 5:00pm yesterday in LA. He went into the bathroom and splashed cold water over his face, dried off, went into the room he called his 'home office' and picked up the phone. He needed information on specific individuals who may or may not have committed any crimes investigated by the FBI, and the best place to find out was the campus in Virginia where a huge data base of fingerprints was stored. If either of these characters had theirs stored it meant they had been flagged by law enforcement at one time, usually in the US, but sometimes as far afield as the UK or Eastern block countries. From there, they could be investigated to find out if they had any common ties in the criminal world.

After speaking to them, explaining what he needed and given the names, he replaced the phone and thought about Bramley. He had been a nasty piece of goods, *pretty much like my brother* he thought. No wonder I sometimes felt almost tied to him in ways. He had had no qualms about cold bloodedly killing Harold Banbury, for what? The old man had put up no fight. Bramley could have easily out-run him and disappeared. *Because he enjoyed the feeling of the knife. I know my brother did. Did I?* His memories were fractured. He was always unsure. His immediate instinct was to open the whiskey bottle when these doubts and conflicted thoughts rose to the surface. Tonight, he supressed it forcibly. He had things to do.

So, did Bramley go straight from the Farrington cottage to his Rotton Park flat? Was he with the two guys and Bonnie? What happened to him that he was found dead on the other side of Birmingham from the flat? Robert looked at his watch. Still early hours, too early to go into the office. But not too early to drive up to Birmingham. The traffic would be light. He would get there by early morning. He would have time to check out the flat for himself before going into the Birmingham Division to find out what the team had found. He needed to go to the morgue to see Bramley's body and speak to the ME. He knew the PM would be pending but there might be something, the tiniest thing he might pick up from a viewing.

The decision was made. He would not disturb Alby now but would phone him early to let him know his whereabouts and intentions.

***

It was well and truly light as his car drove through Rotton Park to the address of the flat. Dudley Road ran through a busy retail area with a variety of food outlets, small businesses, and grocery shops. Most were housed in terraced buildings over which there were flats. Bramley's address was positioned right on the corner of two streets, the crossroad controlled by traffic lights. Robert drove along the street, trying to gauge the feel of the neighbourhood. He saw people going about their early morning business, shopkeepers putting signs out, some setting up displays on the pavement. There was an abundance of lorries and vans delivering goods to the businesses before the shops opened. He braked as a man pushed a trolley across the road, neglecting to look both ways. He waved a 'thankyou' to Robert who tipped him a salute in response. Just an everyday morning in suburbia.

He found a parking spot, locked the car, and walked back towards the crossroad. He saw a newspaper stand where he bought the daily. He opened it as he stood opposite the flat and pretended to read, all the while studying the upper level of the building. Nothing seemed unusual. It had the same plain frontage as all the others. Curtains were drawn covering the windows which he could see from here, needed a clean. There was no sign of life at this time of the day.

Robert crossed the street and walked past the shop on the ground floor, which was closed. It was advertising itself as a property agent and developer. The main foyer door which Robert assumed would be the entry for the flat or flats upstairs was also closed. Robert pushed on it and to his mild surprise, it opened. He let himself inside the dimly lit hallway which had a staircase leading upstairs. He let the door close itself and looked around. Light was penetrating only through a stained-glass window over the door which was dusty. There was a single light bulb hanging but he didn't want to turn it on for fear of drawing attention. After a few minutes his eyes accustomed to the gloom and he looked around, noting the door with the brass handle and letterbox, the wooden floor which needed a polish and the dingy pale lemon walls. There were no sounds inside the building that he could hear, only muffled traffic as the street came to life.

The floor was very dusty but along the centre, the surface had been worn and showed evidence of foot traffic. Then Robert noticed a slight patch near the door which was a shade darker and not so dusty. He took out the little torch he always carried and shone it down to get a better look. He could now see that the wall next to it was a little shiny as if it had been cleaned. He hoped when the Bristol guys got here, they would test for blood because that's what it looked like to him. Someone had bled, leaning against the wall, and recently. Probably Bramley. Robert looked up the stairs. All was dark and quiet.

He climbed to the first floor. At the top was a single solid door with a doorbell and a nameplate which was blank. He rang the bell. Inside the flat it could barely be heard. Ringing several times produced no response. Rapping loudly on the door, he called out.

'Is anyone home?'

There was no answer. He tried the door. It was locked. Descending the stairs, he let himself out into the bright street and walked along Dudley Road. Not far along, he came to a narrow laneway. He walked down it until it turned to the right and continued behind the row of terraced shops and flats. Each one had a rear entrance. Robert could see the end building which would be Bramley's on the corner. The lane was cobbled, quiet and only small windows overlooked it, all bathroom windows which were frosted. He studied the area looking for any small indication that Bonnie had been here. Forensics would scour over it later, but you never knew what you might see. He walked slowly, eyes down, as if beachcombing, something he often compared searching an area to.

One of his few fond memories of childhood was infrequent trips to the sea-side with his mother and siblings where they would trawl the beaches for shells. But today he was not looking for shells, he was looking for...a guitar pick!

Using his handkerchief, he picked it up. *Bonnie had been here, in this laneway! He was sure of it. But where was she now?*

Now, Robert knew what he must do. The Bristol coppers would be here this morning. He would leave the rest to them. He was going to Suffolk. But first, he needed to speak to them, then go to the morgue.

***

Alby arrived at the Yard early as usual. Robert had not arrived. Tired he assumed. He knew his superior. He would have spent half the night going over the case, only managing a couple of hours sleep.

There were memos on his desk. Immediately he saw the report from Bristol and leafed through it. They had found the curtain rod in the weeds between the old cottage and the Banbury's home. It had blood on the end which was a *fleur de lis* shaped spike. Waiting on a match with Bramley. Mrs. Banbury was recovering in hospital and the DS would be able to interview her later today. Good. Their cottage had been thoroughly done over by forensics. The report was pending. It appeared that Bramley had used a dishcloth to wipe everything down as all the door handles, the phone and the hammer handle were clean. However, the one thing Bramley had forgotten to do was the kitchen tap. Forensics had lifted some perfect prints from the tap handle, and they were a match with Peter Huggy Bramley's. *Bingo!* thought Alby. Concrete evidence.

Alby turned his attention to some follow up on the girls from Rick Chambers' files who had disappeared. Their cases were still open but as they had gone without a trace, they had been shelved for the time being. Sadly, there simply were not the funds to keep investigations going when they had reached a stalemate. None of the girls' families, friends or neighbours had seen them since they hadn't return home. None of them had anything suspicious about their lives, possessions, or activities. Everyone who was interviewed denied any knowledge and genuinely seemed distressed and perplexed. They had all simply vanished. The only one whose family had admitted a drug problem was the girl who was found dead from an overdose. In Birmingham. Like Bramley.

Alby wondered exactly where. He found the case notes. The girl was found on the bank of the River Cole near Hodge Hill. She had needle marks and a large amount of heroin in her system. Alby wondered exactly where Bramley was found. He picked up the phone and dialled the Birmingham police asking for the DS who had been given the Bramley case.

Now we're getting somewhere! Bramley's body had been found by a man walking his dog along the path by the River Cole! There was a Cricket Club close by with a car park and a walkway through to the river. It would have been simple to park under cover of darkness, drop the body and disappear. He had asked next if the post-mortem had been done yet and the answer was no. Could they let him know as soon as the drug he OD'd on was identified and how he had taken it? They would do that. Alby looked at the clock. 9:04. Where was Robert?

Alby contemplated where they were at so far. There were so many avenues which still needed tidying up, even though Bramley would no longer be able to be prosecuted for Harold Banbury's death, there were still the questions about his aliases, his business dealings, this unaccountable income, the disappearing girls and of course Bonnie Summer. The phone rang.

'DS Coates.'

'Alby, Robert here. Are you in the office?'

'Yes boss. Been here for over an hour. Where are you?'

'In Birmingham. Just waiting to see the DS up here and check on the progress with the PM.'

'Birmingham? You must have driven overnight!'

'Yeah, I did. Couldn't sleep. Needed to come up here. I think I've got evidence that Bonnie was here near the Rotton Park flat but there's no-one there now. Found what I think are blood smears in the entry hall of the flat. Fresh and someone attempted to clean 'em up.'

Alby chipped in, 'I've just been on the phone to the DS up there. I think we've got a link between the dead girl from Chambers' file and Bramley. Both found near the River Cole. Both dumped on the bank. Both OD'd. Waiting to hear the tox results for Bramley. The girl died of a heroin overdose, injected. Bit too much of a coincidence, don't you think?'

'Good work, Alby. I'm waiting to see him, DS Short, isn't it? Then I'm hoping to see Bramley at the morgue. After that, I'm heading on down to Suffolk. Keep me informed Alby.'

'Suffolk? Lane Byrd's little place? Yep, I will guv. Oh, and they found the curtain rod. Nasty three spiked end on it covered in blood. Waiting on a match. Also, they found Bramley's fingerprints in the Banbury's kitchen. Too bad he's gone. I would have liked to see him locked away for a very long time!'

'Me too Alby. Alright, talk later. Wait a minute, could you pay another surprise visit to our friend Ricky Chambers? It's just a hunch of mine but I have a feeling you won't find him there. Try his home as well, but I think he's away 'on business'. I have a strong suspicion I might find him down in Suffolk.'

'Alright guv, will do.'

'Who are you taking to Suffolk?'

'No-one. Just going to have a peek for myself. Should be back tomorrow.'

'That's a lot of driving, guv. Sure you don't want company?'

'No, you're much more valuable doing what you're doing Alby. I'll see you tomorrow.'

The phone went dead. Alby looked at the handset, shook his head and placed it in the receiver.

Robert still waited in the DS's office, coffee in hand, contemplating his next move. He should be gathering a team together if he truly had enough evidence to support his suspicions, that there was a human trafficking ring operating in the UK, possibly headed up by people in the music business and for the explicit use of very high profile customers. His gut instinct told him Suffolk was a key location and that Bonnie was currently being prepared in that mansion owned by Bramley, alias, Lane Byrd.

His thoughts turned again to the girl. He could visualise those eyes, the colour, the clarity, the intensity, the shape even. They were familiar. From his childhood? A friend, a cousin, maybe a neighbour he used to play with?

His mind drifted to the old village. He and his brother used to cause mayhem in the streets. He remembered how his brother used to set off penny bombs in people's back yards to scare their dogs and cats. Suddenly, he knew exactly to whom those eyes belonged! He could see them blazing with fury at the two boys for frightening the dogs to death! The more he remembered the clearer the resemblance became, but could it be? How? Those remembered eyes were so far removed from this young girl and yet... Now, the need to find Bonnie was consuming him. It could be a matter of compensation for past sins. He had many debts to pay, and this was a small one, but it might be a start.

1953

PHILIPPE

'Into Each Life Some Rain Must Fall'
The Ink Spots

The Alvis pulled up in stately manner at the kerb.

'Here we are, my dear boy!' exclaimed Floyd.

They had stopped in a narrow, one-way street, by a solid stone wall rising to six feet, behind which glimpses of a large home peaked. The second story rose into view above the stone capping of the wall showing the house to be set well back from the road. Pale sandstone, faded in the moonlight, white painted casement windows, tall red brick chimneys and gabled slated roof were visible through tall trees like a partially completed jigsaw puzzle. A pair of wooden gates appeared to be the only access until Petunia saw a small gate nestled in the thick shrubbery.

Philippe unfolded himself from the front seat and Floyd joined him on the pavement. Petunia heard a creak and looked to see the small gate open. A statuesque middle-aged woman ducked her head and emerged onto the footpath, which was dimly lit by an antique, cast iron streetlamp.

'Andrew! How kind of you to bring Philippe home. You must come in for a drink!' The woman peered into the car.

'You too, my dear,' she added, noticing Petunia. I'm sure Andrew will introduce us in good time!' She cast a broad easy smile in the doctor's direction and ushered Philippe towards the gate, her silken, full skirt swishing with a pleasing rustle. Andrew came around to Petunia's door, opened it and helped her out.

'Do you mind, Petunia? Coming in for a drink I mean?'

'No, I suppose not.'

The room adhered fastidiously to the Classic French style with brocade trimmed cabriolet chairs and sofas, matching tables, and thick, intricately woven rugs. In one corner of the large room sat a white, carved, and gilded grand piano. Adrienne Gauthier served drinks from a polished walnut sideboard; every move accompanied by the swishing folds of her voluminous silk frock which was cinched around her small waist with a wide belt of the same rich maroon fabric. Petunia sipped her water with lime, mesmerised by the room and the tall, elegant woman. Her glossy auburn hair fell in waves to her collar and flicked upwards in a carefree manner, but Petunia could tell that much effort had been taken to achieve that look.

Adrienne served Doctor Floyd sherry and Philippe tonic water. 'So how do you know this wonderful man, Petunia?' she asked.

Petunia, who was severely lacking in social graces at this level, shot a terrified look at the doctor.

'We met through a mutual friend, Rennie,' offered Floyd. 'It transpires that Petunia is a great admirer of classical music, in particular the music of Chopin, Liszt, and Debussy. I offered to take her to Philippe's concert as she has not seen him play before, have you my dear?'

'No. I enjoyed the music, madame, Monsieur Philippe.'

Petunia was conscious of her altered dress and lack of *savoir faire,* but she felt grateful to at least have the fur stole around her shoulders. It provided a small touch of elegance. She gathered it together and covertly observed the enigmatic Philippe who stood in one corner of the room.

He appeared distracted. She noticed he made no eye contact, preferring to keep his eyes down while moving constantly from one foot to the other. At times it looked as if he was playing music in his head and Petunia noticed his fingers moving as if over the piano keys.

'Much of Philippe's success can be attributed to Andrew. Philippe has always had the talent of course, but Andrew gave him the means with which to use it,' replied Adrienne.

Philippe nodded rather enthusiastically, causing the wayward quiff of black hair to flop over his face. He said nothing.

'Thank you, Rennie, I have been privileged to have worked with your son. What a delight it was to see the audiences respond to his individual interpretation tonight. Especially the Adagio. You are a painter with the notes, Philippe, creating gentle, blending strokes of quiet beauty and grace. Genius my boy!'

Petunia was now listening and watching with growing interest, although she maintained a quiet and respectful demeanour. Adrienne, on the other hand, seemed more than comfortable discussing her son in front of a stranger.

'You see, Petunia, Philippe has always been different. As a child he did not speak. He was not able to communicate with his father and I, could not attend school and other doctors were willing to label him as mentally retarded or schizophrenic. I refused to accept it. I knew my son was locked away inside, but I had no way of finding my way to him. I knew he understood everything he heard but was unable to respond. I knew he could read and then, one day I heard him in the salon. He must have been four or five, on the piano. He was making up his own tunes, but he could play them over and over and they were quite complicated! I found that if I sang to him, he could play it back to me in the right key, perfectly.'

Philippe did not appear concerned that he was being discussed in such detail. He was smiling and moving from foot to foot, occasionally sipping his drink and nodding agreement.

'When we arrived in England just before the war, and I met Andrew, it wasn't long before Andrew used music as the key to unlock my son's beautiful personality.'

'That's when Rennie asked me if I knew anyone who could teach him without verbal communication,' interjected Floyd. 'I volunteered to try. You understand Petunia that I am no concert pianist, but I have other knowledge and skills I felt I might use. That was the beginning of Philippe's journey into the here and now.'

Adrienne fervently agreed.

'It was a transformation! When Philippe spoke for the first time, he spoke fluently in both French and English! The language had been there, but unable to be used. Philippe has made steady progress although there have been times when he is overwhelmed by people, audiences and has spent time recovering. By that I mean playing in solitude until he is ready to emerge again. I can never repay this man for what he has achieved for us.'

***

Later, in the car, Floyd turned to Petunia. 'I am so pleased you met Philippe. Believe me, Petunia, I was not sure it would happen. As you have seen, he can be one way or the other. I do not make a habit of discussing my patients, but Adrienne and Philippe are both keen to tell their stories. I think Philippe is to be featured in a TIME magazine article on his career and his journey to mental health. What I really need for you to take away from this, is that no adverse situation is insurmountable, no matter how dire you think it is. Petunia, if you will agree to keep working with me on a regular basis, I am convinced you will once more become a whole person. Maybe the person you once were, or perhaps a different but equally valuable person in your own right. I would like you to come to more musical performances as part of your therapy and if you think it might be helpful, I can arrange for you to speak to Adrienne. Not only is she happy to talk about her son, but she is also a very intelligent woman. She used to be a music teacher in France until they came to England. Her husband was appointed curator of one of the art galleries in Wales where some of the paintings from the National Gallery were taken days before the outbreak of the war. By that time Philippe was ten years old, had never attended school but had dispatched several private tutors. Adrienne began helping mentally ill patients by giving them music lessons in the institutions. That is how I came to meet her and her son.'

Petunia had been listening. She realised that for the whole of the evening, she had given no thought at all to her predicament, the child, or the events before. She had to admit she had been carried away by the music and had been in awe of the pianist.

'Alright, doctor. I will continue for the time being. I will attend concerts.'

'I am pleased to hear it. There is one condition you must adhere to, though. You must promise me that each week, or fortnight, whichever it is, when we have an appointment, you will be there, healthy, alive! I must have assurance that you will not do anything to jeopardise our sessions. One small step at a time. Agreed? Make me a promise, now!'

Petunia nodded slowly. 'Alright. I will. I will do as you ask.'

'Excellent! Our next meeting will be Tuesday week in my rooms. Your mother has my card. Will you be there?'

'I'll be there. Yes, doctor. Thank you for this evening.'

There is light at the end of the tunnel, thought Floyd.

1969

'Sinnerman'
Nina Simone

The car sped through the early morning mists, parting the low shroud of fine droplets, leaving curling patterns behind it. The quietly awakening dawn knew nothing of the dark and pressing business of the occupants, nor the disquiet but not fear of the girl blindfolded and secured in the back seat.

A glass partition separated her from the two men in front. She heard no sounds, no talk, music or even road noise. It had occurred to her that this might be a Rolls Royce or a Bentley. It felt large enough, plush enough and quiet enough. She could smell the leather, feel the soft carpet and her heart beating just a little too fast. How long would the trip take? Once more, she needed time to plan.

1969

'I Fought the Law'
The Clash

Alby grabbed DS Wright as soon as he walked in.

'Come on Jim, we've the great pleasure of visiting Rick Chambers again this morning, if he's in. Guv seems to think he won't be. Let's go and have a look.'

They walked down to the carpark. The day was bright, cloudless. The kind of day a person ought to be in a punt on the river with a picnic, a bottle of Chablis and a special companion. Alby had always had a romantic side, much to Deborah's delight. She was apt to receive yellow roses, her favourite, on odd occasions. Once Alby had surprised her with a weekend away in Paris where they sauntered down the Champs Elysees, ate ice creams from the corner shop on Isle St Louis and exchanged a kiss on the bridge over the Seine as they watched the sun dip behind the spires of Notre Dame.

His reverie was broken when Wright boomed in his Yorkshire brogue, ''Ere we are! Want me to drive?'

'By all means, Jim. Watch your head!' as the lanky Wright ducked sharply to avoid the door frame.

***

Once more they took the lift to level three and opened the door to Sharon's reception without invitation.

Sharon was busy painting her nails while listening to a transistor radio playing 'Top of the Pops'. She looked up lazily and on seeing the two detectives, dropped the nail varnish brush on her desk, tried to retrieve it and knocked the bottle over, spilling lurid pink goo everywhere.

'Now look what you've made me do!' she shrieked. 'You're supposed to ring first!'

Wright watched with amusement as she stumbled to her feet, hardly able to balance in her ridiculously platformed boots and went to the filing cabinet where she took out a duster and some nail varnish remover. The men watched as she tried cleaning up the mess, only succeeding in spreading it further, the solvent now stripping the wood finish on the desk.

'Jesus!' she exclaimed in disgust. 'Now what's Ricky going to say? My desk is ruined!' She fixed a glare on Alby. 'What do you want now?' she spat with undisguised venom.

'Is Ricky in? We'd like a chat.'

Sharon narrowed her eyes. 'NO, he's not. Check if you like.' She waved at the heavy wooden door into the inner sanctum. 'He is away. On business.'

'What business would that be?' asked Alby.

'Music business!' replied Sharon. 'What do you think?'

'What kind of music business? Another young thing awaiting, is there? Gone to check her out?'

Sharon pursed her lips defiantly but declined to answer.

'So, what exactly is your job here, Sharon? Every time we're here, you're not doing much productive work. I wouldn't call reading magazines, listening to the radio, or painting your nails productive work.'

'You're not actually Ricky's PA are you?' Wright jumped in, 'Because when I came last time, it was 'John Lennon', wasn't it? What's happened to him?'

Sharon continued to glare at them, pale, glossy lips clamped tightly shut.

Alby went to the door. 'Mind if we have a look?'

They walked into Ricky's palatial office. Everything was neat and tidy, not even a leopard print cushion askew on the zebra skin sofa. The drinks cabinet was well stocked, the walls decorated with framed gold records, his desk featuring a gold-framed portrait of a famous band managed by the company. It was signed, *To Ricky, thanks for the good times.*

Alby tried the desk drawers. They were locked. Sharon was leaning on the door frame.

'Got that warrant, have you?'

'Not with us,' replied Alby. 'Next time.'

'John Lennon' appeared at the door next to Sharon.

'Oh, there you are Stevie. They don't have a warrant,' said Sharon.

'I've called security,' replied Stevie.

'It's alright, we're on our way. So, where did you say Ricky's gone?'

'I didn't!' replied Sharon.

'Let us know when he returns. You've got our number.'

Alby and Wright left the office suite.

Stevie and Sharon exchanged meaningful looks.

'Bloody hell! Things are getting a bit too hot for my liking, Shar. I'll call security, make sure those two leave the building. Talk later?' Stevie asked hopefully.

Sharon rolled her eyes.

***

Robert sat in the noisy, bristling offices where DS Short's cluttered nook nestled against the wall and a window. Robert thought he worked in cramped and noisy conditions at the Yard, but this was ridiculous. Always lack of funding he supposed. Casting his eyes around the room he guessed that at least ten people worked in here, with hardly a chair width between them. With typewriters clattering, phones ringing and intercoms buzzing, speech was barely possible.

Short handed him a hastily typed document. 'Here is a copy of our preliminary report on Bramley,' he yelled.

Robert skimmed over it. He slid an unoccupied chair from the desk next door and jammed it into the tiny space across from DS Short. He placed the report on his lap and contemplated the Birmingham detective.

'What can you tell me about the flat in Rotton Park?'

'We went in this morning, around eight. All locked up and quiet. Forced the door. Obvious that people had been there last night, only just left. Still warm water in the kettle. Water in the sink, fresh food in the fridge. Outside belies inside. Sumptuous, antiques, marble. Food left behind obviously prepared by a chef. Nothing personal found anywhere. Beds not slept in.'

'You think the flat's not lived in?' asked Robert.

'Not permanently. Looks like somebody used it as a stop-off to somewhere else, but we found no evidence of any tenancy. Uniforms went back and yellow-taped it. Put a couple of officers on duty until we can get a forensic team in there. They're still at the river where Bramley's body was found.'

'What did you make of the stain in the entrance, on the floor and wall? Blood?'

'Yeah, it was and very fresh. Managed to take samples, hopefully have enough to test it.'

'I think you'll find it's Bramley's,' volunteered Robert. 'What we have so far is a primary witness in Bristol hospital, who saw two men take a young blonde girl away in a dark coloured car. The girl was Bonnie Summer, and we are sure Bramley was also in that car, suffering an injury inflicted by Bonnie with a curtain rod. I think the four of them were at the flat, which is owned by Peter Farmer, alias Peter Bramley. The fact Bramley was found late yesterday evening suggests maybe he had outstripped his usefulness or maybe he wasn't too well and wasn't worth wasting time on. Or maybe he did inject himself to take the pain away. We won't know until we get the autopsy report.'

'Coroner said the wound was badly infected but probably didn't cause the death.'

'When will the autopsy be done?' asked Robert. He was wondering if he needed to see the body this morning. The fact that they had missed the occupants at the flat by only an hour or two meant time was of the essence.

'Probably today.'

'Right. Thanks for this.' Robert waved the Bramley report. 'Can you send me the autopsy report then when it comes through? And the results of the blood smear in the flat. I want forensics to go through that flat with a fine toothed comb. I found a small piece of evidence in the lane behind the flats which could point to Bonnie's presence there, but we need proof. So, get 'em to do the lane as well; tyre marks, dirt or mud from tyres or under the car, anything to identify the car itself, where it's been, any witnesses who might have seen something in the early hours this morning.'

'Right. We'll get onto it.'

***

Back in his car, Robert checked the map and began threading his way through the Birmingham traffic on his way south when the phone rang. It was Alby.

'Morning Guv.'

'Morning Alby. What have you got?'

'You were dead right. Chambers is 'away on business'.'

Alby emphasised the last, his voice conveying the cynicism regarding the music mogul's business.

'Sharon wasn't talking, and the young Beatle-lad called security. We had a look in Ricky's office anyway but found nothing untoward except all his desk drawers were locked. Before you ask, yes, we did search for a secret drawer but there wasn't one. That desk is an inexpensive copy.'

'Thanks Alby. Birmingham uniforms have been in the flat. We missed 'em. Everything was still warm; food, kettle. Must have only been a matter of minutes, maybe a half hour. I'm on my way to Suffolk now.'

'I'll get a team together ready at the nod from you. Do you think we should alert the local lads and have some back-up on stand-by?' asked Alby. He felt concerned that Robert had chosen to fly into the den of the unknown alone.

'Can't do much until I have a clearer picture. As far as the brass are concerned, the murder is done and dusted. Bonnie's abduction is now at the top of our agenda.'

'That reminds me, guv. We got the information on Bonnie's biological mother. She lived up not far from your old home in Yorkshire. We've got an address. And...' he paused for effect, 'not a peep from the Colemans! Not one phone call, enquiry. In fact, they are not answering their phone. Rae Coleman is being kept up with any developments. She said her son won't even talk to her!'

'Got to go Alby. On the motorway. Got to focus. Talk later.'

Robert hung up. As he fed into the fast lane, he nodded satisfactorily to himself. He had known, hadn't he? After he had found Bonnie, got her to safety, he knew exactly where he had to go.

Getting Bonnie to safety was the primary objective. He was certain now that he would find them in the mansion, Chambers, the two thugs in the car, Bonnie and...who? There were high stakes here and big money; lots of money. The half-way flat was regal enough, lord knew what the house would be like. How much was he paying, this stinking rich sleazeball? Ricky was just a scout wasn't he, oozing around the edges of the beautiful people, always on the look-out for a perfect specimen and Bramley had been his fall guy, putting his name to properties and probably off-shore bank accounts.

It reminded Robert of Bonnie's song 'Field of Flowers'. There was Ricky and dozens of others being paid to search the 'fields of beautiful, perfect, flowers' ready to pick the finest for the clients. Robert shuddered. That thought brought bile to his throat and fear. He still feared his own past deviations. He thumped the wheel. *Damn you father. Damn you to Hell Eric!*

***

Deirdre Coleman caught the midday news on the radio. That disgusting character who had taken Bronwyn away in his van had been found dead in Birmingham, from a drug overdose. *Serves him right* she thought.

She took another slug of sherry and switched off the radio. *Good riddance,* a small voice whispered inside her head as she poured another drink. She settled into her favourite chair to wait until Bob, 'Bob who'll save you a bob or two' arrived home. She hoped that stupid woman, Gwyneth, had something tasty and slimming prepared for dinner.

1969

'Paradise'
The Ronettes

I am alive with anticipation in this quiet room. No sounds reflect or rebound from any surface. I can't hear anything from outside these walls. Conversely, nothing penetrates outside them either. My real existence fades as I take a deeply contented breath, relax my shoulders, arms and drop my head. I close my eyes, but I still see the room, all the features I designed and built using only the finest of materials. I remember how I commissioned the covering on the floor and walls to be made by artisans in the trade of making the finest Persian rugs. I re-live the days spent in the Persian markets, touching, caressing the soft cashmere wools, my fingers feeling every fibre, my mind imagining those fibres touching skin. I shiver a little.

But the ceiling, now that is the piece de resistance. Only a very special few ever see it, but it is worthy of the Sistine Chapel. One perfect sheet of golden mirror, bordered by hand painted cherubins, angels, deities, and visions of Eden. Even though my eyes are closed I still see the glow of the hidden globes behind the cornices, which light the crimson walls almost like rivulets of blood coursing sluggishly to the floor.

Crimson is my favourite colour. Not red, not scarlet, not cherry or rose. Crimson, the colour of kings and queens, rubies, and blood.

Coming here is my catharsis. I contemplate, in my state of semi-meditation that only yesterday, I was racked by frustrations, anger, hatred for the life I am forced to live. Now I am here greedily gazing at my creation, drinking in the blood red colours, the *crimson.* My eyes are open.

There is no real furniture here. I am very minimalistic when it comes to that. I have a bed; I suppose that's what you would call it. It is enormous and crimson, but I don't sleep here. No, not sleep. There is no bed linen, no pillow. Aah! There are other pieces of interest though!

I am waiting now. I have everything in readiness. The wardrobe is full. The crimson and gold bathroom is stocked. I am ready too. My man has seen to it.

I know some would think me totally mad, insane, standing here thinking like this as if talking to someone. I am. Talking to someone. I am talking to you, dear man, the angry one, the one racked with frustrations. I will take you on a new journey soon. Relax.

I glance up to the golden mirror and see my naked reflection. Yes, we are ready!

1969

'I Love the Flower Girl'
The Cowsills

Bonnie thought she must have been in this silent cocoon of a car for two hours or so. Blindfolded in the back, she had lost the sense of real time. The car was so insulated, she had not been able to discern an 'A' road from a 'B' road, or a rutted track from a cobbled street. The driver, whether it be Ed or his accomplice, drove so smoothly that she hardly felt changes in speed and direction. She really had no concept of where they were.

Earlier, when she had been pushed into the back seat of the two-door car, she had decided that she would use the time to try to understand what they were doing with her, and how she would deal with it. It was plainly obvious she had been taken for a reason beyond ransom money. Her dad was wealthy enough, but not *that* wealthy! Besides, she had heard nothing to suggest her parents were involved in any way. So what? Huggy had been very careful not to hurt her and so had Ed and his mate. She didn't think her life was in danger.

Bonnie was sixteen, wise in the ways of the pop world but not in many others. She was not very sophisticated, she lamented to herself. She knew nothing of the real adult world. Although the murder of Hollywood actress, Sharon Tate, by some of the Manson family members was all over the news, Bonnie had not seen any television or newspapers for weeks. Perhaps if she had, she might be much more concerned than she was.

She sat in her capsule, gliding along in the artificial darkness of the black blindfold. Only recently, it had occurred to her that she might be told to give a free concert or performance for some rich guy, but why all the secrecy? Also, she wondered about Huggy. He had been injured and now she didn't know if he was in the car or something bad had happened to him. He had looked rather poorly when she saw him being dragged out of the car, and it didn't look as though even the kindly-faced Ed cared one iota about him. Well, he deserved what he got, she thought bitterly, the way he had treated her!

The more she picked apart the circumstances leading up to this moment, the more she began to suspect she might be in more danger than she could handle. Perhaps not from these two men, but from someone to whom she was about to be delivered.

Where were the police? She had dialled 999 at the cottage and given her name. They would have known where she was two days ago. Did the old lady with the cut on her head see the car or the men taking her? Surely someone had seen something, perhaps in the lane behind the flat where she escaped the boot of the car. Could they be waiting when she arrived at her destination? Then it would all be over. She wondered what her fans must be thinking, missing her Manchester concert, disappearing off the face of the planet. She wished she had a magazine. Had anything been written about her?

But she must think of a plan. As the car slipped silently along like a graceful skater on ice, inside, Bonnie's thoughts churned as did her stomach. Ed. The nice smelling, dimple cheeked, quietly spoken Ed. He had been gentle with her, much more so than the other, whose name she had not heard once. Ed might be the light in the darkness. She realised there was nothing else for it. She must wait to see what happened and formulate a plan from there, beginning with gaining Ed's trust or dare she think, friendship?

The car came to a stop. Dimly she heard the doors open. Her heart hammered.

***

The unpleasant man propelled her along, gravel crunching underfoot, the sun beating down with midday heat on her cropped head. She could discern the perfume of Ed to her left, though he was not actively engaged in escorting her. With the blindfold still in place, her other senses came to the fore. Tall trees rustled. She knew them to be tall because birds were twittering way up above her head. She could smell roses. There must be a rose garden, bursting with blooms, the perfume was so strong. This was mixed with Ed's cologne and the un-named man's more earthy smell, sweat. The ground changed and she stepped onto stone or concrete.

'Watch the step,' growled his voice, not Ed's.

One step, two steps, three steps then flat ground. They must be on a terrace or porch. She heard someone ask them to come inside, not a man's voice, a woman's. Bonnie felt relief. She would be able to talk to a woman. Surely, she would understand how Bonnie was feeling!

The light had dulled as they entered the building. Now her steps fell on a smooth, solid floor, tiles or concrete, and the smell of more roses wafted around her. There were no real clues to help her understand where she was except the trees and birds. She assumed they were in the countryside somewhere.

No-one was talking. She was still being led, blindfolded through the building which could have been a house, a shop, anything, then through a door which she could clearly hear open with a slight squeak of hinges. The door closed. Hands fumbled with the blindfold and removed it. She looked around her, saw Ed and the other man, the driver. The woman had not come with them.

They were in a wood panelled room with lofty ceilings, also intricately panelled and decorated. The squeaky door was tall and wide, wood panelled with brass handle and lock. A huge bay window with thick drapes which were drawn to block any view of the outside. Everything was grandly over-sized from the deep skirtings to the massive chandelier. Pieces of furniture matched the room in size and grandeur. Bonnie assumed this was a drawing room in an exceptionally large, old house. But where and why?

'Where are we?' she asked Ed. He said nothing. 'I want to know where I am and why you brought me here!' demanded Bonnie. 'Let me talk to the lady who let us in. Where is she?' Bonnie made to move to the door. Ed's hand grabbed her elbow, and he shook his head.

'Calm down. We brought you here to meet someone who is eager to make your acquaintance. You'll like him. He has seen your shows, bought your records and followed you on the pop scene. He is very, very wealthy and he would like to give you some gifts. Alright?'

Bonnie scowled. 'Why didn't he just come back-stage at one of my shows and introduce himself then? If he's that cool and digs me that much, I would have given him free tickets and asked him to an after party!'

Both men laughed and exchanged amused looks.

'He's not very sociable; a very private person. When he does go out, he goes in disguise. No, he wanted you here.'

'So, when do I get to meet him? For dinner?'

The man whose name she still did not know laughed again, a coarse guffaw.

'Well? Why are we just standing around in here?' asked Bonnie.

The door opened. Bonnie's eyebrows shot up in complete surprise.

'Rick! Rick Chambers! What are you doing here? I am so glad to see you! I don't know what's going on here. Can you tell them to take these ties off my hands? At long last, I might get to know what's going on, man! Why all the secrecy?'

'Hi Bon! Glad you could make it!' Ricky chuckled towards the two men. 'Trust Ed and Frankie here took good care of you!'

Frankie! That was his name. She would remember that and try to find out their other names. Ricky untied her hands.

'They'll show you to your room where you can take a bath and change into some decent clothes.'

'But I haven't got anything with me. Huggy made me leave everything behind. Even my guitar, so if I'm expected to sing, I won't be able to!'

This was met by a hearty roar from all three men in the room.

'Ha! I don't think he'll be asking you to sing, Bonnie!' laughed Ed.

'Can I talk to you alone, Rick?' Bonnie asked.

'Whoa! Talk about eager, eh Ricky boy!' Frankie leered.

Bonnie ignored him and turned to Rick. 'Tell them to give us a few minutes Rick. I need to talk to you!' she beseeched him. 'Come on!'

Rick threw his hands out and shook his head at Ed and Frankie.

'Go on lads. Won't take long.' He raised his eyebrows suggestively.

The men left the room through the squeaky door. Bonnie caught a glimpse of a panelled hallway but nothing more. She turned to Rick, hands on hips.

'Alright, spill!' she demanded crossly. 'I'm fed up with this. What the hell am I doing here? Who is this dude, the one that wants to meet me anyway?'

Rick watched her with amusement. 'Honey, I organised Huggy and these two dead beats to get you here. 'Course Huggy fucked up, but he was expendable. You're going to find out sooner or later. This guy likes girls, young girls like you, and when he picks one, it's my job to deliver. He's gonna be nice for a while but, sweetheart, you're never going to get out of here. You know that, yeah? Sharon, she bought you some real groovy clothes straight from Carnaby Street. You're gonna impress him alright but he gets bored quick.'

Bonnie was now beginning to realise that she should have been much more suspicious right from the moment Huggy took her away from Devon. She thought back, bitterly understanding now how many opportunities she had let slip, opportunities to escape, to alert the police. Damn, she had been stupid! She regarded Rick Chambers, the guy who had promised the world and he had delivered! Now, the question was, for how long had he been planning this? Had he been the one who got her into the drugs and hippie lifestyle at Notting Hill, or was that an unfortunate mishap as well? Was that how Huggy had 'fucked up? All these thoughts went flying through her mind in the seconds after Ricky had spoken.

'So...I'm to have sex with this guy and then I'm just going to disappear forever. Just because of this one guy? He must be something!'

Ricky seemed a little taken aback at her brashness. He had expected at the very least crying or protesting or begging as was usually the case, but not this.

'Oh, he is, and you would recognise him too, but he always wears a mask when he's with his girls. Look, enough! You need to get tidied up, get some food into you. You're a little on the scrawny side, probably because of that idiot Bramley. I don't think he's going to ask for you until tomorrow. We've got to make sure you're as perfect as we can make you. There is a beautician here, not that she could do much with that hair! One of the things he liked so much. Another of Bramley's total fuck-ups! Come on!'

Rick grabbed Bonnie by the wrist and pushed her through the door into the entry hall where Ed and Frankie lounged, smoking, and chatting quietly.

'Take her up. Give her food. Let her sleep and in the morning, I'll let you know what's going on. Probably get Dora Thorley up to do the beauty shit. Take it easy, yeah?'

Rick's boots clopped on the polished floor as he walked down the long corridor to a flight of stairs. Frankie pushed Bonnie roughly forwards and indicated the stairs.

'Come on then, lots to do. Big day tomorrow!'

1969

The day had turned out to be one of those hazy, late summer days when the sky couldn't make its mind up whether to show its brilliant blue expanse or cloak it with fine misty haze. It was the kind of day Robert could love, if not for the pressing urgency he felt growing as he neared his destination. Although he would never talk about such things to colleagues, he had good memories of days such as this, picnicking with Susan in the South Downs or travelling to Brighton, eating scampi and ice creams on the pier. The only reminder was the cat, Midnight, because Susan had thought he needed an animal to help him develop his nurturing side!

It had all sort of fizzled out. There had been no sudden break-up, no arguments or unpleasantness, no 'other' in the picture for either of them. They had simply seen less and less of each other, until one night when they were dining out for the first time in weeks, Susan had asked him if he minded if she went away for a while. She was a talented and artistic clothing designer who had worked in London, designing for a few sought after labels. She had applied for and been accepted to join a couturier in Paris. She was leaving next week. And that was that. Robert wondered if she would have applied at all if their relationship had had more substance, in other words, if he had put an equal amount of emotional effort into it as she had. But it was too late now, and did he miss her or the relationship? At times he might have liked a partner to go home to, but in truth, how often did he stay at the office until the early hours? How often did he take off for days in the name of the job? Like today! No, he was in no way equipped to manage this career and a wife. And then there was the unspoken dread inside him, still gnawing away at his 'normality'.

He was heading to the southeast of the county, close to the coast, travelling through farming countryside on a two-lane road. Following the map and the address he had, he was looking for a rough track off to the left. There had been a couple, but all had led into farmhouses. Up ahead he saw another clearing in the hedgerow. He slowed and yes, this lane, a two-rutted track, struck out between low shrubs, brambles, and underbrush. He turned in, seeing two closed, rough wooden farm gates, about two hundred yards away. There were quite well-worn tracks here but as he approached the gates, he saw they were locked with chains. A rudimentary sign wired to the gates warned **PRIVATE – KEEP OUT**.

Robert looked around. The gates had no other structures close by, no intercom or cameras! Looking to the left, he could see a house in the distance, through a thick stand of trees. Although very little was visible, he judged it to be a large manor house rising several stories. Casting his eyes around the full circle, he could see there were no other signs of habitation. The rutted road continued after the gates then disappeared around a left-hand bend.

Robert sat in the Merc, engine running, contemplating his next move. He needed to get in and have a look around, but he was not about to boldly put his own life at risk. He felt sure these were very unpleasant characters he was dealing with, if in fact they were here, which was an educated guess on his part. Should he go back into

Lowestoft or even to Ipswich and get some of the local constabulary to back him up? But then it would look like a siege and that's the last thing he wanted. No, he'd have to go in alone and on foot. He needed to find out once and for all if this was the place he thought it was, or if he had been 'barking up the wrong tree'.

He reversed the car out of the lane and drove up the road a little way until he saw yet another tiny lane on the right. Turning in, he found he could drive far enough in to be shielded from the road by the roadside vegetation. Nevertheless, he drove the shiny Merc hard up against the spiky bushes. Oh well, a few scratches on the car won't kill him. He grabbed his binoculars and the keys, then locked the car. Crossing the road, he kept as covered by the hedges as he was able, cursing himself for not having had the foresight to bring more suitable clothes for tramping around the countryside! He turned into the lane and approached the gates which were simply constructed of wooden bars within a frame. He easily climbed over them, even accounting for slippery leather-soled shoes, and continued up the drive.

Suddenly he heard tyres on the rough gravel coming towards him. He ducked deep into the hedge and squatted down among the nettles. A green Land Rover passed him, two men in the front seats. At the gate, the passenger got out and unlocked it, waited for the car to pass through, then re-locked it. Robert watched them turn right onto the bitumen road. That was close! If they had been ten minutes earlier, they would have all met at the gate! Could those men be the two who had picked up Bonnie at the cottage? It was a possibility, but he mustn't jump the gun. He continued warily up the road, the house still not visible to him, therefore, he could assume, his approach was not visible to the occupants. As he walked further towards the house, he executed greater caution, on the lookout for anyone who might catch sight of him, gardeners for example, although he had not come close enough yet to see gardens.

By now he had been picking his way towards the house for about five minutes. He rounded a bend and there stood the house, massive, imposing in size and architecture. There were large, beautifully landscaped gardens with low stone walls, furiously flowering summer borders and willowy trees. He kept close to the edges then, realising he could see windows, he felt it prudent to find a way through the hedge. Leaving the road, he made his way along the hedgerow bordering the meadow instead. Once again, he thought, darkness would have been a better option. There was no movement to be seen but Robert ducked from cover to cover, constantly checking all directions. He was close enough now to see a semi circular driveway and steps leading up to the grand entrance. An expansive rose garden followed the curve, the blooms abundant in every shade, the perfume even from where he stood, dense and fragrant.

He stopped under the canopy of a large oak tree which afforded good cover, took the binoculars, and scanned the house and garden. Nearly all the windows had curtains drawn. A window on the third floor had none but he could see nothing due to the height. He noted how the gardens were well kept, manicured, the house itself in good condition with good slates on the roof, intact stonework, and reasonably fresh paintwork, even on the upper floors. Someone was spending a lot of money on maintenance. Someone very wealthy. Robert reasoned there must be at least half a dozen gardeners and several maintenance men. Could it really have been Bramley, funding all this? If so, what would happen now he was dead?

Staying put until the sun dipped would have been the safest option but he did not have the time to wait. If Bonnie was in danger at all, he must get her out. He began to pick his way closer towards the house, making for the rear, until he could see a large outbuilding. It looked to be stables, but one large door stood open, and Robert could see it housed cars. The open door revealed an empty space, he guessed for when the Land Rover returned. He looked around, saw no-one. All the windows on this side of the house had heavy curtains drawn. He took a chance and sprinted across to the garage, stopped and hid around the corner facing away from the house. He waited, then edged silently around the corner and along the first two doors to the open one. With another glance around, he slowly peered around the wooden frame.

The garage was silent and empty except for the cars. And there were a couple of expensive ones too. There was a two-tone green and cream two-door Bentley. Robert didn't know much about Bentleys but this one looked very new and expensive. On the other side of the Land Rover's space was a brilliant red sports car. Robert didn't know what it was, but it was left hand drive, very sleek and looked fast. He crept over the gap to have a look and saw the name across the bonnet, with a badge featuring a pair of crossed chequered flags. *Corvette.* Next to the Corvette was a Rolls Royce. This one was much older than the Bentley, a classic, he supposed, similar to one the Queen might be driven around in. Occupying the last space in the garage was a Volkswagen Beetle, incongruous compared to the other vehicles. Were these all Lane Byrd's cars? He supposed the Corvette was, because he realised being left hand drive, it must be an American brand. Lane Byrd, alias Bramley was dead. Did the other occupants know? Who else was here then?

He hugged the far-side stone wall of the old stable come garage until he reached the end of the building. Flattening himself against the stone wall, he peered around the corner. He could see the back of the house now, though much of it was obscured by a high wall with a tall wooden gate. He looked around and ducked across the gravel path to the wall. It was at least six feet high. The gate was solid. He dared not try the latch in case someone was on the other side. What now? He moved as quietly as he could, careful to take considered steps which would not crunch on the stones, around the back wall where there was another gate. This one had a latch with a hole behind it. Putting his eye to the hole, he could see the back of the house and a door. A woman stood, leaning against it, smoking a cigarette. Robert ducked and breathed a sigh of relief that he had not tried to open the other gate at the side!

He looked at his watch and was surprised to see it had been an hour since he left his car. He took a chance on another peek through the hole and saw the woman stub out her cigarette and hasten indoors as if she was being called. Then Robert heard a vehicle. It was coming towards the garage. He stayed where he was, behind the back wall and waited, heart thumping in his chest, holding his breath. The car drove into the garage. Doors slammed; footsteps approached. He tried to quiet his heart and waited. He heard the side gate open.

'Think we're all set for tomorrow then. Time for a drink, eh?'

Then the back door closed. Robert let out his long held breath. *Tomorrow.* What now?

***

Inside the house, Bonnie sat on a king sized four poster bed in 'her' room. She would have much preferred the woman to bring her up here, but Frankie was the one chosen to show her around. She guessed Ed had shown a little too much kindness to her. Shame because she really had thought he might be her passage out of here. Now she had an idea of what they were planning, she was certain she must do everything she could to escape.

Earlier, when the three of them had mounted the stairs, Bonnie took note that they turned right at the top, down a long corridor along which there were four polished oak doors She had counted. After the fourth door, there had been another corridor running east-west and they had turned to the left. This corridor looked much the same with similar doors. Hers was the third door along also on the left. In her mind she made a map; *stairs, turn right, up to next corridor, turn left, third door on left.* She knew she would be able to retrace her steps so far.

Her room was huge. The ceiling was domed with carved timber buttresses and the panels were painted with woodland scenes, nymphs, fantastic animals and naked men and women laying in the grassy meadows. The walls were hung with enormous gilt framed portraits of snooty women and men, who all seemed to have a bad smell under their noses. Many were holding dainty handkerchiefs to their faces. Bonnie thought they looked ridiculous. Her bed was enormous, with heavy drapes hung around it, matching the same drapes drawn across the windows. She had noticed there were two smaller doors in the panelling, and Frankie had duly opened them, one to another room which he claimed was the dressing room and the other a lavishly appointed bathroom. Everything had been provided including every item of clothing Bonnie could think of, not that any of it was her taste but she had nothing else to wear!

Frankie had instructed her to bathe and dress for dinner, before leaving and locking the door behind him. Hours later, she had still not done anything he'd asked. She felt distraught that people had paid good money to see her perform that night in Manchester, and she had let them down. What had surprised and horrified her most was that Huggy and now Rick Chambers were all part of this. How stupid and gullible had she been?

The curtains! Bonnie rushed to the window and flung them aside. Not only was the window barred with wrought iron railings, but the glass was covered by a darkly tinted film the likes of which Bonnie had not seen before. She could see very little light through it, and she was certain no-one would be able to see inside. She stamped her foot childishly, then guiltily looked behind her to see if anyone saw her. Of course, they didn't. She was alone. Or was she? A cold shiver ran up her spine to the nape of her neck where her spiky, short hair stood on end. Were there hidden cameras in here, spying on her every move? In the dressing room, the bathroom? Was she safe anywhere?

Bonnie was eternally grateful she had not undressed or taken the bath she had been instructed to do. She had seen spy movies. Where did they always hide the tiny cameras? In the light fittings or table lamps? In the eyes of portrait figures! Yes, she had seen that but surely that was a little farfetched. Didn't they put hidden microphones in the telephone? She looked around. No telephone. She checked the bedside lamps and the table lamp but as far as she could tell, there was nothing unusual. The chandelier hung low from the cavernous ceiling but was still too high for her to see anything.

Now that this unwelcome suspicion had occurred to her, she could not unthink it. She decided to behave as if the whole place was wired. She sat on the bed and waited. With no clocks, no watch, no radio or TV, the time dragged by, the silence and boredom made worse by her brain's insistence on relentlessly trying to formulate plans of escape.

Bonnie sat on the bed thinking. Frankie had locked the door. Had he left the key in the other side of the lock? She thought about checking but stopped herself. If they were watching her, of course that would bring them running, knowing she was trying to find a way out. Wait until dark. She walked into the bathroom and casually inspected the array of beauty aids, creams, lotions, make-up, perfumes, and bathing products. Razors? No, only depilatory cream. Scissors? No. Aerosol hairspray? She thought that could be a weapon, but no. There were no spray cans. She swore to herself. They really had thought of everything! Dammit! The toilet was in the bathroom and though she knew she would have to go soon, she resisted out of modesty, thinking she might be being watched. The silence was broken by the sound of the key in the lock. Someone was coming in.

1969

Robert had decided to walk back to his car. He unlocked it, grimaced at the scratches on the driver's side and drove out of the lane. He picked up the phone and called Alby who answered immediately.

'Guv! Where are you? Everything alright?'

'Listen Alby, I'm at the house, well I have been. Big place, expensive, flash cars but no sign of Bonnie. I just saw two guys leave and return in a Land Rover. They could be the guys who brought Bonnie here *if she's here*. What's more I heard them say they're 'all set for tomorrow'. Something is afoot and it looks like we have less than twenty four hours to get in there and find out. I'd like you to come down. Bring Wright and organise a squad ready to conduct a raid. I think we might need Grainger. We'll need vests as well. There's an old, abandoned barn just near here. According to the map I'm about two miles from Alderwell. As you approach, it's on the right. You can use that as a base. Don't announce your arrival. No lights or sirens please. I'll try to make it there as soon as I can.

'Right, I'll get on to DS Grainger. So, you think they have firearms?'

'I don't know Alby. I haven't seen any, but these people are mixed up in a much bigger organisation than we think. This little operation only scratches the surface. I don't want to take any chances of being caught in the headlights! When you get down here, keep them quiet and out of sight. I want to catch these guys right in it. No point jumping the gun. Meanwhile, can you do a bit more digging about Lane Byrd. See if anything's come back from the US. When did he purchase this place, for how much and where did the money come from?'

'Right. Leave me with it. What are you doing right now?'

'Not much. Can't remember my last meal. Might try to find a sandwich somewhere.'

He hung up and decided to drive until he found a pub. Within ten minutes he reached the outskirts of the village of Alderwell, the main attraction of which was an ancient priory. Everything in the village was named after it, the roads, local hall, school and even the pub, 'The Priory Inn'. Robert parked and entered the old door into the pub. The atmosphere was immediately welcoming, as were most country inns. It featured a huge fireplace, panelled walls decorated with Toby jugs, horse brasses, steins and many references to the old priory including drawings, old scripts behind glass and even recipes for wine and cider.

Robert strolled up to the bar and ordered a pint of lager. As the barman pulled the beer, he eyed Robert's suit and tie. 'Just visiting the area, are you?' he asked casually.

'Yes. I have a friend who lives around here, but he's not home. Thought I'd have a drink and go back a bit later. Do you know him at all? Lane Byrd. Some of us refer to him as 'Chip'.'

The barman continued to pour the beer without a pause, but Robert saw his eyes flicker. He pushed the glass across the bar. 'Two and ninepence, thanks.'

Robert paid. 'Does he come in here at all? We might come back for a meal later.'

'I know him, but he hasn't been in this pub for quite a while. Sorry, I can't help you out,' replied the barman.

'Yes, I remember he got into a bit of trouble in a local a while back. Was that here?'

The barman wiped a glass. 'I think I heard something about it, but I didn't work here at the time.' He narrowed his eyes at Robert and lowered his voice. 'You're a copper, aren't you? What's he done this time?'

'Oh no, I'm not police. Used to know Chip years ago and lost touch. Down in Ipswich on business. Thought I'd look him up, that's all.'

The barman stared at Robert unwaveringly, then he picked up another glass and shone it with gusto. 'Whatever you say. I can't tell you anything except I haven't seen him for a few months. I heard from Mrs. Potts, his housekeeper that he was supposed to be here this weekend. She was getting in supplies this week. Excuse me.'

He turned to another customer, a shambles of a man with unkempt clothes and a ruddy, aggressive expression. The tramp shoved his pint glass at the barman nodding gruffly between the barman and the glass.

'Another one Fred? Time you packed it in and went home to the missus.'

Fred leaned across the bar and forcibly shoved the empty glass at the barman. 'I said, give me another pint o' bitter!'

Robert could see the situation at the bar could be about to become unpleasant. He decided to take his drink into the snug, where he could think and observe without being disturbed.

So Huggy, aka, Bramley, aka Lane Byrd had been expected this week sometime but had not been seen. *Because he has been murdered in Birmingham,* thought Robert. Mrs. Potts was the housekeeper. She must be the woman he had seen smoking at the kitchen door. She had been in here buying expensive drinks. Was she unaware of Bramley's demise or was she buying for someone else? Lost in his own thoughts, Robert failed to see the woman sidle up to his corner seat in the snug, drink in hand.

'Do you mind?' She tipped her head to the seat next to his.

Robert drew back to better see the full height of this very tall, willowy, you might even call 'skinny' woman who towered above him. *Upper crust* thought Robert. Spoke with a BBC accent. He hastened to get up in the cramped booth.

'No, please don't get up. I heard you talking at the bar. Do you mind if I join you?'

'No, not at all, please do!' Robert flopped back into the seat.

'Jane Forcedyke.' She introduced herself, her accent cultured, her vowels the rounded sounds of the upper class. She held out a bony hand, the blue veins pulsing through transparent skin.

'Robert.' He proffered his own hand, declining to give his full name.

Jane sat, almost draped across the seat, her long floral dress brushing the floor, her grey hair immaculately styled and her face unlined and translucent.

'So, Robert, you are a friend of Lane's?' she asked, taking a sip of her sherry.

Robert nodded.

'If you are wishing to visit, you might be disappointed, Mr...?'

'Why do you say that?' replied Robert, ignoring her attempt to discover his last name.

'Robert.' Jane studied him, ignoring his question. 'We both know you are not a 'friend' of Lane's. Why are you here?'

Robert knew how to play this game. It was part of his job.

'How do *you* know Lane Byrd, Jane? Is he a friend of *yours*?'

'Heavens no! Most residents of the district were horrified when that ghastly man purchased the Manor! Modern times, I suppose when new money can buy old heritage.' She took another disdainful sip of her drink.

'So, he isn't a popular man?'

'Hardly! Caused trouble a few times. Drives around in his expensive cars with his nose in the air and what right does he have? Where all his money comes from, no-one seems to know. He associates with lot of high society people. We see them in the pubs and restaurants occasionally. It is rumoured that he even hob-nobs with royalty.' Jane leaned in closer in a conspiratorial manner and whispered, 'I know things happen at the Manor when Lane is in town!'

'Do you really? What kind of things?' questioned Robert in an equally secretive manner.

'My dear friend Lady Thorley, has a daughter who is a beautician.' Jane sniffed a little as if the mere word gave her an unpleasant experience. 'She is sometimes employed by the Manor to attend to guests, obviously women, and they are most often, very young girls!' Jane narrowed her eyes to Robert as if expecting shock or horror.

She continued, 'Why does Lane Byrd invite teenage girls to stay at the Manor? And why are all his hifalutin acquaintances older men? I tell you Robert, or should I call you Detective, Robert?' She smirked knowingly. Robert didn't react.

'There is something very wrong going on out there. Lady Thorley's daughter, Dora has been booked to go out there this weekend. He must have another young lady visitor. I know he has a male guest as well. He arrived in a red sports car. Looks like an aging rock star!'

Could that be Rick? It was a distinct possibility with such a simple but matching description.

'A red sports car? American? queried Robert.

'Yes. Rather vulgar and excessively loud,' added Jane.

'Do you happen to know when Dora has this appointment?' asked Robert.

'Now why would you be interested? Tomorrow, at 3:00pm if that helps. I know because Grace, Lady Thorley, is taking her there herself. Dora does not drive.'

'Jane, can I rely on your confidentiality?' Robert placed his hand very carefully and respectfully on hers to reinforce their conspiratorial meeting. The gesture said, *I trust you because you are a woman of refinement and respectability.*

Jane whispered, 'Oh yes, of course!' She placed her forefinger across her lips. *A childish act for a woman of her age,* mused Robert.

'Do you think Lady Thorley could persuade her daughter to get a description of the young lady. A photograph would be better. I would be very appreciative.' Robert drew out his wallet and opened it to take out some notes.

Jane's sharp intake of breath signalled her shock that he should even consider *paying!* This time she gave her hand to him. 'You can trust us implicitly, Inspector. Implicitly! I have a polaroid camera! I shall instruct Dora myself! Tomorrow evening, here in the snug?'

'Could we make it four o'clock? I have other business tomorrow night.'

'We shall. Goodnight, Robert.'

Robert drained his beer and ordered another at the bar. The beer had taken the edge off his mood. He was feeling less anxious; much more relaxed. A few more people straggled in filling the booths in the snug and the small tables in the cosy room adjacent to the bar area. A young girl stumped in, arms laden with logs and threw them on the hearth with a loud clatter. Adding a couple, she prodded the fire causing a shower of sparks to fly onto the bricks. The fire flared bringing the ambience from cosy to overheated until the initial burn died down to coals. Conversation rose steadily, much of it absorbed by the growing throng of warm bodies.

'Travelling through are ye?'

A voice at his elbow jolted Robert from his reveries, the word 'through' pronounced 'frough'. It belonged to a comfortable man in a tweed coat, corduroy trousers, and cap. He wore a wide smile on his reddened face which had carved deep lines in his plump cheeks, leaving the smile a permanent fixture.

The man elbowed Robert and winked. 'Or are ye on a business trip, ye know what I mean?'

'Right the first time, mate.' replied Robert. He was about to get up and leave the bar, but it occurred to him that the folk around here seemed either very friendly or very nosy and he might learn something new. He decided to stay seated.

'Oh yer, I fought ye might be down at t' manor 'ouse. Sumfink big goin' on this weekend. You know what I mean?'

Immediately, Robert's attention was peaked. Everyone he had spoken to so far had added some detail to the weekend events at the Manor. Village gossip.

'No, I'm not from around here. What sort of 'thing'?' he asked. 'Like a garden party?'

The man winked and tapped the side of his nose, his merry eyes fixed on Robert's. *Nod, nod, wink, wink.*

'And you are?'

'Clive, Clive Baker, at your service. Used to be gamekeeper fer 'is Lordship, not this Byrd chap, the real Lord. Poor chap found it impossible to maintain the place and had to sell after bein' in the family for four hundred years. Yep, worked there fer nigh on fifty years, I did.'

'And you're not employed by Mr. Byrd?'

Clive snorted and puffed his already rotund cheeks. He looked for all the world like a cartoon character, every facial feature over-emphasised and hyper-coloured. 'Not on your life! I wouldn't give that man so much as the time of day. A real nasty piece of work, that one. Know much about 'im do yer?'

Robert's spine stiffened involuntarily. 'No, I don't. Is there something...odd about him?'

Clive Baker's beady eyes pierced Robert's as if he was trying to see into his soul. Seconds passed before he murmured, 'There is noffink normal about 'im. One minute 'e turns up looking like a big time businessman, the next 'e looks like a junkie, hippy or an escapee from Dartmoor. He's got a lot of people follerin' 'im around, different men in sports cars and limos. I'm darn sure I've seen politicians there. Then there's the girls, sometimes lots of 'em, other times only one or two. Dusn't take much to guess what they're up to do it? Some of them girls'd be no more 'n little lasses.'

'When you say you've seen politicians, do you mean you were at the manor?' asked Robert.

'I 'ad a gamekeeper's 'ut in the woods. 'As a back entrance, all overgrown now but I go there sometimes. I can see the 'ouse wi' binoculars. I seen enough to know. You know once they got raided by police but found nuffin'. Must 'ave got warned some'ow. All they found was Mrs. Potts and a cat!'

Robert weighed up whether to confide his status to Clive Baker and decided not to at this point. He wondered how to gain access to the hut without attracting suspicion. Being in such close proximity might provide him with a great opportunity to observe any activity tonight and tomorrow morning. Besides he could do worse than spend the night there. Alby would have to be informed, but it could prove very valuable. He suspected Clive had guessed he had more than a passing interest in the manor and inhabitants.

'Clive,' he said under his breath, 'could you show me your hut? I need a place to shelter for the night and the hut sounds perfect. Just trying to stay out of sight for a while. Don't want to put my name to a room at the pub at this stage. You think you could help me?'

The man pushed the plaid cap back off his forehead and ruffled his course grey hair. He regarded Robert quizzically. A question formed but didn't eventuate and he clamped his mouth and nodded.

'You ready to leave now then? Foller me.'

They left the pub. The sky was turning golden as the sun disappeared rapidly below the horizon. A wonderful fresh chill breeze blew in off the coast. Robert could smell the salt and marsh, even here. He unlocked the car and drove out of the carpark, past the front of the Priory Inn where the lights were now warming the interior and spilling out onto the pavement. He could see people in the glow through the small paned windows. Clive was waiting on the road. Robert followed the tiny red rear lights of the old Morris out of the village, back towards the Manor. *Country pubs; you couldn't beat them*, he thought.

1969

'For What It's Worth'
Buffalo Springfield

The door opened. Ed walked in. He did not appear surprised to see Bonnie still sitting on the bed. He stood contemplating her with a not unpleasant expression, his dimples deepening.

'Bon! What are you doing? I thought we told you to get in that bath, get dressed and ready for dinner!'

'I already had a bath!' snapped Bonnie.

Ed smiled wryly. 'No, you haven't. Come on, I'll have to make you myself.' An easy smile transformed his face. He no longer seemed threatening at all. But Bonnie wasn't fooled by now. Too much had happened.

'NO!' yelled Bonnie. 'You will not! I'm not getting undressed or in the bath.'

'Why not? It's a great bath, gold taps, huge and it's a spa too. Turn on the jets and have a water massage. You'll love it!'

'I want a different room!' Bonnie stood facing him, hands on hips, defiant.

'Why on earth? What's wrong with this one? Fit for a King...or a Princess!'

'You know why! Because it's bugged with cameras! I will not be spied on!'

Ed smiled resignedly. 'I could deny it Bon, but I think you're smarter than that. You're right, the room could be under surveillance, but only for your own safety and I'm sure there is nothing in the bathroom.'

The bathroom door stood open, and Bonnie turned to look through to the marble and gilt decorated room. For a split second she wanted to believe him. Common sense prevailed and she shook her head determinedly.

'Nope. Don't believe you, man. Not doing it. Give me a plain room. Or you could let me out. I just want to do my concerts. I can re-schedule.'

It was Ed's turn to shake his head. 'Not going to happen Bonnie. You are much too valuable, and you know far too much. So, what are we going to do about this situation? Are you going to co-operate, or do I fetch Frankie?'

Fear threatened to overwhelm her, but her new-found inner power won the battle. She was never going to just give in, not after what she had endured in the last week. 'Fetch him if you like. Do whatever. I will not be spied on. Tell me Ed, who would be watching me? Ricky? Frankie, you?'

Ed turned on his heel and marched out of the door, slamming it behind him. She heard the key turn the lock.

***

Downstairs, Ed and Frankie decided to call Ricky in. After all, he knew her reasonably well. Damn that stupid Lane Byrd, Huggy idiot! He should be here; should be the one dealing with this shit. Now they had a minor dilemma. If she refused to play along, they would drug her and get the housekeeper to help, but it wouldn't be as satisfactory. Tomorrow night, *he* would be asking for her. He was already here in his private, secret quarters, preparing himself mentally and physically. The two men didn't know who he was. All they knew was that if his identity was ever revealed to the public, it would mean the end of their money stream, and bring shame to one of the modern world's greatest institutions.

***

Ricky walked in like a thunderclap.

'What is so important you need to get me down here?' he demanded angrily, thrusting a half smoked cigarette in Frankie's face.

'She won't co-operate at all,' explained Frankie. 'She twigged about the bugging. Won't do anything. What do you want us to do with her?'

Rick rolled his eyes. 'That is your job, not mine. I do the securing and the finances. Let me tell you...' He prodded repeatedly, 'you won't get paid if you DON'T DO THE JOB!'

His voice rose to a yell which reverberated off the panelled walls and hard floor. He stalked off, his jack-hammer steps ringing in the two men's ears.

'Go and get Mrs. Potts,' Frankie told Ed. 'I don't know how we're supposed to deal with her, and make sure she's 'pure and untainted'! Jesus!'

Mrs. Potts duly arrived, her face set like concrete, her eyes beady and her mouth drawn into folds. 'Where is she? I'll sort her out.'

'You can't touch her, remember! I know you would love to but...' Frankie wagged his finger at her. 'Hands off!'

Mrs. Potts thrust her hands deep into her apron pockets in a sarcastic imitation of submission.

'She's in her room. She needs a bath, and she needs to come down for dinner. She's hardly eaten anything in the last couple of weeks.'

The woman turned on her heel and stalked off towards the staircase.

***

The key ground in the lock. A woman, older, hard-looking, time-worn, entered the room. Bonnie was relieved. At last, she would be able to talk to someone who might listen to her; understand how she was feeling and perhaps lend her a sympathetic ear.

The woman marched straight into the bathroom without making eye contact or uttering a word and turned the bath taps on. She poured in bath salts and laid the towels out on the end of the massive marble bath. Bonnie followed her into the room, watching.

'What are you doing?' she asked.

'Running your bath my girl. Now, you need to get in here because let me tell you, you smell bad. When is the last time you washed?'

'I don't want to get undressed in here. The rooms are bugged with cameras!' protested Bonnie.

'Absolute rubbish, girl! I don't know where you got that idea from, but there are no spy cameras in this house! Now, if you don't take those disgusting jeans off, I will.'

Mrs. Potts moved towards Bonnie with a determined look on her face. 'Don't push me!'

Bonnie shrunk away clutching her arms across her skinny frame. 'You're wrong about the cameras because Frankie told me so! Who are you anyway?'

'You may call me Mrs. Potts. I keep house here. Right, off with them and in the tub!'

Bonnie looked around as if an escape route might magically appear. The Potts woman grasped her hand and twisted it, just hard enough to make Bonnie squeal.

'Alright, alright!' yelled Bonnie in her face. 'I'll do it.'

She began removing her shirt. The woman was watching her. Bonnie felt acutely uncomfortable. It was exactly the way she had felt when she had sensed Huggy right behind her. She knew that this old bag was paying more than a housekeeper's attention to her.

She shuddered. Every tiny detail about this place had some sinister undertone. She began to wonder if she really would ever see outside these walls again.

'Get on with it! Come on, hurry up. The longer you take, the longer I get to watch!'

Finally, Bonnie ripped of the rest of her clothes and jumped into the fragrant water. Mrs. Pott's eyes sharpened giving her the appearance of a bird of prey, focussed and ready to swoop. The frothing bubbles in the water gave Bonnie welcome cover and she ducked down until they threatened to fill her mouth and nose.

'There's a flannel and a sponge. Hair shampoo is on the end there.' Mrs Potts sounded like the very worst of any schoolteacher, dictatorial, severe and with a want to punish. Bonnie almost expected to hear her say that refusing would mean the cane!

'I'm going to lock you in here. I'll give you fifteen minutes and when I come back, you'd better be out and dressed. Clothes are in the dressing room. There's a connecting door. Don't worry, the dressing room door into the bedroom will be locked too!'

Bonnie was alone but not out of sight, she was sure of that. She washed herself, keeping under the bubbles, rubbed some shampoo over her spiky head and ducked under to rinse. The towels were laying across the end of the tub. Pulling one towards her she managed to wrap it around her as she stepped out without exposing too much for the audience, whoever that might be. She suspected Mrs. Potts would be in the front row. The closet was large with hanging rails, shelves and shoe racks lining each wall. The many items of underwear were nothing like she had ever worn, tiny lacy panties and bras, even suspenders and stockings. The clothes looked like something out of a movie, Italian cut dresses but no jeans or hippie skirts. She picked the most modest underwear she could find and chose a bright lemon-yellow mini dress with a white collar. The mod outfit was finished off with a pair of white tights and sling-back sandals. There was no point combing her hair. She didn't have enough! Looking in the floor length mirror, she thought she looked a lot like Twiggy. She was certainly skinny enough.

What were they planning for her? She was struggling to fathom what this 'admirer' expected from her. A pale, hollow-eyed reflection stared back at her. She blinked, the image blurred for a second and in that tiny moment, she sensed something which caused her to shiver. Suddenly she felt sick. She knew she was going to have to have sex with this man but not the kind she had dreamed her first real sexual experience would be like. That's why she had to be clean and cute and well-dressed but with underwear like a stripper! He didn't want her to sing! What had Ed said? *He'll be nice for a while, but he gets bored quickly.* And hadn't Ricky told her she would never get out of here? This guy was very well known. How could she have been so naïve, so stupid? She had always prided herself on being quite clever, but she had missed putting all the throwaway clues together to form the picture! He would use her and then... well, he would kill her. Her thoughts were interrupted by the unlocking of the door.

Dinner was a strange affair with Bonnie sitting by herself at a long dining table set with twelve places. Each place had silverware, crystal glasses, monogrammed napkins 'LB' in flamboyant script, and flatware. There were water jugs and glasses and yet Bonnie was the only guest. Mrs. Potts brought in the array of food, enough to feed a banquet of thirty or more. Ed and Frankie stood to the side. Neither ate nor drank, only kept watch. Much of the food Bonnie had never seen before. She had no idea what truffles and caviar were. She would have liked some fish and chips but nothing like that was on offer. She picked at a few delicacies and drank the water. Afterwards, Mrs. Potts brought out a huge white mound of something which to Bonnie's horror and then amusement, she set fire to. Bonnie refused to try it, especially with a name like 'bomb' something!

No-one spoke, not one word. Bonnie tried to make an overture, to engage Ed in conversation, to no avail. When Bonnie ceased eating, she folded her napkin and stood up. She was immediately escorted back to her room, where she was unceremoniously locked in for the night without so much as a 'Goodnight, sleep tight!'

Hours later as she lay in the impossibly large bed, sleep refused to come. Instead, her mind was a whirlwind of fears and dreaded possible outcomes. She turned over and over in her mind how she could weasel her way out of this. But the hard truth was irrefutable. She was imprisoned here. Why were the police not looking for her? Surely, they must be after her call from the cottage near Farrington. That detective who came to see her in hospital; he seemed like a nice man. Was he trying to find her? Weren't her mum and dad demanding she be found? What about nana? Finally sleep blurred then blocked her brain's constant turmoil sometime in the early hours.

Downstairs, final preparations for the banquet were in full swing. It had always been intended for an elite clientele.

1969

'Worst That Could Happen'
The 5ᵗʰ Dimension

The gamekeeper's hut was a tiny, wooden slatted construction which had fallen into a dilapidated state. The approach was so overgrown as to be barely negotiable. Robert had ploughed the Mercedes along behind the Morris, which was significantly smaller and more manoeuvrable, through brambles, hawthorn, and foxgloves.

On reaching the hut, Clive had pushed the rotten door open. A lantern hung from the roof which Clive lit giving the interior a dusty glow. The hut was decorated with spider webs and years of dirt and mould. A wooden bed lay against the wall covered by a large sheet of canvas. A small table and two wooden chairs completed the furnishings. An ancient rug, so filthy, it had become part of the pine floorboards in places, mouldered underfoot. The small-paned window was intact and faced the direction of the house.

'Ye can see who comes and goes from 'ere, especially at night when the 'eadlights light up the drive. With a pair o' good binoculars, ye can see the garage and back fence. I've seen a bit of goings on from 'ere, I 'ave.'

Clive tapped his nose again and flashed a knowing grin, revealing a few yellow stumps in his otherwise bare gums.

'I think I will be more than comfortable here for the night, Mr. Baker,' replied Robert.

'There's a privy out there.' Clive pointed away from the house. 'Bit rough though!'

'I'm sure I'll be fine, thank you.'

Clive pulled the canvas off the bed in a flurry of dust. A mouse scurried off the coverlet, disturbed after having settled in cosily for the night.

'Get away with yer,' chuckled Clive. 'Little old mouse won't 'urt yer. Bed's alright.'

'Once again, thank you. I'm grateful for somewhere to keep out of sight for the night.'

Clive leaned forward. 'You're a copper aren't yer? Hinvestigatin' 'im what owns the manor 'ouse!'

'I assure you, Mr. Baker, I am not a 'copper'. Now if you could let me get some rest before the morning?'

'Aye, rest. I'll see yer in the mornin' then?'

'No need. I'll be gone and I'll leave it exactly as I found it. Goodnight and thank you again.'

Finally, Clive left. Robert listened as the little Morris disappeared into the bushes. He intended to get a little sleep, wake up early and be ready to watch for anyone who might arrive or leave. He knew Dora would be coming to 'do' the girl, whom he was positive was Bonnie. He had no idea who else might be coming to the house.

He went out to his car and brought in his small carry bag, the only baggage he had brought with him in his haste to get down here. Taking the binoculars out he trained them on the house and approach. It was dark and he was not able to make out much detail. He thought some of the rooms on this side had lights on, but the curtains were so thick, it was only the faintest hint. He scanned as much of the building as he could, waiting for his eyes to adjust. It was a massive house, thought Robert. How many more windows and rooms on the other sides?

At the very top of this wing, a turret rose above the main roof. Robert followed it upwards with his glasses, working hard to keep his eyes focussed, gathering as much of the indistinct detail as he could. The top floor of the tower had small windows which were showing a faint red glow. Squinting, he concentrated, willing his eyes to gather every flicker of light and enhance the image.

'Hmm,' he said to himself out loud. 'Interesting.'

He watched for a while but there was no movement he could discern. Suddenly, tiredness overwhelmed him, not surprising since he had been on the road last night and had not slept since. He pulled the coverlet off the bed. No more mice. The sheet looked tolerable. He rolled his jacket up for a pillow, laid down and passed out into a deep sleep. An owl hooted. Robert slept on.

***

Susan was snoring softly, and the light was penetrating his closed eyelids. Must be morning. He moved to nudge Susan, but the droning continued as if she was slowly floating away from him. He was about to tell her to roll over when the snoring changed, sounding more like an airplane flying over or a...car engine!

Robert sat up in the darkness. He pressed the light on his watch. Two fifteen. Now he remembered where he was and why. Grabbing the binoculars, he stumbled in his haste to reach the window. Cursing his clumsiness, he trained the glasses in the direction of the house. Car headlights approaching the house. He followed the lights as they disappeared, then reappeared through the trees, until they stopped in the area near the garage. He was unable to make out any detail, but as the headlights died, an outside light blinked on, presumably at the rear entrance of the house.

Who would be arriving at two in the morning? Could it be a secret house guest? Robert sat on the hard wooden chair, watching. The outside light flicked off and there was no further activity. He was about to abandon his post when he spotted more car headlights, visible as a white glow above the bushes and through the trees. *Full high beams, still a distance away,* thought Robert. He watched again as the lights came closer to the Manor and replicated the scenario which had previously played out.

From then on, for at least an hour, cars arrived one after another. There must have been a dozen, though Robert had not counted. A party in the making. By four thirty, all activity outside the house had ceased and the back light remained off. Very soon, the sky would begin to lighten. He might be able to see more, but conversely, if he could see the garage, then it was probable that he might be seen by anyone at the manor house with binoculars. Would there be spotters keeping watch? He didn't know and decided to get out while the going was good.

Back in his car, he crawled along retracing the track without the aid of headlights. Keeping the revs low, he inched out until he reached the back road which would take him to the village. He decided to park in the pub carpark. No-one would think twice, assuming he was a guest.

No-one passed the Mercedes or saw the slumped figure in the driver's seat as dawn came creeping mistily from the east, bringing the salty tang of the marshlands with it. In time, the village awoke, people and vehicles began moving around. The milkman's electric truck buzzed past, then stopped and delivered a dozen bottles to the hotel. Robert got out of his car, stretched his legs, and strolled down the street until he found a small shop, which had opened its doors. He bought a paper and asked if he might buy breakfast this early on a Saturday morning.

'Yes,' the shopkeeper said, 'we can do you some eggs and bacon. Got tables out the back. Would you like tea?'

There are times when a good plate of eggs and bacon, slathered with homemade tomato sauce, and accompanied by a strong cup of tea, can taste better than the finest of cuisines. *This was one of those times* thought Robert as he crunched the bacon, slopped the sauce into the egg yolk and sopped it up with toast, then washed it down with a good slurp of sweet, milky tea. He belched appreciatively, then looked guiltily around to see if anyone heard. He was alone. He wiped his mouth with a paper serviette and decided to see if he could raise Alby yet. It was still only seven thirty.

1969

Saturday morning and Alby had found himself apologising yet again to his wife for leaving her alone. He sighed dismally, recalling how she said it was okay, while her eyes told a different story. At 7:30 in the office, he found Jim Wright already working on a pile of files.

'Morning Jim. First thing, could you get me a phone number for that address, Bonnie's biological mother?' Alby asked.

'I'll see what I can find out,' replied DS Wright.

This was Wright's favourite type of work, poring over lists. He set about it with a will. He knew the area well, having grown up very close to the village himself. He took the directory and without the aid of reading glasses, he was able to scan the minute print, looking for the right address to jump out at him.

Meanwhile, Alby tried contacting the Colemans. He rang the home number, assuming Bob would not be busy selling cars on a Saturday. The phone rang but the answering machine cut in. Alby left yet another message asking one of them to contact CID at

"

Scotland Yard as soon as possible. He then rang Rae Coleman who picked up on the second ring.

'Hello, Rae Coleman speaking.'

'Mrs. Coleman, Detective Inspector Coates.'

'Oh hello, detective. Do we have any news? I suppose you've seen the hoo-ha all over Sunday papers about Bonnie? Are they blowing it all out of proportion Alby, or is it really as bad as they say?'

Alby could tell by the tremor in her voice that Rae might be on the verge of tears, and he didn't blame her. Bonnie had been gone for over a week now with no further sightings since she telephoned 999 from the cottage. Margaret Banbury had positively identified her as the girl who came to her aid after Bramley's attack. She remembered seeing her being taken out to the car. The men had called Bonnie by name, but Margaret heard no other names mentioned. She thought they might have locked her in the boot. It sounded like a boot closing, she explained, but she had remained in the cupboard until well after the car had left, before dialling 999 herself. Since then, nothing but hunches and assumptions. No wonder Rae was beside herself!

'Rae, I must assure you that DCI Turner is doing his utmost to find her and bring her back safely. We all are. If I were you, I would concentrate on information we provide you with and be very careful about what you read in the tabloids! I rang to ask if she has contacted you at all, Rae?'

Rae snuffled on the other end of the line. 'No, detective. She hasn't. I have had reporters here banging on my door demanding interviews and screaming questions through the letter box! I've even had her fans accusing me of hiding her because she's pregnant, and others demanding money because they paid to see her sing. I don't know how much longer I can stay here. I can't even go down the street!'

'Alright Rae. Try to keep calm. What I'm going to do is arrange for an officer to stay outside your house for a while, until we find

Bonnie. Are you agreeable to that? They will field the unwelcome visitors and they can call for more help if needed. I'll send a police-woman who will be able to help you if you need anything. Call me if you have any questions.'

'Thank you, Alby. I appreciate it. I just want my granddaughter back!'

'I know you do. Have you heard from Bob or Deirdre? I have tried to contact them to no avail,' asked Alby.

'Them! No, nothing. My own son! I can't believe him. He is simply her puppet. He does and says whatever she tells him to. I wash my hands of them,' replied Rae crossly. 'You know she was adopted, Bonnie? They, *he*, couldn't father a child. They should have left it at that!'

'Yes, we are aware of that. Rae, I must go. One of us will contact you as soon as we have some news.'

Alby rang off and tried the Colemans again with the same response from the answering machine. He then dialled Rick Chambers' office, though he did not expect an answer on a Saturday. To his surprise the phone connected but it was their answering machine, with Sharon's dulcet tones proclaiming that 'Ricky was feeling groovy, but he was out of the office at the moment.'

Alby was sure he could hear her swap the gum from one side to the other, then, 'If you'd like Ricky to call you back, leave your name and number. Ta very much.'

Alby rolled his eyes and replaced the phone without leaving any name, 'ta very much!' As he was about to grab a cup of tea, Jim called him over.

'I've got it! Got the number.' He scribbled on a piece of paper and handed it to Alby.

'You're a champ, Jim. Thanks.' He dialled the number. It rang. The ring tone on the other end jangled repeatedly. Alby was close to hanging up when he heard the connection.

'Hello?' A female voice, soft as if still grappling with sleep.

'Hello. My name is Detective Inspector Coates. Could I speak with the lady of the house please?'

'Speaking.' A pause. Alby could visualise her checking the time on the bedside clock. Then, 'How can I be of help detective?'

Puzzled? Suspicious? With wakefulness rising, the voice had taken on an edge.

'Could I have your name please?' asked Alby. No information was volunteered. The phone remained silent except for the low level buzz of the lines.

Alby sighed. Why *was* he ringing her? Robert wanted to find her but what reason could Alby give? He couldn't very well ask, 'do you have brilliant blue eyes, and did you put your daughter up for adoption?' He decided this was a job for Robert to deal with.

'I apologise for calling you at this time. Can I give you a number at Scotland Yard? They will connect you with DCI Turner. He would appreciate a call from you at your earliest convenience.'

'Alright. What is the number?'

Alby gave it and rang off. He set about preparing to gather the squad which would be conducting the operation down in Suffolk. Grainger, who was trained with guns and ammunition, would head up a team armed with weapons and flak jackets. Other team members were trained in covert operations including raids. Alby informed the Ipswich Division of what they were planning. He didn't want any accidental investigating on any level to interfere with their operation. He would be ready when the call came. Even with the circumstantial evidence Robert had reported, there was no concrete evidence that Bonnie was even there, that the people at the house were planning anything more than a house party.

***

The previous night, Diedre Coleman had watched the six o'clock news in the informal drawing room. The waning sun had washed through the window and across the cream floral rug, making it look more like a Monet decorating the floor. She had watched while waiting for her husband to return. He had walked straight past the drawing room without a word, upstairs to his study, where he had a small TV. He had probably watched exactly the same news service as Dierdre, a glass of whiskey in his hand. The dinner bell had rung, and they had converged in the dining room where Gwyneth had served grilled fish for Dierdre and a roast with all the trimmings for Bob. There they had sat at opposite ends of the table, deliberately avoiding eye contact or conversation. They had not even mentioned their missing daughter!

After DCl Turner's last visit, they had reached an impasse regarding Bronwyn. Deirdre had completely shut down, refusing to discuss anything which had eventuated from the detective's findings on the adoption. It was as if she wished to erase that whole part of her life.

This morning, Bob had contemplated ringing Turner, but decided against it. The reality was that his existence depended entirely on Deirdre, something he could not afford to upset. Bronwyn and all their friends and acquaintances were unaware that it was Deirdre's family wealth which owned this house, had provided Bob with a business, and held all their assets. Bob was hog-tied. Deirdre refused to budge and had forbidden Bob to answer the phone, even to his mother. Now, when at work, Bob must obey his second in charge, Deirdre's brother, and the receptionist, their daughter, Deirdre and Bob's niece.

Bob loved Bronwyn. He was suffering severe anxiety on her behalf, but all he could do was keep up with the news and hope for the best for her. The whiskey helped, but he knew he was drinking too much in the last weeks. Sometimes he just wished he could go away, disappear, and not come back. Would Deirdre be happy? He thought so.

1969

'You Can Make It If You Try'
Sly & the Family Stone

Bonnie lay in the gargantuan bed, pulling the covers up under her chin and staring in the semi gloom at the draped curtains around the four poster. She knew it was morning, not because she had a clock or watch, but because the impenetrable black cloak of the night had thinned becoming a monochrome veil, as the barest minimum of sunlight squeezed past the curtains. The walls were so thick not even a bird could be heard outside. However, inside the house was different.

Downstairs, people were beginning to move around. Bonnie could hear muffled footsteps on stairs and floors; she could hear low murmuring voices and at one point she thought she heard a car driving away. She waited. There was nothing else she could do. The doors were locked, she had no phone, TV, or radio. All she could do was lie here until someone chose to unlock her door.

Over and over, she went through the escape route to the front door, which had been memorised yesterday. Her eyes glanced up, searching the canopy. Was there a camera up there? She couldn't tell but decided she really needed the toilet.

She slipped out of bed and made her way to the sumptuous bathroom. Using her robe, she managed to preserve most of her dignity in case she was being watched. While there, she once again searched the room for anything she might be able to use against her captors. Thinking about her escape from Huggy at the cottage, she felt proud that she had been brave. She had used her ingenuity to find a way and had succeeded. *Come on* she thought. *What can you see? What could you use? How would you use it?*

She had ruled out hitting anyone. There was nothing light enough for her to lift and wield. The chairs were impossibly solid. The bedside lamps were bracketed to the wall. There were no hand mirrors, hairbrushes or the like. She gathered her robe and tied it up around her waist, flushed and washed at the basin. Nothing here but soap and a small hand towel. The huge bath towels had been taken by Mrs. Potts and not replaced. Acutely aware that she may be under surveillance, she could do no overt searching. She wandered into the dressing room and looked at the array of clothing. She opened the drawers and screwed her nose up at the underwear. Did they, *he,* really expect her to wear suspenders? She picked up a set and twanged the elastic with the clip on the end. Twang, twang. Ouch! She twanged it against her leg. It stung and left a red mark.

She scrabbled through the drawer. How many sets of these were there? Lots! Each decorated in different coloured lace, with frills and some with sequins! A picture formed in her mind of when she and her friends would play a schoolyard game with elastic, jumping in and out of two lengths stretched between two girls. If you missed your footing, you tripped and hit the asphalt. She took out all the suspender belts. There were ten sets, enough for what she had in mind. She went into the darkest corner of the closet where she began knotting them together to form a long elastic cord. The idea had landed in her brain as she had been rubbing the red welt on her leg.

She stuffed the makeshift cord under her dressing gown and returned to the bed, where she hid the cord under the covers, then resumed looking for something, anything. There was only a small water glass on the side table. In the dressing room she pulled on a micro mini skirt and a very skimpy top. Thigh length, black patent, stiletto boots sat in the shoe rack. They might come in handy as a weapon, but she wouldn't wear them, choosing a pair of sandals instead. She sat at the dressing table and stared at herself. *You can do it, Bonnie. Concentrate! What else can you do? Think! You can't just rely on your crazy elastic trip!*

In the next half an hour, she figured out what she would do. She realised that she would have one chance and one only. To guarantee her escape she needed to throw everything at it. Aware of the possibility of cameras she pulled armfuls of underwear from the drawers and spread it all over the floor, then threw the makeshift tripping rope down too. What an untidy girl she was! She tied one end securely to the bed post, about six inches from the floor and disguised it with other items of clothing. She fetched the boots and placed them next to the bed then removed a pillowcase and placed that next to the boots. Afterwards, she filled the shampoo bottle up to the top, mixed it up and capped it. It was a squeeze bottle and would be perfect. Finally, she fetched some leather belts from the closet and casually threw them around near the bed. When she had finished, she found a light cardigan, put it on and sat at the dressing table to wait.

***

'Just taking the breakfast up. Won't be long unless she gives me trouble.' Mrs. Potts was speaking to Ed and Frankie who were eating their breakfast at the scrubbed pine table in the kitchen. The chef busied himself preparing crepes and removing trays of fresh croissants from the AGA. No-one spoke. Frankie nodded.

Mrs.Potts, climbed the stairs her keys jingling on a large, old-fashioned ring hanging from her belt. Reaching the little bitch's room, she placed the breakfast tray on a side table in the passage and turned the large iron key on the lock. She twisted the handle until the door was ajar, then picked up the tray and pushed the door with her foot. It swung open and she marched into the room.

Bonnie, who had darted into position when the lock turned, yanked on her makeshift elastic cord just as Mrs. Potts reached it. The suspender belts sprung up catching the housekeeper's foot mid-stride. Bonnie watched in fascination as the whole thing played out in slow motion. The tray and its contents launched itself into the air. Mrs. Potts pitched forward, throwing her arms out in front of her to try to break the fall. She came down hard, her chin catching the carved foot of the bed. Bonnie thought she heard her teeth crumble as they smashed together. She emitted a low howl but no more. The chin-knock had stunned her. The breakfast tray landed noiselessly on the bed but plates cutlery, the toast rack and a cup of tea all followed their own trajectory. The cup of tea landed squarely on Mrs. Potts' dazed head. Bonnie grabbed the stiletto boot and was about to drive the spike into her, when she thought better of it and gave her a fair hit over the head with the breakfast tray instead. As the woman lay there groaning, Bonnie grabbed one of the wide belts and tied Mrs. Potts' wrists firmly together with it, then used a second to tie her hands to the bedpost. Finally, she took a bread roll off the floor and shoved it in her mouth. By now the woman's eyes were bursting out of her skull with fright. Bonnie took the shampoo bottle and pointed it at her eyes.

'Are you going to give me any more trouble, Mrs. Potts? Do I need to blind you with shampoo?'

Mrs. Potts shook her head. Bonnie decided to give her a spray of the diluted shampoo anyway, then pulled the pillowcase over the woman's head and tied it firmly around her neck with a third belt. Bonnie unclipped the key ring from her belt.

'I'm going to lock you in here. Enjoy my bread roll Mrs. Potts.' Bonnie made to leave then turned to the woman on the floor. 'See you later, in court I hope!'

With that she softly closed the door and locked it. Now to remember the escape route.

****

Downstairs Frankie and Ed finished their breakfast. The kitchen being on the other side of the house from Bonnie's guestroom meant they heard nothing. Their job was to go into town and pick up some last-minute supplies for the party this evening. They took the Land Rover.

The guests were in the breakfast room where they were enjoying a huge continental feast prepared by chef for them. The conversation was animated. No-one heard anything from upstairs. Not one of them knew about the special girl. The day's activities were to include some pheasant shooting in the woods, a gourmet picnic lunch in the summer house followed by either an afternoon siesta, or maybe cards. Dinner would be an early one because the evening's entertainment was to begin at around eight. The girls would be prepped and ready. The party would begin!

1969

'The Happening'
The Supremes

Meanwhile in London, it was Saturday morning and preparations had begun for the trip to Suffolk. Alby, Grainger, and Wright were ready. Alby was expecting a call from Robert but at 7:30 am he was surprised when his phone rang.

'DS Coates.'

'Alby, Robert.'

'Mornin' guv. What's the latest down there?' replied Alby. 'I was thinking of calling you, but you beat me to it.'

'Alby, whatever is going on down here is big. Last night I watched at least a dozen cars arrive between two and four in the morning. The housekeeper has been getting deliveries from the local stores and crates of booze from the hotel, all special delivery stuff. A local woman, a beautician, has been booked for an appointment with a young lady at the house at 3 pm. The locals tell me there have often been parties at the manor since Lane Byrd bought it. They are quite adamant that there are always older men and many young 'lasses' as they put it. One chap says he has seen politicians here for those parties. The clientele are all wealthy, big

285

cars, chauffeurs, splashing around plenty of money in the town but no-one has ever discovered anything untoward.'

'I take it the young girl is Bonnie?'

'I'm betting my life on it, Alby. We might need more personnel to do this right. You're in charge of everything on the outside. I'll be right there, I hope. Wait for my radio call. I want to make sure they're not just playing poker and drinking whiskey. We have to nab 'em red-handed. Today, I've got a plan. I'll try to keep you in on it as much as I can but otherwise, you'll hear from me tonight. Just be ready.'

'Right guv.'

Alby rang off. He had a lot of work to do. It was seven forty-five.

***

Bonnie slipped into the vacant passage and began retracing the well-remembered steps towards the front entrance. Stepping lightly on the plush carpet, she inched her way along when she realised someone was coming up the stairs. Darting a look up and down she reasoned she had heard nothing on this floor outside her room. These rooms must be empty. She tried a door. It was unlocked so she let herself in and closed it behind her. Heart in mouth she turned to face the room. It was empty, another bedroom similar to hers. She squatted and placed her eye at the keyhole. Male voices boomed in conversation as they approached. Two grey-haired gentlemen dressed in satin robes and slippers strolled past. Bonnie heard 'see you downstairs for breakfast' and 'nice day for the shoot, old chap.' They continued down the corridor and Bonnie relaxed. Were there other house guests? Was one of them *him*? She shuddered and opened the door a crack, peering into the corridor. It was empty again. However, she now understood that her chances of being discovered had increased tenfold with many people in the house.

Closing the door again she leaned against it to think. Her plan had been to make for the front door, but it was obviously the main entrance where the house guests would be coming and going. She had to change plans. She needed to find another exit, but having no concept of the floor plans, she was at a loss to know which direction to go. So, the men were going towards where her room had been. She ought to keep going in the opposite direction, besides which she needed to get onto the ground floor. Her mind made up, she opened the door quietly and re-entered the passage.

***

The house was beginning to come awake. Several guests were congregating in the breakfast room, enjoying continental breakfasts, and discussing the day's coming events. No-one spoke of anything but the hunting, or croquet on the lawns. They discussed the dogs, horses, guns, and past shoots. They bemoaned the fact there would be no fox-hunting this time. Pity! Damned animal activists had taken it into their heads that it was animal cruelty! The local keeper of the hounds had sold his pack which meant the end of fox hunting at the manor for the time being.

In the breakfast room, the warm croissants began to dwindle, the coffee and tea too. Someone rang the bell, but no-one came. Someone else cursed. The tables were becoming seriously depleted when one of the guests who was a 'regular' at the manor gatherings offered to venture to the kitchen and find the damned housekeeper.

By the time he returned, some of the guests had left to dress and prepare for the shoot. Other latecomers were hovering around the tables as if willing food to magically appear.

'The housekeeper, the Potts woman isn't there!' thundered the man. 'Chef's there but he's just a frog, can't speak a word of English! Asked where the Potts woman was. All he could say was 'quel?' Course I knew what he meant. France in the war and all that but I'm not lowering myself to speak frog! There is plenty of food waiting to be brought up but…'He shrugged his shoulders as if carrying a tray of bread rolls was something he was incapable of doing himself.

These scornful words of derision had no sooner left his floppy jowls than Ricky made a grand entrance, cigarette in one hand and the morning papers under his other arm. An anomaly in this gracious country manor, with his tight jeans and Cuban boots, his dyed black hair slicked back revealing a face which chronicled a life of excess, Ricky flashed his gold ringed hand around the room.

'Morning gents! Everything to your satisfaction? Papers are here!' He stopped dead, noting that everyone in the room was staring at him as if their lives depended on some action from him. 'What?' he asked. He looked around.

'Where's the damned food, man? Where is the esteemed Mrs. Potts?' demanded the loud man.

'Oh, I see. I'll ring her. Yeah?' replied Ricky.

The man held his hand up. 'Don't bother. She's not there. In the kitchen. Only the chef. Poor form really. Bad organisation!'

Ricky plonked the papers on the table and stubbed the cigarette. 'Right, I'll get onto it. Meanwhile, check out the news!'

Ricky beat a hasty retreat, leaving the guests to the remnants of breakfast and the morning papers.

In the kitchen he found the chef in the process of preparing more trays of croissants with jam and cream, bacon, eggs and sausages and kippers. The kettle was steaming furiously. Ricky rolled his eyes skyward and turned the gas off. Where was she? He knew Frankie and Ed had gone into town. He couldn't ask chef. Ricky had never had the benefit of learning a language at school, in fact learning anything academic at school had been hit and miss for him. He wondered if she might be in the bathroom. Not like her though, just to leave without telling someone. She ran a tight ship. Had she taken Bonnie's breakfast up? That was a definite possibility.

***

In any case, he decided to give her a few more minutes grace before going to look for her. He sat down and poured himself a glass of orange juice, watching the chef labour over the hot plates, sweat pouring off his face mixing with the oil dripping from his hair and the steam from the range. Occasionally he threw a nervous glance in Ricky's direction, between handling trays of bread rolls, but Rick Chambers was studying his orange juice.

Ricky was mulling over the past few days. Nothing had really gone to plan this time. He sincerely hoped the girls were being taken care of by whoever had been assigned as their 'house-mother'! He, Rick, had had nothing to do with them. He was higher up the ladder than that. His task was usually to source the 'flowers', the special ones. All the others were selected from various places by the likes of Frankie and Ed. Many had been off-loaded through Ricky's music business though. Some made it, some didn't. It was inevitable that there would be culling along the way. The ones who made it here would be treated well until they had completed their assignments with the clientele. Afterwards they would be shipped offshore to Europe, where they would be sold into prostitution or slavery. There was no trail left in England. Hundreds of girls went missing every year. The unsolved cases were lying collecting dust in the archives, the girls lives forgotten, except by the grieving families. The clients had no idea and cared not what happened to their entertainment after they had finished with them. The money was very good too, Ricky mused. Funnelled into Swiss bank accounts which belonged to people who were either dead or had never existed. It all worked like a well-oiled machine. He, Ricky would find it difficult to make that kind of money in his legit business. He smoked thoughtfully. Time drifted away.

***

Bonnie made her way back along the corridor towards the staircase which swept down into the entrance hall and the front doors. Once on the stairs she would be completely exposed if anyone were to come out of the front parlour or any of the other rooms off that entrance. As she inched closer, she could hear voices again. They were getting louder, men's voices. It sounded as if there might be half a dozen coming from somewhere within the house towards that front door. Bonnie knew she couldn't risk the stairs. They would have to wait. She peeked around the corner. No-one down there yet. She took a chance and sprinted lightly across the landing to the other side. On this side, the corridor was almost identical to the one she had come from, however, at the first junction there was an alcove with a small door, set well back. She ducked in there and tried the door. It was locked but there was a keyhole. She had Mrs. Pott's keys but there were dozens of large keys, none of which were marked. She peered in and though the light was dim, she could see it was a spiral staircase. *Pity it's locked,* she thought. *Might be an attic I could have hidden in for a while. Never mind, there must be other places.*

And there were. After carefully negotiating several passages, she came to a much less grand part of the house, probably servants quarters of old. She found a small but cosy sitting room which had not been occupied for years, judging by the layers of dust everywhere. She let herself inside and found a large key hanging on the fireplace mantle. It fitted the door. She locked herself in and sat down to contemplate. Had they found the Potts woman yet? Would they be looking for Bonnie already? It was a huge house and searching every nook and cranny would take hours. Bonnie decided to stay here for a while. She began to investigate her new hiding place.

1969

I

t had turned into a glorious autumn day. White puffy clouds rose into towers against the cornflower blue sky. Remnants of the coastal mist still lingered close to the ground in places, dancing in thinning swirls as the car swept past. Robert had left the carpark and was now on the road, which not surprisingly was named Priory Road. He was heading into the town centre where shops and businesses were already doing good trade. He needed fuel and spotted a petrol station up ahead on the left. He pulled in and the attendant began filling up with super, while Robert's instinct was to observe everything around him. In the rear vision mirror he saw a vehicle pull in behind, waiting for the pump. It was the green Land Rover. As the attendant finished, Robert got out of the car. He watched the young, long-haired lad clean his windscreen.

'Oil and water, dad?' the youth said.

'Thank you, no. How much do I owe you?'

In the Land Rover, two men occupied the front seats. The driver waved an acknowledgement to Robert to take his time. Robert nodded and returned to the task.

As he opened his wallet, he covertly took a look at the two in the Land Rover trying to catalogue as much detail as possible through the windscreen. Both had dark hair, dark glasses, and leather jackets. They were the same two he had seen leaving the Manor, he was sure of it.

'Five pounds ninepence thanks.'

The lad held out a grubby, oil soaked hand, the nails long and blackened. Robert pulled out a five pound note and a shilling.

'Keep the change, son,' he said placing the money into the oily palm.

Robert left the petrol station and drove down the street, found a space to pull into the kerb and sat in his car watching the Land Rover until it too pulled away from the station. The morning traffic had escalated by now, but Robert managed to enter the flow of traffic several car lengths behind the men and tail the four wheel drive. Keeping his distance, he followed discreetly, slipping behind when necessary and picking them up again as they visited different places along the high street. Nothing unusual, groceries, the newsagent where they bought magazines, a general store where they came out with a brown paper bag of things unseen.

Robert was considering giving up the tail when the Land Rover suddenly squealed the tyres, executing a sharp left hand turn into a narrow side road. Robert, three cars behind, waited until he reached the road and swung into it to follow them. The Land Rover was nowhere to be seen. The lane was a passage between rows of old brick buildings on both sides, so tall that the light which penetrated to street level was cut significantly. The Mercedes crawled along as Robert looked ahead trying to discern where the road was going, when the green land Rover shot out from a side road, pulling straight in front of him blocking his way. Robert slammed on the brakes and screeched to a halt. One of the men began to get out of the vehicle. Robert threw the Merc into reverse and jammed his foot on the accelerator, sending the car into a reverse swerve back down the lane. The man jumped back into the passenger seat; the driver reversed up. With an ear piercing squeal, he applied full throttle, wrenched the wheel, and slid into a ninety degree turn, bearing down at speed on Robert's reversing car. He accelerated, smashing the Land Rover's sturdy bumper into the front of the Mercedes, which shuddered badly, threatening to send the car into the wall. Robert pushed the accelerator to the floor, struggling to control the wheel in reverse. The other vehicle sped up, accelerating hard and again collided heavily with his car. This time the impact resulted in a sudden gush of water and Robert knew his radiator had been damaged. It exploded in a plume of boiling water and steam. The engine was still running though Robert could hear a clattering sound from under the bonnet. He tried to keep going but the engine was faltering and in seconds sputtered and died.

The two men were upon Robert before he had a chance to open his door. They yanked him out of the car. Although Robert was well trained in defensive tactics, he had been taken in an instant and these two were strong, tough men. He connected a couple of punches and tried in vain to use their weight against them but the two of them overpowered him and frog marched him to their car. There, they shoved him in the back where he was joined by the more unpleasant of the two men. The other pulled some thick tape out of the shopping bag and bound Robert's hands and mouth.

'Now then, who are you and why were you following us?' the ugly one demanded.

Robert shook his head. He was gagged after all.

'Don't worry, we can wait 'til we get you back to the house!'

Robert watched as the man busied himself pouring fuel around his Merc. Returning to the Land Rover, he slammed into the driver's seat, tossed a match at the car, then reversed up and into the cross-lane. Gunning it, he slewed the four by four into a spin, then into the lane in the opposite direction leaving Robert's car with blue and yellow flame licking every panel. As they sped off, a large blast could be heard as the flames reached the fuel lines and travelled towards the petrol tank.

1969

'Bad Girl'
Neil Sedaka

Ricky was roused from his reveries by the sound of a vehicle outside. It was unmistakably the Land Rover. Good, about time! he thought. He waited for Frankie and Ed to enter by the back door into the kitchen. After ten minutes he was wondering what the hell they were up to. Had everyone in this house gone mad? Lost their marbles? He lit another cigarette, crushing the gold box which was now empty and throwing it on the hearth in front of the AGA. About to go outside he was stopped by both men as they came into the kitchen.

'What took you so long? How hard is it to pick up cigarettes from town?' he snarled. 'And what were you up to in the garage?'

Frankie lit his own cigarette and blew a stream of smoke. 'Just a bit of trouble in town. Tell you later. Nothing to worry about.'

'Where the hell is Mrs. Potts?'

Frankie and Ed exchanged puzzled looks.

'Mrs. Potts? Why, what do you mean?' said Frankie.

'She's not here! Do either of you see her? She's gone AWOL!'

'The last time we saw her she was just taking the girl's breakfast tray up,' volunteered Ed. 'Said she wouldn't be long unless Bonnie gave her...trouble. That was at least an hour ago. Shit!' Both men leapt up.

'Jesus Christ! What else?' yelled Rick.

He followed them through the maze of corridors and stairs up to Bonnie's room. The door was closed and locked. They listened but could hear nothing.

'Bonnie?' called out Ed. 'Has Mrs. Potts been up with your breakfast yet?'

No answer.

'Bon?'

Again, no answer, then a faint sound, a moan or sob. Hard to tell. Ed put his eye to the keyhole. All he could see was the opposite wall and the closet door open. The room was so large that the bed was too far to the left to be seen.

'Mrs. Potts, are you there?'

Now the moaning was louder and accompanied by a thump, thump, thump.

'Have you got a key?' asked Ricky pushing forward. He began banging on the door.

'Open the door! Open the bloody door!'

'I'll have to go downstairs and find one.' Ed said. 'You would never break these doors down. Solid oak with cast iron locks. You'll have to wait.'

While Ed sprinted off down the corridor, Rick paced back and forth alternately uttering expletives and yelling through the door. He checked his watch every five seconds, but the time dragged on. After a couple of minutes Frankie volunteered to go down and find out what was going on with the keys. Rick looked as if one of the prominent blood vessels in his temple would explode.

'I'll go. Bad enough with one incompetent moron down there, let alone two!' He stomped off.

Now it was Frankie's turn to pace. He put his mouth to the

keyhole. 'Mrs. Potts, are you alright?'

The thumping resumed. It sounded like someone banging on the floor.

'Right, here's the keys,' Ed shouted as he ran towards the room. He shook a large key ring holding dozens of keys.

'I bloody well hope they're labelled!' Frankie said. 'Here give 'em to me!'

He snatched the keys. Every key had a number yet none of the doors were numbered.

'Is there a list of which key fits which room? he asked Ed scornfully. 'Because how are we supposed to know which key to use?'

Ed, completely fed up, sighed resignedly. 'You will have to try them one at a time.'

Finally, when there were only a couple of keys left, the lock turned, and Ed and Frankie pushed the door open.

Mrs. Potts lay next to the bed, her hands still securely tied to it, the pillowcase still over her head. The banging had been her stomping her feet on the floor. Ed undid the pillow. Mrs. Potts was a mess. Her mouth was still full of bread roll. Much of the softer middle had become soggy with saliva and was spilling out of the corners of her mouth, down her chin and all over her clothes. The undigested crusts still filled her mouth. Her eyes were red and swollen, tears streaming from the corners mixing with the doughy bread.

Ed untied her hands and helped her up. She fled to the bathroom and could be heard coughing and choking for some time. When she re-appeared, she had washed and rinsed out her mouth and dried her eyes.

'Did she do this?' Frankie asked.

Mrs Potts nodded. 'She is pure evil, that girl. She set a trap and caught me. Look! On the floor. All those suspender belts! And she has the keys!'

'How long?'

'Just before you left. As soon as I opened the door, I tripped on *that!* I have no idea what time it is.'

'She could be anywhere, anywhere!' Frankie muttered through clenched teeth. He simply could not believe this had happened. Never had any of the girls or 'flowers' pulled off such a stunt. Finding her could be impossible in this house.

Downstairs, they told Ricky the news. Bonnie had escaped, again, and had the house keys. Ricky grabbed scant handfuls of his long hair and looked as if he would tear what was left of it out. None of them could come to terms with the enormity of the situation. The girl was loose, hiding or lost somewhere in this house of over a hundred rooms. They had a houseful of guests, high profile people here for a purpose. Somewhere in the east wing, there were the girls. Now adding to this, Frankie told Rick about the man they had tied up in the cellar underneath the garage.

'Who is he?' Rick snapped.

'Don't know. He was following us. Dressed like a businessman or a copper. Haven't spoken to him yet.' Frankie replied.

Ricky grabbed Frankie by the throat and thrust his face within inches. 'Did it occur to you it might be one of our guests?'

'No, he's not.'

'Show me.'

Ricky marched out towards the garage followed by the two men.

'You idiots! Do you know who you have here?' Ricky barked, standing at the edge of the wooden hatch door.

The men shrugged.

'He was following us!'

'Frankie, Ed, meet Detective Chief Inspector Turner, the very man in charge of the operation to find Bonnie Summer!'

***

Robert watched the scene play out from his position on the floor of the cellar where Frankie had unceremoniously thrown him.

He had landed hard. There would be bruises, but he didn't think he had any fractures. His hands and feet were now secured with silver tape which was also wrapped around his head and across his mouth. Thankfully he could breathe freely through his nose. He cursed himself for his ineptitude, being caught like that. How many tails had he successfully carried out in his career? Dozens. But this time he had become too sure of his own ability and slipped up. Or perhaps his mind had been too pre-occupied lately. Looking back, he realised he should have driven straight on instead of into the narrow laneway which provided a perfect trap. And here was Rick Chambers. Well, he had guessed as much.

Ever since he and Alby raided the Notting Hill den, Robert's obsession with Bonnie Summer had driven him sometimes blindly, and often knowing his behaviour was bordering on irrational. Now he was in this predicament because of exactly that. Irrational behaviour. He wondered what the others in his Division thought of his impromptu trips up to Birmingham and down here to Suffolk.

'Detective Chief Inspector Turner, the very man in charge of the operation to find Bonnie Summer.' Rick Chambers said.

Robert nodded and voiced a greeting, 'mmnn' through his nose to Rick, who ignored him. Instead, he asked Frankie to remove the tape from Robert's mouth. Frankie pulled the tape which Robert felt sure took a strip of hair from around his head. He refused to cry out, though the pain was acute.

'Now Detective, the tables are turned, yeah? Who hasn't got their ducks in a row now?'

'I have a feeling, things aren't going exactly to plan for you, Mr. Chambers. Where is Bonnie Summer?' asked Robert. He noticed Ricky looked very stressed, his hair in disarray, his hands shaking.

'Bonnie? Why should I know where she is? In Devon I thought.'

'Come now Ricky, don't take me for a fool. Where is she? Let me tell you that I have a crack team heading down here as we speak which is well equipped to take you and everyone involved in this operation of yours down. They know as much as I do,' Robert eyed Ed and Frankie, 'and you and your cronies are going for a long holiday, I can assure you.'

'Why should I believe you? Anyway, what makes you think Bonnie is here? Your crack team will be here raiding a shooting party, that's all. You would be the laughingstock of Scotland Yard, Turner. I doubt you'd be keeping your job, wasting all that public money! Except, you won't be seeing the outside of this place again!'

Ricky's grin moulded his already creased face into a grotesque mask of humour. He pulled out a new packet of cigarettes, opened it and using his gold lighter, lit up, drawing deeply to calm his mood.

'And why would you have me incarcerated in this cellar if you are hosting a shooting party? Perfectly legal, I would have thought. You're scared, Ricky. Very scared and you should be. I intend to make sure you get everything you deserve.'

'Let's go. Deal with him later. Got other pressing business lads.'

The three left without replacing the tape on Robert's mouth. Robert saw the fear on Ed and Frankie's faces. They were not equipped to deal with the way this was developing. They feared a dark future in a dark cell for a long, long time.

1969

'There's Gonna Be a Showdown'
The Johnnys

Cars, vans, and personnel were gathering in Ipswich Police Headquarters. Detective Sergeant Alby Coates was heading up the operation in the absence of DCI Turner.

Alby had waited for contact from him until ten, but none had come, and he had made the call to mobilize the troops. With no communication from his DCI, Alby had had to admit that Robert could be in trouble.

After a detailed reconnaissance, he and the other detectives had formulated a plan of attack. Working on the last information he had received from Robert, Alby assumed the action at the house would be starting around eight or nine tonight. He planned to have his STF, Special Tactical Force, placed around the perimeter of the house on all sides, watching every access and window closely. The rest of them would wait a mile or so away, concealed down a little used side road as darkness came. They would all be in radio contact, ready to swoop on his signal. Alby would be in STF vehicle 1 with Grainger. Adrenalin at the Ipswich headquarters was running high as they checked all the gear, ammunition and went over the modus operandum.

***

In the town, Dora Thorley received a telephone call from the Manor. The beauty appointment had been cancelled unexpectedly. She needn't bother turning up. There was no other explanation and the caller simply hung up. Dora rang her mother, ranting. How did they expect her to just forget about a fifty pound job? Where was the consideration? Didn't they realise she had put off other clients to do this one job? And no explanation! Lady Thorley said she would ring the Manor herself. After repeated efforts ringing the number, she gave up. No-one was answering. She rang her friend Jane Forcedyke to ask if she knew what was going on. She didn't. Jane wondered if the mystery man she had met in the pub would still be meeting her, or if he had anything to do with it. Not knowing anything about him or where he might be staying, she resolved to be at the pub at four o'clock as agreed, to see if he would turn up.

***

Robert lay in the cellar in the semi dark, the only light penetrating through the wooden trapdoor which had deteriorated enough to allow gaps to form between the planks. The thick tape binding his ankles and wrists was beginning to cut the circulation. His feet were aching painfully as were his hands which were turning a strange bluish red. He had to try to release the tape before the loss of circulation went too far. His eyes had adjusted to the dim light, and he searched his surroundings looking for anything to cut the bindings. The roughly bricked floor scraped and tore into Robert's knees as he managed to shuffle across it, stirring the dust until his throat burned and he felt a great need to cough. He fought against it and continued to work his way across the floor, more slowly and carefully now to avoid disturbing the fine powdery dust, the uneven bricks ripping holes in the knees of his trousers.

Those two men, Robert thought, *I don't think they are overly smart, far from it in fact!* Had they checked the cellar before unceremoniously throwing him down here? He thought not. Having to deal with him had occurred unexpectedly. They had needed to make a quick decision.

He continued to search around him. Most cellars would have something that would cut or saw the tape. *Must keep looking* he told himself.

***

Bonnie sat in her small hideaway room, listening. She had continued to hear faint voices, sometimes people moving about close by and then outside, vehicles driving away from the house. As the morning dragged on, all became quiet, and no-one had come close to the door behind which she hid. She had no watch or other way of telling what time it was. She was beginning to feel very hungry, remembering the breakfast tray flying through the air, the food uneaten. Her stomach growled loudly. She turned the key gently in the lock which gave with an audible click. She froze and listened. Nothing. Gingerly she twisted the knob and pulled the door ajar allowing a tiny gap. Putting her ear to it she fine-tuned her hearing. Still nothing. She opened the door into the main corridor and looked around. The corridor, much narrower than those in the main parts of the house was empty. She stepped out. Here the carpets were not as plush, the walls a little shabbier and the lighting simple pendants rather than grand hanging candelabra. She crept back towards the main north south corridor. Although no sounds of life could be heard, the house spoke in soft creaks and groans; *just the voice of a very old house*, Bonnie told herself as behind her, she heard another creak.

She concentrated hard on remaining quiet and vigilant. Suddenly something touched her shoulder, a feather touch and fleeting. She started.

'Do not turn around, Bonnie.'

***

The woman paced the large drawing room, repeatedly checking the silver watch adorning her elegant wrist. 'Eleven fifteen! What is happening?' she asked herself out loud.

She found her silver cigarette case, shook out a slim cigarette and placed it in a long, ebony, and silver holder. She lit the cigarette with a matching black and silver lighter and took a long draw, savouring the calming flavour. She had explicit instructions, as she did every time, to remain in the designated rooms, make sure the girls were prepared and wait for the signal to escort them to the ballroom. By now though, the girls should have had breakfast, but no-one had come. In fact, Eloise, which was not her real name, had not seen or heard from anyone since last night. There was no telephone in their apartment style section of the house and the doors were locked.

Eloise popped her head around the door to the sitting room adjoining the bedrooms occupied by the twelve girls. They were huddled together on a sofa, staring with terrified eyes, clutching at each other, some whimpering.

'Come now, ladies! I'm sure there will be some breakfast soon. Perhaps you would like a shower?' She clapped her hands in their faces. 'Come on! Up!'

The girls shrunk back even further into the cushions, none of them uttering more than a sob or a moan.

Eloise, elegant, beautifully dressed, well spoken, who in fact had once been the manager of a seedy brothel in Birmingham, reverted to her native accent.

'I told you bleedin' scrubbers. Get on with it now or else you know what I will do!'

She spat the instructions, her voice harsh and cruel. As one, the group of young girls, some as young as fourteen, shuffled into the bathroom and closed the door. They did indeed know what she could do, and some had sore joints from having arms bent viciously backwards. One girl had dared to stand up to her and demand they be released. Eloise had wrapped a handful of the girl's hair around her fist and yanked her head around, causing a painful neck sprain and the loss of a tuft of hair. Nothing visible of course. That would never do.

Eloise continued to pace and fret. This had never happened before. She cursed her contact, whom she knew as Mr. White. If he had mucked up this assignment...She smoked the cigarette frantically. She could feel the blood rising.

***

Across the country the papers were now carrying headlines about Bonnie's disappearance. It had now been nearly a week since Bonnie Summer had been reported missing. The Devon story had held somewhat tenuously until after the Manchester Concert debacle which had been cancelled. When Bonnie's manager Peter Farmer/Bramley had disappeared and was later found dead in Birmingham, followed by her record producer, Rick Chambers, vanishing from the scene, the public were desperate for news of their favourite pop star. The police had had nothing more to say after the press release. Bonnie's fans began gathering outside the record company building, bringing flowers and teddy bears. Many were convinced Bonnie had met with foul play and were demanding answers.

The police now knew that she had been taken by Bramley and had escaped him, that she had been able to make a triple nine call near Farrington and that she was no longer there, presumed to have been taken again, this time by two men in a black car. The case had become more and more twisted over the last few days. None of this had been shared with the press, the comment always, that they were doing everything they could to bring her home safely. The operation now codenamed 'Field of Flowers' could so easily be compromised if any of the details were released to the public.

On the outskirts of Alderwell, unmarked police vehicles were gathering in a farmyard. The old farmhouse had been abandoned many years ago. Old crops, gone to seed had begun to encroach through doors, growing inside where soil had been deposited over the years. A sapling had sprung up in one room and was rapidly reaching a hole in the roof where it would flourish in the open, as saplings should. The yard was littered with rusted farm machinery, old washing machines, broken, rotted furniture, pots and pans and the detritus of lives long gone. Now, there was life once more as DS Coates' STF assembled to wait, radios crackling and tensions building. News had come through of a car bomb or similar in Alderwell. Alby instructed the police to attend quickly without attracting any more attention and to dismiss the press by claiming it as an accident caused by a crash and a fuel leak.

*** *** ***

In the cellar, Robert had managed to work his way across the floor to a workbench with sturdy wooden legs, reinforced with steel straps attaching them to the benchtop. He had easily used these to cut through the tape around his wrists and was now releasing his ankles, all the while listening keenly for any sounds of someone approaching. With a last yank on the tape, he freed his legs and was able to stand up, nearly knocking himself senseless on a low beam. He brushed himself down, feeling the tears in his trousers where he had crawled across the rough floor.

The cellar was very dark, even though his watch read 11:55 am. In the few hours he had been down here, his eyes had adjusted well to the low light, and he was able to see the trap door where faint light penetrated. Looking around he saw the cellar walls were stone and red brick. There were no other exits. It looked to him as if this might have been simply a storage cellar, entered as it was from the garage which used to be the stables. He tried reaching up to the trapdoor, but he could barely get his fingertips to the wood. With only the small amount of effort he was able to exert, it wouldn't budge, locked from above. Robert studied the hatch. Some of the wooden boards were showing signs of wood rot. He searched the dim space looking for a shovel or axe, anything to try splintering the boards.

Robert skirted the walls being careful to avoid tripping or knocking things over. He didn't want to make any noise and more importantly, to hurt himself. His fingers traced the rough brick inch by inch as he scuffed his feet along the floor. Suddenly, crack, crack! It sounded like a gunshot, then another, followed by a volley of them. Robert stopped and exhaled, trying to calm his racing heart. The shooting party, of course! That meant less chance of being disturbed for a while, he hoped.

His hand closed upon a handle, round and smoothed by many greasy hands over the years, a yard broom. It was the type with a long, sturdy handle and stiff bristles. The cellar was quiet, other than the background hush of the world outside and now repeated volleys of gunshot. Robert tried not to hurry back towards the hatch with the broom but failed. His thoughts of Bonnie in that house drove him. The handle was long enough and surely strong enough to break through some of the rotting boards but then what? Although the cellar ceiling was low, Robert doubted his ability to lever himself up through the hatch. Frankie and Ed had simply thrown him down there. He had hit the floor hard. The access ladder must be up in the garage.

Robert placed the broom against the wall and continued to squint around in the gloom. He worked his way to the only wall he had so far not explored. The floor was littered with all kinds of items designed to trip him or cause him to stumble. The best method he discovered was to shuffle his feet like an ice breaker through sheet ice. As he neared the wall, something slowly began to take shape, something he knew was his salvation, a step ladder! The time was 12:37 pm.

1969

ANTICIPATION

'Pale Moon'
Frank Sinatra

I stand outside my door in the quiet. The shadows comfort me. The silence calms me. I listen to the silence. It speaks to me, inside me. I slip the key into the lock, but a form, a shape, briefly changes the shadows around me. I turn in time to see the waif, white, ethereal, tiny like a wood nymph. It is her!

I take a breath to quiet myself. I feel the blood swelling in my arteries and veins, racing to every extremity, energising, heating, throbbing, but I must calm it. Too soon! The temptation is enormous. Unable to quell the tide completely, I slide into the corridor behind her. She doesn't hear me. I am close now, close enough to touch. I flick my hand on her neck and shoulder, the white skin sending electric shocks through my fingertips. She shudders.

'Do not turn around, Bonnie!'

I am so close. My tongue wants to taste her neck and trace upwards to the shell ear. It flicks in and out between my lips but does not touch her. Instead, I remove a silk cravat from my neck and deftly bring it across her face, covering her eyes tying it firmly at the back.

'Turn around, Bonnie, slowly,' I say, my voice low and as smooth and silky as the cravat blindfolding her.

Her paleness, ghostlike in this little used corridor, contrasts with the dark woods, carpet, and drapes. She is like a moon moth, fragile, insubstantial, and drawn to my light. She turns her head towards my voice and my breath catches. I place my fingertips, nothing more, on her alabaster shoulders and turn her around in front of me revealing the soft dimples under her clothing. It is too much! I propel her to my door. I unlock the door, barely able to take a breath, and gently push her inside. She utters not a sound.

'Welcome to my secret place, Bonnie. I have waited a long time to meet you.'

1969

Robert scrambled through the hedge on the side of the access road, by which he had earlier arrived in the Land Rover. Shots could still be heard out in the woods, but the yard had been deserted when he had emerged from the garage. He had marvelled at the bright sky, the autumn sun still high and the welcome warmth on his back. His plan was to get to the main road then skirt into town keeping under cover. He needed to find a telephone and reasoned that the pub would be the place to go. His problem was his decrepit appearance, filthy with dust and dirt, trousers ripped, shoes scuffed and knees sporting dried blood.

Now he was at the road, having made his way past the gates without incident. This was not a major road and had minimal traffic, making his progress towards the town more rapid than he had expected. Most of the time he shambled along on the bitumen, only ducking for cover on hearing a vehicle. He continued towards town. His watch now read 1:51 pm. He could see the speed limit sign up ahead and the sign, 'Alderwell: Home of the Famous Alderwell Priory'. He was now passing houses, approaching the beginning of the business area, and felt comfortable relaxing a little. It was unlikely he would be targeted in plain sight. He knew there was a telephone box at the pub, so he headed there. Admittedly, he was drawing some attention, his appearance out of kilter with the other shoppers, commuters, and tourists. Eventually, an elderly woman, bent over a walking stick, thick glasses and wearing a pink straw hat decorated with multicoloured silk flowers, stopped him to enquire if he was alright. She proclaimed to be a member of the local service group which took it upon itself to 'serve and help protect the local community'. Robert explained that his car had broken down and he had taken a fall in the dark. He was going straight to the telephone box to make a call, and he thanked her for her concern.

Finally, he reached the Priory Inn where the telephone box stood on the roadside. He called London, hoping to catch DS Coates. He was immediately connected to Alby.

'Guv!' Alby waved his hand around to the others to 'shush' them. 'Where are you?'

'I'm in Alderwell. Where are you?' replied Robert.

'We're just outside the town at an abandoned farm. We were waiting for your communication. What's going on?'

'Too much to go into the details now. Listen, I've lost my car and my bags. I'm in a bit of a state actually. Would somebody be able to get me a set of clean clothes, anything will do, and pick me up. I'm in the telephone box right outside the pub. When I get there, I'll update you on what I've learned. Bonnie is here, at the manor and so are other girls. Look, pick me up, no marked cars, alright? Then I'll fill you in and we'll finalise our plans.'

'Oh, bloody hell. Alright. I'll get Jones to come down in an unmarked car in plain clothes. You're at the pub, you say?'

'Yes, in the phone box. I'll wait until I see Jones then.' Robert left the box, noticing a park bench on a patch of grass bordered by flower beds, right next to it. He sat, put his head down and waited in the sun.

1969

'Can't Help Myself'
The Four Tops

While Eloise continued to fume with frustration in the apartments, Bonnie found herself being propelled forward through a door by fingertips which felt almost spider-like on her skin.

'Stairs, Bonnie. Take the banister and feel your way.'

The male voice was calm, very low, almost musical but not threatening in any way. She felt un-nerved but not frightened, annoyed to have been caught but curious, nonetheless. Although her hands were free and she could have easily pulled the blindfold away, she did not. It was as if she were hypnotised.

The stairs were spiral. Bonnie counted sixteen of them before reaching a small landing and another door. She heard the key, then the door swing open with a slight scuffing sound and she was ushered through.

'Welcome Bonnie, you may remove your blindfold.'

Her hands rose to her face, her fingers grasped the top of the silken cloth and she slowly pulled it down around her neck. An inexplicable shiver ran through her. Eyes still closed, she waited, her heart thumping in her chest.

'Open your eyes,' the voice urged.

She blinked her eyes open but kept them down. The room was lit by filtered sunlight which cast gothic shapes on the thick carpet at her feet. She could feel the presence before her, but something prevented her from lifting her gaze. He moved towards her, and the spidery fingers took her hand.

'You are beautiful, Bonnie. More beautiful than I had imagined.'

Bonnie looked up. Before her stood a man, not much taller than her, his face hidden by a red and gold mask. Glossy, dark curls framed the mask which covered the face. She noted the exposed skin was also dark. Though he had a cultured accent, British without a doubt, Bonnie guessed his heritage might be Caribbean, Pakistani, African or similar. Insanely, he was dressed in Shakespearean style pantaloons, stockings, and stiff brocade waistcoat. He sported a prominently rotund belly and an equally prominent codpiece.

He continued to hold her hand and she fancied she could see him licking his lips beneath the mask. Instantly the spell was broken, and she wanted to burst out in gales of laughter, but the intensity of the black eyes watching her through the holes in the mask prevented her. *Not only a masked ball,* she thought, *but fancy dress too.* She wondered what outlandish creation had been put aside for her if it came to that. Bonnie did not intend to let it. She would use all her resources to outwit him and escape.

'Who are you, what's your name, man?' asked Bonnie, slowly withdrawing her hand from his.

Ridiculously, he adopted a balletic pose and swept a deep, theatrical bow.

'You may call me William, or Master if you prefer,' he replied grandly. 'Won't you take a seat?' He gestured towards a sofa against the wall of the circular room.

Bonnie understood that she was in a tower. 'What do you want with me, *William?*' she emphasised the name.

'What would you like from me, my darling?'

'I would like you to unlock that door and let me go, what do you think? And don't call me that! How old are you, William? Fifty, sixty? Old enough to be my father!'

'My dear, you have not been averse to sharing yourself with men of my age and I can promise you, that any experiences you have with me will be ultimately more rewarding, special, even exceptional. You have nothing to fear, providing you release yourself to me, and let me guide you through the most sensual and erotic pleasures you have experienced in your young life. Trust me. We will make beautiful music together, you and I.'

The man's voice, almost simpering, failed to persuade Bonnie.

'I just want to go home. My parents and my nana will be missing me.'

A small sigh escaped the mask. 'Bonnie, I know everything about you. Don't try to fool me. Your parents have failed to show any real concern as to your whereabouts. Come through. I promise, you will experience more wonders than you had ever imagined.'

William placed a flaccid hand in the small of her back and guided her to another door. Bonnie shuddered again, but this time with revulsion.

***

Eloise had had enough. She had had no communication since her arrival with the girls. Checking her watch, the time surprised her. A quarter past three! What the hell was going on? She had waited long enough. The doors to the apartments were locked, however, there were windows in the rooms and French doors in one of the salons. Well, she knew what she would have to do. She grabbed a thick towel from one of the sumptuous baths and wrapped it around her fist and lower arm. One firm punch was enough to smash the old glass in one door, then she cleared enough shards from the frame so that she was able to gingerly step through. Out in the afternoon sun, she found herself on a brick-tiled path on the edge of a formal garden, presumably at the side of the mansion. Throwing the towel back in the room, she began stalking purposefully towards the front of the house.

I'll show them not to mess with me, she thought. *Where is that useless man?*

The girls, who heard the smash, crept timidly into the salon where the splintered glass could be seen sprayed across the carpet. On seeing this and the way out, one of the older girls who was wearing shoes, tip-toed to the door and peeked outside. She was just in time to catch the sight of the old woman disappearing around the corner. Turning back to the rest of the girls, she cautioned them to find their shoes as quickly as possible. When they were assembled, she carefully stepped over the glass, through the door frame and beckoned them to follow her. They made for the back of the house, in the opposite direction to which the woman had hurried.

'Don't make a sound,' she whispered. 'And keep down!'

None of them knew where they were or what they would do, except try to make as much distance from the house as they could without being seen. They kept low and quiet. All were young and agile. It did not take long for them to infiltrate the formal gardens and disappear between the rows of hedges and low shrubs. Spasmodic gunshots could still be heard echoing from the woods, the last few determined shooters trying for game. The girls ran on. The older girl, who had assumed the role of leader of the group urged them on, hoping to reach a village or town where they might find a police officer. Surely, they would then be safe.

***

Robert waited on the park bench. He marvelled at how people walked straight past without so much as a glance. He supposed everyone these days had their own busy agenda. People didn't seem to have much time for others. Those who did cast him a sideways glance, quickened their step. No-one wished to interfere in the business of this shabby, down at heel tramp on the seat. He was quite relieved at his anonymity. In fact, it had allowed him to spend the last hour quietly observing the comings and goings of people on the main street, the shoppers, businesspeople, children, and babies.

A sharp tap on the shoulder broke his reveries.

'My goodness, what on earth has happened to you?'

'Jane, Mrs. Forcedyke!' Robert turned to see the tall, willowy woman silhouetted against the brash sunlight of the middle afternoon.

'Were you waiting for me?' she asked. 'We were to meet in the snug at four, weren't we? I'm afraid I have some bad news. I do not have any photographs to show you. Dora's appointment was unaccountably cancelled at the very last minute. But what has happened to you, Robert? You look dreadful!'

'It's a bit unfortunate, Jane. I had a car accident and then took a tumble in the dark. I'm waiting to be picked up by a friend. I'm sorry I would have missed our meeting anyway. So, the manor gave no reason for cancelling the beauty appointment?'

'Well, no. Not that I know of. Lady Thorely said her daughter was extremely upset at losing the booking. It was worth a lot of money to her. Lady Thorely tried to telephone the Manor, however, no-one answered.' Jane raised a suspicious eyebrow. 'I think something is amiss, Detective!'

Robert sighed. 'Is it that obvious? I hope I can rely on your discretion Jane. I'm sure you would not wish to jeopardise an ongoing investigation!'

As he spoke, a white Vauxhall pulled up alongside the kerb. Robert jumped up. 'Sorry Jane, here's my friend.' He leaped into the car, which took off with a small spray of gravel, into the traffic, leaving Jane alone on the pavement.

1969

'Yesterday'
The Beatles

Rick Chambers sat perched on a stool at the country style scrubbed pine table in the kitchen, smoking, the ashtray in front of him overflowing. He was totally at a loss to understand how this 'party' had gone so wrong. Little did he know how much more disastrous his day would turn out to be.

He had deployed Frankie and Ed to search the house for Bonnie and not to come back until they had found her. They must search every single room, closet, bathroom, storeroom, even the toilets. They were to open wardrobes and search under beds and behind curtains. Mrs. Potts was still recovering from her ordeal but had been sent to thoroughly clean the room Bonnie had occupied. It was doubtful the girl would ever return to it and Ricky didn't want any evidence of her occupancy remaining.

Ricky finished yet another cigarette and decided to take a walk around outside. There were numerous outbuildings which needed to be checked, although he doubted Bonnie had escaped outside. All the doors were kept locked. Only he and Mrs. Potts had keys now that Bramley was out of the picture. And Bonnie, he thought ruefully. Damn! He set off from the kitchen door and turned right. The enclosed kitchen yard had no hiding places, being only vegetable patches, a long clothesline set between two sets of posts and a tiny shed which held cleaning equipment such as mops and buckets. He let himself out of the rear door behind the yard, where Robert had taken cover hours ago. Once more turning to the right he headed for the Eastern side of the house.

By now, Ricky could hear voices and realised that the shooters must be at the front of the house. The doors were locked! He sprinted down the eastern side, passing numerous windows and French doors, when his boots crunched, and he noticed broken glass sprayed across the path. He skidded to a halt and gaped in disbelief at the smashed window. The apartments! The girls! Other than the strange one upstairs, the whole reason for the gathering at the Manor! Ricky exploded with a raw scream, guttural like a wild animal. How could this keep getting worse?

Checking inside was futile as he knew the girls would be gone. He ran full pelt around to the front where sweaty, grumbling men were gathering. Ignoring the many jibes and protests, he simply unlocked the doors without explanation or excuses. A terrible feeling of dread surged up his throat. He ran to the garages and straight to the trapdoor where he saw clearly that the door was open. As he miserably peered into the gloom, the stepladder mocked him. Without a second thought, Ricky jumped into the Corvette and fired her up. Attempting to reverse out at speed failed as the cold V8 engine stalled. Rick started her again and forced himself to wait a few seconds while the motor warmed a little, then threw it into reverse and left the yard in a flurry of screeching tyres, dust, and smoke. He had no plan, only to get as far away from this disaster zone as possible. Heathrow might be the best option, he thought.

***

Jones drove Robert out of Alderwell at speed, making for the farm-house which Alby had set up as the headquarters. There, Robert changed into plain clothes after which he called them all into a group and gave them all the details he knew so far.

Bonnie was at the Manor. So was Rick Chambers. There were about a dozen men there for a 'shooting party'. There were probably as many young girls to service the men, although Robert had not seen evidence of them. He only had anecdotal evidence from Jane Forcedyke. There was to be a masked event tonight starting at around eight, according to his informant. The special guest was already there. Then the fact that the beauty appointment had been cancelled and no-one was answering the phone was unusual.

Robert ordered the vehicles to quietly begin moving into position around the Manor.

'When we raid the Manor, I'll be in number two with Wright. We'll find a position to the north of the manor, back in the woods near the game-keepers cottage I slept in. You can see the main road from there, the back of the house and garages. There's access through the rear kitchen garden and back door. Alby and Grainger, you'll be on the south side watching the front, the main entrance and driveway. You can gain access through there.'

Robert stopped and cocked his head. 'Hear that?'

'Sounds like a big motor. V8, I reckon, speeding down the main road,' said Grainger. 'Well, we're not on traffic today!'

'There was a red Corvette in the garage at the Manor. Get on the radio and tell the local division to look out for it. If it is the Corvette, pull it over and take him in, anything will do, excess noise, license check. Whoever it is, we'll deal with it later. Meanwhile, are we just about set to roll out? Let's save Bonnie and those other young girls.'

***

Out on the edge of the woods, twelve girls had managed to escape the house without incident. The older girl whose name was Georgia, gathered them around and they huddled low, under cover of the vegetation. Luckily, the weather was still warm at this time of year as the girls had run without thoughts of warmer clothing.

'Right girls, we need to keep working our way towards the main road so we can flag someone down to help us. I can hear traffic coming from that direction.' Georgia pointed towards the south-east. 'We'll keep under cover as much as we can and maybe spread out a bit. Remember no talking. We've got this far. Let's not muck it up now. Is everybody alright?'

The girls nodded.

'Let's go. We're going to make it. Keep that thought in your mind.'

1969

BONNIE

'Light My Fire'
The Doors

She is spectacular.

I have given her permission to use my bathroom. She thinks the door is locked. She thinks she is alone. But I have my special viewing windows, two way mirrors. All she can see is herself, but I see her in all her splendour.

I witness her disrobe. I watch as the dress slips down over those delightful buds, across her creamy hips to the floor. My stomach clenches as I drink in the sight of soft pink nipples and red downy pubis. I keep my arms strictly to my side and lick my lips. My breath catches but I try to calm myself.

Now she is covering herself with lather, smoothing it all over her delightfully slight frame, across each understated curve and into each fold. My fingers twitch and I feel I may explode, but I have the will. It won't be long now, and she will be mine, my blank canvas, my artwork, my tapestry. The anticipation is almost too much.

1969

'Chimes of Freedom'
Bob Dylan

With the light beginning to soften as the sun sank lower in the evening sky, Alby and Grainger sat in the van, watching, and waiting. Adrenalin was high, anticipation keen. Radio conversation had to be kept to a minimum. Robert did not wish to compromise their covert movement and placement.

After their briefing, all vehicles had moved out making their way for points surrounding the Manor. Robert and DI Wright were parked in the woods near to the game-keeper's hut. There had been no sound of gunshots since they had arrived. Robert assumed the shooters would now be in the house preparing for the evening's activities. He cringed inwardly as he contemplated what that really meant. He had not seen or heard anything to indicate the reality of what he suspected was about to unfold.

'By the way, sir,' Jim Wright said in a hushed voice, 'we tracked down Bonnie Summer's biological mother. I got the word late last night but haven't had the opportunity to get all the details.'

Robert started. Hairs stood up on his forearms. 'What do you know Jim? Where is she?'

'Well, you'll never believe it. She comes from the village next to where I grew up in Brinsworth! I don't know any details, name or where she lived or even where she lives presently, but I'll be interested to find out if I knew her. You came from around there too, didn't you?'

'I did but I don't like to be reminded of it. You must have noticed that I have worked very hard to rid myself of the Yorkshire brogue. My early life is something I would rather put behind me. Still, it is interesting! I wonder which village?'

Robert's mind was in a turmoil. Ever since that first meeting with Bonnie, there had been something, hadn't there? Some connection, a feeling that she was particularly important to him. He had never understood it but here was a piece of information which might help to explain it. Her real mother had lived remarkably close to where Robert had grown up. Could it be that he had known her? He knew he was going to have to wait until this operation had concluded, but the temptation to get on the phone was overwhelming. As he grappled with the conflict of what he must do and what he wanted to do, Wright elbowed him.

'Sir, look, over there!' He pointed through the trees.

In the insipid light, they could discern movement; there appeared to be several of them, slight, shadowy figures crouching, ducking, trying to stay under cover of the foliage. So far, the van had remained unseen. The two men watched as the group moved closer, when suddenly the leader turned to check the surroundings and spotted them. Before she could warn them to flee, Robert and Jim Wright sprung out of the van and darted into the trees.

'Stop! Police! Don't run, we're here to help you.'

1969

'New Town Disaster'
The Dead 60s

Eloise stalked purposefully through the main double doors at the front of the manor. Immediately the atmosphere changed as the cavernous interior of the building swallowed the warmth and light of the exterior. The cathedral-like reception room was deserted, although she could hear voices from all directions. She marched through towards the back of the house, finding a corridor running along behind the twin staircases which led to the first floor gallery. The voices could be heard more clearly here, angry, abusive, shouting male voices. Following the sounds, she found the kitchen where the chef stood gesticulating apologetically towards several older men, who Eloise assumed were the 'guests'.

'Excuse me!' she barked. 'Where is the person in charge? Where is Mr. White?'

The raucous shouting ceased as if cut with a sharp knife. Five faces turned to face her. The chef threw his hands out pitifully and shook his head. One of the elderly men squinted at Eloise.

'Who are you? Who is Mr. White?'

'I am in charge of a group of young ladies who I assume are supposed to be joining some of you gentlemen later tonight.

However, something has gone terribly wrong, and I mean to find out from Mr. White what I should do. I have had no contact or instructions since last night and it just will not do!' she finished pompously.

'As you can see, we too are trying to find out what the dickens is going on here. I know of no Mr. White. Rick Chambers is missing as are his two lackeys. There appears to be no-one here who has a clue where they are or what is happening.' replied the man.

'Je ne sais pas! Je ne comprends pas! Je suis désolé!' the chef whined, rubbing his greasy hands together as if praying for a miracle to free him. He cowered behind the scrubbed table, his eyes darting between the back door and the angered group in his kitchen. Sweat dripped from his brow as he pleaded his ignorance.

'Oh good Lord! Tell him to quit his snivelling,' Eloise dismissed the chef and faced the men. 'Let me tell you, the chances of those girls staying in this place now are zero and none. You may as well write off your investment and scarper!'

In her anger and frustration, Eloise had inadvertently reverted to her northern accent. She threw the men a disparaging look and turned to leave the kitchen. The man she had been addressing lunged and grabbed her arm.

'Where do you think you're going? You're not leaving here until we know exactly what is happening. You're coming with me. We're going to look for the fodder. That's what we like to refer to them as.' He guffawed lasciviously.

Eloise was dragged along with him, while a couple of others followed behind. The group narrowly missed a head on collision with Ed and Frankie who skidded into the kitchen.

Confronted with the utter state of confusion here, Frankie yelled, 'What the goddamned fuck? Will somebody tell me what in hell's name is happening?' Eyeing Eloise, he took two deliberate steps and jabbed his face into hers. 'And what are YOU doing here?'

The man holding Eloise released her from his iron grip, threw his hands in the air and stalked out, leaving a trail of expletives in his wake. The other guests followed leaving only Frankie, Ed, and Eloise. No-one noticed the chef who had shrunk against the wall and was trying to inconspicuously slide towards the door.

Eloise stood her ground against Frankie's threatening stance. 'I am looking for Mr. White. I have had no contact from anyone, locked up in those apartments for two days now. No phone, no food, no idea! I broke out and I'll bet a million quid those bleedin' little tarts have gone.' She waved her arms expansively. 'Out there somewhere by now I should think. And what exactly do you have to do with anything? Where is White?'

'I have no idea who you're talking about. Of the two in charge here, one is dead and the other, Rick, has disappeared. The housekeeper, Mrs. Potts has also disappeared as have two other very important people. Unless Rick turns up soon, I'm afraid we're going to have to abandon the event altogether.'

Frankie turned to Ed. 'Do we even know for sure that the primary client is here? And where is Bonnie?'

Ed shrugged. 'I was told he was here. I suppose he's in the tower. But we don't have a key to the door at the bottom. Only he does. And we don't have a phone line to his apartment up there. As for Bonnie, we've searched this place top to bottom. I think she's probably escaped. With her gone, the other girls gone, and Ricky nowhere around, I think we know what to do.' He nodded towards the direction of the garages.

'Take me with you!' Eloise snarled. 'If you don't, I promise you I will spill everything!'

In one sudden move, Frankie grabbed her and smashed her head against the wall. She fell like a stone and remained down, blood streaming from her head. Frankie kicked her again and again, mercilessly pummelling her limp body until Ed forcibly dragged him away.

'Enough! You'll kill her! Come on let's go while we can. If any of those girls or Bonnie make it to the town, we're done for.'

1969

'All Along the Watchtower'
Jimi Hendrix

In the tower bathroom, Bonnie took her time, languishing in the suds, trying to steal time to think and plan. She looked at her hands. They were crinkled and red. She must get out of the water. Thus far, she had not come up with a real strategy. It was rapidly becoming less likely that she would escape. She knew the tower was three stories or more and there only appeared to be one door to exit the small suite of rooms up here. So far, she had seen the circular reception room and this bathroom. What else could be here? There must be a place William would take her to fulfil his grandiose promises.

'Bonnie, you may finish bathing. I have laid clothes out for you in the annexe to the right.'

Bonnie turned to face him, but he was not there.

'You have ten minutes.'

The voice was coming from speakers in the corners of the ceiling. *He has been watching me,* Bonnie thought. *Alright, here goes.*

I've done it before, and I'll do it again! I can beat him. I will get out of this! She climbed out of the tub, wrapped herself in the voluminous towel and marched into the annexed room off the bathroom.

Behind the mirror, the watcher dropped his chin and closed his eyes, took deep breaths, and calmed his racing pulse. Not long now.

1969

'The Good, The Bad & The Ugly'
Ennio Morricone

Once the girls found they were safe, they had agreed to stay with Robert and Jim Wright until another van arrived to take them to Ipswich. There they would be admitted to the hospital for health checks and subsequently interviewed. Their families would be informed which would be both a great shock and a huge relief as some of the girls had been missing for months.

While waiting for the van to arrive, Georgia, who had appeared to have taken upon herself the role of leader or caretaker of the others, told Robert what she knew about this event. She explained that it was not the first time for her and a few of the others. Not wishing to divulge details, she preferred to focus on where the girls had been living and what they were told of the 'jobs'. Georgina had been in no doubt as to their futures. They had heard tales of other girls who had simply disappeared after so many events. She assumed they had either been killed or sent somewhere else, probably Europe.

Now Robert and Wright were on the radios to the rest of the units placed around the manor. The time had come. 18:00. Robert had decided that with the latest developments, he did not want to wait any longer. They must get in there and find Bonnie and the despicable man who had paid for her!

'Is everyone ready to roll? Alby, you're on the main entry to the Manor. We're coming in from the hut to the eastern side. Everyone else converge on the manor. Use all means at your disposal to prevent anyone leaving. Keep in contact and as soon as you have Bonnie, let me know. Alright, go, go, go!'

Wright gunned the van down the rutted track towards the manor under lights and sirens. Sirens could be heard wailing from far and near as every unit began making for the manor at speed.

Just as Frankie and Ed dragged Eloise outside to leave, the peace of the surrounding countryside was split by the sound of multiple sirens wailing from all directions.

'What the fuck?' yelled Frankie.

'They're everywhere! He was telling the truth, that detective! Must be dozens of 'em and they're coming here! Quick, garage. We'll take the back lane out past the old hut.'

The two men yanked and dragged Eloise across to the garage. Chef threw his hands into the air and ran in random circles around the yard, screaming French expletives at no-one. Less than half a mile away, the police van careened down the track, scraping bushes, rocking, and rolling on its spongy suspension. As they neared the manor, the strident sound of sirens filled the air.

Frankie had the Bentley running and was reversing out of the garage when Ed rapped his knuckles on the window, frantically gesticulating towards the direction of the hut.

'Flashing lights, through there. They're nearly here.'

'Fuck, fuck, fuck!' Frankie beat the polished steering wheel. 'Get in, we'll make a run for it.'

Ed shoved Eloise into the back seat, dove in beside her and slammed the door. Frankie poked the huge engine which responded by lurching the car down the driveway at speed.

'Go, go, get going!' Ed shrieked, panic beginning to take over.

One hundred yards, two hundred then, 'FUCK! Here they are. Ahead, coming straight for us! Go round, go round.'

'I can't, too many trees and ditches. We'll never make it,' roared Frankie.

He slammed on the brakes and threw the transmission into reverse. Pushing the accelerator flat to the floor he began reversing crazily back towards the manor. The police van was closing fast. Frankie lost control. The huge car spun, then wheels skidding and brakes screaming, it crashed heavily into a large tree, completely crushing the rear and one side. Petrol began pouring from the ruptured tank. Eloise, suddenly revived by the crash, frantically tried to open the rear door which was bent and crushed. The other rear door was now jammed against the tree trunk. Frankie had managed to get his door open, get out and was making a run for it.

The police van jerked to a stop allowing the armed officers to pile out. Frankie was thrashing through the thick bushes. Ed was still in the car as was Eloise. As they were taken into custody without resistance, Ed heard someone shout, 'Stop, police.'

Frankie continued to fight his way to freedom. A gunshot sounded, whistling close above his head. He crouched low into the grass.

'Stop, police. There are weapons aimed at you. We do not want to shoot. Turn around, hands in the air, walk slowly towards me and you will not be hurt.'

Frankie didn't move. His eyes darted, looking for a way out. He leapt up and dashed a few yards. Another shot.

'Stop! Turn around and walk towards me, slowly with hands in the air. You are surrounded. Your accomplices are already in custody. You have no-where to go and things will only get worse.'

This time Frankie decided to do as asked. He stood slowly, raised his hands, and began walking slowly towards the men and the van. He could not see Ed or Eloise, in the van he supposed. He kept walking, the gun still trained on him. He knew once the whole operation was exposed, he would not see daylight again for a very long time. Suddenly he dropped his hands and sprung into flight, turning, and hurtling towards the hedge. The gun fired. He felt an impact on his left shoulder, which slammed him off balance and down. He tried to get up, but something was preventing him. He simply couldn't make his legs work. Although he thought he had been hit in the shoulder, there was a massive crushing pain in his lower body and his legs were numb. He tried again to push himself up. He looked down and saw blood streaming into the grass and then he realised why. When the impact of the gunshot had thrown him forward, he had fallen across a dead tree branch, the sharp spike of which had impaled him. That was why he couldn't move; why he couldn't feel his legs.

He slumped feeling the branch move, gouging his stomach. Now there were footsteps, shouting, someone feeling his neck, the light fading and the sirens wailing off into the distance. These were Frankie's last sounds and sensations as he lay dying in the scrubby bushes at the side of the road approaching the Manor.

The Bentley, still running, with fuel flowing freely into the grass suddenly drew the attention of a couple of police officers.

'Quick,' urged one, 'turn 'er off and get away.'

Someone used a fire extinguisher, and the very last things Frankie knew were the faint whooshing sound of the foam, and the smell of petrol.

1969

'The Court of the Crimson King'
King Crimson

Bonnie could hear music, old fashioned music. It sounded like a harpsichord. She knew what a harpsichord sounded like because she had listened to The Yardbirds song 'For Your Love' which featured a groovy harpsichord sound. This was much more classical and reminded her of some of the stuff nana listened to. Ordinarily, she would have enjoyed it, but her current situation demanded she focus her whole attention on survival and escape.

She had draped herself in the diaphanous gown, which had been the only piece of clothing left in the annexe for her. It really was beautiful if only it had been for a fancy dress party. Made of sheer fabric so fine and translucent it reflected beautiful colours, pink, mauve, aqua and gold which reminded Bonnie of the colours in soap suds. Considering what William had been wearing, the music and this gown, she assumed they were to be acting out a pre-sex drama born of William's twisted imagination. She sat on a crimson, deeply buttoned cushion, not wanting to invite his attention, yet knowing it would come.

'Ahh, my Titania, my faerie queen!'

The mellifluous voice rose above the music as her captor appeared in the doorway. He was holding one hand out to her, a regal invitation to go to him. Bonnie didn't move. 'Come, my lovely. Do not be afraid of me.'

He sashayed across the floor and took her hand in his. Bonnie quelled a shudder. She could not shake the feeling of being courted by a giant, globular spider. As she resisted his beckoning, he grasped her hand tightly and pulled her off the pouffe. The coal black eyes behind the mask disclosed his counterfeit affection. He led her with false tenderness out of the annexe. Dragging behind him, she noted the shiny, black curls, the exaggerated swagger and the left hand adorned with an enormous gold ring. She tried to focus on that ring but could not see enough of it to describe it.

She was escorted into another room off the main circular reception room. The massive door, crimson panelled, and gilt framed swung open.

'Welcome to my private chamber of secrets.'

The voice behind the mask, rich and cultured, maybe a very slight accent, reminded Bonnie of someone she had heard, but where, she could not think. Her senses were immediately overloaded by the room. Everything was red except the ceiling, which was mirrored in polished gold and bordered by paintings of angels. There were no windows or visible lights, but the walls glowed with falling rivulets of glowing red, *like blood*. Her bare feet sunk into thick carpet, richly patterned in shades of red and gold. Her eyes, however, were drawn inevitably to the only piece of furniture which dominated, an enormous gilded four poster bed. It looked like no other bed she had ever seen with no bedding, only satin cushions. On each of the four posts were tied silk and satin sashes. The walls were bare of decoration.

Bonnie searched the room for exits and found there was only the one by which William had brought her in here.

'William!' She tugged her hand out of his. 'Let me go! Look,

I have money! I'll pay you whatever you paid for me. It will be our secret. You can still boast to your friends about me. I won't tell, I promise. Just let me go.'

William shook his head sadly. 'Oh, my lovely, you misjudge me. You are here only for pleasure. I do not boast or discuss my liaisons. As for the money, it means nothing to me.' William walked to the wall and pressed a panel which sprung open revealing the source of the music, a sophisticated sound system. He changed something and now soaring voices filled the chamber.

'Handel,' he said by way of explanation. 'One of the most beautiful pieces of music ever written. Have you heard it, *The Messiah?*'

Bonnie ignored him and leapt for the door, searching frantically for a handle, latch or button but found nothing with which to open it.

'Enough!' growled the voice.

Bonnie was grasped by both arms and propelled to the bed. She struggled and fought but this chubby man had a strength which surprised her. He threw her down and taking one of the satin sashes he deftly wrapped it around one wrist and secured her to a post. With her free arm she managed to claw at his face, trying to dislodge the mask or gouge his eyes, but he was remarkably quick, grabbing yet another sash and tying her other arm. With the music rising and falling in glorious crescendos, Bonnie was bound to the plush red bed with the softest, finest satin, the gossamer folds of the robes falling around her like shimmering insect wings.

From somewhere deep inside her, a strength of will engulfed her, as if she had known this before and understood what she must do to survive. She fixed her stare on William who was now caressing her through the filmy material. Like a crab crawling over dips and folds in sand, his fingers explored her. He had not shown any sign of undressing himself as yet still wearing the full Elizabethan regalia. William was so close to her face. She could see his eyes, fancied she could hear him salivating and sucking in hitching breaths. His left hand was manipulating something. Dread filled her. He was freeing himself from the codpiece. She squirmed and writhed but felt his hot skin through the thin fabric of her robes.

The music filled her head and gave her an internal escape from reality. The soprano voice held an impossibly high note, pure as gold then faded with controlled vibrato. Again, it rose and fell. Bonnie was so focussed, she now thought there were more voices.

Her mind afire with sensations, sharp awareness overcame her like a freight train. The sounds were more than a soprano. They were sirens. Police sirens. They had come! Finally, they had found her and come to rescue her. She began to scream. She screamed until William lay on top of her, crushing her, and completely covering her mouth with his. If he had heard the sirens he ignored them, obviously secure in the knowledge that no-one would be able to find them up here. No-one had a key, except him.

1969

Now the units had converged on the Manor. They had stormed the house, arrested several men and were in the process of clearing every room, one by one. Chef had thrown himself at them, begging and pleading in his native language. He too had been handcuffed and escorted into the van.

Working their way through all the rooms was a laborious task with so many small closets, annexes, and hidey-holes. The main objective now was to find Bonnie and the man who had paid for her. Robert was in radio contact with the different units who checked in with him as they covered each wing or suite. He had received news that Chambers had been stopped on the way to Dover, presumably planning to cross the channel. His hope was that they had managed to secure everyone who had been in the house. The driver of the Bentley's death was unfortunate collateral damage, but he was relieved that death had come by misadventure rather than a gunshot from one of his team. There would be an investigation, of course. The other two in the car were now on their way to Ipswich, where preliminary interviews would commence. Any information which could help them find Bonnie at this stage would be valuable.

Forty minutes after Robert's crack team entered the Manor house, they had cleared the cellars, ground floor, first and second floors and were preparing to check the attic rooms, accessed by narrow staircases hidden behind doors concealed in the panelling.

So far there had been no sign of Bonnie or anyone else. The house was relatively quiet, other than the crackle of radios and sparse conversation between the personnel conducting the search. Robert, Alby, Wright, and a few others had set up in the dining room. Calls had gone out and they were expecting a forensic team any minute. The ambulance had arrived to collect the body and a lorry was coming to take the crashed Bentley away for testing. They had sent twenty-six people to Ipswich, the girls to hospital, the men, Eloise, and Ed, in cuffs to be placed in custody. Ricky Chambers was also on his way to join them. Robert felt he had done as much as he could up until now, but Bonnie was still missing. Was she here?

'I'm going up with them to keep looking for Bonnie. Alby, you're with me. Jim, hold the fort down here. I must find her. I have a bad feeling.'

'Yep, will do, guv,' replied Jim Wright. 'Be careful. Are you covered? Have you got a vest on?'

Robert patted his chest. 'I certainly do, and I've got this as insurance.' He indicated a revolver concealed in his jacket pocket. 'Come on Alby.'

They began up the stairs, Alby leaping two at a time with his long legs, Robert following a little more slowly. The house was now echoing with the sounds of dozens of men moving around, beginning to collect and bag evidence and to carry boxes of evidential articles down to the waiting vans. The two men reached the second floor, then ascended to the third up a narrower staircase which led onto a corridor much less grandiose than the lower floors. Here the dust was ever present, the carpet worn and the décor shabby. Men were moving along looking for extra nooks and crannies.

One officer called out, 'Here, I found another room at the end. Looks like a servants' parlour.'

Robert and Alby followed the voice. 'What have you found?'

'Looks like someone has been in here recently, sir. Look, it's thick with dust but there are marks in the dust on the table. Someone sat here and there is a key in the lock, on the inside.'

Robert spotted a bag on the old single bed. A woven, hippy style bag. 'I think Bonnie has been here. Look at that bag! Get forensics to dust for prints and don't touch anything,' ordered Robert. 'Bag that,' he added, indicating Harmony's shoulder bag.

The room was so small it was plain to see that no-one was hiding here, but he had a feeling that they might be getting closer. Just then he thought he heard something, very faint.

'Quiet!' he hissed. 'Listen, do you hear anything?'

The four men stopped still and yes, very faintly; they could hear music. It sounded as if it might be coming from above.

'The Tower!' Robert exclaimed. 'Of course. Come on!'

***

Bonnie lay, bearing William's weight until she could barely breathe. He released her mouth leaving wet, sticky saliva. She desperately wanted to scream but had no breath in her lungs. William rose from the bed to adjust the music again. This time Nessun Dorma by Puccini, one of the most famous arias ever written.

'I thought this was supposed to be pure pleasure,' Bonnie gasped trying hard not to see what he had been stroking and prodding her with.

The powerful tenor spilled out of the concealed speakers.

'Does this not fill you with wonder? Do not resist me and we can begin again.'

Bonnie, regaining her voice, hoping that the sirens had brought the police who would be at this minute searching the house, screamed as loudly and shrilly as she could, until a dark hand was clamped over her mouth.

***

Robert and Alby ran frantically, searching for the door which might lead to the tower. They followed the sound which became clearer, and they knew they were heading in the right direction. The small door was well concealed. The music was much louder here, opera. Robert recognised it instantly.

'He's here. That's him. He's got Bonnie. Get that door open!'

The two officers lunged against the door, but it was solid and immoveable. Again and again, they tried without budging it.

'Get down, cover your eyes and ears!' urged Robert and withdrew the firearm. Aiming it squarely at the lock he fired, the shot splintering the timber and blowing the lock apart. The men charged up the spiral staircase. The door at the top looked to be as heavy and secure as the one below.

'Can't risk shooting. Don't know what's behind it,' said Robert. Come on, all four of us. Ready? On my count. One, two, three!'

***

William was once more stroking himself.

'I have waited for a long time Bonnie. I will come to you and...'

Even above the enormous, swelling sound of the music, they both heard the crash. William leapt up and charged into the parlour where the remains of the door lay flat on the floor and four men were storming into his tower room.

'Don't move!' ordered one of the officers, weapon aimed fairly at William.

'Where is she?' shouted Robert, charging past the others. 'Where is Bonnie?'

'In here, help me. I'm in here!'

Robert raced into the red room. Bonnie lay on the bed, arms spread and tied to the posts. For a split second, Robert saw a fragile mayfly thrashing back and forth in a gossamer web.

'I'm here, Bonnie. Detective Turner. You are safe now. Let me untie you, then go and find some clothes. We're not going anywhere without you.'

He deftly undid the sashes, removed his jacket and handed it to her. She put it on and hurried out. Taking a glance around, Robert noted the lack of furnishings, windows, and the golden ceiling. Seeing the panel open in the wall, revealing the stereo, he turned the music off, then re-joined the others in the parlour.

William stood, handcuffed but still masked.

'Take it off, the mask. Let's see who we have here.' commanded Robert. 'Alby, you can do the honours.'

Alby stepped up to him. William shrunk away but was powerless to stop him. Alby pulled the ornate mask away. And stared. 'You!' he exclaimed. 'You! I thought you...' Alby faltered, lost for words.

'Alby?' Robert looked questioningly at the other two officers who were standing on either side of William. They raised their eyebrows. 'Do you know him?' Robert asked them.

They nodded slowly, disbelievingly.

'I can't believe it. You bastard!' spat Alby. 'To think I idolised you growing up in Puerto Rico. I watched every game you played. You were my hero. I always thought if I worked hard enough, I could be as good as you, who knows, even playing in the big time, like you!'

William offered nothing. His dark eyes were hooded, his lips full, set in a childish pout.

'You're a disgrace to your country and the greatest sport on the planet! I shall have the utmost pleasure in seeing you incarcerated for the rest of your life. I can't wait until the press gets hold of this!'

Robert, whose scant knowledge of the game was in its infancy did not know to whom Alby was referring. 'FIFA?' he asked.

'Yep, played ten seasons. Only the most famous player to have ever come out of Brazil, guv. Makes me ashamed to be a fan!'

'Take him away!' Robert ordered the men. 'Right, we need a policewoman up here. Alby, radio and ask for PC Stewart to come up. When Bonnie has gone, we'll start the examination of this hideous den. I wonder how many more secret panels there are in these walls, and what's behind them?'

'God only knows!' sighed Alby. 'I just can't believe it Robert. I just can't!'

'You never know what you might find in this job, son. You never know.'

AUGUST 1969

PETUNIA

'Hey Jude'
The Beatles

Today was her fiftieth birthday. Friday. There would be no celebration today but tomorrow she would be attending a concert in Sheffield. Philippe would be playing a composition of his own, a sonata for piano and oboe. The tickets were a birthday gift from her good friends Andrew Floyd and his wife. Philippe's mother Adrienne (Rennie) and his father Henri would also be there, all people with whom Petunia now felt comfortable. Perhaps it was partly because they were all in their sixties and early seventies. She found it easier to relate to older people.

It was nine years since she had lost her mother. She had never fully reconciled with her even after seven years, but they had achieved a level of companionship in their co-habitation of the Old Vicarage. Joan had finally given up bemoaning her lost grandchild. Petunia had continued therapy with Andrew and had reached a point of stasis, where she was able to not accept but bury what had happened. She no longer wanted to die, but she still felt that it was a delicate balance between sanity and insanity.

After Joan had died, Petunia had sold the Vicarage with the help of Andrew and had purchased a smaller, detached house in Brinsworth, not far away from the village but far enough. She had never returned to teaching in the Catholic school or any other school. That was a step too far for her, but she had taken on private tutoring for children with diverse disabilities. It had come to her attention, primarily through Adrienne, that many children who had been diagnosed as 'retarded' were often simply locked out of the world, like Philippe had been, just waiting for someone to find them. She tutored six children in their own homes, ranging in age from four years old to sixteen. She had found that regardless of the severity of the intellectual or physical disability, all her children had found something in their lives which had been formerly denied to them, music, art, drama, poetry, science, or mathematics. Every one of them had a special key.

More often, the key was music or art. Children who could not express themselves in words, could often use paints or pencils. Children who could not co-ordinate limbs, could keep a steady beat and move in time to music. There had been revelation after revelation for the parents and Petunia felt validated once more. She was needed. Life was becoming more than tolerable.

1969

'Colour My World'
Petula Clark

Robert knocked on the door. It was now two months since the raid on the Manor and Bonnie's rescue. All the men at the house had been arrested and jailed. Some had been bailed, some not. William, which was not his real name, was in prison awaiting his trial, having been refused bail. The trial promised to be drawn out and difficult although he had the best lawyers. They were arguing that due to his fame, he would never be able to get a fair trial. He was trying to be repatriated back to Brazil.

Most of the young women were back with families but some had no family to go to. Their futures were uncertain. Both 'Hon' and 'Lennon' had been completely taken aback when the door to Rick Chamber's office had burst open and dozens of police officers had crawled through everything, taking many cartons of files, paperwork, and records. Both were considered accomplices.

The fallout from that single raid was enormous, stretching from England to America, and Europe. The abduction and exploitation of minors for sex was only a small part. There were ties to organised crime with money laundering, supplying illegal drugs and even corrupt law enforcement to be investigated. By now it was far beyond the realm of Robert and his team. They had returned to more local pressing business.

As for Bonnie, her path did not track smoothly after her release from hospital. She had wanted and expected to return home to Menston. Robert remembered her room at the Colemans, completely cleaned out, devoid of any of Bonnie's belongings. He recalled thinking that Deirdre had cleansed it. With that in mind, he investigated whether Bonnie might stay with Rae for a short while. Naturally, Rae was delighted, Bonnie confused. Robert explained that Devon would be quieter, giving her more chance to recuperate. The past two months had taken a huge toll on her both physically and mentally, compounded by the constant demands on her by the police investigation and by the media for interviews. When Bonnie had settled, Robert travelled down to Devon to catch up with both her and Rae.

'Come in Inspector, so nice to see you,' Rae exclaimed warmly. She ushered him into the cosy sitting room.

Although autumn had arrived, the weather was still mild down here, the skies blue and waves tipped with froth. He watched the gulls through the tiny windows and considered whether he could retire to a place like this.

'Bonnie is in her room. She has taken up playing a guitar again and writing too, I think. She is alright I suppose. I can't imagine what she's been through, but I haven't pushed her to talk about it. She's had enough of that with police interrogations!'

Rae busied herself in the small kitchen making tea. Just as she placed the tray on a small table in the sitting room, Bonnie appeared.

'Bonnie! How are you?' asked Robert.

A smile spread across Bonnie's face, her blue eyes sparkled, and she skipped across to Robert and hugged him fiercely. 'DCI Robert! I really don't know how to thank you and your men for getting me out of that place! I tell you; I was really running out of ideas!'

Robert, somewhat taken aback, held her at arm's length. 'You look well Bonnie. The Devon air suits you. Your nana tells me you are playing and singing again. Wonderful!'

They sat to take tea and biscuits. The three chatted, Robert steering any conversation away from Bonnie's abduction. There would be plenty of that in the coming months. Bonnie talked animatedly about her new guitar, all the ideas she had for new songs, the fact that two big record companies had approached her to sign with them. Suddenly she became subdued, left the room, and returned with an envelope which she handed to Robert.

'What is this, Bonnie? One of your offers?' he asked her.

'Open it.'

Robert slid a folded piece of paper out of the envelope and looking at Bonnie for reassurance, he unfolded it. He read:

Bronwyn,

After much consideration, your father and I have decided to inform you of something important.

Bob and I were not able to have our own child. We decided to adopt. You are that adopted child. We took you when you were only days old. Your mother was single and unable to take care of you.

After the last few months, we are aware you wish to pursue a different life to one that we wish to support. In addition, Bob and I are separated, and I will be filing for divorce. He is to remain in the house while the business wraps up. I shall be moving to my mother's apartment in Earl's Court. You will be welcome to stay in Devon for as long as you need to.

During your disappearance, the police made inquiries regarding your biological mother, to investigate any connections between her and the abduction.

Therefore, we give you full permission to contact her.

Detective Chief Inspector Turner will help you with details.

We think it would be for the best if you stay with nana Coleman. There is a substantial sum in a trust fund which you will be able to access when you turn twenty-one. You can thank Bob for that. The money you have earned with your singing is a matter for the court to sort out, or so we have been informed. We have authorised you as the recipient of all communications from them from now on.

Bob and I wish you all the best for the future.

Best Regards,

Deirdre and Robert Coleman.

Robert contemplated the letter. Bonnie's incredible eyes were fixed on him. He turned to Rae. 'Have you seen this?'

Rae shook her head. 'What is it, Bonnie?'

Robert handed her the letter. 'It's difficult reading Rae.'

Robert had been informed that Alby and Wright had identified Bonnie's biological mother but had been so completely immersed in the case that he had not had a chance to follow it up.

'Bonnie, you do not have to make any decisions in a hurry. How did you feel when you read that? This must be an enormous shock for you, especially after all you've been through. I cannot understand how Bob and Deirdre thought this was acceptable!' he said addressing Rae, who was solemnly shaking her head.

'Do you know what, Inspector Turner?' said Bonnie. 'It didn't surprise me at all! I often wondered why I never had a brother or sister. I always felt sort of different to them. I don't even look anything like them! No-one I know has red hair! I might like to find my real mum. Maybe we would be like each other. After all, it sounds like she didn't want to give me up, she just couldn't keep me.'

'Take some time Bonnie. We will need to contact her first. The desire to meet must be both ways. She could have a family, children of her own. Perhaps bringing the past back would be a major trauma for her. So, I will get the wheels in motion to make the first approach and keep you informed. If at any stage you decide not to go ahead, then we will not pursue it. OK?'

'OK. I feel sort of excited though!'

***

Back at Scotland Yard, Robert asked Alby for the information he had on Bonnie's biological parents. Alby handed him a file. Robert retired to his desk in his small office space and opened the file. Running his eyes down the page, the name leapt off the page. He knew it! He knew the name. He knew who she was, Bonnie's mother! His memory of those eyes when he and his brother had tormented the dogs was true.

His mind whirled. He felt as if the wind had been knocked out of him as he was struggling to take a breath. The page swam before him, and he momentarily thought he might pass out. But the enormous truth of what he was seeing slowly seeped into his consciousness and he sucked in a huge gasp of air. Now, his feeling of connection was validated. His underlying certainty that he *knew* those brilliant blue eyes and that flaming hair made sense. He realised, seeing the name, Petunia Jackson, that Bonnie was, in fact, his niece. His niece, who was conceived from his brother Eric in the vilest of circumstances.

He remembered that time well, when his brother had been found dead, lying on top of the woman he had tortured, raped, and abused; the woman who had, with a mighty will, used her very shackles to strangle him. Robert had carried the shame ever since. The need to compensate for his brother's shocking crimes had driven him to where he found himself today and yet, hadn't he always suspected that he carried the same evil gene? Was that not why he had never been able to sustain a relationship, because he didn't trust himself?

Alby knocked. 'You OK guv?'

Robert nodded and waved him away. 'Need to do something. I'll be out of the office for the rest of the day and tomorrow. I'll catch up with things when I get back.' He held up his hand. 'Don't! I'll fill you in later.'

***

And so, he found himself here at her door, unannounced, not even knowing if she would be home. He knocked again. From inside the house, he heard deeply excited barking. Seconds passed. The door opened a crack, held by a security chain. A large black dog stood swaying its tail back and forth and trying to bark through a mouthful of felt arms and legs, a golly. A woman with chestnut hair and a pale face peered out.

'Can I help you? I'm sorry, but if you're selling vacuum cleaners, I already have one.'

Robert, slightly taken off guard replied, 'No, no, I am not selling anything.'

The dog continued pushing its muzzle through the gap, trying to thrust the toy at Robert.

'Stop it, Hugo. Sit!' said the woman. 'I'm sorry, Flat-coated retriever. They must always have something in their mouth! What can I do for you?'

He showed his badge.

'Petunia Jackson? Detective Chief Inspector Robert Turner. May I come in?'

Petunia closed the door slightly. Robert thought she was closing it in his face, but he heard the chain on the other side and the door opened.

'Please come in Detective,' she invited.

He followed her and Hugo into the front room of the cottage. Hugo settled, now convinced the visitor was welcome. Petunia stood regarding Robert quizzically.

'May we sit down Miss Jackson? I have something I need to tell you or ask you, I'm not sure which yet.'

Petunia stared at him. 'Did you say Robert Turner? You look familiar. Are you...?'

'I am Eric's younger brother, yes. I know this may be a shock for you, but I have a good reason for being here,' said Robert gently. 'Believe me, I do not wish to upset you at all. My reasons for coming to see you are difficult for both of us. All I ask is that I may talk with you.'

Petunia heaved a sigh. 'You'd better sit down then.'

Two hours later, they still sat, cups of tea finished and forgotten, with so much said and so much still to say.

'So, who is the girl you say is my daughter and why is she suddenly so interested in finding me? I have worked long and hard to accept what happened. I have spent many years in therapy to achieve this and I am still prone to episodes of depression and self-loathing. I do have a wonderful group of people to whom I will forever be indebted; people who have stood by me and picked me up when I have fallen. I have my work and have regained my life to a great extent. Why would I wish to tear it apart again, Robert? What does she want from me? What can I possibly offer her?'

'Petunia, the last thing I want is for you to feel threatened in any way. And rest assured I have made it clear that unless you are one hundred percent in agreement, it will not happen. But I have grown to know this girl, my niece. Since I first met her, I have felt a deep connection without understanding why. She has your mother's red hair and intense blue eyes. She is a free spirit, a product of her age, but she has inherited your incredible strength of will and determination. She is also very talented, musically, and artistically which has given her a substantial independent income. She has displayed amazing resilience. I am immensely proud of her and would dearly love to be able to tell her so, but she does not know that we are connected at this stage.'

Petunia listened, carefully digesting each piece of information. 'You say, you only recently met her. How did you meet her? Was it in the context of your job, as a Detective? Is this girl in trouble?'

'Petunia, there is much I cannot discuss. Have you heard of the abduction case which has been in the news lately? A young girl?'

'Yes, of course. One could hardly miss it, on every TV news program and in all the papers. Why? It's not her...is it?'

'Yes. Her name is Bonnie Summer and I think, if you can find a tiny place in your heart, she is a part of you.' Robert stopped, 'I am so sorry Petunia. I don't mean to pressure you. I withdraw that last comment. I think I had better go before I make things worse. I only ask that you give some consideration to this girl, who has, like you have, suffered terrible trauma and succeeded in overcoming it. She is a wonderful, strong, resilient and intelligent girl. She needs nothing from you. She might want to simply share with you. Are you alright?'

Petunia nodded.

'I think I have much to consider. May I contact you if I need to discuss things further?'

'Absolutely you may. Anything, anything at all that I can do.' He handed her a card with his private number. 'Goodbye Petunia. I look forward to speaking to you soon.' He held out his hand which she took briefly.

'I'll show you out. Thank you for the card.'

'Anytime, Petunia. Just one question. This couldn't possibly be the Hugo that I remember, could it?' He wrestled the golly with the enthusiastic dog.

'Oh no, of course not. Once a flat coat owner, always a flat coat owner. This is Hugo the Third. He is only eighteen months old.'

Robert ruffled the dog's head. 'Goodbye Petunia.'

1969

'You Can't Hurry Love'
The Supremes

The group entered the University of Sheffield Concert Hall. The beautiful, old building housed this intimate performance space where Philippe felt perfectly at home these days. Everyone sat on floor level, but luckily the family and friends were in the front row with a perfect view of the artists. Philippe was to perform his sonata for piano and oboe again. This time, Petunia had invited a guest to accompany her.

The lights dimmed, the spotlight lit the piano and a single music stand with a soft orb of light. Philippe walked on, flicked his tails over the piano stool. The oboist walked on, acknowledged Philippe, and stood at the stand. Philippe lifted his hands, in perfect control. He took a breath, paused then his fingers fell like rain on the keys and the music poured over the audience transporting them to other dimensions. The oboe complimented his music with its peculiarity of timbre, lending a subtle middle eastern feel. Both musicians executed such brilliance, they left the audience gasping.

Petunia sat with Robert. Over the last few months, an easy familiarity had developed between them, a shared love of classical music had been the catalyst. Later, Robert had introduced Petunia to Italian cuisine, she had shared her love of art galleries with him and had introduced him to the Gautiers, Henri, Adrienne, and their son Philippe.

As the last strains of the oboe faded accompanied by Philippe's final chord, Petunia laid her hand on Robert's. She leaned in towards him and whispered, 'I want to meet her.'

1970

CURTAIN CALL

'Blackbird'
John Lennon & Paul McCartney

The people rose as one as she stepped onto the stage. A deafening roar filled the Wembley Stadium, surging on and on, not taking a breath. The sound became a living, breathing entity, enveloping everyone in its path. The crowd itself surged and pulsated like a swarm of locusts, it's voracious appetite for the feeding frenzy to begin, for the devouring of the prey. As in a locust plague, no individual could separate itself from the whole. The mass threatened to consume her. Ushers and security people tried in vain to stop the crushing movement within the body of human flesh. Someone grabbed a microphone and shouted for quiet. The massively amplified voice was lost amidst the screaming.

Suddenly, she was rushed off stage by burly minders. The space was empty now, but the crowd roared on for minutes, their waving arms like antennae. Gradually the realisation that the object of their adoration had gone penetrated the collective consciousness, and the sound abated until the stadium became quiet and still. The MC came out with the mic to centre stage.

'Good evening, everyone.' The rumbling began and he held his hand up, waiting. When it subsided, he continued. 'Miss Summer wants to let you know that she does want to perform for you tonight...' A huge cheer began to which the MCs hand went up again to quieten them. 'She does want to play and sing.' once more the hand to control. 'But she felt very nervous, in fact frightened by you before. She will not appear if this continues.'

People exchanged looks and murmured but no rising cacophony this time.

'Let me say again, she will not come out here unless she feels safe. Please be reminded, she is young; not as tough as some of you. She has survived an unthinkable trauma in the last months. Take care of her. Let her sing. Let her play and most of all; please enjoy the incredible Miss Bonnie...SUMMER!'

With a swish of his hand to welcome Bonnie back to the stage, he made a flamboyant exit to the side. Bonnie walked across to the mic stand, guitar slung over her shoulder. Her flaming red ringlets, now halfway down to her waist again, complimented by a red and gold satin and chiffon pantsuit with bell-bottoms swishing around her platform gold sandals. The fact that the outfit was semi-transparent in places caused her Nanna' sharp intake of breath, as she sat in the front row VIP box with Robert. She nudged him and he smiled and nodded resignedly. This was pop stardom in full bloom.

Bonnie played an E minor and the crowd clapped and screamed. She stopped. They quieted. She began the opening chords of 'Field of Flowers' as a glowing peace symbol rose dominating the back-drop and shivered slightly in the breeze. Stepping right to the microphone, her lips caressing it, she sang, the breathy, sweet voice floating over the crowd from large speakers on either side. The audience listened in raptures. 'The voice of an angel' is how she had always been promoted and tonight she was bringing those words to fruition. She reached the vocal and lyrical crescendo of the song before her voice fell away to a soft whisper, hitching gently as the words painted the picture of the dying flowers on the graves of the fallen. The peace symbol faded dramatically as she strummed the last plaintiff chord. The lights dimmed and she took her bow. Wembley Stadium, packed with eighty thousand people erupted.

Rae Coleman glanced at Robert. She smiled as she saw tears in his eyes. She placed her hand over his and squeezed.

'She is so lucky to have you Robert,' she said. Though he didn't hear the words, he understood and nodded. *I am lucky to have found her.*

Up on the stage Bonnie began strumming a riff well known to her followers, another smash hit in the last twelve months, 'Come Along'. She turned to face her band, played it again and the drummer executed a roll followed by the bass player bringing in the grinding rhythm. The crowd picked up on it and began moving as one to the beat. They swayed and sang with her through the chorus.

Come on, come on, come along with me.
I promise you we can be free.
Come on, come on, come along with me,
Come into the light with me.

The words, so simple, but sung to a powerful rhythm over and over, took the crowd with her. She covered all of the stage, strumming and singing while the band improvised, clearly enjoying themselves. Bonnie invited her fans to join in. They did. The auditorium now moving as one. Bonnie stopped playing and singing. The crowd sang on. They were hypnotised by their angel. The band ramped up the sound, the drummer's sticks pounding at light speed, his brow dripping, his biceps flexing. Bonnie came in for a grand finish.

Police kept busy watching out for crushes and fans trying to jump on to the stage. Rae, Robert, and the Gauthiers were safely enclosed and guarded near the front. Each one of them watched in complete amazement, the small figure holding this enormous beast of a crowd in her tiny hand.

The band hammered the last chord; the percussion fill pulsed from the small toms to the floor tom and back, again and again. Bonnie threw herself into a deep and prolonged bow. The audience screamed. She acknowledged the band. The audience screamed. She exited the stage and the audience screamed. Rae had never experienced anything like it.

***

Later, much later, Robert sat in his apartment after bringing Rae back. She was staying the night in his guest bedroom. Bonnie might not be back for a while but would be home when the after party had wrapped up. She would be OK; of that he was certain. He had Alby on the job, and he knew she was safe.

He sat back with a whiskey, contemplating the last twelve months again. Was he a different man to the one he had been when he had first set eyes on his niece? Yes, he thought he probably was. He no longer suffered the feelings of guilt. He felt he had appeased the devil in him to some extent. If the steely knife had been hiding in the folds of his subconscious, it was now sheathed and safe, never to re-appear...he hoped. Finding Bonnie, her mother and the family ties had given him a real and important reason to live a good life, to value himself as a worthwhile person; to give and receive love in the purest way.

The doorbell sounded. He pressed the intercom and saw Adrienne, Henri and Philippe Gauthier waiting. Just as he invited them up, Deborah Coates opened the outer door.

'Everyone, come up and I'll introduce you" said Robert.

He glanced at his watch. Over at the sideboard, he poured a glass of champagne. She would be here soon too. She had declined going go to the concert. She was still grappling with dealing with crowds. She would share the excitement with them here, at home. Sipping the whiskey, he pondered the months since he had first visited Petunia. After that initial contact, he had telephoned to check on her since learning of her daughter. She had remained non-committal but had followed up with a call to Robert, asking him if he could come up to talk. What followed was a series of phone calls and visits to Brinsworth for Robert.

At this point in his contemplations, he took a gulp of his drink, drained it, and poured another. It is true; he had been shocked how accepting Petunia had been of him. She had been able to disconnect him, as a person, from his brother, the animal who had abused and nearly killed her. Why was that? He was reticent to admit it might be that he *was* a different person to his brother.

His friendship with Petunia had grown and in truth, Robert had found himself becoming emotionally connected to her. He could not reconcile if it was because of Bonnie, or his sympathies for Petunia, or could it be he was falling for her. On her part, Petunia always greeted him warmly, even affectionately. They had shared their interests and outings. Not too long ago, they had shared a tender kiss goodnight. Yes, thought Robert, since then, they had been behaving more and more like a couple, and he had finally come to the realisation that that was exactly what he wanted. He hoped she did too.

The guests entered through the lift doors. Robert greeted them with undisguised warmth. 'So very glad you came. Let me take your wrap Adrienne, and your coat Henri. I'll get us some drinks. Andrew and his wife will be here shortly.'

No sooner had he spoken than the bell rang again as Floyd and his wife appeared on the intercom. 'Come on up.'

The gathered people, who until recently Robert had not known, were chatting in subdued tones, the occasional amusing comment followed by soft laughter, but all eyes were on their watches, glancing often to the lift doors waiting for the guest of honour to arrive.

This time there was no intercom. She had her own key. The

lift doors slid open with a hush, and Petunia walked in. Robert took her hands in his, drew her to him and greeted her with a kiss. Henri handed her a glass of champagne while Philippe grinned and shifted from one foot to the other, his dark eyes shining through the wayward lock of dark curls. Petunia smiled around, greeting her friends, then approached each and exchanged affectionate embraces. Tonight, she looked stunning in sapphire blue satin, a diamante clip holding back her glossy chestnut waves, which by now were tinged with grey. Robert thought she had never looked so beautiful, her face alight, her eyes sparkling.

'You're looking lovely tonight,' he commented.

She smiled warmly. 'When is she coming home?'

'She'll be here soon. She was wonderful. You should be so proud. Rae is here. She's in her room having a lie down, but I'll get her to come out when Bon gets home.'

'I wore the sapphire to complement her. I don't have the eyes, but I hope this is alright?'

Robert embraced her again. 'You are the most wonderful person I have ever known, Petunia. Whatever you do is 'alright'!'

Petunia sought Deborah, Alby's wife and employed her newfound confidence to initiate conversation.

***

Bonnie arrived with Alby in tow at around 2:30 in the morning. When the lift doors opened, there arose a collective 'aahh' from the room. Robert and Petunia rushed to enfold Bonnie, hugging her fiercely with love and pride.

Robert called out to Rae that her granddaughter had arrived.

'Good work Alby and thank you for taking care of her.' He clapped Alby on the shoulder.

'Oh, she's a bit of a handful, guv! No! Not seriously! She's an angel, hadn't you heard?'

Rae had come in and on seeing Bonnie, she rushed over and crushed her in her arms, exclaiming, 'Oh Bonnie, you were wonderful, wonderful!'

'Did you really enjoy it nanna, with all the noise and screaming?' asked Bonnie, concerned because she had always known her nanna to love the quiet life.

'Yes, love. Every bit. You've made your old nanna very proud!'

Robert stood up. He chinked his crystal glass with a flick of his middle finger.

'Can I have a bit of shush please?' The murmuring ceased and all eyes looked his way. Robert gestured to Petunia to come to his side. Philippe nodded happily.

'Now we're all here, can everyone raise your glass? To Bonnie!'

'To Bonnie!' chorused everyone and sipped their drinks.

'Now,' said Robert, 'everyone is here and there's something I want to do. I have been wondering when I should do this and tonight seems to be the perfect time, with the people who are most important in our lives here, all together.'

Alby winked at Rae. She responded with a quizzical look.

'Petunia,' Robert bent to one knee and took her hand. 'With Bonnie's blessing, and the blessings of everyone here tonight, will you do me the great honour of accepting my proposal of marriage? Petunia, will you marry me?'

Petunia blinked as tears filled her eyes. She stared at him, unable to utter a sound. Everyone held their breath. Petunia cupped his face in her hands.

'Yes, yes, YES! I do, I mean I will. Yes, I will marry you!'

'Dieu merci! Thank goodness! Tu m'as inquiété!' Henri always reverted to his native French when under stress.

With that, Robert drew a ring box from his pocket and opened it. He placed the square cut sapphire ring on her finger, took her in his arms and they kissed as Bonnie, Rae and the entire room applauded and cheered.

Alby clapped him on the shoulders. 'Well done boss! Better late than never, eh?'

The newly engaged couple were surrounded by their dear friends and family.

'Excellent, old chap!' from Floyd as he caught Petunia's eye and imperceptibly nodded his satisfaction.

'Fantastique, félicitations, vous deux!' from Adrienne.

'Yes, yes,' agreed Philippe as he gave a bow to Robert and an awkward, stiffly executed hug to Petunia.

Bonnie squealed with delight.

'My mum and my uncle, getting married. Wow! Like WOW! Soooo groovy. I love you both soooo much! Can I be a bridesmaid? Can I?'

She twirled and capered around the room, nearly knocking the champagne glasses over.

'That's for you and Petunia to figure out!' chuckled Robert. 'Your mother and I have much to think about now, where we will live, how we will fit our work lives into a marriage and so much more. Nevertheless, one thing we both want is for you, Bonnie, to be in our lives from now on, in whatever way you want. You will always have a place in our homes and our hearts!'

'Of course, Bonnie.' Petunia hugged her daughter. 'We have so much to share, and I hope we can be your family!'

Bonnie twirled again. 'A real family. My family!'

∗∗∗

Rae Coleman, eyes wet with tears of happiness, still found a corner of her mind wondering what had become of Deirdre. Bob was a shell of the man he was, she knew. Living in a council flat, selling cars for a small, private sale yard, he missed Bronwyn but had neither the will nor the way to do a thing about it. Bonnie spoke to him on the phone occasionally. The conversations were brief. He was embarrassed.

Rae decided she would not tell him about the wedding or Robert and Petunia's offer. He would find out soon enough. It occurred to her that two sad lives had traded places. Petunia and Robert had found love while her son and his wife had lost theirs. *That's life,* she thought as she watched Bonnie twirl. She had heard Bonnie sing the song:

'*Turn! Turn! Turn! (To Everything There is a Season)*' *The Byrds.*